continued . . .

Other Historical Novels
by Diane Haeger

"In Haeger's impressive Restoration romance, King Charles II and his mistress . . . leap off the page. . . . Charles and Nell are marvelously complex—jealous and petty, devoted yet fallible. Haeger perfectly balances the history with the trystery." —*Publishers Weekly*

"Engagingly deep romantic historical fiction." —*Midwest Book Review*

"Romantic . . . filled with intrigue and danger." —*The Indianapolis Star*

"Set against the vivid descriptive detail of Rome and Trastevere, Haeger's tale of how the ring came to be obscured in the Raphael masterpiece resonates with the grandeur and intimacy of epic love stories. . . . This romance is first to be savored as the wonderful historical tale that it is." —*BookPage*

"Lush . . . [a] rich yet fast-paced story." —*Historical Novels Review*

"Spectacular. . . . Haeger explores the fascinating, rich, exciting, and tragic life of Henry II's beloved. . . . Lush in characterization and rich in historical detail, *Courtesan* will sweep readers up into its pages and carry them away." —*Romantic Times*

"With her wealth of detail cleverly interwoven into a fabulous plot, Diane Haeger has written a triumphant tale that will provide much delight to fans of historical fiction and Regency romance." —*Affaire de Coeur*

The Queen's Rival

IN THE COURT OF HENRY VIII

DIANE HAEGER

NEW AMERICAN LIBRARY

NEW AMERICAN LIBRARY

Published by New American Library, a division of Penguin Group (USA) Inc., 375 Hudson Street, New York, New York 10014, USA • Penguin Group (Canada), 90 Eglinton Avenue East, Suite 700, Toronto, Ontario M4P 2Y3, Canada (a division of Pearson Penguin Canada Inc.) • Penguin Books Ltd., 80 Strand, London WC2R 0RL, England • Penguin Ireland, 25 St. Stephen's Green, Dublin 2, Ireland (a division of Penguin Books Ltd.) • Penguin Group (Australia), 250 Camberwell Road, Camberwell, Victoria 3124, Australia (a division of Pearson Australia Group Pty. Ltd.) • Penguin Books India Pvt. Ltd., 11 Community Centre, Panchsheel Park, New Delhi - 110 017, India • Penguin Group (NZ), 67 Apollo Drive, Rosedale, North Shore 0632, New Zealand (a division of Pearson New Zealand Ltd.) • Penguin Books (South Africa) (Pty.) Ltd., 24 Sturdee Avenue, Rosebank, Johannesburg 2196, South Africa

Penguin Books Ltd., Registered Offices:
80 Strand, London WC2R 0RL, England

First published by New American Library,
a division of Penguin Group (USA) Inc.

First Printing, March 2011
1 3 5 7 9 10 8 6 4 2

 REGISTERED TRADEMARK—MARCA REGISTRADA

LIBRARY OF CONGRESS CATALOGING-IN-PUBLICATION DATA:

Haeger, Diane.
The queen's rival: in the court of Henry VIII/Diane Haeger.
p. cm.
ISBN 978-0-451-23220-5
1. Blount, Elizabeth, ca. 1502–1539—Fiction.   2. Catharine, of Aragon, Queen, consort of Henry VIII, King of England, 1485–1536—Fiction.   3. Henry VIII, King of England, 1491–1547—Fiction.   4. Great Britain—Kings and rulers—Paramours—Fiction. 5. Mistresses—Great Britain—Fiction.   6. Ladies-in-waiting—Great Britain—Fiction. 7. Great Britain—History—Henry VIII, 1509–1547—Fiction.   I. Title.
PS3558.A32125Q46 2011
813'.54—dc22   2010039719

Set in Simoncini Garamond • Designed by Elke Sigal
Printed in the United States of America

For Kelly,
With love and gratitude

Prologue

July 1536
Greenwich Palace

"*I* tell you, it *is* her!"

"That such a strumpet would have the courage to return . . . It is scandalous!"

It had been years since Bess had been at court, and even longer since she had walked this vast carpet-lined gallery leading to the king's privy apartments. But it was not so long that she had forgotten how it felt to be whispered about loudly enough so she could hear. Neither the king's second cousin Lady Hastings, nor Lady Margaret Bryan—aging noble magpies in rich velvet, strings of pearls, and red and gold brocade—had changed at all.

Determined, she held her head high and ignored them. Time and years, more than two decades, slipped away. In those days she had simply been Bess Blount. But she was no longer that pretty, young, innocent girl; yet neither was he, the man she had come to see, the dashing young ruler he once was. But he was here, and he needed her.

As she made her way forward, the tall carved doors before her were parted by two stiff Yeomen of the Guard in green and white livery and silver breastplates. Each bore a tall, flashing gilt halberd. A line of elegantly clad servants and curious courtiers on the other side bowed deeply or dipped into formal curtsies as she advanced. Like waves, one after another, they acknowledged her as the venerable Lady Elizabeth Clinton, whose reputation well preceded her. Then they backed away in a kaleidoscope of movement—rich Tudor green, white, blue, red, and yellow velvet; brocade; and pearls combined with glittering gold. The tunnel of light, sounds, and fragrances drew her back in time even more deeply. There was no place on earth that smelled quite like the court of Henry VIII: rich, musky, complex—very like the king, the man, and the legend himself. Ironic, Bess thought, that it was here in this very presence chamber that she had first seen him. Here, she had first touched his hand . . . and had first fallen in foolish, childish love when she was barely fourteen.

The empty throne before her was polished and heavily carved, placed beneath a tall silk canopy fringed in gold and emblazoned with an H and J intertwined. J was for Jane Seymour, his new—and third—queen. Bess was relieved not to have to face her newest rival today of all days.

"Elizabeth, Lady Clinton."

Hearing her title announced by the herald, Bess fell into a deep curtsy herself. The rich amber-beaded velvet of her skirt, edged in gold thread, pooled around her as Thomas Cromwell, the king's chief minister, approached. Then Bess heard the whispers flare again, but she did not recognize the voices this time—those of two women and a man. Still, the sentiment was all too familiar.

"What will the new queen say, knowing that the mother of the king's son has dared to return?" one of the women wondered aloud.

"They shall likely say she looks surprisingly merry for her age, though she must be past thirty now," the oily-voiced man replied.

"Ah, it seems only yesterday that she was a fresh-faced and eager threat to the queen," remarked the second woman.

"Back then everyone in a dress was a threat to the Spanish queen," quipped the man in return.

"Not so much a threat as Bess Blount. He very nearly married her, they say."

As Thomas Cromwell, a stout middle-aged man in a black velvet robe and cap and a heavy gold and jeweled baldric, extended his hands to her in greeting, the conversation ceased.

"My Lady Clinton," he said somberly.

"My Lord Chancellor," she returned deferentially, acknowledging the king's most influential adviser.

"While I understand that this is the hour of your greatest grief, I am afraid His Majesty does not wish to be disturbed by anyone."

"His grief is my own, my lord."

There was a slight pause as he studied her, his gray beetle eyebrows merging. "'Tis true, I suppose. Under the circumstances, *you* are not just anyone."

Bess pressed back the tears that filled her eyes, refusing to cry at his acknowledgment of what had brought her such notoriety. *Mother of the king's son.* There had been rumors all across England less than a month before that Henry had actually been about to take the unprecedented step of formally naming his natural son—*his only son*—heir to the throne of England over Katherine of Aragon's and Anne Boleyn's daughters.

No one would ever know now if he had truly meant to do it.

His son; her son—precious Harry had been destined for greatness. He was meant to be Henry IX.

As Bess followed a porcine, tottering Cromwell down the long private corridor, her mind, still full of memories, caught and eddied on bright, sharp moments and images through the years. They tugged at her, bidding her to remember how a tender girl from the Shropshire countryside had wound up here at the court of Henry VIII, so naive yet so full of ambitious dreams—mistress to a king; mother of the King of England's only son.

Oh, yes, I shall go to court one day. . . . She heard her own voice echo across time, tumbling forward through her memories. *When I grow up, I may even meet the king. Just you watch and see. . . .*

When they reached the small rounded door, Cromwell turned back to her. His face was full, his snub nose was red, and his expression bore the barest trace of empathy.

"There is a secret staircase leading to the king's bedchamber beyond this door, my lady," he said. "You may be some comfort to each other, if he will see you."

"He shall see me. And I know well the way," Bess replied, turning the handle, its movement taking her very swiftly back in time. Each shadowy, winding step was like a year she had passed as the woman Henry VIII had met, loved, and had very nearly made his queen. . . .

PART I

The First Step . . .

A journey of a thousand miles
Must begin with a single step.
—Lao Tzu

Chapter One

June 1513
Kinlet, Shropshire

"*B*ess, wait!"

Hearing nothing but the wind, she raced back across the broad, waving carpet of emerald grass dotted with rich bluebells, a full pace ahead of her siblings. A canopy of azure dipped low to the horizon, meeting the shadowy stand of oaks ahead, on this Midsummer's Day. Her rich rose-colored skirts billowed out behind her so fully that she felt as if she might actually fly as the image of their father blossomed in her mind, kindling the excitement of seeing him. Of the six Blount children, she was his favorite, and these months had felt a lifetime to a girl of fourteen. Her mother had just returned from King Henry's court, where she served in the queen's household, and now her father was home from the war in France. All would be well with the world—at least with their own little world here in the countryside.

Tell us of the king, Father! Do tell us again!

Words echoed across memories, and images tumbled between them as her heart raced. In her mind, she was sitting on her father's knee, rubbing her forefinger over the smooth plane of his square jaw. He had always resembled a statue, she thought—chiseled, young, magnificent. Surely there could be no other father like Sir John Blount. Shortly after that, he had nobly gone off to France to fight alongside the king in order to reclaim English land. It was like something from a great romance, her mother drawing him to her and whispering devotions in his ear with tears in her eyes and her chin quivering as his great warrior bay stood ready in the distance. Bess and the other children had lingered silently nearby.

Mother had been home for only a few hours to be with her beloved. Still, that must have been something of a sacrifice, Bess thought, leaving the exciting court and its romantic, fascinating sovereign.

"He's a handsome sort, tall as a tree, and trim. His Majesty can hunt and sing—"

"And joust!" Bess had chimed, knowing the details well, yet still loving how her father recounted the tale, as he did with Lancelot and other magical adventures he read to them, filling their heads with fantasy and possibility.

"Yes, after jousts he can dance on into the night, besting everyone!"

Bess was faster than the others now, and more eager, as she dashed up the brick steps outside the house and scrambled through the vast entry hall, her footfalls softened by the Turkish carpets. She was determined to be first to greet her father once they had heard the sounding of the trumpet announcing his return. It had been almost a year since he had left.

George and Robert, her two brothers closest in age, were not far behind. Their little sister, Isabella, fell back and cried out again.

"I shall tell Master Clarke, and he is going to flog the lot of you properly for leaving me!" the little girl stubbornly warned, using their sour-faced tutor as a threat.

Predictably, they all ignored the stout, rosy-cheeked little girl behind them, who always insisted on tagging along. Bess keenly felt the thump of anticipation in her slim chest as she sailed around the corner and into the drawing room, which bore a massive wall of leaded windows with panes shaped like diamonds and a heraldic panel in colored glass. Then she stopped so suddenly that both boys crashed into her as if she were a wall. The wounded man, covered in blankets and lying on a litter, was not her father, her mind said, yet her heart knew that he was.

For a moment, Bess stopped breathing. Her hands fell limply to her sides; her lower lip dropped. She could not force herself to move forward. He frightened her, this old-looking man with the gaunt cheeks, gray skin, and hollow dark eyes. He did not even sense her presence or call for her approach as he usually would have done.

There's my poppet! Come give us a proper kiss.

The memory of his kind voice, so full of command from a year ago, shook her now, and Bess squeezed her eyes to chase it away as she fixed her gaze on someone who was not the man she remembered. This man was weak, defeated, and without the shine of the sun that once had so defined him. This was the last thing she expected. He seemed a stranger.

A heartbeat later, the boys pushed past her and ran to him, past the ring of Blount servants crowding the doorway. The litter on which he had been carried had been set on the sweet-smelling rush-strewn floor. Their mother was beside him, along with the steel-haired physician, Dr. Thornton, who had long attended the family.

"He really should be put to bed," Thornton dourly advised. "Sir John has had a long journey home, and he is not the better for it."

Catherine Blount held her husband's hand and glanced up at the kind-eyed family friend. "He said this was the view of Kinlet that kept him alive in France. He wants to look upon it for a moment longer. Then he will let us take him upstairs," she explained.

"Very well, but only a moment more," the doctor said, bargaining with her. "He must rest if there is any hope of a full recovery."

"What's happened to him?" George asked bluntly. He was the first of the children to draw near their father.

Two years older than Bess, George Blount could well have been her twin. He was slim and blue-eyed, and the color of his hair was exactly the same as her own—like wild honey kissed by sunlight, their father always said poetically. Finally catching up, Isabella pushed past the boys and fell to her knees beside the litter, but Bess remained beside the doors, stunned. It was like looking at a ghost of someone, she thought, feeling a shiver so powerfully that she almost could not look. She wanted her real father back.

"Shh," Catherine admonished. "Father has been wounded in the war, but by God's grace he has been returned to us."

Bess glanced at him again, lying there motionless, his expression unchanged. It did not appear that he had even heard his wife, who had returned from court as elegant and graceful as ever.

As if Bess's thought alone had brought the censure, Catherine Blount turned suddenly to look with reproach upon the prettiest, most willful, and eldest of her daughters.

"Bess, pray, do present yourself properly to your father. Do not cower there like that. It is not at all becoming or respectful."

Her legs felt like lead as all eyes descended on her and she moved slowly forward.

"Come, child," her mother urged with a note of irritation. "He wishes to see you. You know how he delights in you."

George reached back, clasped her hand, and drew her forward, knowing too well that their mother's level of patience did not match her serene beauty. In addition to their father's support, George's she could not do without, so she complied, kneeling along with the others, beside the litter. When she took his surprisingly cold hand and gave it a gentle squeeze, Bess was surprised that, at last, their father opened his eyes. Bloodshot and weary, full of war stories she could never understand, they gazed up at her. At last, some small spark of the father she had known appeared.

"Bess," he murmured in a raspy voice that did not resemble the one she remembered.

"Welcome home, Father," she managed to whisper. When she felt the slight tightening of his hand in hers, tears began to slide in long ribbons down her smooth, pale cheeks. The bond, the unspoken connection between them, was still there. He would always be her father, the man she idolized, and a man who actually knew the King of England.

As their father rested upstairs, Bess organized her favorite pastime—one into which her siblings were endlessly coaxed. By the hour, the music room became their presence chamber at court; a high-backed chair was her throne. George became Lord Chamberlain, Robert was her steward, and she, of course, was Queen Bess. Rosa, who was eight, and Isabella, who was seven, were her maids of honor. At not quite three, Agnes was too young yet to participate, but she was allowed to sit and watch the fantasy come to life. No one played the king since that seemed disrespectful. And after all, Bess reasoned, there could only ever be one King Henry VIII.

A copy of his portrait framed in heavy wood, a gift to the family from the king himself, hung prominently in the entry hall. Early on, Bess had committed each of his handsome features to memory.

She would stand before it especially whenever a long shaft of butter yellow sunlight moved across the paneled walls and made his image shimmer, almost as if he had come to life. And when Bess was certain no one was looking, she would smile shyly and make her best curtsy before it. Practice, her father said, was essential.

She would be prepared when her turn came to go to court.

"Must we play again, Bess?" Robert whined. "I do not at all like being a servant."

Her hands went to her hips and her tone became one of reproach. "You must work your way up at court, use all of your talents to get ahead. 'Tis what Father always says."

"What talents do I have?" he pressed. "I cannot sing or dance like you and George, and you always remind me that I am not at all clever."

Bess tipped her head. The expression she made became exactly like her mother's—serene, indulgent, and full of confidence. They looked so much alike, mother and daughter, with their smooth, milky, apricot-colored skin, wide blue eyes, small, perfectly shaped mouths, and golden hair.

"Then we must find what you are good at, or you shall not survive the rigors of court life," she exclaimed so authoritatively that she sounded as if she had actually been there.

"I am not going to court," Robert declared, his ginger curls stirring as he shook his head. "And neither are you. This is only a game, Bess."

"Not to me," she quickly countered.

"What are *you* so good at?" Robert asked belligerently as he crossed his arms over his chest.

"She *is* awfully pretty," said Rosa. "Is that not enough?"

"Mother says court is full of pretty, empty-headed girls. So it is most definitely not enough for me. I intend to go there and make the most splendid match with some great baron or earl. Just wait and see if I don't. That is why you must keep up your dancing lessons and your singing, and you really must improve the way you play the lute," Bess warned Rosa, who seemed only to be half listening, bored like the others with the repetition of the pointless game.

"I heard Father say that neither singing nor dancing is what the king fancies most in a girl," George quipped, suddenly sounding older himself. "And he fancies plenty of them!"

Bess shot him a glare. "That is a vulgar thing to infer. But he *is* king, after all, and he can do precisely as he pleases with all of us. Whatever his pleasure with any of us might be," she said, even though she really had no idea what that meant.

"Well, you get what you deserve if you ever go there," he warned.

"Riches and adventure? Those I would gladly take."

"And all that goes along with them," George shot back.

"I shall take my chances," Bess declared, asking herself, at that moment, what harm could ever come from the great honor of living in the presence of the handsome king at his grand and romantic court.

Bess had been called upstairs alone by her mother's maid. Such a summons was never good, although she could not imagine what she might have done that would have displeased either of her parents. Father had been home for only a few hours, and she had taken the other children and occupied them all, making certain they were not too loud. She lingered for a moment outside the door, straightening her rose-colored dress, then adjusting her posture. She glanced down at the lace of her flat, tight bodice, remembering there was a small stain of gravy there. She said a silent little prayer that Father would not notice. It had always been important to her to be perfect for Father—as perfect, at least, as he had always seemed to her. If he should notice and remark about it, Bess was certain it would sadden her for the rest of the day. His disappointment in her really was the greatest punishment.

"Come in, child," he called to her in that kind, cultured voice of his that was so reassuringly familiar.

Her mother was sitting beside him on the bed, but as Bess drew near, Catherine stood and clasped her hands before her in a more formal posture.

The bedchamber was suitably large, dominated by a grand tester bed and a vast armorial wall tapestry. There was a large table draped with fine damask silk that held a collection of thick candles and a stack of leather-bound books. Most prominent among the books was the volume of Chrétien de Troyes's *Lancelot* from which John Blount frequently read to his children, filling Bess's head most especially with romance. She stopped at the foot of the bed but quickly cast down her glance, trying to press back the coming flood of tears with which she was doing battle at the sight of him. It was difficult to see her strong and handsome father like this, wounded and vulnerable. A moment later, he held out his uninjured hand to her.

"Sit with me," he bid her as her mother stood silently in her elegantly embroidered gown with turned-back bell sleeves, beadwork, and a heavy rope of pearls hooked onto the bodice.

"Your mother and I have been speaking, and we want you to know, since I will be unable to return to court for a while, we have decided it will be better for the family that she remain here in Kinlet with me."

Bess could not help it. Her reaction was swift and instinctual. "Not go back? No! You cannot both retire from court! I shall lose my chance, and there shall be no opportunity for me to be presented to Her Grace if neither of you—" Bess lurched forward, her words spilling forward and her tears drying suddenly in panic. "Father, I do beseech you!"

"Now, my dear, you must not react so strongly, or he will think I was wrong about your being ready. Young maids of honor to the queen have control, not only over their emotions, but over their words and actions," her mother calmly reminded her with only a hint of a smile turning up the corners of her lips.

"Ready?" Bess looked back and forth at each of them. "Me?"

For a moment both were silent, each waiting for the other to speak. "My lord uncle Mountjoy, as you know, is the queen's chamberlain," John finally said. "I believe there is a very good chance that once I have written to him of our family circumstances, he shall invite you to function in Her Grace's household in your mother's stead. At least until she is able to return."

"At court? But when?" The four words leapt from Bess's mouth in a staccato rush, and her heart began to beat like a hummingbird's wings against the tight plastron front and square neck of her dress.

"As soon as possible, before there is any loss of place," her mother replied.

"I would go to the king's court as a . . . maid of honor?"

"That would be our hope," her father answered.

Bess sprang back to her feet as her face flushed with excitement. "I have dreamed of this forever."

"We know," her mother mused. "Your father is not as convinced as I that you are ready for the pace and the complexities of life there, but we haven't much other choice at the moment."

"Oh, I *am* most ready!" Bess replied excitedly. "I promise you I am. I will be the most extraordinary maid of honor, you shall see!"

"Settle down, child. Remember what I have told you. With this queen, it will not do to be too extraordinary, or too eager. She has yet to give the king a son, and everyone whispers that she has begun to fear competition."

"From her own household?" Bess asked with naive surprise.

"Especially there. The king and his friends are all young and healthy men, and their flirtations are a daily challenge past which the queen's ladies must navigate."

Bess tipped her head. "A challenge?"

"To maintain the balance between not offending any of them with rude rebuffs, yet not angering our extremely pious young queen with disrespectful or flirtatious games."

Bess felt her excitement pale just slightly as she tried in vain to understand and accept her mother's words of caution. The king was a married man, after all. Katherine of Aragon was said to be an exotic Spanish beauty, the daughter of the glamorous and powerful Queen Isabella and King Ferdinand. Their story was the stuff of legends. Their daughter could not be anything less than magnificent, Bess was certain, and her marriage as romantic as a verse about Lancelot.

"Teach me, Mother, before I go," she finally said. "You know I am a swift learner."

"That I do." Catherine Blount smiled with maternal pride at her daughter, so much like herself.

"I know I can make you both proud of me and keep your place for you until you are ready to return. And I shall keep the family honor as well."

"Lofty goals for a girl of only fourteen," her father observed as Catherine leaned down to give him another sip of wine.

"I am up to the task, I promise you! And I might even surprise you by attracting my own powerful man one day."

John Blount chuckled wearily. "Do not get too ahead of yourself, my little minnow. Let us first see if Lord Mountjoy can secure you a place in Mother's stead, shall we? And if he can, then we shall need to pray you do not irritate the queen with all of your ambitions and youthful excitement once you get there."

Chapter Two

*T*he redbrick palace lay across the river and above a great broad meadow before her like an enormous glittering jewel, with its commanding series of turrets and great towers, both round and square. All of it was surrounded by a wide, mossy moat. Bess gazed at it all in wonder as the party drew near the drawbridge entrance down the long tree-lined causeway. Lord Mountjoy had sent an escort to Kinlet to accompany her, and although the royal guards and the two stout court maids had been largely silent, they had made it apparent that she was a person of value, superior to them, and accorded respect. At her young age, that was a heady sensation for a girl whose dreams alone had been her guide until now.

Bess held herself proudly as she sat unmoving in her blue silk gown, the back of her hair held by a matching silk caul lined with delicate pearls. She was feeling almost grown-up as they crossed the stone bridge on horseback and neared the central gateway. Yet all the while she was trembling. It was more awe than fear brewing within her as she tried to remember all that her mother had tirelessly taught her, and each thing about which her father had warned her, over the last two months. Her heart quickened almost in time to the click of the horses' hooves as they finally passed into the wide cobblestoned courtyard, with its grand statuary, splashing fountains, and formal ring of conically shaped yew trees. Just seeing it, Bess knew, no matter what, there was no going back now. She wanted to be a part of the court's elegance, grandeur, and excitement.

The groom who approached her horse was a formal young man dressed in the king's green and white livery. A crown and pretty Tudor rose were sewn prominently onto the front of his tunic. But he did not smile or welcome her; he only helped her down, then nodded perfunctorily and turned away. There were other grooms-men around them who did the same for the others in her traveling party, then silently led the horses toward the grand stables.

Just then, two richly dressed ladies emerged from an open door at the top of a small flight of stone stairs in the palace's east wing and swept toward them. Bess was stunned by the elegance of their gowns. One was dressed in blue brocade with a square neck cut very low to her ample breasts, pearl ornamentation, and fashionably long, turned-back sleeves. The other wore a gown of topaz-colored silk with an underskirt and wide, puffed sleeves of sable-colored velvet. Both women wore gabled hoods and an abundance of pearls and beads. Neither of the young women smiled as they approached, but the one in brocade extended her hand, which was softer and more strikingly smooth than anything Bess had ever touched.

"I am Anne, Lady Hastings, Mistress Blount," she said as Bess made a proper curtsy, which she had spent a lifetime perfecting. "And this is my sister, Elizabeth, Lady Fitzwalter. We are the king's cousins, and our brother is the Duke of Buckingham."

Bess had already heard plenty from her mother about Edward Stafford, the Duke of Buckingham, who was Lord High Steward.

It was the highest ceremonial position at court, and his influence would have been unparalleled had there not been whispers about the king and Buckingham's married sister, Anne, who stood before her now. Catherine Blount had told her daughter that such an estrangement had developed between the two men over the girl's flirtations that the only means of healing the fissure had been for the duke, as a show of fidelity, to follow the sovereign into battle, where both now remained.

Bess tried to look a little more closely at the elegant girl without staring once she remembered the story. Lady Hastings had a smooth face free of wrinkles or scars, but her dark eyes were wide set, her nose was long and prominent, and her mouth was too small to balance it all. Looking at her now, a liaison with the great and dashing king seemed slightly preposterous to Bess when he had such an undoubtedly wonderful queen. Lady Hastings's sister was slightly more attractive and younger. Bess knew they were highly placed attendants to the queen and both were well regarded. She turned slightly then and honored Lady Fitzwalter with the same proper and well-schooled curtsy.

After the introductions and a chilly welcome, the sisters turned unceremoniously, as if their duty had been fulfilled, then went together back up the stairs, the intricate trains of their gowns sweeping along the steps behind them. That Bess should follow was implied, not stated, and she scurried to keep up, trying awkwardly to brush the dust from the hem of her own dress as she did.

"We are to show you to your accommodations. There, you may change and rest," Lady Fitzwalter said in a glacial tone, without turning around. "Presumably you have something more suitable to wear when you are introduced to the queen later today?"

"Yes, my lady," Bess replied nervously, wondering which of her three dresses, all far more plain than theirs, would be considered suitable by either of them.

Her mother had told her that since she was now one of the youngest maids of honor, and certainly the prettiest, she must not incite any sort of envy among the others. Sabotage was a pastime she would not know how to battle, and the family was depending on her. Looking at the backs of Lady Hastings and Lady Fitzwalter, their elegant gowns sweeping across the tile floor of the first long gallery, Bess herself was quite certain that was true.

The gallery in the east wing led to a wide-open loggia in the Italian style, with a view down to the king's intricate knot garden, ornamented with fountains, benches, topiaries, and stone statuary much like the courtyard. It was almost too much to take in so quickly, and Bess was not even sure where to look. Kinlet was elegant, but this was grandeur on a massive scale.

The walls of the gallery around her had the fragrance of fresh lime wash and were decorated with torches and vast Flemish tapestries on heavy black iron rods. The tile floors on which they walked were laid out in a beautifully intricate mosaic that resembled, almost perfectly, the shape of the knot garden below. The soaring beamed ceiling above was painted in a brilliant azure and decorated with the same crowns and Tudor roses as the servants' livery.

Just as they were turning toward a prominent, sweeping staircase, a young girl about her own age and a boy, dark curls spilling onto his forehead, came stumbling down the stairs, laughing and chattering. Quickly and without missing a beat, the girl made a proper curtsy and the boy dipped into a bow, their laughter ceasing only as long as it took to honor Lady Fitzwalter and Lady Hastings before dashing past.

"Typical," Lady Fitzwalter grumbled, rolling her eyes.

"If that empty-headed churl's father were not one of the king's closest friends, I do believe she would have been ousted long ago."

"Who was that?" Bess asked, biting back a smile at the very last thing she expected to see amid the seemingly structured and rule-dictated court.

"'Twas Elizabeth Bryan. Her father is Sir Thomas Bryan and her mother, Lady Margaret, is one of us. It was a foregone conclusion that their little terror of a daughter should be placed as a maid of honor. But personally, I believe the child needs a sound flogging," Lady Hastings declared.

"And the boy?" Bess dared to ask.

"Gilbert Tailbois," Lady Fitzwalter said with a sniff as if his name alone were objectionable. "The wastrel boy lives by some mysterious connection to Thomas Wolsey. Appointed to the cleric's household at the king's pleasure, the frightful little urchin nevertheless seems free to roam the halls of court, disturbing whatever he wishes whenever he pleases."

"His father is not of sound mind. You know that, Sister," Lady Hastings amended as they began to climb the same staircase the youths had only just descended.

"See that you do not model their behavior, Mistress Blount. The queen has no fondness for folly," Lady Fitzwalter warned.

"Nor patience for it," added Lady Hastings.

"I shall keep that in my mind always," Bess dutifully replied in the way she knew she was meant to.

At the end of a second tiled gallery, hung with portraits of various ancient dukes, lords, and kings, they came to what Bess realized must be the queen's apartments. A collection of elegantly dressed ladies was gathered beyond the open double doors in the watching chamber and in the presence chamber beyond. Her heart quickened again, so near to the absolute pinnacle of England's power and importance. *At last*, she thought as they moved into the queen's actual privy chamber. Before her lay the glamour, the music, the excitement of the queen's world . . . and by some miracle, she was about to be a part of it!

Bess moved more tentatively, however, behind Lady Hastings and Lady Fitzwalter. She was mindful of her mother's warning, even though she was secretly relieved to have seen at least one other noble maid, Elizabeth Bryan, with her same sense of spirit. If God favored it, perhaps they could one day become friends.

The queen's privy chamber, like the rest of the palace, was impressively vast, with one whole wall of windows, ornamented by cornices and columns, facing the gardens below. The other wall was lined with massive hunting scene tapestries and paintings hung in heavy gold frames. Beneath them were carved chairs cushioned with red velvet and gold fringe. Chairs of the same style were also placed in the center of the room, grouped at small carved tables where many of the queen's ladies sat sewing. But the thing beyond all else that struck Bess, as they moved inside the chamber, was the absolute silence surrounding her. There was no singing, no laughing, and no music. The occasional softly spoken word or whisper in Spanish was the only sound.

His eyes always glittered with excitement when her father told her stories of the gaiety of the king's apartments. There were endless card games, dice, and laughter, and the sovereign was never without music—a lute player, pipe, dulcimer, tabor, or a performance on the virginals by one of the royal musicians. Bess tried to press back the surprise and disappointment of reality as two more women approached. Both had dark hair and darker complexions, and their dresses were ornamented only by prominent silver cross medallions hanging from heavy chains. Lady Fitzwalter introduced them.

"Mistress Blount, this is Doña Maria de Salinas. She is Her Royal Highness's senior-most lady, as well as her dearest friend. It is to her authority you must answer above all others."

Bess dipped into an especially solicitous curtsy and remembered to keep her eyes lowered properly as she rose.

"And I am Doña Agnes de Venegas. My husband is Lord Mountjoy, your father's uncle and chamberlain over this entire enterprise," the other dark-haired woman said in an accent heavily laden with her Castellón roots. "It is by his favor that you are here. Remember that."

Again Bess curtsied. When she rose, she wisely did not smile. While both were young, they were sour-faced, serious women who set the tone for the queen's household, which clearly Bess was meant to adopt. Her romantic fantasy faded a little bit more.

"I have informed my husband that you have arrived, and he hopes to find time to meet you later. If not today, tomorrow."

A flurry of other introductions followed with names she struggled in vain to keep straight: Lady Percy, Lady Bergavenny, the Countess of Oxford, the Countess of Derby. Few of them smiled and fewer still acknowledged Bess in return. Even the flat-faced, plain Marchioness of Exeter, the daughter of Agnes Venegas and Lord Mountjoy, and thus her own cousin, seemed unimpressed by her arrival. It was not hostility Bess felt as she followed Lady Hastings from the room, but definite antipathy. In spite of all her dreams and hopes, Bess was apparently just another girl to fill out the queen's suite. And unlike the others, Bess did not even bear a title. She was merely plain Mistress Blount, an unimpressive maiden whose moderately connected father had called in a favor with a well-placed, distant relative. Everyone knew it, and there was no doubt that she was meant to know it as well.

Bess had not expected the overwhelming wave of homesickness to hit her, or so swiftly. She could not remember a time when she had not longed to come to court. She had dreamed of it and planned for it as if she had known it was the one wish in her life that would come true. Now, washed and changed from the long journey into a new gown and fresh headdress, she walked slowly and full of hesitation, back toward the queen's vast apartments.

Her dress was a suitably modest one of scarlet velvet with tight sleeves and white embroidery at the square collar. From the girdle at her waist, an enamel rosary hung. Her honey blond hair was swept up into a small, proper gold mesh caul. She was the picture of sweet elegance. Again, the silence in the queen's apartments startled her. Although the rooms were filled with court ladies all sewing or reading as before, they did so without laughter and with only a minimum of conversation. Bess did not realize it until then, as she stood at the fringes of the activity, that the ladies were sewing banners and copy after copy of the Royal Standard. Clearly, they were to be sent as encouragement to the English troops at war in France. It was a noble, if slightly dreary task that surprised Bess nevertheless. Even though she knew the king had named Queen Katherine as regent in his absence, Bess had expected Her Highness to be engaged in far more entertaining pastimes than those strictly of duty, like this, and prayer. Upon seeing the girl called Elizabeth Bryan, who, seated at one of the tables near the warmth of a charcoal brazier, was sewing a standard with another young maid, Bess felt safe enough to approach.

"May I sit with you?" she cautiously asked. When they both glanced up, Bess said, "I am Elizabeth Blount, but I am called Bess."

"Splendid. Because I am Elizabeth Bryan, and there can only ever be one of me." The declaration had been flippantly delivered, but it was followed by a sweet smile. "Yes, do sit with us. We could use some fresh conversation. This is Jane Poppincourt. She is friends with the king's sister, the Princess Mary. But occasionally Mistress Poppincourt deigns to entertain herself with less important maidens such as I."

They both giggled softly then, and Jane put her finger modestly to her lips. She was pretty with pale hair, gentle eyes, and a kind smile. Neither girl seemed to possess the same haughty demeanor of the other court women, and Bess was glad of that.

"Your uncle is Lord Mountjoy?" Jane asked as she handed Bess a needle and some red thread. Her accent was thickly French, but her voice was soft and appealing. There was none of the condescension she had heard earlier from the others.

"My father's uncle," Bess clarified. "Apparently the Lord Chamberlain took pity on my family since my father was wounded fighting alongside the king."

"We are all here as a favor to someone," Elizabeth observed. "Most of the queen's ladies do not fancy me at all, but my father and the king are inseparable, so, alas, they are forced to tolerate me, poor things." Elizabeth Bryan smiled a bit more broadly, clearly proud of herself and the place she had made.

"I saw you coming down the stairs when I first arrived."

"So you did. With Gilly. I am being punished by Lady Hastings for that bit of fun with no supper. Never mind, though, he is entertaining enough to be worth it."

"Are you and he—"

"Gilbert Tailbois and I?" She giggled at the notion and cut a glance at Jane who lowered her eyes with a shy giggle of her own. "Great heavens, no. He is just entertainment in this dreary place."

"My father always told me such stories of the dancing and the music here, the great and clever jests, and all of the magnificent banquets," Bess said a little dreamily.

"That is the king's merriment, not the queen's. When Her Highness is with child, as she is now, we must put aside all fun. So we sit silently, murmuring prayers for a living son this time, and we sew flag after flag to be sent for the men to take into battle," Elizabeth calmly replied.

It seemed a dangerous way for her to speak in the queen's chamber, and yet it felt deliciously brave as well. Clearly, Elizabeth Bryan was not in the least intimidated by her royal mistress. Nor was Jane Poppincourt, who stifled another soft giggle with the back of her hand. In spite of herself, Bess smiled, too, and the homesick sensation began to wane just a bit in the glow of the first small spark of excitement at making friends.

"So, how is it that Lady Hastings can scold you if your father is so powerful?" Bess asked.

"'Tis not power my father wields so much as a subtle influence," Elizabeth corrected. "The king wisely leaves the maintenance of the queen's household to the queen. Doña de Salinas worries after Her Grace, and Lady Hastings worries after all the rest of us."

"Because the king fancied her," Jane said in her soft voice.

"And because the Duke of Buckingham, her brother, is his most powerful minister?" Bess asked.

"Power wound and knotted like a fine skein of yarn," Elizabeth replied in agreement. "Lady Hastings played the game particularly well, and at the end kept a wealthy husband along with the admiration of her former royal lover. We all could learn from her."

Bess did not hide her surprise. "So the gossip was true about her and the king?"

Elizabeth leaned forward across the table, lowering her voice to a gossipy tone. "Well, naturally we cannot say for certain." She glanced furtively around the room. "But what I *can* say is that after spending a great deal of time in the king's company, Buckingham gained enough power to have his sister sent to a nunnery over the rumors. But she was quickly and quietly returned to court, to his dismay, and her position is even greater now. So naturally the rumors continue."

"Surely the queen has heard them; yet she tolerates a rival in her own household?" Bess asked.

"That, Mistress Blount, is the importance of power *and* influence. By some means or other she has won the king's favor, and no one, not even the queen, dares go against that."

Bess had never considered that a woman might be more influential than the queen, and it surprised her to imagine the prospect now. She picked up two pieces of fabric and began to sew them skillfully together, but her mind was far from the task. It seemed to her a dangerous thing to go against the very person in whose household one lived. But Lady Hastings certainly had a haughty-enough spirit for Bess to believe she was doing just that, and gaining power, riches, and influence along the way.

Admiration for her spirit and ambition mixed with pity inside Bess for Katherine of Aragon as she contemplated the poor pregnant young queen who had to tolerate the daily presence of a beautiful rival. Just as the thought moved across her mind, everyone in the chamber stood suddenly and fell into deep, silent curtsies to the swish of stiff silk and heavy petticoats near the door. As Bess mirrored their movements, she saw entering the room a young pregnant woman dressed in dun-colored satin, with a heavy gold cross ornamenting her square neckline bordered in gold thread. Doña de

Salinas was on one side of her; a pretty, fashionably dressed young woman on the other.

The queen was not what Bess had expected. Although her Spanish olive skin was smooth, her face was plain and square, and her dark eyes were wide and bulging, especially with her hair entirely hidden beneath her tight, stiffly gabled hood. As she approached, Bess properly lowered her eyes and remained in her curtsy.

"You are Mistress Blount," the young queen said in English deeply laced with a Spanish accent.

Slowly, Bess rose and faced the woman whom two English kings had taken as their queen. She seemed to Bess an uninspiring choice. "I am, Your Royal Highness."

"I see by your expression that I am not what you expected."

"Your Highness is far more than I expected."

"You lie like Mountjoy." The queen sniffed. "While it is less difficult to tolerate in one so young and obviously inexperienced, see that you do not make a habit of it. I do not suffer falseness gladly."

"I shall, Your Highness."

"Now then, are you suitably settled in?"

"Very well, thank you, Your Highness."

The queen had a small mole on her chin and hairs growing out of it, and she smelled thickly of musk. It was the scent of a man, not of a woman, and least of all of a queen. She was not at all like Guinevere in the romance *Lancelot*, which most powerfully had guided her to this place. Bess tried her best not to stare, but the mole was distracting.

"Then you shall attend me now at prayer."

It was four o'clock in the afternoon. Bess had been told that the queen attended matins each day upon rising, then returned to the chapel at midday. Did she truly mean to pray a third time in one day?

"Yes, Your Highness," she responded as dutifully as she could manage for every other thought swirling around in her mind.

Silent sewing. Repeated prayer. An absence of gaiety. Duty without pleasure. This was not at all the court Bess had envisioned, or the life. Perhaps things would be different once the king returned to England. *Please let them be different*, Bess found herself praying.

Anne, Lady Hastings watched the Blount girl follow the queen and the other young maids back to the chapel. *Good*, she thought as she asked for a cup of wine and received it from one of the queen's esquires. *A few blissful moments to myself without having to fawn over Henry's bland wife*, she thought as she lowered herself onto a carved oak armchair at one of the unoccupied tables heaped with flag fabric, as yet unsewn, left beneath a window. It was only a moment more before her sister joined her. The chatter that always rose up when the queen was gone now made their conversation inaudible to others.

"She is a pretty little thing, is she not?" Elizabeth, Lady Fitzwalter observed as she picked up a half-sewn banner and absently examined it with no intention of sewing any longer.

"If one values doe-eyed youth, I suppose she is."

"Half of the king's men do value just that, if not King Henry himself."

"His Highness seemed fairly pleased with my skills before he left for Calais."

"Brother always says beauty is power. When mixed with youth, it is generally a far more lethal combination than any that maturity could provide."

Anne frowned at her. "On whose side precisely are you, Sister?"

"The winning side, *Sister*. As any good courtier would be. You taught me that."

"Then you would do well not to antagonize me. His Highness shall return to court soon, and, when he does, I fully plan to return to his heart, my maturity not withstanding."

Lady Fitzwalter chuckled. "I do not think his heart was the part of him you captivated."

"Well, whatever it was, it gained Sir George and me a lovely country house, and this ruby that is the envy of all."

She proudly touched the huge stone in the center of a medallion accented with four shimmering pearls that lay against her tight silk plastron.

"Payment for your body makes you no better than a Smithfield whore," Elizabeth parried.

"You are only jealous the king never wanted you," Anne sniped.

"Are you so certain he will still want *you*? They say King Henry values most the thrill of the chase. You were hunted and caught long ago," her sister tauntingly reminded her.

"Your analogy bores me."

"Did you not see how many times his eyes rested upon pretty, virginal Lady Bryan at that final banquet before he left for France?"

"She is a child, and dull as dirt."

"Youth and beauty." Elizabeth smiled, reminding her sister. "Our dear older brother, the Duke of Buckingham, truly does understand a great deal more of our king than the one part of him you were allowed to know."

"You are poisoned by envy," Anne scoffed, and turned away.

"Rather, I have a realistic nature, Sister. And I am looking to keep my own fortunes sound when yours begin predictably to wane."

Anne stiffened. "I'll not share the king with a chit like Mistress Bryan, or Mistress Blount, for that matter."

"Will you have much of a choice?"

"There is always a choice when one knows how to play the game," Anne countered.

Elizabeth leaned toward her sister, then lowered her voice. "You would not do anything to either of them, would you? I mean, truly, Sister, they are only silly little girls."

Anne touched the ruby at her chest once again, then glanced up, her eyes narrowing. "Did our good brother not also say that all is fair in love and war?"

"Well, he certainly did not say anything about carnal relations."

"He well should have," Anne quickly countered. "After all, is it not all one and the same? And like all good warriors, I, too, protect what is mine. I tell you, no one is taking away what I captured for myself. Certainly not without a fight."

There had been a bland and quiet supper with the other maids of honor in a small, private dining hall, then a fourth journey to the chapel for evening prayer with the queen and her attendants before Her Highness at last retired. As the young queen read her dispatches and news from Calais, her servants were finally excused.

Bess lay exhausted in the small bed in the plain little room above the queen's apartments. The whirling thoughts in her mind had finally begun to slow, and she felt the heavy pull of sleep just as she heard a click of the latch at her door. The sound startled her, and, disoriented, Bess sat upright in the dark, her heart racing in fear. "Who's there?" she called out in a whisper.

Footsteps, breathing, and the faint scent of roses filled the cool, dark room. It was a feminine presence, though Bess could not see anyone in the dark. Suddenly, a candle flame ushered in a second person, the glow revealing a sweet-faced boy with a mop of dark curls that hung down onto his forehead. In the candlelight she could see that the girl beside him was Elizabeth Bryan.

"Are you prepared for your initiation?" she asked.

"I do not understand," Bess murmured.

"Mistress Poppincourt is standing guard just outside. We must see if you are one of us before we trust you with our friendship. Thus, the initiation," Elizabeth explained.

Bess now recognized the dark-haired boy as the one called Gilbert Tailbois. He was modestly handsome by this light, she thought; tall and lanky, his bearing as straight as a small tree. His face was long and narrow and dominated by his eyes, which were round and as black as his hair, framed by remarkably long, dark lashes.

"What precisely would you have me do?" Bess asked warily.

"Only as much as the three of us have done. You shall steal into the king's bedchamber by way of the secret staircase to which we shall lead you, then report back to us some detail of the room that will prove you were there."

"By my lord, I cannot!" she gasped.

"Of course you can. We will show you," Elizabeth said with a laugh. "It is an ancient staircase, which no one but the king ever uses; and he is away, so it will not be difficult."

"Then why do it?" Bess asked, still clutching the bedcovers and trying frantically to think of a way to dissuade them.

"Why do anything? Because you can get away with it," Elizabeth answered with a beguiling little grin. "And because it is a bit of fun in this dreary old place, which is far too dull with most of the men away at war."

Gil gave a little huff of indignation at the slight that was buried in her response, and Elizabeth tossed him a carefree glance. "No offense to you, of course, Gilly," she added, still smiling in a way that seemed capable of winning her just about anything she desired. "So, will you join us then?"

Had she any other choice? Bess wondered. They, alone, were befriending her, and the alternative—a solitary existence—was not a pleasant one, considering the other women she had met.

Silently, the four youths stole quickly down the torch-lit corridor, Bess in a hastily donned pair of slippers and a gray cloth cloak to cover her white linen nightdress. Her heart was racing as they neared the entrance to one of the several round palace turrets that housed a steep staircase, but it brought with it an unexpected sensation, which she liked. There was pleasure and novelty in excitement— the first she had found at court.

Suddenly, Elizabeth Bryan stopped, and the others backed up behind her. A quiet, nervous laughter followed.

"All right, this is where we leave you," Elizabeth declared.

"But why?" Bess asked, her sense of panic beginning to rise again.

"That is the point of the game. Beyond that little door is a staircase. At the top are another door and a grand tapestry like a drapery past which you shall find the king's bedchamber."

"Bring us back an account of something or small token proving you were brave enough to enter there, and you shall be one of us for life," Gil added with the gravity of one advising a military maneuver, in spite of the adolescent sprinkling of pimples she now saw spotting his cheeks.

Bess glanced at each of their three faces lit by golden torchlight, all gone quite serious. "What if I am caught?"

"Have courage," Jane replied on behalf of them all. "But just in case, you are to say it was entirely your own idea."

"Implicating us," Elizabeth added gravely, "would be unfortunate. And it would immediately void our offer of friendship."

For a moment, Bess considered objecting or declining the challenge completely. The risk would be far greater than the gain if she were caught and sent back to Kinlet. And yet Father always said that in life there were risks. The spoils generally went to those who were brave enough to confront a challenge. *Father . . .* She thought longingly then, wishing he were here to tell her what to do.

"It will be dark. How will I see?" Bess asked, stubbornly willing her voice not to break.

Elizabeth and Jane exchanged a quick glance as Gil explained. "The turret is lit by moonlight through several small windows, the bedchamber by half a dozen larger ones."

And with that, she was pushed through the door, like a lamb from a pen, and she was on her own.

Bess's heart pounded beneath her nightdress and cloak as she held on to an old rope handrail, fed through iron loops, to steadily make her way upward. Although it was summer, the turret was dank and musty, making it apparent that the secret staircase was rarely used. *Good, at least I have that,* she thought, trying to still her heart enough so that she would not entirely lose her faltering courage.

The bedchamber she entered at the top of the stairs was vast and full of frightening shadows. As the summer wind blew the trees outside, the shadows danced before her. Pressing back the overwhelming sense of panic, Bess tried to focus on the task at hand so that she could scramble quickly back down the stairs victoriously.

The bed at the room's center was massive, raised high on a platform, with a tall, crimson velvet tester emblazoned with a gold H.

Beside it, on the wall, was a mural depicting the life of Saint John. Bess tried quickly to survey the rest of the shadowy chamber for a distinctive detail that would prove she had been inside. A large round table with turned legs holding a stack of books was near the grand stone hearth. The soaring buttressed ceiling bore painted oak beams and a crown. There was an ornately carved cabinet, a small writing table near the window, tapestries on the other walls, and a grand portrait of the king's father, Henry VII, in armor, dressed for battle.

Bess moved toward the table carefully, feeling the wood floor beneath the carpets creak with each careful footstep. She could not still her heart, but she had stopped trying. This was simply going to be terrifying until the moment she escaped.

She glanced at the table piled with books. Prayer books sat stacked along with volumes by Petrarch, Aristotle, and the work of John Skelton, all of which she herself had at least partially read. Each was bound in rich black or crimson leather, the titles tooled in gold. She picked up a small, black leather-bound volume of *Lancelot*, the old epic story of chivalry and romance her father had read to her when she was young. So the handsome young king had a romantic heart, she thought as she scanned the familiar pages—a heart challenged, no doubt, by war, and many other matters of office.

Suddenly there was movement. She heard the click of a door handle. The sound of heavy, controlled footsteps followed. Someone was entering the darkened bedchamber behind her. Struck by a new surge of fear, and with her means of escape—the secret door across the room—suddenly blocked, Bess instinctively scrambled beneath the massive bed.

She had thought this game a mistake—now she knew it. The very best she could hope for was simply to get out in a single piece, and without being caught.

The footsteps, as they neared, were commanding, full of purpose—not tentative like her own. It was a man's heavy-footed stride that shook the cold floorboards onto which she pressed her face and felt her heart slam. Carefully, still holding her breath, Bess lifted the velvet skirt of the bedcover and dared to peer out. There was a swish of black satin, and the man was beside the book table, in the very spot she had stood, now lit by a candle lamp, which he held. He was tall and thickly set, dressed in clerical garb. His nose was long and hooked; his face defined by prominent jowls.

Suddenly there was a flash. Candlelight illuminated a ring on his finger, making it sparkle. And she knew. This was the famous cleric Thomas Wolsey—Henry VIII's Almoner and key adviser, as well as the architect of the war in France. Her father had described the important players at court so well that she knew them all. Wolsey was unmistakable.

She watched him more keenly now, moving past her own great sense of panic to wonder what he was doing alone at this late hour in the king's private bedchamber. In his long cassock, buttoned to the floor, close-fitting sleeves, white rochet, and biretta, he moved methodically. The strong scent of ambergris swirled around him, invading the room. She kept silent watch as he flipped through each of the books as if searching for something hidden between the pages. He moved next to the tall, ornately carved cabinet.

Stories about Thomas Wolsey played through her mind as she watched him. In great detail and with much gesturing, her father had told her of a boldly ambitious man, the son of a merchant from the village of Ipswich, who had found not only his calling in the clergy, but his path to greatness. An unattractive middle-aged man, who seemingly presented little outward threat to the other ambitious courtiers, Wolsey had become the king's private Almoner, a member of the Privy Council, and eventually, and determinedly, an intellectual counselor whom the king had come to trust implicitly. But, as Bess studied him from beneath the bed, she felt instant distrust. Knowing he was here in these private quarters when the king was away seemed to confirm her feelings.

Suddenly, her thoughts were distracted by a small, soft slip of lace fabric edged in silk bunched up on the floor beside her. Bess pulled it to her in the shadowy darkness, as there was some sort of embroidery sewn into the center in small, neat stitches. She watched Wolsey open the cabinet next and begin rifling through one of the drawers there. She did not move, and she tried to not even breathe too loudly. But she watched.

The prelate took a small blue velvet pouch, heavy with coins, and she watched him withdraw several, as if they were his own, before replacing the pouch. Next, he took a small brick of crimson wax and a gold stamp and put them into a pocket in his ankle-length black satin coat. Did he really have this sort of access, Bess wondered, or was he actually stealing from the king?

She had heard some of the women saying that after victories at Thérouanne and Tournai, young King Henry was now seeking appointment for the older Wolsey as Bishop of Tournai. Perhaps Wolsey had returned early to watch over the pregnant queen now that victory belonged to England? Bess knew she had much to learn here, and she could not be certain of any of the players enough to trust them. She clutched the lump of fabric and waited until he finally left the room. Only then did she scramble back out from beneath the bed as she dived for the secret door, anxious to be out of there.

In the corridor at the bottom of the turret, Bess expected to see Elizabeth, Jane, and Gil waiting for her, but they had vanished.

As the panic came at her in another powerful wave, Bess tried to remember from which direction in the black maze of hallways they had come so she could make her way back to her chamber. In the dark, the corridor, which ran in two directions, was impossibly long and forbidding. If she went the wrong way now, she could easily become lost and at greater risk of being caught. Neither path before her looked familiar. Yet with the sturdy determination of a Blount, she chose one, exhaled an unsteady breath, and moved forward.

"Lost your way?" a deep-voiced man called out behind her.

Bess's heart stopped. She froze where she was. She was afraid to turn around. When she did at last pivot back, tucking the fabric into a fold in her skirt, she saw that it was her father's uncle, the balding and formidable William Blount, Lord Mountjoy. She had met him at Kinlet on only two occasions, but the family resemblance to her father, particularly the cool blue eyes, was unmistakable.

"My Lord Chamberlain," she said, curtsying properly, as she knew her father would wish her to do, even as she wondered what he was doing here so suddenly.

"You may call me uncle, Elizabeth. It may smooth your way around here a bit."

She was relieved by the courtesy he was showing her in spite of her surprise at his appearance here. She thought about asking him, in return, to please call her Bess, as the rest of the family did, but she decided against it. Perhaps that was just as well. Mountjoy was a stranger to her really, and a forbidding presence. He was only doing a duty having her in the queen's chamber. And when her mother returned to court, Bess was likely to be sent home to Kinlet. She had only a brief chance to make an impression, and she must not do that by being too familiar with the man who held so much power over her.

"So, who put you up to it, Mistress Bryan or young Master Tailbois?" Mountjoy asked as they began to walk.

Bess was surprised that he knew. Then again, Mountjoy did oversee the queen's entire household. "I do not believe they were being malicious," she carefully replied.

He shook his head. "I should have known. Those two are as thick as thieves, and together they are twice as dangerous."

"But they seem so pleasant."

"Few at court are as they seem, Elizabeth. You must be vigilant about that, constantly assessing. Our king and his queen may be spirited souls, but they take loyalty seriously."

Hearing him speak of loyalty, she thought then about mentioning Wolsey's apparent midnight theft from the king, but she decided against it, at least until she knew the players better. When Mountjoy walked her in the opposite direction from the one she had intended, it was a symbolic reminder that, at the moment, she really was in need of all the guidance she could get.

Her father's uncle then bid her a good night at the door to her little room above the queen's apartments and informed her that she must rise early the next morning to attend matins with Her Highness. In spite of the objectionably early morning hour, it was an honor, doubtlessly one he had secured for her, and she must not be late. While Bess still found her very formal uncle an extremely intimidating man, now she felt a tiny glimmer of relief that there was an adult here at court upon whom she might actually come to depend.

When she opened the door and went inside, Bess was surprised to find Elizabeth Bryan sitting alone on the bed, her skirts pooled around her and her face bright with a smile.

"You abandoned me," Bess declared angrily.

"Yes, well I am sorry about that, but it was unavoidable. The king's Almoner, who is also Gilly's benefactor, Thomas Wolsey, returned to court unexpectedly today, so Gilly was called upon immediately to attend him."

"At this late hour?" she asked skeptically.

Elizabeth Bryan chuckled. "You shall learn soon enough that courtiers—particularly important statesmen—have little sense of time, or duty to it. We all serve at the pleasure of our masters."

Bess closed the door, moved forward, and slipped off her shoes and cloak. Her entire body ached, and her mind was still spinning. "Why has Master Wolsey returned from France without the king?"

"Apparently our sovereign wished a trustworthy accounting of the queen's health, and of her pregnancy. The queen badgered him into naming her regent while he is away, but since there has been so much trouble bringing a royal child to term, the king is said to have realized the gamble. He trusts Wolsey to the exclusion of all others to tell him how his wife truly is."

"My father said Wolsey battles for place with the king's child-hood friend, Charles Brandon."

"In truth, he does. But Wolsey's advantage is his tie to the Church. Where Brandon feeds his spirit, Wolsey feeds his soul, and he does it with aplomb."

"You doubt the cleric's devotion?"

"It is more that I understand his ambition," Elizabeth clarified.

"I feel far too young to understand the ambitions of grown men," Bess said as she began to unlace her gown.

"Wait until you are here for a while. You will understand them well enough."

"Then what drives a man like him, do you think? A man who has been given access to the King of England? What would a man like him hope to gain?"

"As much as he can, I suspect. Just like the rest of us," Elizabeth pointedly replied. Bess sank wearily onto the bed beside her as Elizabeth twisted her head, changing the subject, and asked, "So then, did you complete the task we gave you?"

"Of course. I have the article right here to prove it."

Elizabeth tipped her head. An incredulous smile broke across her small face. "You took away something?"

"Only some scrap of cloth from beneath the bed, just to show for certain I was there."

"Gilly thought he saw spark enough in you that you might actually go through with it," she said with a chuckle.

Bess felt a surge of anger at the sound of Elizabeth's laughter. "Oh, he did, did he?"

"Gilly said he thinks that great beauty brings courage along with it, so he will be glad to know he was correct."

Bess sprang indignantly back to her feet. "Oh, will he?"

"Oh no, do settle your tail feathers, Bess. It was all just a bit of fun."

"At my expense! What if I had been caught?"

"You are far too clever for that. Even I could tell that from the first. You take after your mother, whom we all like a great deal."

Bess knew that flattering her mother was a ploy, but her homesickness allowed it to work predictably. "Do not do anything like that to me again," she warned a little more tepidly.

"It is a promise. Now then, what exactly did you fetch?"

Bess held up the article then, looking at it herself for the first time. In the light she could see that it was a baby's cradle blanket. The embroidered initial she had felt in the dark was not an H but an A sewn in gold thread with a crown embroidered above it. The A was clearly for Arthur, the king's older brother, first husband of Queen Katherine. For a moment, both girls gazed at it in awe. The king's bedchamber was not a place an infant's cradle ever would have been placed or stored, so it had likely been secreted there intentionally—a link perhaps to a lost son or brother by this king or the last. Bess considered the romantic thought. It was a poignant reminder of the humanity and mortality behind the grandeur of the ruler Bess had yet to see or meet.

"The women in the queen's suite always speak of how close the brothers once were. Perhaps it remains there as a comfort and reminder," Elizabeth offered, losing her smile and sounding, for a moment, almost like an adult.

To have married his own brother's widow must have brought a certain amount of guilt, and even a sense of betrayal, Bess thought, knowing well of the sibling bond between herself and George. She could not imagine George gone forever from her life, or what small token she might wish to keep as a reminder.

"That is so sad," Bess said softly.

"Some whisper that the king's marriage is cursed because he married Arthur's wife, which in Leviticus the Bible expressly forbids, and that is why she has not yet been able to give him a living child. It is said he might well believe this himself."

"My father always says the marriage bond is the most important thing. I cannot imagine going outside of that."

"Here, there is very little fidelity. You shall see that soon enough," Elizabeth warned.

"So, do I pass the test from you and Master Tailbois?" Bess asked, changing the subject.

They both glanced down at the baby's cradle blanket she had

taken from a king. "Indeed you do. Actually, for that, we should well call you our new leader," Elizabeth said with a clever smile.

Gil knelt and removed Wolsey's lambskin riding boots from his thick, blistered feet and placed them neatly beside the chair. Then he stepped dutifully back beside the fire to pour the cleric a cup of warm ale. Wolsey had grumbled to the boy already that his journey had taken him two arduous days, traveling from Calais back to Richmond. It was three hours on choppy waters, crossing from Calais to Dover, then another long ride over hard, rutted roads, stopping only for fresh horses that would see him to his duty. By the time he had arrived, it was dark and the queen had already retired, so Wolsey would have to settle for speaking with her in the morning after matins, and then begin the exhausting return journey. Such was the level of his ambition to please the king who had sent him.

Gil prepared a basin of warm water for Wolsey's feet, then brought it to him. "Your feet and ankles are blistered from the stirrups."

"And they shall be so again tomorrow as I return to Thérouanne."

"Can you stay no longer and rest, perhaps?"

"I have my duty, boy, as you have yours," Wolsey answered gruffly.

He watched the youth flinch at his words, which were delivered in a clipped tone. Thomas Wolsey had not intended to sound harsh, but softness was weakness, he reasoned, and that could only get in the way of his ambition.

In the beginning—a lifetime ago now—he had taken responsibility for the boy out of guilt. He had retained him as a ward out of affection. Wolsey touched Gil's head as he felt the warm water's relief. The boots really were too tight, but they were of hand-tooled

Spanish leather, from the same maker the king himself often used. Wolsey was a vain man. Few knew that about him because he hid it well behind his greater show of piety. He hid many things well. The road to court from the life of a simple rural priest in Norwich had been a long one, and he had made many mistakes along the way. The greatest threat to his wild ambition was his continuing hunger for women. He glanced again at young Tailbois, still tenderly washing his feet. The lad did not seem to know that particular variety of temptation—or, perhaps, just not yet.

Thomas Wolsey had not so much desired to join the clergy as he had accepted it as his sole path to a life of prominence and riches. And once decided, he had trod that path well. He had greedily taken every opportunity, attending Oxford, befriending the powerful Marquess of Dorset, and eventually becoming rector in Somerset, where the marquess was patron. But, as with everything, Wolsey had done it all by taking careful shortcuts and using other unconventional means, and satisfying himself along the way with more than one mistress.

Then, ten years ago, he had found himself chaplain to the great Archbishop of Canterbury, and thus in the direct pathway to the new young monarch, Henry VIII. And nothing—nor anyone—was going to get in the way of that.

"Is that better?" Gil asked, drying Wolsey's feet and carefully pressing them into soft black velvet slippers.

"'Tis far better, actually. My thanks."

Wolsey watched how the reply, casually spoken, worked like a balm to heal the sting of his earlier words. He could see it in the boy's face. He idolized him.

"I am glad. I can only imagine so arduous a journey."

"Yes, lad, it was that. And I shall be forced to depart as soon as I have spoken with the queen."

"When will you return for good, now that you have so masterfully arranged for the king's victory in France?"

Thomas smiled in spite of himself, and his meaty cheeks puffed into two round balls above full red lips and below coal black eyes.

"You did do that, after all. I know it is your victory," Gil proclaimed.

"'Tis true enough, I suppose," Wolsey said, voicing his agreement with a boastful flourish as he again drew up the cup of ale. "And it was no simple task with Brandon always in the way."

Charles Brandon, the king's affable childhood friend, was Wolsey's nemesis in all things—and the single greatest impediment to his complete dominance over the sovereign. While Wolsey was stocky and ruddy faced, Brandon was slim, muscular, athletic, and handsome. While the king's Almoner was serious and intense, the king's friend was blithe and witty. These past months in France had been a daily struggle for Wolsey to keep himself in the forefront before Brandon. The selfless offer to ride home to check on the queen was the culmination of that struggle. The taking of a few coins from the king's private stock had not been out of need for money so much as to prove that he could get away with it whereas Brandon could not. He, alone, had such unfettered access to the king. It was not behavior befitting a royal Almoner perhaps, but behavior certainly expected of the scrappy son of a commoner, one not to be underestimated by anyone.

"The king has it in his mind to meet with the emperor's sister. But after that rather meaningless show, we shall all ride back to England, triumphant, drenched in our victory, prepared, at long last, for the birth of the royal heir," he said with a sneer.

He liked Katherine well enough. She made a tolerable queen, if not a stunning one. But he, like the rest of England, had already begun to grow weary of the wait for a living heir to secure the monarchy and the country. Certainly, there was no one else to be blamed for that but the queen. Marguerite of Navarre was said to be beautiful and witty, which Wolsey knew was the real reason Henry was keeping his army in Thérouanne longer than necessary. But the boy did not need to know that when he was still innocent about many of life's more harsh realities. That veil would be lifted the moment Gil found someone he truly wanted but could not have.

Wolsey knew all too well the pain of that.

A light knock sounded at the door then, and Thomas set down his cup. "You may leave me, lad. I am certain you are tired."

"I should see you to bed first."

Wolsey stood as the door clicked, then slowly opened. A slim middle-aged woman with a narrow face, prominent nose, and straight, unbound russet-colored hair walked into the room. She was wearing a cambric nightdress, a blue velvet dressing gown, and a matching cap.

"Forgive me, my lord. I believed you would be alone by now," she said, seeing the boy still kneeling at Wolsey's feet.

"So did I. That shall be all for this evening, Master Tailbois. You may retire now," he declared, drawing one of the king's coins from a pocket in his coat and handing it to him.

Certainly the gesture was more than generous, but silence was golden, and keeping the lad's tongue, as well as his loyalty, was worth the price. He watched Gil regard the woman, then look back at him. For the first time in a long while, the boy's expression did not reveal what he was thinking.

"Shall I return in the morning to attend you, sir?" Gil finally asked as he moved slowly to the door, openly clutching the valuable coin.

Wolsey made certain not to look at the woman as he responded. "That shall not be necessary this time, lad. But thank you just the same," he replied in a calm, well-schooled tone, betraying nothing of himself beyond the words.

The next morning just before dawn, Bess was awakened by a young servant girl who quietly helped her into a modest dress of beaded yellow satin with white lace frills at the wrist and wide, hanging sleeves. Once again, she was to attend the queen for matins. Everything at court was much more somber than she had imagined. Bess dressed her own hair by lamplight at the small polished looking glass framed in etched silver on a table next to her bed. Carefully, she pinned on a plain cap with a white linen fall that met her shoulders, and topped that with a gabled hood. She studied her reflection for a moment. Her skin was smooth and pale, her eyes were wide and vivid blue, and her nose was small and turned up sweetly at the end. She had always known she held the promise of beauty. But who might think her beautiful when there were so many sophisticated women at court, she could not imagine.

Gathered in the presence chamber among ladies-in-waiting and other maids of honor as the sun slowly rose, pale pink, through the leaded windows, were Elizabeth Bryan, Jane Poppincourt, and Mary, the girl she knew to be the king's younger and favorite sister. Bess lingered near the door at first, uncertain of her place among the elegant players. Elizabeth moved among the women with such grace and ease that it only increased Bess's discomfort. Bess linked her hands at her waist, uncertain what else to do with them to stop their trembling. If there could be one friendly face, like that of her brother George, she could stop longing so desperately for the predictability of home and enjoy her limited time here. As yet, she did not trust Elizabeth Bryan.

"I never thought you would do it. I am sorry we asked that of you."

The voice, young, male, unsteady, and whispered, came from behind her. Bess pivoted slowly. It was Gil Tailbois. He had entered the vast rooms with Thomas Wolsey, who had continued into the presence chamber just as Queen Katherine came out of her bedchamber through an arched doorway and drew near him. Bess watched the king's stout Almoner bow reverently to the queen and then embrace her affectionately. Their inaudible whispers forced Bess to turn her attention back to the slim youth with the dark curls, and even darker eyes, who stood before her. The reference to the previous night set her even more on edge.

"Do you and Mistress Bryan test all of the new girls at court this way, or was I the only fortunate one?"

Clearly surprised at her sharp tone, Bess watched him shrug his shoulders, then run a bony hand behind his neck. "'Twas only a game, mistress."

"One that well could have seen me ejected from court altogether. I find little humor in that sort of game."

"More's the pity when you are so splendid at it," said Elizabeth Bryan, who had come up beside them in a sweep of amber-colored brocade, a gold and pearl pendant glistening at her throat.

People here seemed always to be doing that, listening and lurking about, Bess thought angrily, remembering not only Wolsey but her own uncle. It was off-putting, to say the least.

"We were wrong and you know it," Gil suddenly said to Elizabeth. "Our boredom is not a sound reason to risk another's position."

"Mistress Blount is going to discover that no place at court is ever without risk. She may as well find that out sooner than later. I believe we did her a service," Elizabeth parried.

While Wolsey continued speaking with the queen, Bess watched the Princess Mary whispering and laughing with Jane Poppincourt. Their light chatter was in direct contrast to the constant restraint, fear, and oppression Bess felt. She had clearly prepared her tourdion and her pavane for nothing; all anyone seemed to do here was sew or pray. For her, there was no reason to laugh or smile.

As the queen linked her arm with Wolsey's and headed toward the door for prayer, the rest of the court ladies and younger girls silently assembled behind them. As it was with everything else, the procession was a grave and orchestrated undertaking.

When Lady Hastings nodded to her, Bess slipped into the line where she was directed beside the king's sister. At eighteen, Mary was poised and breathtakingly pretty, and she seemed to Bess more elegant than anyone else in the queen's household. It was difficult for Bess not to turn her sideways appraisals into stares as the collection of women walked silently out into the corridor, across a rich inlaid tile floor, and advanced down a twisted staircase to the king's chapel. As they neared the open doors, the ladies before her all steepled their hands solemnly, and Bess followed suit. The queen and Wolsey were still speaking in low tones at the head of the line. Childish curiosity made her long to know what they were saying. Lines from *Lancelot* and sweepingly romantic images moved through her mind, and she nearly fell out of step before she steadied herself by looking at the back of Gilbert Tailbois directly ahead of her.

He walked beside Elizabeth Bryan, her pretty amber brocade dress sweeping over the tiles. He was not unattractive, Bess decided, as they moved in a silent double-file line into a small, cold chapel, a sanctuary with a very high vaulted ceiling and far fewer chairs than ladies. It became obvious that those behind her and the princess would be required to stand. Bess had no idea how someone so young and new at court as she would have been given such prominence of place, but she was old enough to realize that those behind her would not like it. The thought only set her further on edge.

Instead, she tried to focus again on the young man in front of her—the only male, besides Wolsey, in their company. Gil seemed taller than most young men his age, certainly taller than George, her brother. He was not quite gangly, yet youthfully slim. His rich wheat-colored doublet bore slashings at the puffed sleeves, and a dagger and tassel were slung from a belt at his waist, in the current fashion, all of which seemed to wear him, rather than the other way around. Yet he walked with a certain confidence bespeaking his feelings that he belonged precisely where he was, however mysteriously. Bess liked that about him, even though she was still angry about the challenge.

She was too aware of the people around her after that to hear much of the service, making sure to know for certain who each lady was, her title, and level of importance at court. She silently catalogued each of them as the cleric at the altar droned out the prayers. It would be dangerously easy, her mother had warned, to insult someone if she did not.

After the early-morning service, they returned to a large, elegant chamber beside the queen's apartments for breakfast. It did not come as any surprise to Bess that the meal was simple. There was baked fish, porridge, and bread served at a large tapestry-draped oak trestle table in a room overlooking the bowling green. The queen did not join them; neither did Wolsey nor Master Tailbois. She was disappointed at that since, besides Elizabeth Bryan, Gil seemed the only spirited soul at this rather dull court, and the comparisons she was continually making between them had begun to remind her of George.

Bess sat between Elizabeth and Jane, eating silently as she tried not to stare at Princess Mary, who sat on the opposite side of the table. Such elegance fascinated her. Her dress was rich pumpkin-colored velvet, the square-cut necklace outlined with a border of gold, set with jewels. At her breast was a heavy gold square pendant adorned with four pearls. Her pale copper-colored hair was caught up above her neck in a gold mesh caul. Even for matins, Mary looked noticeably lovelier than the other girls, and still there was a spark of fun about her. It made Bess wonder if her brother, King Henry, possessed the same spark. He certainly had that reputation.

After the silent meal, the ladies returned to the predictable task of sewing more banners and flags. As it had been the day before, it was largely silent work, and Bess was certain she would soon go mad from the tedium, when a commotion exploded in a flurry of Spanish in the privy chamber just beyond the doors. Murmurs, whispers, and serious cutaway glances occurred all around her, but no one dared move from their places.

A moment later, one of the queen's stewards bent down behind Mary. After he whispered something to her, she pressed back her chair, stood, and went alone in a swish of velvet skirts into the presence chamber next door.

Bess glanced at Elizabeth. "What is happening?" she whispered.

"I heard this morning that the Scottish are attempting to use the king's absence as an opportunity to attack England in the north. The troops are collecting there, and the queen is planning to lead them herself against King James."

"But the queen is with child!" Bess exclaimed, stunned by such a possibility.

"That is what's causing everyone's concern now. Her Highness waited until Wolsey left for France with his report of her health for the king. Now she wishes to go into battle like her mother, the warrior Queen Isabella."

"Will she go, do you think?" Bess asked with wide-eyed surprise.

"Her aides as well as her ladies are trying to counsel her against it. But the queen is a stubborn woman once she sets her mind to something. And she believes having had the king name her regent in his absence, before he left, is a great honor that should not go untested."

"She seems so mild mannered."

Elizabeth smiled. "She does, does she not? But the daughter of Ferdinand and Isabella is not someone I would wish to go up against."

"I shall take that as a warning."

"You would be wise to do so," Elizabeth Bryan concurred, glancing back at the open door. They could still hear arguments back and forth in both Spanish and English.

"Will she go, do you think, even risking the royal child?" Bess asked again.

"I believe it is likely that her warrior side will trump her maternal side for now."

Each girl went back to the banner she was sewing, trying to eavesdrop on a conversation all of England would soon be privy to if Queen Katherine got her way. From that moment, Bess had new respect for the proud Spanish queen, a seemingly plain and understated woman. She had much to learn, Bess thought as a warm summer wind blew through the open windows, ushering in the scent of wisteria and wildflowers from the garden.

The next morning, the women and young girls of the queen's household peered out open windows and collected in the courtyard below. They watched as Henry VIII's wife, four months pregnant, was helped onto a proud Spanish Jennet, which waited, elegantly draped in red velvet with gilded stirrups, at the head of a uniformed contingent of the king's guard.

Bess turned around to see Gil, who stood towering above her beside Elizabeth.

"The king would not let her go if he knew, would he?" Bess asked.

"Unfathomable. He wants a son. Yet she wishes to be a part of her Spanish legacy. Wolsey always says that. I think it was the biggest reason he returned," Gil said.

Bess came away from the window, and he followed her. "The king does not trust her?"

"I think it is more that he understands the circumstances," Gil replied.

"So shall we have a bit of fun, finally?" Elizabeth proposed, wrapping an arm over Bess's shoulder as the trio moved toward the door.

"While the cat's away?" Gil said with a chuckle.

"Of course," Elizabeth countered blithely, and Bess was happy to be included in whatever sudden merriment the two might conjure, even if she did not quite trust either of them yet.

Running down a brick pathway, her dress flying out like a sail behind her, Bess laughed as she struggled to keep up with Gil and

Elizabeth, who knew well their way. In the queen's absence, the three of them were free to explore the vast palace grounds in the still, balmy air of late summer.

One pathway led to another, and Bess was quickly lost among the fountains, trees, and hedgerows, but even that was better than the monotony of the queen's household and the silent drudgery there. They ran until the brick became gravel paths, bordered by daylilies and wild marigolds. Near a flint wall covered with clematis, they tumbled onto a spongy bed of clover, laughing and out of breath. Bess gazed up at the broad blue sky, the thick billowing clouds moving quickly by as she tried to make shapes from each of them.

"What do you dream?" Elizabeth asked of neither of them in particular, and Bess was uncertain of how to answer.

"I dream I shall one day be a duke," Gil said fancifully. "And I'll have no walls or fences to keep anyone out or in. I shall eat my supper at midnight, only because I can, and I shall never wake up before dawn for anyone's prayers!"

Elizabeth giggled, but Bess was afraid to show amusement because she had been warned she must never say or do anything to jeopardize her family's standing. Secretly, however, she daydreamed of a life like Guinevere's, full of romance, excitement, and even a bit of danger. Ah, that she might find her own King Arthur, as she dreamed at home in quiet Kinlet.

"I dream of being kissed on the lips very slowly by Master Brandon," Elizabeth finally revealed.

Gil spit out a laugh and sat up. "Charles Brandon? The most notorious jackanapes at court?"

"That title would belong to the king, by your leave," Elizabeth responded, parrying the question with a false little sniff of indignation.

"Brandon has eyes only for the king's sister; everyone says that," Gil teased. "So you dream of being second choice?"

"As long as I was chosen."

"For a kiss?" Gil asked.

"For anything," Elizabeth replied.

They began to chuckle naughtily at that, and, in spite of herself, Bess joined them.

"So, now you, Mistress Blount," said Gil. "What do you dream of?"

She drew in a breath, then exhaled. "I dream of my father being well again and of both my parents being here at court with me."

Everyone was silent; the only sound was that of geese overhead. "A noble, if less than creative response," he remarked.

"Come now, Bess," said Elizabeth. "Surely you can do better than that."

"No, truly. That is what I dream of. My father was wounded at Calais."

"And yet if he were here, then your mother would be here with him, and you would not be," Gil observed. "And I, for one, do not at all fancy the prospect of that."

"Truly, Gilly." Elizabeth chuckled. "Your flirtations are clumsier than a farmer wrestling his pig in the mud."

"Thank you very much indeed," Gil said haughtily, his face flushed with indignation. "Being pleasant does not have to mean flirtation, you know."

"It does not have to mean that," Elizabeth quipped, "but in your case it does."

Bess watched his pale cheeks grow even more crimson as the friends exchanged a little glance.

"Tell us whom you *really* would not mind kissing then, if you fancy embarrassing *me*," Gil pressed.

"That was just harmless, personal fantasy," Elizabeth defended, her smile and blithe tone quickly fading.

"By my troth, no matter what she says of Master Brandon, our dear Mistress Bryan dreamed more than once of kissing the king," Gil revealed in order to match her cruelty. "The married young king, I might add."

"Yes, as if we did not know that. Well, he *is* incredibly handsome and dynamic. What more need I say?" Elizabeth defended. "If you were a girl, you would dream about him, too. He is humorous and clever, and those eyes of his pierce you right to the core if you are fortunate enough, even for a moment, to have them gaze upon you," she said dreamily.

Gil laughed. "I do wonder what our warrior queen might be driven to do if she heard you speaking like that of her husband."

"He may be her husband, but he is *my* king, and I most certainly would serve him any way he pleased."

Gil and Bess exchanged glances, smiling. She liked the way his eyes crinkled at the corners above a long, relaxed jawline. There was an innocence about him, not unlike her own. He was different than the others. She could see that.

"Go ahead and laugh, the two of you," Elizabeth said. "But you shall see what I mean about the king when the men are home from France. Believe me, you will see."

By the time Katherine of Aragon arrived near the border of England and Scotland, the Battle of Flodden was over, the English troops were victorious, and the Scots' King James already lay dead of his war wounds. The price Katherine had paid for her dedication to England and her young husband was the miscarriage of another royal child. To convalesce and to mourn, she did not return to court, but instead went to Windsor. Only her ladies to whom she was closest were summoned there to attend her. Bess, Jane, Elizabeth, and Princess Mary were to go on to Richmond Palace with the others to await the triumphant return of the king and his collection of soldier-courtiers, all of whom Bess had heard about but could not begin to imagine. That, however, would come soon enough.

Chapter Three

October 1513
Richmond Palace, Surrey

*H*e led the three of them blindfolded, holding hands and giggling beneath a little vine-covered trellis. The aromas were a delicious mix of late-blooming roses and the burning of raked leaves coming from the great fields beyond. Bess was the first to remove her blindfold, Jane and Elizabeth following suit, so that they all saw the feast of sweets at nearly the same time. Before them on a small table, covered in white linen, was a cornucopia of gingerbread, marzipan, and crystal dishes full of jam and plump berries. There were chargers, ewers, goblets, and finger bowls. It was quite a display; one fit for a king. The girls gasped with delight, then began to giggle again when they realized he had done this especially for them.

"However did you pull this off? It is magnificent; definitely one of your better ones, Gilly," Elizabeth exclaimed, clearly impressed.

Bess watched them closely to see if she could detect anything romantic between them; a glance, a smile, or a flirtation. But Gil looked at Bess instead.

"Did it surprise you?" he asked her.

"Completely," she replied, smiling with the same delight as the other girls. She had only ever tasted marzipan once at home two years earlier when Lord Mountjoy had paid them a visit.

"Gilly does things like this for us all the time," Jane remarked, nonplussed. "The king, of course, would have laid it all out on silver."

"Obviously, I am not the king," Gil replied, and Bess could hear the disappointment in his voice.

"Well, since I have no idea what the king would design, I think it is glorious. May we try some?" Bess asked. She watched his smile return.

"Try the gingerbread first while it is still warm." He grinned as a greedy bee droned beyond the trellis. "I had Agnes prepare that especially for you."

Elizabeth and Jane sat down on the little iron garden bench behind the table, and each took up one of the confections.

"Agnes?" Bess asked, letting Gil lead her to one of two little stools he had placed on the opposite side of the table.

"The king's favorite baker. She has been at court, she says, since he was a child, and she likes to spoil him."

"And you?" Bess supposed, once again surveying the impressive display spread out carefully in bowls, dishes, and plates.

"I suppose you could say she fancies me a bit as well."

"Nonsense," Elizabeth put in uncharitably as she took a rather unladylike mouthful of gingerbread. "In true court fashion, Gilly flirts with anyone and everyone to get what he wants."

"Untrue." He smiled slyly. "But I do study diligently from our good king."

A moment later, everyone began to laugh, and realizing now that this casual banter was simply the way they were with one another, Bess relaxed and felt free to delight in the first taste of warm gingerbread in the crisp autumn air.

"So what other surprises have you managed, Master Tailbois?" she asked with a smile as Jane and Elizabeth began to chatter excitedly about the king's imminent return. "Since it was your idea that I steal into the king's private chambers, I imagine they are all quite creative."

"I do what I can to be noticed by comely girls. Believe me, it is not always easy with the stiff competition here. So, if you don't mind, I shall guard my ideas."

"I could simply ask the two of them," Bess said, indicating Jane and Elizabeth.

"You could," he countered, plucking a small piece of marzipan from the dish for himself. "Or you could wait and see what might be in store, which would be much more fun."

In spite of herself, she laughed. Bess was not drawn to Gil Tailbois romantically, but he was sweet, kind, and even a little clever, she thought.

A fanfare of trumpets announcing the king's return suddenly broke their carefree idyll, and both Jane and Elizabeth excitedly sprang to their feet.

"They've returned!" Jane gasped. "Pinch your cheeks, Elizabeth. I imagine that Master Carew shall be riding out front beside the king."

"Nicholas Carew does not know I even exist," she replied, straightening her gown. "Nor would I care if a coxcomb like him ever did."

"Well, one as pretty as you could certainly change that," Jane countered, and they began to giggle to themselves in a way Bess envied. "Come, we must be there when they arrive in the court-yard!" Then Jane pivoted back with an afterthought.

"Thank you for this, Gilly. As always, your little surprise was delightful."

The two girls ran ahead down the gravel path as Bess stood with Gil, his disappointment obvious. "Shall I help you collect everything?" Bess asked.

"Thank you, but I shall have someone sent down to do it. Perhaps you could keep me company while I organize it a bit, though?"

The moment after that became awkward as they stood alone in silence beneath the trellis, very near to each other. The thunder of horses' hooves from the king's massive cortege in the distance grew louder.

"Well, thank you, Master Tailbois, truly. It was such a lovely surprise, and the gingerbread was delicious. May we do it again sometime? I really would like that."

From the gravel path beyond a low-hanging evergreen, Elizabeth Bryan called to her, "Are you coming, Bess? 'Tisn't every day you get to see the King of England for the first time!"

When Bess looked back at him, Gil only shrugged. "Go on ahead," he said. "I suspect there will be a lot of 'firsts' ahead of you from now on. But I shall be around."

"Thank you," she said with a smile. Bess felt a little spark of guilt for turning away just then, yet she was too excited for what lay ahead to stop herself from joining them.

Covered in dust, his black leather boots caked with mud, King Henry leapt from his great warrior bay, lurched into the open arms of Mary, his younger sister, and claimed her in a broad and powerful embrace.

"I've missed you, Hal. 'Tis never the same without you," she said against his bare, sweaty neck as she began to chuckle. "Yet adore you though I do, you are surely in need of a bath."

"And you, sweeting, are a sight for very sore eyes."

They laughed together as he pulled her more closely into his embrace. "Are you well?" she asked.

"Only tired, but other than that, I am right as rain. There is zest in victory."

"I can imagine." Mary smiled up at him with that same sweet smile their mother once possessed—one in which Henry had always found great comfort. That was, until he saw the little glance she exchanged with his best friend, Charles Brandon, who had come up beside him. *Bull pizzle!* He had believed that little dalliance of theirs would have run its course while they were in France. It was a blessed thing that it could not amount to anything more since Brandon was already betrothed to his own little ward, the wealthy Elizabeth Grey. Perhaps this thing before him was just a court flirtation. *Of course, that was it. . . .* He was just being foolish, thinking it could actually be more. Charles was a notorious scoundrel and dreadful flirt, as he himself was. There was nothing to worry about.

As Henry walked across the cobbled courtyard with Mary, he slung his other arm over Brandon's shoulder. If he could have chosen a brother after Arthur, Brandon surely would have been it. They were close. They had total trust in each other. It was a rare gift for the king to bestow on anyone, save Wolsey. But the bond with his cleric was a very different thing.

"I am surprised you did not go to Windsor with the queen,"

Henry said as they walked beneath a carved wooden portico and into the first cavernous hall with its oak-beamed ceilings painted in blue, red, and green.

"She wished only for Maria de Salinas and Doña Elvira to attend her," Mary replied.

"Well, she should not have gone, endangering the child like that," he scoffed.

"She went to Scotland for you," Mary reminded her brother, who still wore a field costume, a brocade tunic with hanging sleeves, padded gauntlets, padded hose, a dagger, and tall, black leather boots.

"Wolsey came here himself and told her not to go. Now she is still a childless queen, and I am an angry king because of it."

"You both are young, Hal. There will be others. That was an act of loyalty."

"It was an act of stupidity! Perhaps I should have listened to those who warned me against marrying my brother's wife in the first place," he petulantly declared, beginning to stalk rather than walk.

"Our brother's *widow*, Hal. Katherine is a good wife to you."

"I shall be the judge of who is good for me," he said peevishly, glad all of a sudden that young Mistress Poppincourt had not gone to Windsor with the queen either.

Bess stood breathless in the courtyard, her heart still racing, as the stewards and esquires unloaded trunks and supplies, and the liveried equerries began to lead the vast collection of horses away to the royal stables. She was stunned, so that for a moment she almost could not move. The king was absolutely magnificent. He was everything they said he was, like Lancelot come to life. Henry VIII was very tall and muscular, his shoulders impressively broad and his calves as sturdy as the trunks of two trees. In the sunlight, his tousled copper hair looked like silk crowning a chiseled, square face that held her gaze riveted to him as he had leapt from his horse, greeted his sister with a broad embrace, and walked toward the open palace doors. Katherine of Aragon was the most fortunate woman alive, Bess thought, since that human god, their king, belonged to her and her alone. Bess's adolescent heart soared with the images of what Katherine's life must be like; the riches, the jewels, the private attentions of a man like that.

With her heart racing, Bess thought very little of the courtier with curly copper hair who approached Jane then and whispered something to her that Bess could not hear. But it struck her how Jane glanced across the courtyard at the king. He turned only briefly, nodding to her before he advanced toward an open door surrounded by aides, friends, and servants.

"Very well, let's go. He is gone for now. So shall Master Brandon be. He follows the king like a lapdog," Jane Poppincourt declared.

Bess watched Elizabeth straighten into an oddly defensive posture. "He does what we all must do, Jane, whether or not we declare it to others."

"You're only angry because you thought it would be you and not me. But obviously there are some circumstances where your Bryan family lineage does not trump all."

Elizabeth gave a little indignant huff after that and spun around on her heel, her nose tipped up. There was something more between the two girls, something not at all clear to Bess, but whatever it was seemed to involve the king more directly than anyone at the moment was willing to say. "My lineage will be victorious soon enough. A pity you might well be back in France by then and not see the grand life I shall have once you are gone."

The flaring of tempers that followed Gil's wonderful surprise and the king's triumphant return was confusing to Bess. She did not understand what they were arguing about. She still understood little so far of the intricacies and rivalries of this new world, and she even despised what she knew was her own sense of naïveté. But one thing she understood completely: It was a world she had every intention of conquering, as Elizabeth Bryan also planned to do. What path Bess would take, however, was still a complete, and rather exciting, mystery.

The court burst back to life that same evening as the king hosted a grand celebration in the banquet hall with all the flair and magic Bess had imagined. Dressed in a pretty brocade gown with puffed slashed sleeves and a yolk embroidered with beads, she sat, admiring all the activity. Henry VIII was not only celebrating the English victory over France, he proclaimed, goblet in hand, but also his return as host of all the beautiful ladies of his court. He did not mention the queen. It did not seem to her that Katherine of Aragon even existed at all.

The somber queen's court was entirely overshadowed in a single day by the brilliant, festive environment the king preferred. The high, painted beamed ceiling of the banquet hall echoed back the melodious strains of rich, happy music coming from musicians collected in the gallery above. Between the linen-draped, flower- and herb-strewn tables, a group of elegantly dressed courtiers danced while everyone else was taken up in boisterous laughter and happy conversation. But from her place near the back of the hall, Bess focused solely on the young and handsome king, who sat while talking, laughing, and greeting friends and embracing the most beautiful of the ladies as they filed before him for a moment of his attention.

In an odd comparison, she remembered then when her mother had only just lost a child, the heavy pall that had descended on their house, and how somberly Father had sat alone in the library for hours, refusing to speak with anyone. Perhaps the king's own grief was a thing he felt duty bound to hide from his subjects, Bess considered as she watched him. The jewels on his ornate slashed sleeves glittered in the golden flickering lamplight as he tipped his head back and laughed heartily at something Wolsey had said. The royal Almoner was on his right; Charles Brandon on his left. Her father had told her they were the two most powerful men in England, second only to the king, and they fought each other daily for supreme dominance. As different as the two men were, she could see what her father meant.

Wolsey was a stout, unappealing man, but he seemed better at keeping the king's attention—particularly when Brandon was so taken up by Mary, the king's pretty sister, who sat, radiating beauty, on Brandon's other side. It was interesting to watch it all play out. It was like attending a performance, with all of its players, and she had no idea yet how the story would go.

"They *will* end up together, you know." A voice beside her startled her back to the moment, and Bess turned to see that Gil was now suddenly sitting beside her, fingering a wine goblet with an unadorned hand. "Brandon has as much of a reputation at court as the king for getting what, and whom, he wants. It has been a good-natured contest between them for years."

"And what he wants is the king's sister?" she asked.

"That is certainly the gossip."

Bess could easily understand it if it were true. Brandon may have been strikingly handsome, but, with her beauty, Mary met him equally. Her graceful neck, vibrant green eyes, and abundance of jewels, made the adolescent country girl feel instantly plain and unappealing when she dared to compare herself to the princess.

"My father says she is betrothed to Charles of Castile," Bess stammered.

"They say King Henry has now lost interest in that match since the war with France, and by the look of it, Lord Lisle means to seize the moment."

Bess had been educated enough by both her parents to know that a key political pawn like a king's sister would never be wasted on someone politically inconsequential, even a personal and dashing friend like Charles Brandon. Bess's mind worked quickly to put more of the key court players into places that made sense.

"Will you dance?" Gil asked then as he extended his slim hand, interrupting her thoughts.

"Are even we permitted to dance, not just the important few?"

Bess realized, like so many other things, that she did not have any idea of what one might do in front of the king.

Gil only smiled at her question. "Wolsey says the king prefers dancing to the lot of us sitting here, staring at him."

Bess could feel the heat of her own blushing. It made her straighten in her seat. "I was not doing that."

"Ah, but you were," he affably countered. "Everyone does when they first come to court. It is rather unavoidable really since he is so majestic and handsome."

"He is that," Bess replied, cautiously daring to agree.

She let Gil lead her out into the area where others were dancing, and the fabric of her skirts brushed against all the other luxurious fabrics and folds. Well schooled at dance, they both slipped easily into the steps of a branle. Happy to feel confident at something at last, Bess smiled. They were surrounded by dancers, courtiers not just of importance, but of such skill and grace, that it felt daunting and yet rather fun as well. Moving flawlessly around her were the king's impressively stylish friends, Sir Edward Neville, Sir Henry Guildford, and Sir William Compton, who was the curly-haired young man she had seen whispering with Jane in the courtyard. All of them were brilliantly arrayed in velvet, jeweled doublets, and matching puffed trunk hose. Gil named each of the courtiers carefully, and Bess quickly memorized their faces in case she should be introduced. Chief Gentleman of the Bedchamber, Esquire of the Body, Keeper of the Sewer; their titles were daunting to a girl of fourteen. The women, their partners, she knew by now. But these were the men of great wealth, power, and influence. They were the true keys to everything, Gil explained. This applied particularly to Compton, who, as Chief Gentleman of the Bedchamber, was in a position to control every person going in or out of the king's room. Bess considered that, and her mind eddied on a thought. She remembered Compton talking privately to Jane earlier, and the catty exchange with Elizabeth that had followed. But she pushed away the unthinkable thought, flatly refusing it, before she could reach its natural conclusion. She looked away, seeing Charles and Mary— preferring that vision to the one pressing in from the back of her mind.

They were partnered together nearby in the dance, and he was smiling down at her with something akin to admiration, Bess thought. Perhaps it was even love. Surely the king could see it, as everyone else could, and a magnificent young man like Henry could not be without a heart for romance. That much seemed impossible.

Just as that new thought blossomed in her mind, Bess saw the king across the dancing area partnered with, of all girls, Jane Poppincourt. The thought she had tried to press away came forward forcefully again. Jane was dressed far more elegantly than usual. Tonight her gown was of azure velvet over brocade. Very large turned-back cuffs revealed brocade sleeves, and at her throat was a heavy gold pendant surrounding a large emerald. Jane was laughing quite boldly, Bess thought, and she was gazing up at the king with an odd familiarity. Thinking now what she was trying very hard not to, she felt a strange burst of pity just then for the queen—childless and in mourning alone at Windsor Castle. Bess was young and inexperienced, but she was not a fool. It was easy to imagine wanting to flirt with the King of England and attract his attention. But Jane was a part of Katherine's own household, and her laughing so overtly like that seemed a betrayal.

"You are scowling, you know," Gil observed as the dance neared its end.

"Am I?"

"It does look a great deal like envy."

"Envy for Jane? I have only just met her."

"'Tis not serious, you know. Wolsey says he truly loves the queen."

"Then why would a girl do something so unwise as flirt with him, or he with her?"

"A courtly pastime. And because she can. Mistress Poppincourt is rather comely."

"I can see that."

"Surely your parents explained all of that to you." Gil laughed as he led her back to her place at the table.

She was not entirely certain that they had, at least not fully. "Well, I for one think it is awful," she declared with a little huff as she watched the king leave the hall with Jane very noticeably on his arm. Again she thought of Jane and Sir William Compton's familiarity with each other. "I would never do something like that to the poor queen."

"You are young, Bess, and green as grass to the ways of a court like this one. You would be wise not to declare yourself so forcefully just yet. At least not until you have met our sovereign," Gil said.

Over the next days, Jane began to spend more of her time with the king's sister, walking with her in the garden and sitting beside her as they sewed. And they were always whispering. Elizabeth Bryan was left to seek out Bess's company as a result, which was fine with her because Bess liked Elizabeth. Their temperaments were similar, they were the same age, and both had courtier parents. As they sat together one afternoon watching the king and Brandon dashing back and forth at tennis, Elizabeth was surprisingly vocal.

"Fortunate little moppet, Elizabeth Grey," she remarked under her breath.

"Who is that?"

"Lord Lisle's ward. She is our age, yet if you can fathom, they are betrothed to marry. The formal nature of the betrothal has already made Master Brandon a viscount, thus his title. I would shudder to be in that poor girl's slippers!"

"I thought it was Master Brandon you fancied?"

"I said that for Gilly's benefit, of course, because I knew he would tease me worse than he did if he were certain of the truth. No, Charles Brandon is far too cockish. He plays boys' games with women. His dearest friend, the king, however—now *he* is quite decidedly a man. Just look at him!"

Bess watched the king sprinting magnificently across the court in a loose muslin shirt with leather laces, and padded suede breeches, his muscular chest shining with perspiration. She felt a reaction deep within herself for the first time in her life, and the sensation took her breath away. At twenty-two, Henry VIII was an adult, and she most decidedly was not. She was a silly adolescent girl, but that mattered little in fantasy, she thought, smiling devilishly to herself.

"Do you not think he is glorious?" Elizabeth asked.

"Glorious, indeed. And I would imagine *he* would be a glorious kisser, too, just like Lancelot," Bess replied with a mischievous chuckle.

Elizabeth looked at her with an expression of surprise. "I knew you could not be so different from the rest of us when faced with that royal, godlike perfection. They do say experience is the best teacher, and I am certain he has had plenty of that. They may look alike, but there could not be more difference between Brandon and the king. You know our Lord Lisle, as they already call him, has lived quite the scandalous youth. He is as ambitious as he is handsome, and he has already had two wives to further his standing."

Bess looked at the king's opponent more closely. Brandon was attractive, it was true. Tall, taut, and auburn-haired, he looked as if he could be the king's brother. Bess watched the two of them laugh and sprint and yell when the other missed a volley or a serve. All too soon, to Bess's mind, the match was over, Brandon having dared to beat the sovereign. Still, their arms were slung over each other's shoulders casually as they approached Elizabeth, Bess, and the few other maids of honor who had collected to watch.

"So you witnessed my humiliating defeat, did you, Mistress Bryan?" the king asked with an open, affable smile as he and

Brandon stopped directly before them. Both girls curtsied, as the others did around them.

"Your Highness played splendidly," Elizabeth replied. "I actually thought you won."

"Brandon cheats," Henry declared with a little wink as his storm green eyes landed at last upon Bess. "And whom have we here, Mistress Bryan?"

"I am Elizabeth Blount, Your Royal Highness," she replied for herself, though the words stuck suddenly in her throat and were delivered on what felt like a miserable, high croak as she dipped into a painfully awkward curtsy, then rose back up. The king smiled at her youthful embarrassment, which made it that much worse.

"Ah, yes, you're Sir John's girl."

"I am, sire." Bess averted her eyes as the reply left her lips, feeling her cheeks flush hotly. She was unable to look into his confident, handsome gaze a single moment longer. She felt like such a fool, a hopelessly inconsequential child in his presence, with his gaze bearing down upon her. His casual smile had seemed absolutely blinding.

"How goes your father's convalescence? He is missed here at our merry little court."

"My mother writes that he is swiftly improving, sire."

"That is splendid news." He seemed to be studying her, she thought, when she forced herself to look back at him and he had not looked away. "You do very much resemble your mother, you know."

"I am told that."

"You shall be a great beauty one day. You certainly hold promise. Do you not agree, Brandon?"

Charles Brandon, who seemed bored with the entire exchange, was glancing off toward the gardens as if he had barely noticed her. He did not even regard Elizabeth Bryan, whose confidence and beauty were already apparent. She certainly did not seem intimidated, Bess thought, feeling a sudden spark of envy toward the girl.

"Brandon!" the king barked.

"Yes, of course, Your Highness. Lovely, lovely," Brandon blandly returned, still never looking directly at Bess either. She must be too far beneath him for that, Bess thought a little ruefully, finding no admirable comparison between Lord Lisle and the king beyond appearance, just as Elizabeth had indicated.

"I am sorry if it has been dull for you here without the queen, but she shall return soon enough," the king suddenly said to her.

"Not dull at all, Your Highness. There has been much for me to learn in her absence."

Henry's smile widened. His teeth were white and straight, and as magnificent as the rest of him. She could not push the legend of Lancelot from her mind as she looked at him girlishly. "Ah, an optimist, are you, Mistress Blount? That pleases me greatly."

"They tell me I get that as well from my mother."

Bess forced herself not to look away this time, but it was a bit like looking at the sun, brilliant and blinding.

"Well, there is much for you to learn at my court, whether the queen is here or not," Henry said decidedly.

"I am discovering that, Your Highness."

"Mistress Bryan here is a splendid teacher. Mistress Poppincourt as well. Learn what you can from each of them. Take their advice, too, since both might be ahead of you in many ways," he said with a wink. Bess made a proper nod in return to the surprising gesture, but when she looked up, she saw that the king and Brandon had unceremoniously turned and were already walking away.

"That went pleasingly," Elizabeth remarked. "And you did not even say anything too foolish to embarrass yourself, or me."

Bess thought of saying that Elizabeth's adoring and silly adolescent gaze upon the king had done that well enough, but she decided against it. Bess knew she needed what friends she could find here.

"Does he always depart like that, without so much as a fare-thee-well?" she asked instead.

"Often, yes. He is the king, after all, Bess." Elizabeth chuckled. "He has quite a lot more on his mind than two inconsequential girls. I am surprised he said as much as he did. Perhaps it was my new dress that drew him over here."

"Of course that was it," Bess said with a smile as they left the tennis court in a line behind the other girls.

Secretly, Bess did not care what had brought the king to her side, or caused him to speak. She knew only that it was a defining moment in her life. And she would wait eagerly and full of fanciful thoughts for it to happen again, somewhere, sometime. While she waited, she would try very hard not to resent the very fortunate queen for marrying him before Bess had even fully grown up.

"What are you moping about for, lad?" Wolsey asked with an irritated sigh as Gil came away from the window through which he had been gazing for the better part of an hour. It was a window that shone down onto the royal tennis courts and the knot garden beyond. The king's match with Brandon was only just over.

He was a good boy, Wolsey reminded himself, doing his best to finish his letter, but Gilbert was completely distracting him with his endless pacing and dramatic sighs. Wolsey knew the signs well enough. He had been a love-struck lad himself once, before his ambition had begun to speak more loudly to him than the call of his heart. Gilbert Tailbois was his one reminder now of that other world, his other life, and perhaps even love. It was a world he tried not to dwell upon too much on days like this, when a skillfully written letter to the Princess of Navarre, thanking her for her hospitality, seemed far more important.

Gilbert ambled tentatively toward Wolsey's writing table then, and, with a little thud, sank onto the leather chair opposite him. Wolsey lifted his eyes but kept his chin down.

"Are you planning to tell me what and who?"

"No."

Wolsey let a small, contained smile pass his lips. "I didn't think so. But whoever it is, she must be quite remarkable to have you in such a sorry state at the moment."

"She is remarkable. But she is no passing thought, Father."

Wolsey dropped his pen onto the parchment. It clattered, and ink sprayed onto the desk and his hands. He lifted his thick chin and frowned at the boy. "You know perfectly well you are not to call me that."

"Not saying something does not change the truth of it. Is that not what you always say?"

Wolsey sank back against the high upholstered chair and wrapped his hands over the carved arms. Most of the time he saw so little of himself in the boy that, throughout the years, he had frequently doubted his paternity. But then there were moments like this—the small stubborn streak that flared, the set of his mouth, defining him—that dispelled all doubt.

"Be that as it may, you refer to me as 'my lord' and 'sir,' as we have agreed."

"When I remember to."

He stiffened. "Well, remember it. You are a Wolsey, not a dolt."

"Very well, Father." The boy smiled at him then. The expression was not disrespectful, but one that showed he held a powerful secret in the palm of his hand and seemed to know how to use it. He could not blame the spirited lad for that. Seizing opportunity was a Wolsey trait. Gil would have a brilliant future, the cleric silently reminded himself, if he did not let the wrong girl turn his head. The court was brimming with temptation for everyone, and falling in love could be wildly dangerous. Gil might be a bastard son, but he was still his son, and Wolsey would never allow that to happen.

Wolsey had seen the longing glances he had given the new Blount girl. He had nearly been able to feel them. In the first few days, Wolsey had assumed it was only adolescent infatuation. Now, he could not be so certain. But she must have nothing to hold against Gil, nothing to threaten his future, or change his life, just as Elizabeth had changed his own life long ago with the advent of their child. Wolsey must be certain. He must confirm to have any peace. He excelled at fading into the woodwork. And he would do that tonight when he searched her room for assurance.

"Is there anything I can do to help things with her along, lad?"

Gil glanced back like an afterthought. The soft laughter of young girls came up softly through the windows below. "I wish there were. But this is something that would be better if I did it on my own," Gil replied.

Wolsey nodded his approval, yet silently he wondered if his son—this gangly, shy boy—was up to such a daunting task, especially if she proved to be as remarkable as he claimed.

Later that afternoon, Gil rode a horse from the royal stables alone out to Hounslow to the hospital there. Since George Tailbois was one of his royal Knights of the Body, the king had offered Sir George accommodations at court while he recovered from his battlefield injuries. But, fearing that the mental collapse might be permanent and that his condition might cause the sovereign embarrassment, Gil had declined the offer on behalf of the man who had raised him.

George Tailbois had always refused to acknowledge the story of his son's true conception, and so Gil knew little about himself, or even why George had taken on a child as his own. What he did know had come to him in bits and pieces grudgingly imparted by Thomas Wolsey.

After he was named Dean of Lincoln sixteen years earlier, Wolsey had met a woman called Elizabeth. Only Wolsey's tone, when he spoke her name, gave Gil any indication at all that he had ever truly cared for her. She had been married off shortly thereafter to the sheriff of Lincolnshire and Northumberland, Sir George Tailbois. Gil had always been forced to draw his own conclusions about how and why the noble family, with a claim to the barony of Kyme and the earldom of Angus, had agreed to take Gil on as their own. Then, several years later, when he was still a boy, both Gil and his adoptive father found places at court among the king and Wolsey's staff. Thus the ruse had been cemented, and Gil had realized the Tailbois family had been driven by money and position. Gil's loyalty to George Tailbois, thus, was born not fully of affection but of gratitude for having given his mother and him a name if not the tenderness he still craved.

Gil was shown now by a stone-faced guard into a room locked from the outside. It looked to the fifteen-year-old boy more like a prison cell than a place where anyone could recover. There was an icy draft in the spartan room with only a single bed, a small table, and a window that let in noise from the street below and just a sliver of afternoon sunlight. The room smelled heavily of urine.

"He has been yelling for two days, although no one can quite make out the words," the guard said matter-of-factly. The jangling keys seemed to rouse him.

"Who is it?" came a clotted, rheumy voice from the bed, but the man was buried beneath a mountain of blankets.

The guard returned to the door. "'Twill be safer for you if I lock you inside. Just rap on the door when you've finished your visit, lad."

The well-groomed boy gave in to a small shiver of panic. He drew in a steadying breath and moved forward. "'Tis I, Father."

"Who? Make way for the soldiers, lad! And mind the lances!"

"Father, you're not in France. You're safe back in England." He moved tentatively nearer the bed just as George Tailbois bolted upright, casting off the blankets and wrestling them like an enemy onto the floor, his body sharp with tension.

"Careful, boy! He's dangerous, that one! He's got a dagger!"

Gil felt his eyes fill with tears. No matter what he thought of this man who had teetered on the edge of sanity for years, and embarrassed him more than once with his outbursts, George Tailbois had given him a name and legitimacy, if also not the privileged life among dukes, earls, and beautiful noble girls like Bess Blount that Wolsey had. He sank carefully onto the edge of the bed, forcing himself to be brave. "'Tis all right, Father. You stopped him. He's given up."

"Bollocks! Never trust the enemy. They'll play dead as a sturgeon, then rear up and gouge your heart out without even a thought. Who'd you say you were again?"

"Gilbert, Father, Gilbert Tailbois."

"Gilly?"

"Yes, Father."

He waited, almost not breathing, as a veil seemed to lift from the thin, haggard man's watery blue eyes.

"It is you."

"It is."

Gil reached out and struggled not to recoil from the sour odor as he took the hand of his adoptive father.

"Forgive me. I must have been dreaming."

"You must be very tired," Gil said gently. "I brought you a sliver of marzipan."

The older Tailbois smiled. "Ah, 'tis my favorite."

"I remember."

The formerly powerful sheriff, and servant to the king, took the small confection like a greedy child and pressed it between his lips. The taste seemed to bring him back a little, Gil thought.

"Thank you, Son. How is your mother?"

"She writes that she is well, sir."

"And your sisters?"

Girls who were only half sisters. "My mother writes that they are well, also."

George's eyes filled quickly with tears. "I miss her so. . . . How many years has she been dead now?"

"She is not dead, Father. Mother wrote to me only a few days ago. She is home safe at the estate in Kyme with my sisters, eagerly awaiting your return once you are well enough."

As quickly as the tears had come, they dried on his ruddy cheeks and rage took their place.

"Do not lie to me, Captain! 'Tis war!" He tensed again and sprang from the bed, but he lost his balance just as quickly and fell back.

Hearing the commotion, the guard opened the door again with another clattering of keys. "Everything all right in here?" he asked.

"He is just a bit disoriented."

"A bit?" The guard chuckled unkindly. "He has been mad like that since they brought him here, weeping one moment, calling out wildly the next."

He may have been only fifteen, but indignation brought courage. "Sir George Tailbois is a servant to King Henry, and thus, you are to show him the respect he has earned, do you understand?"

"Easy, lad. 'Twas no harm intended."

"Is there nothing you can give him?"

The guard struggled and shook his head. "Whatever the doctors do seems to help him less and less."

Gil felt a strange mixture then of pity and cold detachment. He bore the man's name, certainly, but not his blood. Pray God, he would not somehow share George Tailbois's slow descent into lunacy as well. One last time he took George's hand and gave it a reassuring squeeze. "I shall return soon," he said.

"Who are *you?*" asked George Tailbois with a frightened, disoriented voice in response.

Very late that evening, after everyone had retired and Bess was at last free to be alone with her thoughts, she sank onto the edge of her small bed. She gave a weary sigh, then drew up from beneath the bedcovers, where she had hidden the delicate cradle blanket. She still could not reconcile the man who would keep such a sentimental object with the carefree, handsome sovereign she had met that day. But she knew well enough that blood ties were indelible and complex. This blanket made the untouchable king seem real. And it made her miss her own brother the more.

Tomorrow she must write to George. There were so many things to tell him. She must say that she had met the king, that he had actually spoken to her, and that she had begun already to make friends. She must confess to George that she still had possession of something she had stolen, since the guilt weighing upon her was tremendous. Most of all she must tell her brother she missed him desperately—William, Isabella, and Rosa, too. She so dearly longed for the simple games she had played with her siblings, and the days of fantasizing about what life at court would be like. Bess was quickly discovering how serious, and complicated, it was to succeed here with so many people clambering after the king, willing to do whatever it took to be first in his life and heart. As much as she liked it here, Bess could not imagine herself ever doing the same.

The next morning after prayer, Bess, Elizabeth, Jane, Princess Mary, and Mountjoy's daughter, Gertrude, Marchioness of Exeter, entered the queen's apartments together, famished. The meal to break their fast was decidedly more appetizing now than when the queen was in residence, and they looked forward to it with great relish.

"Her Royal Highness believes that self-sacrifice is pleasing to God, and that it will show Him her determination to give her husband a healthy, living son," Gertrude explained.

"And while she makes deals with God, the rest of you must eat like prisoners while I am more often permitted to dine with the king," Mary quipped as they walked amid the swish of skirts and the echo of their collective footsteps across the long pathway of tile. "That is not to say that she is not a splendid and loyal wife to my brother."

"Perhaps, at times, a bit naive," Jane boldly observed.

Bess watched Jane exchange an odd little glance with Mary, and she wondered how many things the two of them knew that she, as yet, did not. She was young, and still largely untested, but she was determined to change that by listening well and learning quickly.

"Mistress Blount."

The man's voice booming suddenly behind her was deep and menacing enough that her determination vanished as she flinched. So did the carefree smiles on the faces of the girls around her. Bess turned around to see Thomas Wolsey, the king's stout and towering Almoner, his full face compressed by a frown, clutching in a single meaty hand the cradle blanket she had taken.

Bess felt her face burn. She had thought it well enough concealed beneath her bedding. She had not counted on anyone going through her personal things, but his boldness should not have surprised her after what she had witnessed in the king's bedchamber. She had been caught, and there would be a harsh penalty handed down to her.

"By your leave, Mistress Blount, explain how it is that this article found its way into your chamber."

Her heart beat like a drum against her rib cage. The punishment might well be so severe that even her parents would not be allowed to return to their positions. Her family could sink to ruin because of her. Taking the cradle blanket and then keeping it had been as foolish as it had been careless. A dozen images moved through her mind, foremost the look of grave disappointment that would darken her father's face when she was relieved of her duties and returned home in disgrace.

"I—I," she stammered, but no other words would come.

"Forgive me, my lord; it was my fault." The surprising admission came from Gil Tailbois, although she had not even seen him enter the room.

He stood tall and self-assured beside her now but with just the

right amount of contrition in his expression to balance the confidence. Bess marveled at him. Was he really about to take the blame
for her?

"Master Tailbois, what precisely is the meaning of this?" Wolsey
asked in incredulity, his full cheeks mottled red as his accusatory
expression changed to one of anger. "You have never done a blatantly bad thing in your life."

"And I did not mean to do it now. Strangely enough, I found it
in a pile of other linens on the back stairs when Mistress Bryan and
I were having a bit of fun there; just running about as you know too
well we do. We took it to show Mistress Blount and must have forgotten it when I was told of your return to court. She, in turn, must
have forgotten that I left it behind."

The silence that fell around them was sudden and heavy. Bess
dared not even look at Gil for the masterfully easy lie he had just
told in order to protect her. She had never been more shocked in
her life.

Wolsey's discerning gaze moved critically from Gil to her and
back again.

"Is that the truth, Mistress Blount?" he asked sternly.

"My lord, I cannot honestly—"

"You cannot honestly take the blame for me; that is what Mistress Blount was about to say," Gil said, interrupting her. "But it was
a noble gesture."

The nobility belonged entirely to him, but she was too stunned
to say more.

"Very well, Master Tailbois, I shall deal with you later. Mistress
Blount, my apologies for any offense," Wolsey said, nodding perfunctorily, the tension of the moment quickly defused.

"None taken, my lord, I assure you," she replied in a much

softer voice than she normally used, since her mind was still reeling. Bess had no idea what Gil was even doing here in the queen's apartments, let alone at that critical moment to save her. Nevertheless, she was grateful.

After Wolsey and Gil had gone, and the girls sat down to take their meal, Bess turned to Elizabeth, leaning in as she did so no one else would hear. "Why on earth would he have done that?"

"Because it was our fault in the first place," Elizabeth replied simply, and with seemingly uncharacteristic charity. "Gilly may not be much to look at, but he is a man of honor. Or he will be—once he is a fully grown man." She chuckled, pleased with her own sense of humor. "And he has a way with Wolsey. Everyone says so."

"Gilbert would seem a good friend to have."

"How appropriate." Elizabeth Bryan laughed a bit more loudly. "Because he says the very same thing about you."

Chapter Four

*I*n the spring of Katherine and Henry's fifth year of marriage, the queen was pregnant for the fourth time, and once again, all of England waited cautiously for a living heir. Since it was not thought safe for the queen to participate in court activities at this stage of her pregnancy, the dynamic young king sought companionship and entertainment elsewhere.

Increasingly, that included pretty fifteen-year-old Elizabeth Bryan.

As Mistress Bryan's presence beside the king, at tennis matches, hunting parties, garden strolls, and at the frequent banquets, was phased in, so Mistress Poppincourt's presence was seamlessly phased out. Like smooth steps in a courtly dance, the movements and changes were subtle. Where one of the girls had once been seated at the table nearest the king, the other was now directed. Where one had ridden beside the sovereign, or joined him in his personal barge for journeys down the river, the other now kept his company.

Bess might not have noticed at all if not for being increasingly placed beside Elizabeth at these events.

In the year since coming to court, Bess had learned well the players to befriend and those to avoid. Of all the courtiers around her, she trusted only two: Elizabeth Bryan and Gil Tailbois. Owing to the king's dependence upon him, and his subsequent appointment as Bishop of Lincoln, Wells, and Bath, Wolsey's attention was in demand to attend and advise the sovereign. Gil came along to attend Bishop Wolsey, so Bess had around her daily those upon whom she most depended.

True to his word after the victory at Thérouanne and Tournai, Henry VIII made plans to conquer all of France. Until he learned that his allies—the queen's own father, Ferdinand, and the Emperor Maximilian—had deserted him and signed a peace treaty with their enemy, the French King Louis XII. Only Wolsey's words seemed to temper Henry's anger, advising him to form some sort of alliance with the French monarch in order to rescue his world reputation. Henry's desire for war did not help the royal marriage, and it set into motion a series of events that would change the lives of everyone at court.

"I trusted the queen's father most of all!" Henry raged. "I should have been able to rely on his daughter's loyalty as well!"

"The queen has been most loyal, Your Highness," Wolsey cautiously countered. "She cannot be made to pay for the actions of King Ferdinand, so far away in Spain."

"Having her father betray me, nevertheless, is like my own wife betraying me. Foolish woman, if she were not already carrying my child, I would divorce her! Perhaps I should look into that as a matter of course, anyway."

Wearing a long velvet coat edged in gold, Henry stalked back and forth the full length of his shadowy private gallery, his pride pierced and his mind swimming with thoughts of revenge. Wolsey sat on an ornately carved bench, his legs crossed, and waited for the rage to quiet. At the age of twenty-two, Henry was still largely untested as a ruler and often more full of fantasy than sense. Wolsey's job, as he saw it, was to channel those fantasies into useful actions.

"I do not believe that will be necessary, sire," Wolsey calmly replied, fingering the large ruby ring set in gold on his chunky forefinger—a recent gift from the king. "*If* you vanquish them at their own game."

Henry stopped beside a large map of the Netherlands fixed to the limestone wall. His expression was one of incredulity. "And how would you propose I do that, Wolsey, when that triumvirate has already indisputably damaged my reputation, making me appear a complete fool?"

"You do have something none of them has—a beautiful, desirable sister to offer up, one who could make you and Louis not only allies but brothers."

"I cannot consign Mary to an ancient lizard like the French king!" Henry bellowed.

"Can you go on without doing so?" Wolsey pointedly asked as the king stopped in his tracks, the folds from his rich velvet coat swinging at his knees before he pivoted back.

Wolsey knew it was a risk even to propose such a thing. Henry loved no one like his sister. The death of their brother, Arthur, had forged the bond that the loss of their parents had sealed. But a beautiful young princess was still a bargaining chip like no other, especially lovely Mary, with her chaste reputation. Due to a failed betrothal to Charles of Castile, it was a stroke of good fortune that she was now free to utilize.

But Wolsey saw the glances exchanged between her and that

ambitious prig, Brandon, just as he had seen Gil's interest in the Blount girl, because he made it a point to look for such things. Now that Brandon, newly raised by Henry to the peerage as Duke of Suffolk, was amassing power and great fortune at an alarming rate, it would not surprise Wolsey at all if Brandon still had designs on the king's sister. In spite of his betrothal to young Lady Lisle, for which he had earlier received the title of Lord Lisle, though their marriage had never been formally executed, Charles Brandon's appetite for grandeur knew no bounds. Additionally, Brandon had never let a little thing like rules or the law stand in his way before, so it was unlikely he would do so now if Mary was what he desired. It would serve Brandon right if at least that one door to his ambitions, and such an alluring one, was forever closed. Pleased with himself, Wolsey bit back a smile and waited patiently for Henry to adopt the idea as his own.

"It would not be completely unexpected to her. Mary has, after all, been raised, as I was, to know her duty."

"Indeed, sire."

"Very well, Wolsey. Look into it then." The long sleeve fell away from Henry's hand as he flicked his wrist with the directive. "I am late as it is for the hunt, which is why we came to Eltham in the first place. Brandon, Carew, and I have some pretty young ladies to impress before they grow tired of waiting."

Young was right, thought Wolsey petulantly, even as he bowed to the king. The word characterized most of the new crop of naive contenders who were unsuspecting candidates for the plucking.

Bess was shocked, yet excited, to have been invited.

Henry would be a magnificent hunter to watch as they galloped through the woods, all thundering hooves, clattering harnesses, glittering jewels, and carefree laughter. The Duke of Suffolk was always witty, and Master Carew could never quite take his eyes off Elizabeth Bryan. Not that she ever noticed, for she and Bess watched the king's every move with pure adolescent devotion. When Henry spoke to either one of them, they would chatter on about nothing else for days.

Wolsey usually joined them, but everyone knew there was increasing tension between the cleric and Brandon, so Wolsey declined this hunt. As a result, Gil did not come downstairs to see them off. It was just as well, Bess secretly thought. He was a good friend, but Gil could become moody and quiet when she and Elizabeth giggled over the king, and she had to admit it did rather ruin their fun.

The little hunting party collected now in the courtyard, a light spring breeze swirling around the young ladies of the queen's household, including Bess; Elizabeth; Margaret, Elizabeth's older sister, Lady Guildford; Princess Mary; and Mary Stafford, Lady Bergavenny, daughter of the Duke of Buckingham. Also included were Anne Stanhope and Joan Champernowne, two other maids of honor. Conspicuously absent, once again, was Jane Poppincourt, whose prominence of place beside the king had steadily diminished.

Henry strode through the tall carved doors a moment later in elegant green velvet ornamented with gold cord, and a jaunty matching cap plumed with an ostrich feather. He was with Charles Brandon, Nicholas Carew, Henry Guildford, Henry Norris, and William Compton. They were laughing at some great unheard joke told by Sir Guildford, whose responsibility, as Master of the Revels, it often was to set the mood.

When the men looked their way, Bess felt the heat deepen in

her cheeks and she lowered her eyes, still not entirely comfortable with attention from a group of handsome noblemen. Elizabeth did not suffer the same weakness, and, when Bess looked up, she saw that Elizabeth and the king were smiling at each other. Bess looked back and forth. The gaze between them was now an open flirtation. Clearly, it was the same look she once had seen between the sovereign and Jane. Even though the court was full of these games, and everyone seemed to play them, her next thought, as it had been the last time, was of the pregnant queen upstairs. But, surprisingly, it did not prevent her from wishing that she, rather than Elizabeth, had caught the king's eye as a part of this little intrigue, and she looked enviously from Henry and Elizabeth.

"Are we ready, my ladies?" Charles Brandon asked with an affable wink and grin as he donned his tooled leather riding gloves.

Brandon wore the very same plumed green velvet hat as the king, which made them, with their copper hair, look like brothers. Yet even that was not a coincidence; clothing to mirror the king signaled one's position and power. Then Bess saw Brandon and Princess Mary exchange the same unmistakable look and smile as she had seen before. *Such open flirtation*, she thought to herself. They all seemed such experts. The only one who ever smiled like that at her was Gilbert Tailbois, and Bess had long ago decided he did not count—not for that, anyway.

When the horses were brought from the stables, Bess was helped by one of the young liveried grooms onto a sleek gray mare saddled in gilded Spanish leather. Elizabeth was assisted by the king himself, as Mary was by Brandon. Bess wondered if either man fully realized the impression they had on young girls. Their handsome smiles, witty jokes, and carefree confidence would have been enough even without the seductive power swirling around them.

She could not imagine why the queen wished so rarely to be in his company.

If I were queen to Henry the Eighth, she thought fancifully as the royal party passed the guard tower, then crossed over an emerald rise behind the palace, *I do not believe I would ever let him out of my sight.*

Enviously again, she watched Henry lean over in his own gilded saddle and murmur something to Elizabeth, who laughed with kittenish delight. Bess marveled at how easy it seemed for her friend to converse with the King of England as if he were just like anyone else. All afternoon she watched them, daring in her most private thoughts to increasingly imagine herself in Elizabeth's place. When she did, she would laugh out loud, mocking her own foolish hubris. Even though the king addressed her from time to time, he did it in the most perfunctory of ways—casually, blandly. She was simply another maid of honor to him, another inconsequential adolescent girl at a vast, fast-paced court with more beautiful—and mature— women than she could count.

After a stag was impressively cornered, then killed by the king himself deep inside the lush forest, the royal hunting party retired to a little wooded glade, carpeted with pine needles. There, an army of servants had laid a spectacular feast on long tables, complete with linen, tapestry cloths, gleaming silver plates, and jeweled goblets. As the custom had become, Bess and Elizabeth were seated beneath a lacy bower of shade trees beside the king and Charles Brandon. Even Princess Mary was not so well placed to dine. That struck Bess as curious, but she was too enamored of her own steadily growing good fortune to do anything but sit and enjoy it.

The king was still whispering to Elizabeth Bryan, both of them laughing at some private little joke as Bess bit into a moist piece of grilled venison.

"So then, Mistress Blount, how did you find our little adventure?" Brandon casually asked her as a servant once again filled the wine goblet he had already drained.

"I found it fast paced and exciting, Your Grace."

"As all things at my court should be," the king interjected suddenly from the other side.

Devilish glances were exchanged between the two men. "If it were any more fast paced, we would both be dead, certainly," Brandon returned.

"The killing was not too gruesome for such a demure young lady as yourself?" the king asked her.

To Bess's surprise, his glittering green-eyed gaze had descended fully on her, and his mouth was still turned up in a handsome smile as he waited for her reply. In spite of herself, her heart began to race as it always did when he looked at her, and she felt herself begin to blush. Bess said a silent prayer that he would not notice, because she knew it made her seem like a silly child, certainly not the clever young woman like the others she longed one day to be.

"Mistress Bryan and I are the same age, and it does not seem to affect her," Bess replied, careful to modulate her tone so her voice did not quaver as it always did around these worldly men.

"Mistress Bryan has a bit more experience than you do, Mistress Blount." Brandon chuckled.

"At the hunt, you mean," the king added with an odd little wink.

"Yet it is Mistress Poppincourt who trumps us all in experience," Elizabeth interjected tartly.

Bess's gaze darted among the three of them, looking to gauge their reactions. Then she forced herself to laugh blithely along with them, as though she were a part of the great private joke that had been made at Jane's expense, although she did not understand it at all.

"If it is true what they are saying about Jane and the duc de Longueville, that resourceful girl will find a way to return to France with him once he is released," Brandon said.

Bess longed to ask him precisely what that meant, but she held her tongue because everyone else apparently knew and she could not bear to go on looking naive.

"Of course it is true, Charles," said the king. "They have been secret lovers for weeks now. You think I do not know what goes on in my own court, especially with a noble prisoner, who is more guest in my court than any sort of captive, yet one I personally took on the battlefield in France?"

"Our Jane certainly does not hesitate to try new things!" Brandon affably joked.

Once again the two men laughed, and then suddenly, as the king looked at Elizabeth, Bess saw his hand drop down to Elizabeth's knee, disappearing beneath the table cover. She felt a jolt of shock; then something else caught her attention from the corner of her eye. It was another glance exchanged across the table between Charles Brandon and Princess Mary. At first, Bess was amazed that the king did not notice the exchange, for it was the most open of glances and lasted longer than was appropriate, but he was whispering something so closely to Elizabeth's ear that he was almost grazing her neck.

"So, Mistress Blount, do tell us all something interesting about yourself that we do not already know," the king suddenly bid her. "You are definitely the most quiet of the girls in the queen's household."

"Does Your Highness no longer find mystery enticing?" Elizabeth cleverly interjected.

"Unraveling a mystery can be as tiresome as hunting if the right prey is not captured. I must know whether it is worth my time."

Brandon chuckled, as did the king. "Is there not some juicy little detail you will share with us, Mistress Blount?" Brandon echoed. "Mistress Bryan is an open book to us now, so we must look elsewhere for something new."

Bess's heart beat like a bird's wings against her ribs, because she knew she must think of something on the spot. This was her moment to please them and show, like all of the other girls around her, how clever she could be, but it had come too suddenly, and she was unprepared.

"I am not certain I want to be captured," she said in a soft and careful tone.

The king bit back his smile. "I have a large enough collection of exotic creatures at Greenwich, Mistress Blount. I think you are quite safe from capture. I shall have to show them to you one day."

"I shall look forward to that, sire."

"Indeed you would be wise to. As I will look forward to your great secret when you decide to reveal it. Suddenly, I have a feeling it shall be worth the wait," the king remarked, just before he turned his attention back to Elizabeth Bryan, whose bright and clever smile had dimmed.

Gil was waiting for them when they returned. He was outside Elizabeth's small room, and he followed them inside, closing the door behind them.

"Tell me everything," he bid Elizabeth and Bess, "and spare not a single detail."

The girls exchanged a glance, then smiled at each other. "There is really nothing to tell. Just the usual; kill a stag, then dine and dance and laugh for hours. Merriment is so exhausting," Elizabeth replied tauntingly, since she knew how badly he had wanted to join them. "Still, the king could not be more handsome, which makes up for everything else."

"Or more clever," Bess added, as they both began predictably to giggle.

They had been there only moments when a knock sounded at the door. Gil went to open it.

"Mistress Blount, you are to come with me," declared a young page dressed formally in Tudor livery of green Bruges satin with gold buttons. His words held an ominous note. He did not smile or even bow to her. Suddenly she feared the worst, that she had somehow displeased the king with her first, adolescent attempt at clever evasion. Her heart began to pound again, and her throat went very dry at the possibility.

"May I ask why I have been summoned?"

"I was told only to bring you, mistress. Not the reason."

Elizabeth clasped her hand for a moment in silent support and then smiled. Bess's expression was stricken as she followed the page from the room.

"You are very transparent, you know," Elizabeth said once they were alone.

Gil came back and stood beside her. "Am I?"

"Quite. She really has no idea how you feel about her. I shall keep your secret, though, if you will keep mine. I am dying to tell someone."

"I thought Bess was your confidante."

"Not with this." There was an awkward silence for a moment as Elizabeth Bryan attempted to summon her courage. It was one thing to want to confide in Gilbert Tailbois, whom she had known most of her life, but it was quite another, she found, to actually speak the words aloud, giving validity to them.

"You were right all along. I am hopelessly in love with the king."

Gil unlatched the little leaded glass window beside the bed and opened it. "Is not every young girl at court?" he asked nonchalantly.

"Perhaps. But I have actually been his lover, so I suspect that makes my affection a bit above par."

She watched his expression carefully as he came to sit beside her. There was strained silence between them as a bee droned just outside the open window and footsteps passed by out in the corridor beyond the closed door.

"The gossip was that he was bedding Mistress Poppincourt."

"That was true until last spring," she said simply.

"Why have you not told Bess instead of me?"

She straightened her back and primly fluffed the folds of her burgundy and gold skirts. "Bess Blount believes in the image of the king and queen, their happy marriage, and equates everything she sees here with the romantic tale of Lancelot. She looks at our king as a legend and a fantasy, not a man. Who am I to ruin that for her?"

"And you are afraid she will learn from you, as you learned from Mistress Poppincourt, how to catch the king's eye herself."

She frowned at that. "I really do love him, Gilly."

"As futile an exercise as whistling in the wind."

"And yet did you not tell me yourself just this morning that he told Bishop Wolsey he was considering a divorce?"

"Angry men say many foolish things."

"Even powerful kings?"

"When you were gone, Wolsey told me the king might consider his suggestion to allow the French king to marry his sister. In that case, all anger would be forgotten between Henry and Ferdinand, and divorce would not be necessary."

"Mary will never agree to that," she scoffed. "She is in love with the Duke of Suffolk, and he with her. Everyone knows it."

"Love has nothing to do with marriage, Elizabeth. You would be wise to remember that. Bess would tell you the very same thing."

"Well, you must not breathe a word about any of this, especially to her. Promise me, Gilly. At least not until I know for certain where I stand with the king."

He lowered his eyes judgmentally upon her. "You have no intention of stopping, do you?"

"Not for as long as he will have me. I cannot. It might be as futile for me as things with Bess are for you, but you know neither of us is going to give up," she said. He did not answer, because he could not disagree. He was only sixteen, but Gil Tailbois knew it was true. He was hopelessly in love with Bess Blount.

Bess was led silently by the page down a twisted flight of stone stairs and along a corridor to a chamber concealed by carved double doors. Her heart was pounding with dread as she waited for the boy to knock. What she did not expect was whom she saw on the other side once the door was opened. Bess gave a little shriek of surprise, engulfed by the warm, familiar scent of her father, John Blount, as he drew her into a hearty embrace.

"Why did you not write to me that you were returning?" she sputtered, tears blurring her eyes as she laid her head against his noticeably slimmer chest. He felt more fragile, still weakened, she thought. Yet he was here. The post of Royal Spear, bodyguard to the king, was a demanding one, so he must be returned to good health.

"And miss that expression on your sweet face?" he said with a chuckle.

"We wanted to surprise you."

The voice behind them, sweet, gentle, and female, belonged to her mother. Bess gasped in disbelief at Catherine Blount, who stood in a pretty topaz satin and beadwork dress with delicate lace at the square neckline and sleeves, her face framed by a smile. She was slimmer as well. Bess did not need to embrace her to see that; yet still she did so, and heartily. She went to her mother's open arms with all the love of a child who had lost her way, and only now had found home.

"Apparently the surprise pleases our beautiful daughter." Catherine Blount smiled serenely. "Just look at how you have grown in a year's time. And we have heard much about you from Lady Hastings."

"I do not think she likes me very well," Bess confessed as they stood together in the center of a room with a high ceiling ornamented with heavy beams and two tall windows filled with colored glass.

"The Duke of Buckingham's sister likes you well enough to write to us that you have been elevated to an impressively prominent place at the king's table when he dines in public."

"That is only because I am friends with Mistress Bryan, whom the king favors most especially as a dining companion. She is, after all, very clever and beautiful."

Her parents exchanged a glance. "Sir Thomas's little daughter?" her father asked, but it was not really a question. "Bollocks! He has boasted for years about parading her out before the king the very moment she was old enough to be matched, not caring for the consequences. I always thought he was joking. Unseemly, is what it is."

"She certainly deserves a proper match. I always thought she was such a pretty girl," said her mother.

Bess studied each of her parents, much aged in the last year by her father's convalescence and her mother's constant care of him. Both looked a little less elegant than she remembered, yet it was so wonderful to have them back here with her. She did not want to dwell on Elizabeth any longer.

"How are you truly, Father?" she asked, gazing into eyes that were more deeply sunken than a year before. "Are you certain you are strong enough?"

"Fit as ever, dear one. Not to worry. Returning to my post will be the perfect medicine for me."

They were both smiling at her so happily that Bess had no choice but to believe them.

"Does the queen know you have returned?" she asked her mother. "She calls for me very little these days."

"I went to her first, of course. As you know, she is most uncomfortable at this stage of her pregnancy, and she finds it a comfort, she says, to be in the company only of women who have endured the same process. It also cannot be easy to know that such pretty young girls as you and Mistress Bryan keep her husband's company while she cannot."

"We are not to refuse His Highness's invitations. You and Father told me so yourselves that he and his friends enjoy the social company of pretty girls. *Be always at the ready to obey the king and queen*, was what you said," Bess defended, remembering the king's gaze upon her during the hunt earlier that day, but refusing even now to think of it as anything more than a game.

"You have done what is right, child," said her father, calmly intervening. "The act of balancing the varying motives and ambitions here is difficult at best, and we are enormously proud of you."

She felt a small sliver of relief, which made her smile.

"Only take care that nothing you do insults the queen, since it is our family connection to her household, through Mountjoy, that allows you and your mother to attend at court in the first place," said John.

"I love the queen. It is always my honor to serve her," Bess returned, meaning it. What she did not say was how greatly she envied Katherine of Aragon for the man she had captured and would have, forever.

After their reunion, Bess returned to her room as her parents went to get settled in. Bess still had not changed her costume from the hunt, and she could not go into the queen's apartments wearing dusty shoes or a riding hood. She half expected to see Gil still there with Elizabeth when she returned. Because of his connection to Wolsey, he was such a fixture in these chambers and corridors whenever she and Elizabeth were there. And secretly she did enjoy his company. Although she never quite knew what it was, there was something different about him from the other young gentlemen at court, and she liked that. She would have liked it better, she told herself as she removed her own shoes, if she knew how to identify her feelings for him. They were certainly nothing like what Guinevere felt for Lancelot, or Isolde for Tristan. That much she knew.

Only when she sat down on the edge of her small bed did she see them. A little bouquet of primroses lay on her pillow, bound by a strip of green silk ribbon. There was no note, no hint of who had left them. As she picked them up, Bess felt herself smile. Her mind raced back to the hunt that day, and to anyone who had paid even the slightest attention to her and might have left them, besides the king. However, he seemed a highly unlikely source, she thought, laughing sheepishly at herself for even considering such a preposterous thing.

It was late, and she had been asked to accompany Lady Hastings and her sister, Lady Fitzwalter, at prayer for the queen. While Bess had seen very little of the powerful Duke of Buckingham at court, she had learned well that his two sisters were not women she would want to defy. Quickly, she changed her shoes and donned a prettier cap, making certain her hair was properly tucked beneath the lacy fall. She pinched her cheeks, glanced in the little mirror on the table beside her bed, then dashed out of the room. She left the flowers lying beneath her riding hood and gloves, as forgotten as the question of who had left them there, or exactly what it was that drew her to entirely trust Gil Tailbois.

PART II

Step. . . .

*Alas, alas, if you only knew, I am sure you would never
allow me without interference to be led away a step.*

—Guinevere, *Lancelot*

Chapter Five

"*I* must be rid of Mistress Bryan," Henry announced to Wolsey matter-of-factly as they stood together on the archery field, a warm summer wind ruffling the plume of his cap and the edges of Wolsey's black cassock. The field was far behind the palace, just beyond the apple orchard, where Henry knew no one would hear them. They were alone but for pages and stewards who waited at a distance with wine and perfumed, dry cloths, to attend him when they were finished.

"She pleases Your Highness no longer?" the stout prelate dared to ask.

"She pleases me a little too much. But I am bored with the girl, Wolsey," he grumbled. "She is always lurking about, always laughing too loudly at my jokes, always smiling and flirting and waiting for me to call for her."

"Forgive me, sire, but that is bad precisely how?"

"It is desperation, Wolsey, a most unappealing quality in a woman, even one so young and pretty as Elizabeth Bryan." He set down his bow. "Things with her have run their course. Katherine will deliver me a son soon enough, and I have a need to be ready to get her with another as soon as possible afterward. But I cannot risk insulting the girl's father. I am not a fool to this sort of thing. Sir Thomas is one of my dearest friends, and I know he has turned a blind eye to this dalliance for months out of deference to me."

Henry ran a hand behind his neck, feeling the heat from the late-summer sun as heavily upon him as his conscience.

"That may be a problem," Wolsey observed. "He could make an issue of it, unless Your Highness provides an appealing alternative for his daughter."

"A marriage?" Henry asked as he signaled for the waiting steward to bring them each a goblet of wine.

"Why not? The girl is fifteen already."

"Have you anyone to propose to me, Wolsey? You know I trust your judgment in all things."

The bishop with the full cheeks and small eyes took a long swallow of wine before he replied. "Brandon, whom you trust equally, might advise you differently, but Master Carew is the right age, nearly eighteen, and unmarried. I used to see the little glances between them. I am certain, due to his standing with you, Sir Thomas and his wife would approve."

"Nicholas Carew is quite a rake now. There are few girls at my court with whom he has not dallied."

"Which makes him eminently suitable to accept the less-than-virginal Mistress Bryan, does it not?" He arched a brow and waited for Henry to consider it fully as he placed his empty goblet back onto a silver tray the steward held beside them.

Marriages really were the most prudent way to solve a multitude of complications, Henry thought as he picked up his bow once again and drew an arrow from the tooled leather quiver across his back. The old French king Louis XII had happily agreed to marry his sister Mary, a month earlier, easing England away from the need to return to war with France that summer, as he had thought to do. By the alliance, he was also saving face after Ferdinand and Maximilian, behind Henry's back, had brokered their own deals with Louis XII. That betrayal still stung.

If he thought about it too long, Henry felt guilty about giving someone so young and beautiful as Mary to an ailing widower like Louis XII. But his advisers had told him Louis was too ill to survive a vibrant young queen for long, so she would have the opportunity to find love in the next marriage he arranged for her. Infuriating as the circumstances were, one must not be stymied by such details but always be open to all options, he had resolved.

Tonight was the banquet celebrating Mary's marriage by proxy. His noble prisoner, the duc de Longueville, a guest really, was to stand in for the French king, who was not well enough to travel to claim his own bride. All of the players were as intricately woven together as a fine Flemish tapestry, he thought as he drew back the arrow and steadied his arm. He knew all about de Longueville's secret encounters with Jane Poppincourt, and he had kept quiet about them for the same reason he found himself considering Carew for Elizabeth Bryan. Women were always less of a problem when they were not cast aside outright. In time, when he found someone new upon whom to grant his favor, and Elizabeth was well married, perhaps they would even be friends. The fact that there was no one right now who interested him was of little consequence to Henry. There would be someone soon enough—certainly the next time the queen was with child, he thought as the arrow jettisoned directly toward the bull's-eye, shaking the target.

Even though she was pregnant, the queen had decided to attend the banquet that evening to celebrate Mary's proxy marriage, so all of her ladies and young maids of honor were called upon to attend her. Bess had seen little of the queen in the past month as Katherine still preferred the company of her older companions just now, so Bess knew how important it must be for her to leave her intimate surroundings.

Along with Jane, Elizabeth, and Gertrude, her cousin, Bess was to attend the important ceremony but stand well behind the queen; Maria de Salinas; Agnes de Venagas, who was Mountjoy's wife; and Bess's mother, Catherine. Two of the youngest maids of honor, both new to court, were invited as well. Mary and Anne Boleyn, the daughters of Sir Thomas Boleyn, passed in front of Bess, whispering and giggling inappropriately. Instinctively, Bess did not like or trust either of them. Both girls were as impudent as they were pretty, and she intended to stay well out of their way.

It was rare for a queen visibly with child to attend such a public function, but Bess saw how Katherine wore her devotion to the king on her sleeve, and in every expression on her face. Bess had been too young to recall much about her own mother's pregnancies, but now the process fascinated her as the culmination of great love, like the one between the king and queen, or even between her own parents. She could not quite fathom loving anyone enough to happily bring that upon her own body, yet Bess secretly hoped she would wish it one day, and out of love rather than duty.

After the solemn and formal ceremony, and a Nuptial Mass, there was a celebration in the great banquet hall. Beneath plastered beams, the walls were hung with cloth of gold embroidered with the arms of France and England. The warm summer breeze through open windows made the candles and lanterns shimmer as everyone danced. Bess sat beside Gil and Elizabeth. She felt suitably elegant in a formal gown of mauve-colored velvet with turned-back sleeves and a small pearl-dotted coif.

Beside the king sat a gouty man with a clipped little gray beard whom Bess did not know. She had seen him infrequently at court, but then only at a distance. When Gil saw her staring at him, he casually said, "That is the Duke of Buckingham, just returned from his estates. Wolsey and he do not like each other. It is always like a great chess match when Buckingham returns between the duke, Brandon, and Wolsey to see who will have the most influence with the king."

"Tonight it would appear to be the duke," Bess observed.

"I certainly will hear all about it later before I retire." Gil rolled his eyes and smiled.

"The bishop confides in you to that extent?" Bess asked, letting the note of surprise in her voice come through.

"Only from time to time, if there is no one else about."

"Oh, *do* tell her the truth," Elizabeth interjected from beside them. "Bishop Wolsey dotes on you as if you were his own son."

"'Tis true enough that he is fond of me," Gil quickly responded. "Quite likely, it is only because he is unable to have a family of his own."

"You do look a bit like him," Bess observed, noticing the resemblance for the first time. Elizabeth returned her gaze once again across the vast room to the king, who was laughing at something the Duke of Buckingham had said. Bess watched with surprise as Elizabeth lowered her eyes and smiled flirtatiously, clearly trying to get the king's attention.

"What if the queen notices her doing that?" Bess leaned nearer to Gil to ask.

"I would imagine Her Highness is accustomed to it by now. There have been girls doing it for as long as I have been at court."

Bess was embarrassed to admit to herself that she was secretly one of them, one of many silly little girls nursing childish fantasies. It made it all the more pathetic to see the king turn then and gently brush the back of his hand along the line of his wife's jaw in what looked like a show of concern. All of it was nothing more than a courtly game, she thought.

"Mistress Bryan, would you join me in a dance?"

Bess saw Elizabeth glance perfunctorily at the handsome young man who had asked the question before she said, "I do not like the tourdion, Master Carew. Perhaps Mistress Blount would be a more fitting partner since she dances so brilliantly."

Nicholas Carew, dressed in a fashionable gray doublet with silver silk slashings, gave a strange little pause before he replied. "The king wished me to request a dance on his behalf from Mistress Blount at the same time, since I meant to come over here to ask you, Mistress Bryan."

Bess felt the surprise blossom on her face in a warm rush. "But what of the queen?" she asked.

"Her Highness cannot dance in her present circumstance, and she plans to retire for the evening soon anyway. She does not begrudge the king a bit of fun when she is unable to give it herself," Carew added. The sting of rejection made his words sound sharp.

When Bess glanced back, she saw the king nod to her in acknowledgment, then smile as a page drew back his chair for him, and he stood. In response, Elizabeth shot Bess an oddly angry look, tipped up her chin, then stood as well.

"Come, Bess. One mustn't keep the King of England waiting. Especially not when he wants something—or someone," she said tartly.

Elizabeth then curtsied to Carew, her pale blue dress pooling around her, before she rose again.

"What did I do?" Bess whispered in a panic to Gil, who had time only to shrug his shoulders as Elizabeth reached back, clutched her by the wrist, and drew her along to the place where King Henry stood waiting.

"Good evening, Mistress Blount," Henry said with a little nod and a slightly twisted smile that made her forget to breathe as she stepped into the dancing area. "So tell me, how does your tourdion fair?"

"Tolerably, Your Highness."

"Shall I be the judge?"

"I shall pray you do not judge me too harshly."

"Such beauty would make that impossible."

Elizabeth gave a sudden little grunt at the exchange as she brushed past the king, and Nicholas followed her.

"Do they not make a handsome couple?" asked the king.

"A couple, sire?"

"Mistress Bryan and Master Carew. They are a great deal alike," Henry said, taking her hand and leading her toward the other dancers. "Both spoiled, willful, and full of expectation. They might make a good match, if they do not kill each other first."

"My father always says that a healthy challenge brings the best reward."

As Henry laughed, his green eyes crinkled at the corners, and suddenly Bess could see nothing else. God, but he was handsome, and so remarkably clever. "I always did like your father. How is he?"

"Returned to your service, sire."

Henry paused for a moment just after he had taken her hand. The feel of it was warm and full of power. "I was not told. I shall have someone punished." His tone bordered so close to seriousness that Bess could not discern if he meant it, and she felt a shiver of panic.

"Oh, please, my lord, do not!"

He leveled his eyes on her again as the music for the tourdion began in the gallery above, and dancers began to move around them, swirling silk and layers of velvet, along with the heavy scent of mingling perfumes. "What shall you give me, young Bess, if I grant you your wish?"

He was toying with her, like a cat with a mouse—she could feel it now. And she knew that some witty retort was what he was after, just like the last time when she had left him wanting. But, to her horror, Bess was still too inexperienced to know what might please or insult him.

This was a game for adults, and she was not quite sixteen.

The king must have seen in her eyes what she was thinking, because suddenly his smile faded and his eyes filled with sincerity.

"You are lovely indeed when you smile," he said, taking her hand again and leading her to the very center of the other dancers.

"I am honored Your Highness would find me so," she replied, lowering her eyes demurely.

"A man would have to be blind not to find you so, Mistress Blount. The man who one day wins your heart shall be heaven blessed indeed."

They turned in time with the music and with the other dancers, linked hands, then turned back the other way.

"What sort of man do you believe you shall fancy?"

A man exactly like you, she thought foolishly. "My father always warned me I shall have little choice in the matter of my husband, so I have not given it much thought."

Henry arched a brow. "That is true in marriage, but not in love. No one can control your heart, Mistress Blount. Remember that."

She realized for the first time that little Bess Blount from Kinlet was keeping up with the King of England, and he was still smiling at her as if he were enjoying it. He always danced eventually with the various ladies of his court, young and old, Gertrude once told her. No doubt he saw it as his duty. Whatever his reason, Bess thought, just as the song came to an end, this definitely was the most wonderful moment of her life, one she would never forget for as long as she lived. At last, it had been her turn.

"Would you do me the honor of joining me at my table for a while, Mistress Blount? Your friend Mistress Bryan seems occupied just now, the queen is about to retire for the evening, and I will be frightfully bored if you do not. You may take her seat if it pleases you."

If it pleases me? She looked across the dance floor and saw Bishop Wolsey speaking with Elizabeth and Nicholas Carew and exiting the banquet hall. Across the room, the queen and Maria de Salinas stood. Those around her stood as well and bowed or curtsied to her. Bess saw her cast a glance back at the king, stiffen, then turn to depart just as the king himself had predicted.

"Does Her Highness mind that you danced with me?" Bess asked.

"My wife understands well that a king's burden is a heavy one. She is pleased when I enjoy myself. Come now, soon we shall take Princess Mary and her proxy husband to the bedchamber to consummate their union, but sit with me until then."

Bess longed to ask if that meant the duc de Longueville was required to actually bed with the French king's new wife. But no matter what the answer was, she knew having someone so handsome and powerful speak of intimacies to her would be difficult to endure without entirely embarrassing herself.

The dukes of Buckingham and Suffolk both stood then and acknowledged her as she approached. Suffolk smiled; Buckingham did not.

"You look lovely this evening, Mistress Blount," said Suffolk, though she still thought of him as Charles Brandon. He was always so kind to her, but tonight he seemed distracted. It did not take long to realize that he was preoccupied with looking, once again, at the king's newly married sister. Yet he had been at court long enough to be charming before everything else. "The color of your gown is most becoming against your skin."

"Thank you, Your Grace. 'Twas a gift from my parents."

"Your family has excellent taste."

She felt herself blush, marveling at the believable tone in his courtly flattery.

"Buckingham, you know Mistress Blount," said the king as they all sat down and the music for a new dance began. A silver ewer of wine was brought and a goblet was poured for each of them.

"We have not had the pleasure of an introduction, sire, although she and Mistress Bryan do make themselves well-known to all," he smoothly replied.

Buckingham, the small, brittle-looking man, wore more jewels than the king, had a more neatly cropped beard, and was certainly more intimidating. His tone, so different from Brandon's, was clipped. The pitch of his voice was higher than most men's, Bess thought, sharp and more nasal in quality, which made him seem even more formal than his slim, stiff bearing suggested. He was a powerful man, she knew from her parents, and he was not friends with either Brandon or Wolsey. Rather, they were polite, relentless competitors for power and royal favor, which was obvious to her now. Gil always said it was best, if possible, to stay well out of their way. She did not like Buckingham. He frightened her.

"So tell me, Mistress Blount," said Brandon, "will you be sailing with us for France in the wedding party?"

"She and Mistress Bryan are to remain at court," Henry answered for her. "I know not what I would do without such jolly company and two such lovely faces, of which I am quickly growing quite fond. Nor would the queen," he said as an afterthought.

Bess saw that he was looking at her again as he spoke, and with an increasingly intense gaze. But of course she was imagining it. Her own secret daydreams of the young sovereign were becoming embarrassing fantasies. Suddenly she missed Elizabeth and Gil and the comfort and reassurance they brought. When she glanced back across the room, Bess saw Gil sitting stone still, in the same place she had left him. His eyes were rooted upon her, and he was most definitely not smiling. For a moment, seeing his expression shook her so that she, at first, did not hear the ribald laughter or the jokes between the men around her. Certainly Gil was not happy.

Then suddenly a trumpet fanfare peeled through the vaulted hall, announcing the king and Buckingham, who bowed to each other with courtly formality and smiles. Each then drew off his formal beaded coat, and led the court in an impromptu country dance, wearing their more casual doublets and hose, as the crowd raucously cheered. Her concern for Gil vanished as Bess was transfixed by the dance. Henry's long legs beneath his hose had the muscles of a warrior, yet he moved with grace and skill to the music. She could not take her eyes from him. More of the court men joined the king, but Charles Brandon remained beside her.

"You are a sweet, gentle girl, Bess Blount. Take care while I am gone, will you?" he said oddly.

When she looked at him this time, she saw that Brandon's expression was no longer clever and easy but full of a strange sincerity.

"You sound as if you are trying to warn me of something."

"Perhaps I am."

"Perhaps you would be better off with me simply coming out and saying it. I am not as clever or experienced as some of the other girls here."

"Precisely why one might wish to warn you," said Brandon as they watched the king and Buckingham continue to show off for the rest of the court. "You are always with Mistress Bryan, I see."

"Much of the time, when we are not serving the queen, 'tis true."

"And does she speak to you familiarly?"

His tone made it obvious that he was trying to get at something, but she had no idea what. "We speak as most young girls do, Your Grace, with some degree of familiarity, yet I would not claim to know her heart, nor she mine."

Brandon leaned back in his chair, fingering his goblet. He seemed to have discovered what he wished to know, since his expression eased. He glanced over at the king's sister once again, then back at Bess.

"You are different, Mistress Blount, not like the other girls of the queen's household. There is a gentle spirit about you that might be mistaken for naïveté. But I do not think you are naive so much as inexperienced."

"Are they not one and the same?" she asked.

His studied nonchalance began to fade beneath a stronger air of sincerity. "One can become experienced in an instant. Knowing which experiences are good for you or which are dangerous requires strong instinct. I believe you have that."

"You have faith in someone you barely know?" she asked him.

"Ah, well, I am neither naive nor inexperienced. My own instincts tell me when I am in the presence of someone I should help to protect if I can. I wish I was not going away just now, or that you were joining us in France, for I fear I know only too well what will happen while I am away."

"I wish Your Grace could be more specific," Bess said, feeling the rise of frustration at his vagueness more than any fear his warning might bring.

"I wish I could as well. But I value my place, and my instincts tell me not to threaten that just now, especially when I have my own challenges ahead of me," Charles Brandon replied as he finally caught the eye of the king's newly married sister, who met his gaze with what Bess thought was a strangely sad smile.

Gil did his best to comfort her, but it was a pointless exercise. Elizabeth wept in his arms, her body racked with childlike sobs. The plaintive wail of disappointment and betrayal coming from her seared his soul, yet there was nothing either of them could do. The choice, quite obviously, had been made by the king himself. Gil had seen something like this coming from the moment she confided in him, but there was nothing he could have done to convince her to stop. He had been as powerless then as he was now, because Elizabeth Bryan believed she was in love with a married man—a king.

A soft rap sounded at the door then. A moment later came the voice they both knew well. "'Tis Bess. Are you all right? May I come in?"

"Please do not tell her of it!" Elizabeth begged Gil in an urgent whisper.

"But she is our friend. Does she not deserve to know? Besides, is she not likely to hear about it anyway?"

"That will only be gossip. You were my friend first, Gilly. Pray, have you not some loyalty for that?"

Elizabeth straightened herself on the edge of the bed and wiped away her tears with the palms of her hands, but her nose was red from her weeping, and she still could not quite catch her breath. Her body was still trembling as Bess opened the door and came inside.

Beautiful as a painting, Gil thought as she drew near. He noted the remarkable angles of her face and the widest cornflower blue eyes he had ever seen. Yes, her eyes still stunned him. Her small, soft mouth was one he had dreamed of kissing more than once. She was, quite simply, perfection. He had thought that from the first moment, and in her year at court, his opinion had gone unchanged. Unfortunately, it seemed fairly clear to him that Bess Blount did not return his affection.

"What has happened?" Bess asked him, concern spiking in her eyes and causing the words to come quickly as she sank onto the bed beside the two of them. It was close enough for Gil to smell the scent of lavender on her skin. Controlling the physical reaction he always had to her was a challenge. He drew in a breath to steady himself before he explained.

"She is betrothed to marry Nicholas Carew. She was told of it only tonight."

"Told, not asked, by Master Carew?" Bess wanted to know.

"Informed by Bishop Wolsey and Sir Thomas Bryan of the decision already agreed to by their families."

Bess tipped her head, and Gil saw she was trying to decide what to say. "Well, he is very handsome indeed, and he seems a nice enough sort; clever, witty. . . ."

"Nicholas Carew is an incorrigible rake," Gil gently amended. "Women have been playthings for him since the moment he realized his effect on them."

"I do not love him, nor will I ever love him!" Elizabeth hotly declared. "Even if I am forced to become his wife!"

"This seems so sudden," Bess said, looking from one to the

other of them as they all sat on the same edge of her small bed in the shadowy little room.

The leaded window before them was open, ushering in warm summer-night air and the chirp of crickets in the hedgerow below. For a time, that was the only sound.

"It does seem an honor, since Master Carew is one of the king's closest friends," Bess cautiously observed, trying to be helpful.

"I've absolutely no choice in it, so I might as well try to see it that way. My father certainly does." Elizabeth looked at Bess then, tears still rolling down her cheeks in ribbons made bright by the candlelight. "It was just something of a surprise." She sniffled, trying in vain to collect herself.

"At least you have the duration of your betrothal to know him better," Bess offered hopefully.

"The king has commanded that we marry before his sister departs for France. My father wants the new French queen still here in England to add importance to the union."

"You do not believe that is the reason for haste?" Bess asked with a little tip of her head and a glance at Gil that was so gentle and innocent, it made him shudder.

"What I believe is just as unimportant, Bess, as what I desire. I just did not realize how unimportant until tonight."

"Is there someone you would rather marry? Has that upset you the more?"

Elizabeth shot Gil a little warning glance, urging him not to reveal anything about her affair with the king. But she need not have done that. She knew he was a young man of honor. Gil had given her his word, and he meant to keep it. Whatever Bess found out about the workings of this court and this king, she would do so on her own.

Chapter Six

August 1514
Dover, Kent

*B*ess could not quite believe the honor she had received. She was to attend the new French queen in the royal party that would see her from Greenwich to Dover, then bid her farewell at the dock amid a grand procession. She did not mind at all that the honor would end there and that she would not be continuing on to France. That seemed a strange land anyway, with a language she had never learned to speak well. Better to leave that journey to a few of the older, more experienced women of the court—and to Mary and Anne Boleyn. Those churlish little sisters boasted daily about how brilliantly sweet their French sounded because the tutor their ambitious father had retained for them was actually French. Besides, Bess thought as they stood gathered where the banks of the bay met the dock and nine great French galleons were anchored, Elizabeth Bryan would need her as confidante when she returned from her wedding trip.

Poor Elizabeth; the prospect of marriage had changed her from the carefree, clever beauty who had challenged her to steal into the king's bedchamber, and Bess missed their camaraderie. At least there still would be Gil, sweet, dependable Gil, she thought, as she felt the salt air move through the fabric drape behind her neck. She was grateful to have it cool her. The brocade dress she had chosen for today was her most elegant, but it was too heavy for August, and she regretted wearing it.

As the king and his sister walked alone out onto the long dock to where the great royal ship sat bobbing at anchor, Bess turned back to Charles Brandon. His expression said absolutely everything. All Bess had suspected was never more true than it was on his face at this moment. It was indeed far more than a harmless courtly flirtation between them. He was deeply in love with Mary.

But with the realization came pity.

How pointless it was to fall in love with someone promised to a rival with whom one could not hope to compete—a waste of not only a life, but a heart.

It really was no different, she thought, than with Jane and the duc de Longueville, the noble battlefield prisoner who was now being released and allowed to return home to his obligations in France, but returned without his far less noble mistress. Looking around her, there was enough misery to make Bess vow that she would never be so foolish with her own heart. Unlike Elizabeth and Jane, and so many others around her, she would wait with her maidenhead intact for her father to choose a suitable husband for her. He would choose wisely, she knew.

Bess had no intention of ever wearing the same bereft expression she had seen on the faces of Jane Poppincourt and Charles Brandon.

That evening after the ship had set sail for the shore at Calais, the royal party that had remained was welcomed at Dover Castle, the great twelfth-century fortress perched on the vast white cliffs. The massive castle, wrought of ancient gray stone, with a drawbridge entrance, fortress wall, and great square Norman tower, was lovely and welcoming inside. It held massive, warming fireplaces, tapestries, and a sweeping view of the sea. Bess had never seen an ocean, or taken in the pungent salt air as she did now, standing alone at the edge of the jagged, rocky cliff. The wind blew so strongly that she removed her hood and let her long blond hair dance in ribbons around her face. The early-evening wind was warm and the sensation was so freeing, she could not help the small indulgence.

"I miss her already."

Bess gave a startled little jump. When she turned around, she was surprised to see it was the king standing there in the same magnificent black and silver doublet he had worn at supper. But without his cap, there was nothing to draw attention away from his eyes, or his handsome face, which seemed so troubled.

"Foolish, I suppose, since Mary is a grown woman with a duty to fulfill," he added with a heavy sigh.

Bess paused, uncertain if he meant for her to respond.

"I miss my brother George as well. I know he is happy where he is, yet still I miss him," she eventually replied with some hesitation.

"The sibling bond is deep," Henry said knowingly.

"Like no other," she replied in agreement.

He linked his hands behind his back and gazed out at the sea along with her as the very last crimson strip of the sunset dipped below the horizon before them.

"But I am pleased to hear that you are happy with your place at court."

"I am indeed, sire."

"I had a brother once. He was called Arthur," he said a moment later. The words were so casually spoken that she thought he might have been any other ordinary young man in England making a passing reference to his brother—not someone meant to be king.

"Yes, my lord. I have heard of him."

"He died when you were very young, but you would have liked him. You have a similar way about you."

Bess was surprised by that, and she guiltily hoped that the little blanket she had taken had eventually found its way back beneath his bed. "Your Highness flatters me by saying so."

"There was the same reserve about Arthur that you possess, but there was always much beneath the surface, for those who took the time to see it."

The king's eyes were haunting to her now as they settled deeply upon her, the warm wind stirring their clothes and hair. Such a deep and fathomless green, they were eyes Bess knew, even then, she could lose herself in, if she allowed it. He was everything a young girl from the country ever dreamed about. The thought frightened her, because he was a king, yes, but more than that—because he was irrevocably linked to another woman: his wife.

"Did the queen see what you saw in Arthur?" she asked, surprising herself. His marriage was much on her mind these days, but she found that she truly did want to know.

"You mean when Katherine was his wife? Yes, she did. We all loved Arthur so dearly."

She watched Henry's eyes mist with tears just before he turned and gazed back out at the sea. "I have no idea why I just told you that."

"Yet I am flattered that you did, Your Highness."

"Sire. Your Highness. My lord. All such wearisome appellations," he said, sighing and sounding much older than his twenty-two years.

"Would you think me less of a flatterer, and perhaps more a fool, if I told you that the great King of England who stands before you keeps an article of his brother's, almost as if it were a talisman, hoping to bring him back? It is a small cradle blanket in which he was wrapped as an infant. Sometimes I feel, when I touch the delicate fabric, that he is near to me again. And that feeling somehow lightens the burden of being king."

"That is very dear, not foolish at all," she said, meaning it. But this time she could not bring herself to pull her eyes from his. Henry's gaze had a strange command over her, and Bess knew, at that moment, she must work very hard not to fall beneath its powerful spell. No matter the harmless, courtly flirtations she had seen, he rightfully belonged to Katherine of Aragon, Bess diligently struggled to remind herself. So strong was the sensation that his nearness brought, and so complex were her feelings, she did not think to wonder what had brought him out here in the first place to this rocky cliff to stand alone with a girl he barely knew.

"Dear." He repeated the word with a little scoffing laugh that Bess thought surprisingly brittle. "Well Arthur loved his wife, and she loved him. They were well matched, even for ones so young." The king seemed like an ordinary young man with weaknesses of his own. His words gave her the courage to be bold.

"And you, my lord, are you well matched with your queen?"

"Katherine was the right woman to become Queen of England after Arthur died," he finally replied with a burdensome sigh. "Without a child, though—without a son—I do sometimes wonder if I displeased God by believing that."

"I pray God you did not displease Him and that this next child will be a son for you both."

Henry looked at her deeply then, almost studying her. "You really are a different sort of girl, are you not?"

"I am not certain what Your Highness means, exactly, but my brother George always said I was full of thoughts that only I would ever understand."

Henry smiled his dazzling smile at her response, which then faded into a soft look of sincerity. "I understand you perfectly well, I believe."

"Do you?"

"As I understood Arthur. Bess, sincerity is rather easy to see. You may well be young, but your sincerity is strong, apparent, and a comfort to be around."

She felt a shiver at the sound her name made on his lips. It was strangely intimate to her, a kind of communion between them, and thus totally inappropriate, both because of her youth and because he was married. She must not forget that.

Bess glanced back up at the grand castle, wondering who knew they were out there alone together. Most likely everyone knew.

"I am truly flattered that you would find me so." She struggled against the powerful attraction she felt. His gaze told her he was feeling the same. She glanced a second time at the stone manor up above the winding gravel-covered path.

"In such a complex world, am I less of a comfort to *you,* Bess?" he asked deeply as he closed the gap between the two of them in a single movement.

"Not because you are the king, my lord, but because you have a wife." Bess was not certain from where the words had come. The declaration had been bold, but the words had pushed their way out before she could deny them. She had thought and dreamed of little else for months, but how different she would feel if he were an unmarried man. Bess so loved the fantasy, but just now she valued loyalty to her family more.

Henry smiled again, and this time the expression was full of easy confidence as he reached up and very gently touched the side of her face with the back of his hand. The sensation was so charged that Bess grimaced as she felt her face grow very warm. Her body was weakening, no matter what words she had managed to force past her lips.

"It is precisely because I am king that I require a wife and, by extension, a son."

She tipped her head as she studied him. "You are not saying that you do not love the queen, are you, sire?"

"She is my heart's duty, if not my heart's desire, so at times I suppose I am drawn to something more," he said philosophically.

His tone surprised her nearly as much as the admission. Even though she had seen evidence of it and long suspected it was true, of course, there was a harsh reality to the confirmation, which seemed far-flung from the romances, like *Lancelot*, in which she still so wanted to believe. "So you do take mistresses then?"

"That is not at all what I meant."

The wind was tossing their hair and masking their words so that only the two of them could hear. "But I do find myself powerfully drawn to you, Bess, and I am at a loss as to how I might temper the attraction."

His voice had become melodic, keenly seductive now, and somehow he had moved close enough that she could feel the rise and fall of his chest against her own. Again, he ran his hand along the side of her face, tracing the line of her jaw down near her mouth. Bess knew she should protest, but she could not.

"Do you feel nothing at all for me?" he asked.

"I feel my duty to the queen more." Her body had begun to ache in a way it never had before, and the urge to melt deeply against him was unrelenting.

Henry smiled again. "Care to tell me how much more?"

She could not contain her feeling, and she smiled. Why had God set before her like this someone so clever, so handsome, so desirable, and so far beyond her reach?

"No, I do not care to tell you."

"No matter." He chuckled. "Your eyes have shown me, even if your words do not. Not to mention your body," he added, glancing down at the way she had yielded, pressed against his doublet.

Embarrassed, Bess stepped back. Her parents would be livid if they knew.

"Too late," he gently quipped, not surrendering the intimacy between them. "This is just the beginning."

"Beginning of what?"

"Only time shall tell, Mistress Blount."

"Not 'Bess' any longer?" she asked with a sudden flair of spirit.

"Not 'Bess' again until I know hearing it on my lips, in the way I mean to say it, is what you desire, as much as do I."

She bit back her smile as they stood together in the last vestiges of daylight. "And what if that day never comes?"

"Oh, it shall come," Henry glibly said. "Of that I have no doubt."

Bess half expected to find Elizabeth or Gil waiting when she returned a few minutes later to her small bedchamber, which had a wonderful view of the sea. She missed them both here in Dover, so far from court. There was so much to tell, yet there was no one but

Jane Poppincourt in whom to confide—and even Jane was mysteriously nowhere to be found.

Bess stood at the single open window, letting the night air and the rhythmic sounds of the sea wash over her. It had been a strangely unnerving day of battling her conscience and her desire. Her father had warned her about this world. Mountjoy had as well. These were powerful men with even more powerful desires to use beautiful young girls as playthings in meaningless games of courtly love. But never in those warnings had anyone adequately prepared her for the possibility that one of those men might ever be the married King of England.

She closed her eyes for a moment as the cool night air dried the perspiration on her neck and the hollow between her breasts, beneath her velvet gown. She did not even like Jane overly much, yet Bess longed to tell her about the evening anyway. She longed to tell someone in case she woke up tomorrow and it had all been a dream. And it *was* a dream of sorts—a dangerous one. Gil would not hesitate to warn her of that. Better to have him back at Greenwich with Wolsey and the queen, Bess thought with a little spark of defiance, and better for this to be an incredible, delicious little secret for her alone.

The roads were especially muddy and rutted by summer rain, and they had slowed the journey back to court to a jarring, neck-aching crawl. Bess longingly anticipated a soft, still bed as she climbed the last staircase, then twisted the iron door handle that led to her chamber. What she had not anticipated was who would be waiting for her when she arrived.

For the first time in more than a year, Bess gazed in surprise and disbelief at her favorite brother, George, standing beside her bed, smiling. He was here without warning, just as her parents had been.

"How?" The single word was all she managed to shriek as she flew into his arms.

He held her tightly for a moment, then kissed the top of her head with great affection. "I was summoned very suddenly. A servant to the king came to Kinlet and told me I must come at once."

Two days earlier, she had stood on a cliff with the king and they had spoken of brothers. This was an obvious gift to her from King Henry.

"I have missed you!" she cried as tears made little pathways through the road dust that covered her face.

"And I you, Bess."

"How long will you stay?"

"I have not yet been told, and I did not want to endanger anything by asking. But I am so dearly glad to be here." He held her out for a moment at arm's length then, his smile widening. "Look at what a beauty you have become in a year. I can scarcely believe it. You look like a proper lady now, and a grown woman."

"Thank you, Georgie," she replied, giving him her best, serene court smile until they both began to giggle and then collapsed onto her little bed. "Do Mother and Father know you are here?"

"They showed me to your chamber."

"They must be thrilled, Father especially."

"You are their hope now, Bess. There is great family pressure on you to make an important marriage, you know."

"No," she said honestly. "I did not know. I assumed I would be sent back to Kinlet soon, now that Father is well recovered and they are both returned."

George smiled at her, with that smile full of so many memories and happy times. "I believe it is safe to say that plan has been forever changed by the brilliant match your friend Mistress Bryan made with Master Carew."

Bess's smile faded. "I do not know how brilliant she would say it was. Elizabeth wept the entire morning of the ceremony."

"A coltish bride is no surprise, Father always says."

She gazed up at the ceiling, feeling constricted now by her tight stomacher, the heavy velvet gown, the shoes, and the proper head-dress, all of which she longed to cast off. "It was more than that, Georgie. Although she refused to speak to me or our friend Gil about it, I always believed she had designs on someone else."

"Gil, is it?" he asked with a twisted smile. "Do you mean Master Gilbert Tailbois, ward of Bishop Wolsey?"

"How do you know of him?"

"I have always been a good student of our parents' lectures on the key players at court, lest I be called into service. Or even for just a visit such as now, where I might make an impression. So then, what about you and Master Tailbois? Since he is the aide to one of the king's most trusted confidants, Father and Mother must be hoping he will consider you."

Bess felt herself blush discussing this with her own brother, no matter how close they were. "Gil is sweet and kind, that much is true, but I assure you there is no feeling of romantic connection between us. I do believe I would be the last girl he or the bishop would consider."

George turned his head to look at her as they lay beside each other, her now-hoodless blond hair fanned out between them on the bed. "Is there someone, then, with whom you *do* have a romantic connection?"

Bess met his gaze for a moment, wanting to push past the

awkward sensation in order to confide in the one person she knew without question she could trust. "Promise you'll not laugh?"

"I promise."

"It is impossible, of course."

There was a little silence then. "Oh *Jésu*, no."

"He has done absolutely nothing improper, but I believe King Henry brought you to court in order to please me."

"You and the king?" George began to laugh as if it were the most preposterous statement in the world. "Little Bessie Blount from Kinlet and the King of England?"

She felt herself stiffen at the slight. "Is it really so difficult to believe?"

"That a handsome, powerful sovereign, one with an equally important queen to whom he is devoted enough to name regent, would think of my little country sister as anything beyond a dalliance? Yes, Bess, it is very difficult to believe, indeed."

She sat up with an indignant little huff and pushed her long hair back behind her shoulders. "The king is a serious man with serious intentions. He told me so himself. Why else would you think he would suddenly bring you here other than because I told him I missed you?"

"You were having that sort of intimate conversation with our married sovereign and you do not believe me? Whom else have you told about this?"

George was sitting up now as well, but she would no longer look at him.

"No one."

He exhaled deeply. "That, at least, is a relief. See that you keep it that way, or you shall endanger not only your own position here, but Mother's and Father's as well."

George took up her hand then and held it tightly. "The truth is, I can understand the lure. But do not be a fool, Bess. There is nothing he could offer you beyond what the others have already gotten."

"He may be a bit bold with his flirtations, but he told me he does not take mistresses, and I have no reason not to believe him," she countered with adolescent stubbornness.

"Mother told me herself it was whispered that your friend Elizabeth Carew was one of them," he put in very gently. "Perhaps the tears you saw at her wedding were of innocence lost?"

"Elizabeth may have flirted with him like the rest of us, or even, I shall grant you, joined him in his chamber, but she would never have compromised herself fully like that."

"Perhaps if she once believed the same things you now do—"

"Stop!" Bess cried, and bolted for the window. As she tried to collect herself by glancing down into the courtyard, she saw that most of the horses used on the long journey to Dover had been led back to the stables and only a few servants remained. They were still unloading the carts that had accompanied the massive royal entourage. The king. Dover. *The cliff* . . . Finally, Bess drew in a steadying breath and turned back around. "I am happier than you shall ever know that you are here," she said with a slight tremble to her voice. "But there are some things you simply do not understand."

"And even more things that *you* do not. Sister, please. I'll not tell anyone, but I bid you, take great care."

"No matter what I may feel, my loyalty is to the queen, who allowed me to come to court, and I told him as much myself."

George Blount slapped his forehead then, his eyes rolling to a close. "You have spoken that familiarly with the king?"

"I do not expect you to understand someone you do not know," Bess snapped in reply.

"And you do? Pray, take care with this *friendship*, Sister," he warned, "or you may get well more than you ever bargained for."

They stood looking at each other stubbornly, both angry, and at an impasse that had come as suddenly and swiftly as their reunion.

"I shall be careful, I promise," she finally said, knowing even as she spoke the vow that she was flirting with danger. Bess was a different person now in more than appearance, changing every day into the kind of woman who courted danger, no matter the risk.

To Gil, it had felt a lifetime that Bess had been in Dover.

He had missed everything about her, and he kept his mind on the details of her, picturing them over and over, until he could make her real again—her golden hair that always looked to him like silk, her wide, expressive blue eyes, her slight countryside accent that she tried her best to conceal. He even missed her charming naïveté. Yes, Gil knew without a doubt, especially now, that he was hopelessly in love with Bess Blount. There was no one like her, and tonight at the banquet he planned to take her aside, risking everything, including his pride, and tell her so. The timing seemed particularly suitable since Elizabeth Bryan, now Carew, was not here to warn him against it. Either way, the draw to gamble was far more powerful than any fear that might have stopped him.

He glanced down at the ruby and pearl pendant that had once belonged to his mother. It was a modest piece of jewelry by court standards, but it was dear to him, and he meant to give it to Bess tonight when he told her that he loved her.

Excitement, fear, and anticipation, a potent brew, worked swiftly inside him now. Gil had been planning every detail of the scene almost since the moment Bess had left for Dover. Somehow he would draw her outside with him for a breath of cool night air, and there beneath the stars he would finally confess his love. He wanted desperately to tell her that he had thought of nothing and no other girl since they first had met. He laughed at himself and at the slightly pathetic image his thoughts conjured as he stuffed the pendant back in his pocket and began to look around the banquet hall for her as it slowly filled with courtiers to celebrate the king's return. Perhaps all of that would be a bit much for one night, he silently amended, shaking his head. It would be enough for now to give her the token, Gil decided instead, and to see where that might lead them.

The queen was not at the banquet that evening since she had begun her formal lying-in in preparation for the birth of the royal child. Elizabeth, who had not returned from her wedding trip, was not there either, so Bess felt a hesitation she had all but forgotten concerning the evening ahead. She was still a little angry at George who all her life, until today, had understood her. But he loved her, she knew it, and she was grateful that tonight he would be there to support her, no matter their disagreement.

Her dress for the evening was a new one. Rich burgundy and gold brocade was styled over with ivory lace at the hem and square neckline and along the fashionably long bell sleeves. Her small cap was to be worn at the back of her head so that the front of her blond hair still showed slightly above her forehead in the latest fashion from France. Bess checked herself in the mirror one last time, then pinched her cheeks to brighten them while George waited, dressed elegantly in a silk doublet and trunk hose, which she knew must have cost their parents a small fortune, much like her dress. But, as they always said, one must look the part, no matter what. Such was the requirement of succeeding at court among princes, dukes, earls, ladies, and duchesses.

When they arrived, the banquet hall was already brimming with glittering courtiers, ambassadors, and noblemen, so Bess and George were able to slip virtually unnoticed beneath the beamed, vaulted ceiling and into the very center of everything. The music was light, played from a minstrel's gallery above, but the summer air was already thick and full of a noxious mix of sweat and perfume that made Bess quickly feel like escaping.

She missed the cool country air of home at times like these, but her attraction to the king trumped everything else. Since Dover, Bess had played their private conversation over in her mind a thousand times. She had closed her eyes and felt his hand on her face and ignored all the things that separated her from him—his position, the age difference, and his marriage. In her fantasies, none of that mattered, just the words he had spoken to her on that windswept cliff like lines from a book.

"Is it like this all the time?" George asked her of the elegant crowd, bringing her out of her private thoughts.

"Whenever the king feels the inclination for a public banquet it is. He seems to have that inclination rather often lately. And if there aren't banquets, there are masques or pageants, hunting parties, or jousting tournaments. Very few moments at court are dull."

"I cannot wait to catch a glimpse of him for myself. All of my life I have imagined what a king actually looks like." George began to search the crowd excitedly.

"Oh, you will know when he has arrived," Bess said with a chuckle. "There will be no mistaking that. But he really does look just like a normal man, albeit an incredibly handsome one."

As George rolled his eyes at her, Bess felt the press of a firm hand at the small of her back. When she turned, she was met with Gil Tailbois's good-natured smile.

"There you are at last," Gil said, and his cheeks seemed to flush at the sight of her.

Or perhaps, she thought, with a little rush of humility, it was only because the hall was so warm already. Yes, she would prefer that to have been the cause of it, rather than herself.

"You must be George," Gil said, turning his attention smoothly to Bess's brother. "I heard you had come. The family resemblance is remarkable."

"Considering my sister's great beauty, I shall take that as a compliment," George replied with a suddenly easy smile of his own.

"It is meant as one. I am Gilbert Tailbois, ward and aide to Bishop Wolsey, and fortunate enough to have become a friend to Mistress Blount."

"My sister seems the fortunate one," George returned.

The trumpet fanfare announcing the king's entrance was a welcome distraction from Bess's thoughts. She knew where things would go from here. Her brother would be anxious to dissuade her from indulging in her infatuation with the king. She could tell that Gil was quickly becoming an attractive option for him.

"I have something for you," Gil said, leaning in to whisper to her as everyone dropped into formal bows and curtsies. "But I would rather give it to you later if there is a quiet moment."

"You did not have to do that."

"Oh, but I did," Gil replied with a little wink.

The king had never looked more handsome, Bess thought, as he smiled and nodded and strode past her with Bishop Wolsey, tall and stately, beside him. The king was near enough now that she could smell his personal scent, a heady combination of musk, civet, and ambergris. Her heart quickened. His doublet was sewn of sapphire blue velvet, trimmed in gold, and ornamented with glittering stones. His legs looked even more long and muscular in white beneath his padded blue trunk hose. When he looked at her directly, Bess thought herself the most fortunate girl in the world that a man like the king knew her and acknowledged her in public.

"You were right," said George as the chatter rose up again. The king had taken his seat at the head table beneath a long blue silk tester emblazoned with an H and a crown above it. "There is no mistaking the king, but I have to disagree that there is anything ordinary about him."

"Indeed, there is not." She chuckled. "On second thought, I suppose you are right."

Watching the king's every move, eager to have him catch her eye again, Bess leaned toward her brother as they were shown by a gentleman usher to their seats; the tune played on a lute, harp, recorder, and pipe softened.

Beneath the ceiling, brightly painted with Tudor roses and hung with decorated banners, there was a cornucopia of food and drink laid out in bowls, flagons, and goblets. Wine from Gascony flowed from intricate silver ewers, along with Malmsey and claret; sturgeon baked in steaming pastry was brought out and served on gleaming platters, set beside roasted peacock, spiced goose, and ginger veal. The flames from thick white candles on the tables and blazing torches in iron sconces on the walls made the hall seem almost magical in the evening light. Bess was simply unable to stop herself from taking everything in as if it were her first banquet.

She was so filled with excitement that she did not notice at first Gil take the chair on her other side. All she saw was the king's gaze continually light upon her, move away, then return as he was brought into one conversation after another around him.

Is he staring? she wondered as he looked at her again, or was she so increasingly drawn to him that her mind was making too much of the moment?

She was studying him so intently that she did not see that her own parents were seated beside George now, or that Gil had drawn something from his doublet and was nervously clutching it in his hand. Nor did she see Lord Mountjoy watching the scene from across the room, scowling and shaking his head at her. At the very moment when Gil lifted his hand and leaned toward Bess to speak, a heavily carved silver goblet was set on the table before her. The deep-voiced, liveried esquire behind her leaned over her shoulder.

"His Royal Highness bids you enjoy the contents with his compliments. It is from his private collection," the young servant said.

"The king sends you wine?" George asked in surprise.

"He never has before."

When she glanced over at the king, he lifted his own goblet to her and nodded as if they were sharing a toast. She lifted the cup to her lips then, and, tipping it, she tasted not wine but instead felt something cold and hard hit her lip. It was a gold and pearl necklace dotted with a small, perfect cabochon ruby that she poured into her palm with a little shriek.

"What the devil?" George gasped.

"Aptly named," Gil remarked beneath his breath.

The king smiled and once again nodded to her. This time there had been no mistake. The King of England had given her a costly gift and undercut Gil's moment completely.

"This is absolutely a dream. It cannot be happening," Bess murmured, feeling a flush of excitement warm her cheeks.

"More like a nightmare, if you ask me," Gil grumbled. "But it does not surprise me at all."

"You make too much of a small gesture," she weakly defended, caring little at this moment whether Gil Tailbois found it a nightmare or not. Naturally, he was only envious that the king was not bestowing favor directly upon him, and in such a clever and casual way. At least, that was what Bess told herself so that she would not feel another rush of guilt for the queen, who could not possibly approve of her husband settling tokens upon her young maids in her absence. But he had told her he did not take mistresses, and Bess wanted desperately to believe that. She wanted to believe that this attraction between them was unique and that she was unique to him. After all, he had confided something very personal to her about his brother. That had to have meant something. It had certainly meant something to her.

Bess saw him lean in toward Wolsey then. A moment later, Wolsey turned his attention to her as well. Her heart was racing furiously and her mouth had gone so dry that she almost wished there had been wine in the goblet instead of a necklace—almost.

"Take care, Sister. This could put the entire Blount family at risk if it goes any further," George gravely warned in a whisper as he sat, helplessly watching the scene play out.

"Or it might bring rewards none of us can yet imagine," Bess countered, suddenly feeling the full power of what was beginning to happen.

"He already has a queen," Gil added flatly.

"There are other roles I might play."

"Believe me," Gil quickly countered. "You do not want the obvious one."

"And why would I not?"

"It is beneath you, Bess. Beneath the life you are meant to have."

"Who but God himself knows what I am meant to have?"

"Can you truly say you could settle for being a man's mistress?" George asked her from the other side.

Suddenly she felt defensive, and she did not like it. George and Gil were like hostile little bookends, pressing her to feel extremes of guilt she did not truly feel—at least not yet. For now, excitement and surprise tempered every other emotion.

It felt like no more than a moment before the gleaming platters, dishes, and cutlery were whisked away and the king himself rose, in a few bold strides sweeping to the center of the banquet hall to play a tune on his lute. The conversation fell to an excited hush, and Bess straightened in her chair with anticipation. She had heard from others that the king loved to entertain his court, but she had not yet heard him. She watched as he settled into a tall chair and balanced the lute on his knee in the sudden silence. She heard a cough echo out from the crowd before he began to play a haunting tune. Bess was riveted by his skill and grace. She felt a deep ache just looking at him. Everything about him drew her. She felt hypnotized. Bess studied his face more closely—the smooth, square jaw; perfect nose; and penetrating deep green eyes.

"His Grace wishes you to sing a tune with him."

She recognized the masculine voice behind her. It belonged to Bishop Wolsey.

"Your father has been most generous in his praise of your talent, Mistress Blount," Wolsey said coolly.

Gil stood and faced his benefactor with a familiarity that was full of tension. "Surely no good can come of it, my lord," he said to the cleric in response.

"Nevertheless, boy, 'tis by the king's desire."

Bess began to straighten her skirts and the fabric of her long bell sleeves, feeling a strange dread build in her chest, then move up to her throat. What if she sang out of tune or did not remember the words? What if she blushed too deeply for his liking or giggled or tripped over her own feet on the way to meet him? Elizabeth would know what to say. She was accustomed to this sort of thing, and she alone would know how to talk her through the sheer terror Bess quickly felt settling in.

"I do not know if I can do this," she managed to say in a sputtering tone just as the king's first song was at an end and he began to acknowledge the adulation with nods and a cool smile.

"I am afraid you haven't a choice," Gil said coolly. "The bishop is correct. If the king desires it, then it shall be. Just as everything else."

She glanced back at Wolsey who stood unmoving, his strong face a mask of indifference as he waited for her to accept the inevitable. A moment later, Bess complied and followed Wolsey through the maze of chairs and servants and a sea of faces marked by surprise to the center of the tables, where Henry VIII awaited her. As she approached him, a tufted stool was brought and set beside his chair. Henry stood with a smile and extended a hand to her.

"I thought it might be amusing to see how you respond under pressure," he said so softly that only she could possibly have heard.

"And if I respond poorly?"

His smile became strangely sly. "I suppose I could cut off your head."

It was such an oddly surprising thing to say that she paused for a moment to consider whether he was serious. When he saw her expression, Henry began to laugh. "Fortunately for you, I am open to persuasion from a pretty girl."

"Has Your Highness a dark side then?"

"Impossibly dark."

"Perhaps I should consider myself warned," Bess shot back swiftly.

"Perhaps you should. Yet there is a side that is equally light. The trick would be to keep me there. No one has managed that for long, so far."

"Someone may surprise you."

"No one I have known so far in all my years has surprised me much at all."

She saw the jaded side of him then in their brief exchange, but his complexities only drew her more.

"Do you know 'My Heart's Desire'?" Henry asked her as they sat down together and the crowd once again fell to a hush.

It took her a moment to realize he was asking about the song. She nodded with what she knew was a foolish, eager-to-please smile for which she silently chided herself.

"Sing it with me then. It needs a sweet female voice."

"I shall do my best."

As he took the lute back up onto his lap, Bess caught a glimpse of Gil that stunned her. His expression was unusually cold as he stood to the side of the hall, arms crossed over his chest. From this distance, she thought it was even contemptuous. The odd moment vanished as Henry struck up the tune. Bess knew she must put all of her effort into her best performance, and focus only on that. Not only were her parents and Mountjoy watching, but so was Bishop Wolsey, who would be a force to be reckoned with if she did not please the king.

Their voices blended nicely and the words and tune came far more effortlessly to her than she had expected. In what felt like an instant later, it was over and the king's guests were applauding, wisely calling for another duet from the pair.

"Well, well," Henry said above the roar of the crowd. "I do believe you have surprised me, Mistress Blount."

The way he said it—somewhere between admiration and desire, made Bess shiver, and she fought not to show her pleasure. "I am honored Your Highness would find it so," she said demurely.

"Oh, I do find it so. The little token from earlier shall be your reward for making me look good before my courtiers."

Bess remembered the exquisite necklace then, which made her blush, but she fought the urge to lower her eyes, wanting desperately to appear poised and mature.

"Your Highness does not need me for that," Bess said with a little smile.

"You might be surprised by what I need."

"Might I?"

"A king, after all, *is* human, Mistress Blount. Although I would thank you not to tell anyone I ever admitted that." He leaned closer as a clever smile lengthened his lips. "Admitting fallibility makes it difficult to rule one's subjects."

Bess nearly laughed, but she quickly thought better of it. "The necklace is extraordinary, but will the queen not mind that you gave me something so extravagant?"

"The queen is my wife, Mistress Blount, not my keeper," he replied with just a note of irritation. "Besides, the token is from Brandon, who asked to be remembered to you and Mistress Carew, who also received one. At least that is the story I shall maintain unfailingly. Now, shall we give them another tune?"

They both knew who had actually sent the gift. Brandon was in France, and though he was still not wed to Lady Lisle, and thus was as yet an acceptable potential suitor for many women at court, Bess knew it was not her favor he sought. The furtive glances between him and Princess Mary long ago had confirmed all that for her.

Bess's eyes met the king's once again. Like a lovesick fool, she could see nothing else but him. Yes, she would sing another tune with him, no matter who might disapprove—including her own family. She was absolutely powerless to deny the king anything he asked of her now, or anything he might ask in the future. Of that she was certain.

As the king and Mistress Blount sang, Thomas Wolsey watched Gil. The poor, foolish boy was in love with the girl. He had seen the signs before. But he also knew the king, and what doubtlessly lay ahead for the girl in the next year. Thomas knew Henry's type almost better than Henry knew it himself, since the cleric had helped to extricate him from more than a few liaisons over the years.

Henry found no harm in a brief and discreet dalliance here and there when the queen was pregnant, but his conscience, or his interest level, seemed to preclude anything of the heart from ever developing. That these doe-eyed girls allowed themselves to be used for a man's pleasure, even if some did not have much of a choice, made them unsuitable for Gil, who deserved someone untainted, Wolsey determined with a proprietary little huff. Mistress Blount had just joined those ranks.

Amid the warmth of the flaming torches and the crackling fire, Gil twisted the little pearl and ruby pendant between his thumb and forefinger. Seeing him fling it to the floor in a rage once Bess had joined the king, Wolsey himself had silently retrieved it, exchanging only a small, sympathetic glance with the boy as he did. Although Gil believed otherwise, it was actually Wolsey who had given the little token to Gil's mother when he was young, lovesick, and equally as foolish as Gil was now. He had been conflicted in those days. Wolsey remembered his fascination with the Lincolnshire country girl, but he also remembered his own ambitious path to the Church, which had led him away from her. He knew offspring were a risk of any dalliance, and there had been other women and there were children he had sired along the way, but what he had not bargained for was coming to care for one of them—as he had for Gilbert. That lunatic father to whom the boy had been given over had brought out every paternal instinct Thomas had. Long after he had stopped loving Gil's mother, Elizabeth, he had provided comfortably for her, for the boy's sake, and he had promised himself then that he would protect any child of his however he could. When Thomas Wolsey came to court, the boy came with him. If it seemed more coldhearted to the Tailbois family, so be it.

Thomas shifted now in the stiff dining chair and pressed the pendant into the folds of his long coat as he watched Mistress Blount curtsy to the king, then make her way back to her seat. He saw the king watch her walk away and the crowd around him whisper about her ripening beauty. Yes, her path into Henry's life was as predestined as his own, Wolsey thought. And while poor Gilbert may already have made the mistake of falling in love with her, he would not be allowed to waste his life, or his heart, on a girl destined to become the king's whore—and thus the queen's rival.

Not if he could help it.

Chapter Seven

A few days before the yuletide festivities were to begin, the court trekked on horseback and carts across the cold winter landscape through vast woodlands, used in spring for hunting, to Greenwich, where the king liked to pass the holy days. Bess was excited because Elizabeth and her new husband were at last returning to court after their wedding trip. She had missed the camaraderie with her friend, and it felt like ages since she'd had anyone to confide in or share her secrets with.

When they arrived, Bess looked at the luxurious blue velvet dress that had been brought for her, laid out meticulously on her bed in the little chamber she had been assigned to share with Jane Poppincourt. The identical dress had been laid out on Jane's bed. The style was the height of fashion, the Savoy velvet accented with gold cloth. Beside each was an intricately designed gold mask decorated with pearls and tiny jewels. Bess pressed a finger against her lips and with her other hand touched the sumptuous velvet of the dress. Tonight she and Jane were both invited by the king to perform in a masque in the queen's chamber.

"We are to dance a tourdion for the queen," Jane announced. "There will be only four of us, along with four men. Since the queen is with child, she prefers her entertainment on a smaller scale. Pray that she can give the king a living child at last, and, by God's grace, a son so there can be a bit more merriment here when she returns to us."

There was a distinct note of displeasure, or condescension, in her words—something Bess could not quite identify. She turned back to the silent servants who were in the midst of transforming her from a country adolescent into an elegant, courtly beauty. She sat very still for the application of creams, perfumes, pins and stays. But no matter how she dressed, or what jewels adorned her, she would always be Bessie Blount from Kinlet, a simple girl who loved her family, books, and dreams of romance. It was something she had not fully known about herself before coming to court, but she was growing increasingly proud of her commitment to her values, especially when she was in the company of worldly girls like Jane Poppincourt or Elizabeth Carew.

After they had been properly dressed, their hair collected up into matching blue velvet French hoods, Bess and Jane donned their masks, then went out into the corridor to meet the other two girls, both pretty, young maids of honor as well, who would join them. Joan Champernowne and Anne Stanhope, dressed in the same gowns and masks, were already waiting. Their backs to Bess, they were gossiping rapidly.

"I cannot see how she continues to take such a prominent place with the king. She is the most inconsequential girl at court," the ivory-skinned Anne Stanhope remarked snidely as her mahogany eyes glittered.

"But she does have her mother's beauty," pale, freckle-faced Joan Champernowne observed with a smile.

"Blount's beauty is country beauty. If the king pays court to her, we will all know why."

"Did you never hear that gossip makes you ugly, Mistress Stanhope?" Jane suddenly intoned, to Bess's surprise.

"And have *you* never heard, Mistress Poppincourt, that it is dangerous to defend the indefensible?" Joan Champernowne icily returned.

"Perhaps that is why your lover abandoned you rather than take you back to France with him," Anne Stanhope said cruelly, her button nose and dark eyes trained on Bess all the while.

The accusation stopped Jane in her tracks. Bess saw the color drain from her smooth, porcelain face. Bess had heard the gossip that Jane's relationship with the married de Longueville had been a tempestuous one. His return to France had altered her life, no doubt. Bess had begun to imagine the pain of loving another woman's husband, and knowing a future could never be. One must show compassion for that, if not approval.

"Shall you not defend your friend, Mistress Blount, as she has sought to defend you? Or is that beyond the acumen of a country waif?" Joan Champernowne asked with a cold little smile, as if she had read Bess's mind.

"In the country, mistress, we are taught forbearance."

"Oh, dear, is such naïveté actually attractive to men?" Anne Stanhope laughed cruelly. "We did not intend for you to answer, Mistress Blount, since you have absolutely nothing of value to say. Remember that, will you?"

Bess was absolutely stunned. Both of the women, young maids of honor with her since she had arrived at court, had always been outwardly cordial to her. She was forced now to wonder if all of the other maids felt the same condescension. She had tried so bravely for more than a year to fit in. But even after all this time, it was very clear that she was nothing more to them than an overreaching country girl.

"I will indeed remember everything," Bess replied without inflection, not for an instant breaking her gaze from Anne Stanhope, who she had always believed before now had the most innocent of smiles.

They were joined at that moment by four tall, muscular young men in blue velvet doublets and jeweled velvet masks to match their own. Each bore a flaming silver torch. The light around them danced, casting enough shadows that identifying any of them was difficult. One of the young men paired himself with Jane, another with Anne Stanhope, and a third with Joan Champernowne. The final tall, well-built young man drew near her, stood beside her, and silently took up her hand. His grip was so firmly possessive that Bess felt her heart start to beat very fast beneath the long, tight plastron of her dress as two court musicians in tunics and hose, one with a flute, the other with a tambourine, drew up behind them. They were playing a tune as they led the way to the queen's apartments.

The mysterious partner beside Bess began a lively tourdion with a skip, then a practiced step, as they entered the apartments. She was glad once again that she had paid attention at home when their father had insisted they learn proper dances, even as George and Robert had complained. She bit back a little smile and wished George had not had to return home. She missed him. She would always miss him.

As they danced blithely into the presence chamber, flaming torches in hand lighting their faces, the queen was seated with her Spanish companion, Maria de Salinas, beside a roaring fire in the massive stone hearth. Bess thought the queen did not yet appear pregnant, but Katherine was noticeably heavier now than she had been when Bess had first come to court. Although a maid of honor in the queen's household, Bess had seen little of Henry's wife since her last miscarriage. She kept mainly to her privy chamber, still comfortable in the companionship of only Maria and Mountjoy's Spanish wife, Agnes de Venegas. But now that the queen was newly pregnant, there was renewed excitement, and many of her English ladies had been brought back to attend her.

As Bess and the other masked revelers danced, she saw Lady Hastings, Lady Fitzwalter, the Countesses of Oxford and Derby, along with Elizabeth Carew and her own mother, seated elegantly around the queen. Bess was relieved that they were all smiling, whispering, and pointing as they wondered who was behind each of the masks, which was a great part of the game.

The group danced a second dance, and Bess remained partnered with the same masked courtier, who moved faultlessly beside her. She liked the constant and firm grip of his hand and his smooth, perfectly timed steps that matched her own. The twirl and swish of skirts in the glitter of torchlights in time to the sweet music made it magical. Since the queen tapped her finger on her knee and seemed pleased with the performance, Bess felt herself breathe more deeply and smile, allowing her to enjoy the experience, even after what had happened out in the corridor.

When the dance was over, the queen and her ladies applauded as the masked dancers all dipped into deep curtsies or swept into formal bows. Then, to Bess's surprise, the gentleman still gripping her hand drew off his mask to gasps of delight from the queen and her ladies. She'd had no idea her partner had been the king. Following his lead, everyone else then drew off their masks, bowing again as each identity was revealed. Jane had danced with the king's friend and the Chief Gentleman of the Bedchamber, William Compton. Joan Champernowne had been partnered with the king's friend and gentleman waiter, Henry Norris. Nicholas Carew, the newlywed, had joined Anne Stanhope. Only Bess's presence, she quickly realized, seemed a revelation and brought an expression of panic from her own mother, since the king still had not let go of her hand.

Bess felt her face flush with an embarrassment so fierce that she could no longer look at the queen. Her husband was devoted and wonderful, having organized this for Her Highness's pleasure, yet Bess was keenly aware of how it must have appeared. In the instant after seeing her mother's expression, she instinctively wrenched her hand from the king's grip and lowered her eyes. Her bright smile fell. She had been warned repeatedly that court was a dangerous place where she walked a fine line. Tonight she was a witness to just how true that was.

As the king went to the queen, Bess turned and fell into Elizabeth's embrace. She hugged her back tightly, relieved to see the face of someone who was truly happy to see her.

"I have been dreadfully bored without you!" Elizabeth whispered as she drew Bess even closer. "You must tell me everything that has happened while I was away."

Bess tried to smile. "I shall."

Yet true honesty was impossible.

What she felt for the king was wrong, absolutely adolescent and foolish, not to mention dangerous. And to make more of his attentions than mere courtesy allowed would have been to avoid the inevitable. Bess could never be anything more to the King of England than an amusing little dance or singing partner, she repeatedly told herself. He already had a queen, a wife . . . a soul mate in Katherine of Aragon. She must stop the infernal fantasies and someday find a soul mate of her own. She was determined to make that her goal . . . after tonight.

No hay mal que por bien no venga. . . . There is no bad from which some good does not come. That wise saying always came to her mind, and to her heart, when she saw it happening again. Katherine was not a fool. She loved her husband with every fiber of her being, but Queen Isabella had made her daughter not only a warrior for the things in which she believed, but a pragmatist as well. It was always easier to battle a known enemy, and Katherine's primary rival was not one particular girl but rather the elusive enemy of infidelity.

Katherine knew that, in his way, Henry loved her. He whispered too sweetly in the darkness, and mourned too deeply with her each time she lost a child. But he was a man, not only a king, and one with desires that went well beyond her ability to keep him to herself. Katherine knew he had held that pretty Blount girl up tonight as proof of that. She also knew perfectly well, as did the rest of the court, about his dalliances with Lady Hastings, Mistress Poppincourt, and Mistress Carew. Whatever he felt now for Mistress Blount was certainly nothing new.

The only way to vanquish an enemy, her mother had always said, was to acknowledge and understand it. Only then could the key weakness be found. She had been advised that Mistress Carew and Mistress Blount were friends. That could be a useful tool, Katherine thought, as Henry came near to her after the dance, wearing a broad smile. She nodded to her husband, forcing herself to match his smile as ideas skittered across her mind, forming into a rough plan.

"My queen," Henry said, taking her hand. "Pray, tell me, did our little entertainment please you?"

"It is always pleasing to me when I see my husband enjoying himself."

"I wish you would dance with me," he said flatteringly.

"Yet you know I must do absolutely nothing to endanger our child. The journey to Greenwich was already taxing enough."

And she knew it herself. Katherine was determined to sit like a bird on a nest for the next two months if that was the requirement for giving Henry the son he craved. Then perhaps, if she was not pregnant for a while, he would cease with his attentions toward the other women. Perhaps then, pray God, she could be enough for the man she adored. . . .

No hay mal que por bien venga.

Maria de Salinas stood, then bowed silently to the two of them, freeing her chair for Henry, who had been standing beside his wife. He sank into it and took up his wife's hand.

"How are you feeling?"

"I am well, as is our child," she replied in her heavy Castellón accent.

"Splendid. You know that I worry."

"I do know that, Hal," Katherine said softly, needing his reassurance this time more than before. "And I miss you."

They both knew what she meant.

"It shall not be long till I may return to you," Henry reassured her in a soft and surprisingly tender tone.

"It seems like an eternity to me, as it always does."

She saw his eyes darken. His tone hardened as swiftly as it had softened a moment before. "I need a living son, Katherine."

And I need my husband just as much, she thought. But she did not dare say that.

Katherine followed his gaze across the room to where the

collection of young girls stood laughing and gossiping, their bodies still slim, healthy, and untouched by repeated pregnancies—their faces full of too much innocence and optimism for her taste now. *They have not a care in the world*, Katherine thought bitterly.

If this child within her did not survive, she was not certain what would become of her. There had already been rampant gossip and murmured rumblings about the young king's political frustrations with Spain, and by extension, with her. Agnes de Venegas and her husband, Lord Mountjoy, had loyally warned Katherine that the Spanish ambassador was being forced almost daily to defend England's alliance with his country. Since Henry would not visit her bed while she was pregnant, she could do almost nothing to protect her marriage or to defend the now-fragile tie between her two countries.

Suddenly, Henry stood and bowed to her. The tenderness was gone and the move was perfunctory. "You will excuse me?"

"Certainly." She nodded compliantly. *Te quiero con toda mi alma*, she was thinking. And Katherine of Aragon did love her husband with her whole soul, for all the good it would do her if she could not produce a living heir, she thought, as he turned and walked away.

Very late that evening, after a banquet and more dancing, Gil, Elizabeth, and Nicholas Carew accompanied Bess to her own little room above the queen's apartments. They were laughing and joking, their moods light. It was so good to have her back, Bess thought. Elizabeth even seemed a bit softened now to her marriage with Nicholas Carew, defined by little flirtatious exchanges and quiet laughs between them, where once there was frosty compliance. And Bess was glad of it, since she did not want to think of her dear friend so unhappily married as both of them had thought she would be.

Jane was conspicuously absent from their group that evening, having mysteriously disappeared not long after the king retired for the evening, which set the gossips abuzz. It seemed impossible for Bess to believe any of it because Jane had wept so uncontrollably after de Longueville had returned to France; she was certain they had been in love.

"Love has very little to do with the king's fancy," quipped Nicholas as he flopped down happily, and a little drunkenly, onto Jane's bed, which sat beside Bess's bed in the same little room. It gave in to his masculine weight with a low creak. "His fancy lands upon many," he said with a chuckle. "He is a bit of a scoundrel, our king, not always the fairest person when it comes to ladies."

"Yet why should he be? He is young, brilliant, impossibly handsome, rich—and can have anything, and *anyone* he pleases," Elizabeth remarked.

"He *is* to be envied for that," her husband returned.

"Does the king still fancy Jane, then, do you think?" Gil asked.

The question came as a complete surprise to Bess. Everyone glanced at one another in awkward silence. Gil and Elizabeth exchanged a particularly knowing look.

"Well, when the queen is with child, as she so often is, it is well-known that our good sovereign must find entertainment elsewhere. It does not make him a bad husband," Nicholas added philosophically. "Only a predictable one."

"How fortunate for you, Lady Carew," Gil quipped.

Elizabeth playfully batted his arm in response.

"My experience with husbands had well better be different than the queen's," Elizabeth said, biting back a smile. "Is that not true, Master Carew?"

"Indeed, wife, it is," he replied with mock gravity.

"Still . . . Jane and the king?" Bess remarked, trying to sound nonchalant. It was difficult to keep the disappointment from her voice. "I am still truly surprised. I thought it was an evening or two, just one of the court flirtations I heard so often about as a child."

"Then you are the only one," Nicholas replied.

"It *is* only a dalliance, Nicholas," Elizabeth said, quick to counter. "Not a love affair, certainly. Jane is ambitious, and he is bored."

"And what were you?" her husband asked sharply.

The sudden silence was palpable. "Naive. Nothing more."

Bess was stunned at Elizabeth's words. Though she had seen the way the king had periodically favored Elizabeth, and Elizabeth's connection to the king's Gentleman of the Bedchamber, Bess had never been entirely sure of the nature of their relationship. She wanted to take Henry at his word when he said he never took actual mistresses. Bess wanted to believe he simply indulged in harmless flirtations—or at the worst, momentary dalliances. But it was difficult to ignore the conversation heatedly swirling now around her.

What shocked her even more was that Gil did not betray the slightest hint of surprise, and she wondered if he had been privy to confidences she had not been. The thought stung.

"It is time to retire," Elizabeth announced in a clipped tone. "Are you coming?"

Nicholas stood more slowly but did not look directly at his young, beautiful wife. "Of course, my dear. As always, whatever is convenient for you."

"Do I even want to know what that was about?" Bess asked Gil once the Carews had gone.

"Court games, as you supposed. Nothing of gravity."

Bess walked the short distance to Jane's bed, reached beneath it, and withdrew a small red leather pouch of gold coins. The pouch bore the letter H sewn in silver thread. This was in addition to the exorbitant two hundred pounds per year Bess knew Jane already received as a member of the queen's household staff.

"I believed him when he said he did not take mistresses. Am I truly such a foolish girl that even after all this time here, I understand little of what goes on around me?"

Gil pulled her gently down onto the edge of the bed beside him and drew up her hand. It was nothing like the king's firm, sensual grip, but there was warm reassurance there, and she needed that at the moment.

"A trusting girl, Bess, but no, not a foolish one."

"Too trusting. Jane is nineteen now, and she knew all along I looked at the king through the eyes of a little girl. Yet she never said a word in warning."

"What could she have said to you, Bess, truly? Theirs is a unique relationship, based on boredom and convenience. Not love. If the king told you that himself, I supposed you should believe him."

A moment later, she wrapped her arms around his neck, feeling every bit the girl she still was. Forgetting completely the odd exchange between the newly married Carews, she leaned against him for the reassurance she so craved.

"What would I do without you?" Bess asked as she saw a strained little smile finally lift the corners of his mouth.

"I hope you shall never discover the answer to that."

Bess sat back for a moment and dropped the pouch of coins onto the bed. "Speaking of gifts, did you not say you had something for me?"

His smile disappeared as quickly as it had come. "It was not important," he replied dismissively. "Besides, it shall keep."

Bess tipped her head to the side, studying him for a moment. "You'll not tell me what it is?"

"Perhaps one day I shall," he replied, finally letting go of her hand. The expression on his face was intense. It was one she had never seen before. "I shall know if the time is right."

"You are being so mysterious," she said with a chuckle as he suddenly stood to leave.

"Not so much mysterious, Mistress Blount, as realistic. I think you shall have to grow up for me just a bit more first."

"Difficult to avoid, it seems." Bess smiled.

"Many things will be. Much more than you know," Gil returned.

Bess did not say anything after that as he left. Tonight she had realized he was probably right. There was obviously a great deal for her to learn, even after a year here, and to do that, she must grow up. From now on, thoughts of the king were to be avoided, in all but the most pure and respectful of ways, Bess decided firmly.

It was frigid all across England for the Twelfth Night celebration, and the ground at Greenwich was thick with an icy winter frost. The landscape, as Elizabeth Carew gazed out the window, was bleak. The tree branches in the courtyard below were twisted and bare, and only the flock of crows flying past lent any color to the landscape.

Gil Tailbois silently watched her, waiting for her to speak.

"So, what precisely did you tell her while I was away?" Elizabeth finally asked him. Her back was to her friend, hands framing the cold glass panes, and an icy draft worked its way through the stone.

Gil thought about how much she had changed since he had first met her, and even more in the months since becoming a wife. Her hair was still that lush red-gold, and her eyes were still blue, but the soft, girlish shape of her face had begun to show more definition. There was now a purposeful set to her mouth, and her body was defined by curves.

"Do you mean Bess?" he asked.

"Of course. What does she know?"

"If you are asking me whether she knows about your brief interlude with the king, the answer is she knows it not from me, if at all."

She turned around then and leaned against the windowsill as the sky steadily darkened and a light snow began to fall past the leaded panes of glass. "Many thanks," she said.

"Would it really matter so much though if she did?"

There was a little silence as Gil noticed her elegant new gown that matched his own green velvet doublet, both with full brocaded sleeves and bright, multicolored beads designed for tonight's masque.

"Bess is the only one at court who does not look at me with pity because the king married me off to be rid of me."

Gil went to her at the window and pulled her into his embrace, and they stood like that silently for a while—friends who trusted each other. He was tall and still so youthfully thin that for a moment the embrace felt awkward, but they had shared so many adventures and milestones that there was a reassuring familiarity there for both of them.

"I just feel such a fool for ever having cared for him."

"He is rather a difficult force to avoid."

"Still, I should have known."

"You were too young to have known, and he favors variety."

Elizabeth came away from the window and from his embrace. She sank down at the little rosewood-framed looking glass set at her dressing table. Pretty enough to catch a king, he thought, just not interesting enough to keep him.

"Have they bedded yet?" she asked Gil through his reflection in the mirror.

"She would have told me if they had."

"She still does not know you are in love with her then?"

"No, since I would be a rather pitiful replacement for a handsome young sovereign. She continues to have those youthful fantasies guiding her."

"As did I."

He settled a hand on her shoulder and paused for a moment as the door opened behind them. It was Nicholas Carew dressed in the same style of green velvet costume as Gil and Elizabeth, since he would be partnered with his wife for the evening's festivities. Gil felt her tense at her new husband's presence.

"But I did get her a Christmas gift," Gil said as he proudly drew a small red leather volume from a pocket in the folds of his heavy doublet.

Elizabeth took it from him. It was a copy of *Lancelot*. "Bess loves that tale."

"I know," Gil replied with a small, reserved smile. "Do you think it will please her?"

"How could it not?" Nicholas replied for his wife as he clapped Gil soundly on the back, man to man. "Are you waiting for just the right time to give it to her or something? 'Tis not much left now that it's the Twelfth Night." Carew winked.

Gil looked away. "I tried to give her something else once and the timing was all wrong. I have not been able to rally the courage since."

Elizabeth stood and her husband wrapped an arm around her waist, but she drew away from him and turned around. Gil noted that movement as well. It was a pity really, he thought. "We shall help if we can," she promised encouragingly. "But you really do not want us to give her a hint? Something that might help your cause?"

"It would not be best for either of us if it were to happen like that," Gil said as stoically as he could manage, "and perhaps it would be best as well if she grew up just a bit more first. I told her so myself."

They all walked together down the long, torch-lit corridor, across an intricate tile floor, and down a twisted stone staircase that echoed their steps. At the bottom, they met other courtiers, dressed as they were, in green velvet, who also had been invited to participate in the king's evening.

When they arrived in the banquet hall, Gil saw her almost at once. She was holding her mask, not wearing it, and smiling at something the man beside her had said. She looked so beautiful, he thought, and he was eager to give her the book—until he saw that the man was Charles Brandon, recently returned from France. Brandon, he thought, with a little grunt of competitive disgust. The man was an insufferable rake, far worse than even the king. Gil rolled his eyes. What women saw in him, he could not fathom. Yes, Brandon was tall and muscular with a square jaw, thick copper hair, and deep brown eyes full of feigned sincerity, but should there not be something more? He laughed at himself, self-deprecatingly, for even having the envious thought.

Gil stood back a pace then, and watched the revelers organize. Bess moved to the front of the group, her velvet skirt brushing against a sea of other green velvet skirts as she moved. He saw that she held her head high and proud. She would be partnered again with the king, he thought, and she seemed to realize it. Gil stepped back, again, out of sync with the moment. God, but she was lovely—still so young; still so entirely unaware. Yet she had a new kind of confidence; the same as Elizabeth, and Jane before her.

It was like watching an unavoidable cataclysm take shape before his very eyes. But the most he could do was wait . . . and hopefully pick up the pieces after it was over.

He glanced at Brandon again, leaning casually against the paneled wall, one leg crossed over the other. Vile showman, he thought, especially when all Brandon truly wanted was the king's married sister in France. But what, and whom, would he take in the meantime while he waited? Apparently any young innocent who was besotted with his royal best friend would do. Gil did not have a chance against either man.

Suddenly, the king, wearing a highly embellished version of the same costume as Brandon's, emerged through a rounded side door. Rare jewels and pearls glittered on his doublet and full slashed sleeves. The girls included in the evening's entertainment swarmed toward him like bees to sweet honey. Henry smiled a crooked smile and greeted each of them. When he saw Bess beside Brandon, Henry's smile fell by a degree. It was a nuance noticeable only to Gil, who had been watching particularly for it and had felt the same thing. The two handsome friends had long been rivals when it came to women, and he seemed to sense a challenge.

In response, Henry suddenly turned from Brandon and Bess and went to Jane Poppincourt. He drew up her hands, kissed each of them, and his smile broadened. Henry was a resilient man, if a little brooding. They were partnered for the celebration dance, which, like the last, the pregnant queen would view. When the king's trumpet fanfare sounded just beyond them inside the banquet hall, Nicholas Carew took his wife's hand. Gil was paired with Anne Stanhope, who was nearest to him. He would have given anything for it to have been Bess. Gil watched her tip her head back and laugh blithely at something Brandon said. Seeing her innocent flirtation, and how attractive she was, made his blood run cold. Apparently, she still had absolutely no idea how he felt.

The group danced the intricate steps of a galliard before the queen, the Spanish ambassador, Buckingham, and Wolsey. There were dozens of other nobles privileged enough to have been invited to court for the Twelfth Night festivities in the soaring hall set aglow by candles and torches like a winter fairyland. Yet Gil was aware only of Bess. He watched her graceful steps, the elegant turn of her slim neck beneath the drape behind her little pearl-dotted hood, as she stepped in perfect time to the music. Brandon would never be good enough for her. Neither, for that matter, would the king.

The only person in the world who could have distracted him at a time like this was Wolsey. Gil watched him speak with a liveried page, then bolt from his chair like a shot, his face gone pale with surprise. Immediately, he directed the servant to the Duke of Buckingham, Lord High Constable, seated with equal prominence on the opposite side of the king's vacant chair. Wolsey then bent down and spoke something quietly to the queen seated beside him. Something was most definitely wrong. All of their faces showed it.

Gil was careful not to miss a step as he watched Buckingham rise as well, and, when the dance was finished, the two men went to the king. There was so much laughter and conversation that at first no one noticed, but when the three of them quickly left the hall and the same page went to Charles Brandon, the gossip began.

"What is it?" Bess asked when she saw the strained expression on the face of her dance partner. "Has something happened?"

"The King of France is dead. The King of England's sister is a widow."

Brandon's tone was telling, she thought. He did not sound particularly sorry. Rather, the expression on his face was one of guardedly pleasant surprise. She remembered then the gossip all that year about the Duke of Suffolk and the Princess Mary and what she had seen for herself at Dover.

"I am sorry," she murmured respectfully, uncertain of what else to say.

"I most certainly am not. He was old, foul-smelling, and lecherous. I saw that well for myself."

Of course. Brandon had returned just recently from France, staying longer than the Duke of Buckingham, or nearly anyone else from the wedding delegation. The rest of the dancers began again, but Bess and Brandon moved off to the side near a large tapestry of a hunting scene, hung on a heavy iron rod. His expression seemed to quickly become one of agitation. His gaze darted around the room, and his body had tensed perceptibly following the news.

"Will she remain in France now, do you think?" Bess asked him.

"The new king will hope so. He is more of a lecher than the old one. But she'll not remain, if I am allowed any say in the matter."

Brandon's feelings were becoming clearer with every word, and Bess longed to speak something of encouragement to him, a passage from *Lancelot* about the determined, romantic warrior, but her father's volume was old, tattered, and back in Kinlet; and her memory of the exact wording remained there with it.

Charles Brandon turned to face her fully as he conjured a sincere smile. "Please forgive me for abandoning you this evening. It is horrid of me, but I really must find Wolsey and the king at once." He pressed an innocent kiss onto her cheek. "Watch yourself around this place if I happen to be gone again for a time, Mistress

Blount. There are many men at court whose ambitions for a young beauty like you are not so pure as my own."

Bess smiled back at him. Her blue eyes were very big. "That sounds odd when so many here have said the very same to me of you."

He laughed deeply at that, then squeezed her small hand in his much more powerful and large one. "I was never a threat to you or anyone else here. With a great blessing from God, the reason for that shall be revealed to you soon enough."

Entirely caught up in the romance of a young and beautiful widow, and a dashing lovesick duke, Bess leaned toward him one more time so she could speak softly, as if they were the dearest two friends in the world.

"You are going to France after her, aren't you?"

He paused for a moment, struck by her words. "Pretty *and* bright as well, you are. That shall be a lethal combination at this court before too long." He chuckled. "Take care of yourself while I am away."

"Good fortune to you in it, Your Grace."

"Thank you, Mistress Blount. Lord knows, in this I shall need all of the good fortune I can get, and perhaps a miracle or two as well."

Across the room, Gil Tailbois had not taken his eyes from Bess, or from the revoltingly intimate little scene with Charles Brandon, although why Brandon was leaving the banquet without her after that little display was unclear. Perhaps they were meeting somewhere later. So much for Brandon's great love for the king's sister,

Gil theorized in an impulsive burst of jealousy. His gift to her of a romantic tale, given under these circumstances, would have made him more pathetic than he already was. He had felt bile rise as he watched her laugh with Brandon and hold his hand. All along, Gil had feared the king and had never once thought his real competition might be the worldly, handsome young Duke of Suffolk as well. He did not possess the strength to do battle with them both.

As the dancing concluded and everyone began to take their seats before the meal was served, Nicholas, who had watched him draw the leather-bound volume from the pocket in his doublet, settled his gaze on Gil.

"You really should not jump to conclusions, you know."

"Say not a word more." Gil held up a hand in angry admonishment just before he stepped toward the blazing, massive stone fireplace, a gilded H and crown emblazoned above it. Without another word, Gil surrendered to the flames the small, rare volume he had saved up his pay to buy, and which he had intended for Bess. That was where the book, and his feelings for her, belonged. He would have to force himself from now on to remember that, he thought, in the coming days.

Chapter Eight

The court had been in an uproar since the previous winter, and just now, as summer drew to a close, had things at last begun to settle down. Not only had Katherine lost yet another child in the interim, but the king's best friend had betrayed him. Without royal permission, or even the knowledge of Henry VIII, Charles Brandon had gone to France as part of the funeral delegation for Louis XII. Two months later, in March, Brandon secretly married the French queen. As winter then fully descended upon England, Henry felt the full force of rage and betrayal over the treasonous act—not only from his beloved sister but from his closest childhood friend. The two, who had renewed their love affair in France, had subsequently eloped in spite of Brandon's assurance to Henry that he would do no such thing. For weeks the couple was not permitted to return to England under penalty of death, the king angrily decreed, even though Mary was already pregnant.

It had not helped Henry's mood on the matter either that, once again, the queen's child had been stillborn, causing him to begin feeling increasingly cursed by his marriage. Not only was he to be punished with the lack of an heir, but also during that period he had been forced to deny his growing attraction to the ripening Blount beauty.

Throughout the winter and into the spring he had forced his attentions, for duty's sake, back upon the increasingly pious and unappealing queen in an attempt to see her pregnant yet again. He could not tempt himself by being in the company of any of the queen's ladies until he knew for certain that he had once again done his duty. By June, he was told he had succeeded.

During those last warm summer days at Hampton Court, Thomas Wolsey's recently purchased showplace on the banks of the Thames—a glittering symbol of his growing wealth and increasing power—a spark of life returned to the youthful king. As his intimate group of friends joined him to hunt, eat, and drink, Bess and the others noted how much he had been affected by Wolsey's sage and caring counsel. She had heard gossip that the prelate had taken it upon himself daily to plead with Henry to allow the newly married lovers to return home and be a comfort to him once again. He had done so alone, as the rest of the Privy Council—Brandon's chief rival, the Duke of Buckingham most fervent among the group— reminded the king daily that Brandon's actions amounted to treason.

Wolsey's dogged perseverance and calm advice had eventually, however, won out, and the king began to feel a small sliver of forgiveness. Provided Brandon paid to the Crown a massive fine for his treasonous act, in May, Henry had allowed Mary and Brandon to return to England and be married again in a family ceremony at Greenwich. As the September sun now warmed the thick limestone corridors and tile floors of the newly elevated Cardinal Wolsey's palace, Henry fully let go of his anger, dared to hope again for an heir, and felt free to socialize, most particularly with the ladies of his court. Bess herself certainly noticed his transformation, about which everyone whispered.

Hands linked behind his back, and moving in long-legged strides over straight brick pathways, Henry walked beside the queen through the fountain court, just a pace ahead of Bess and Elizabeth Carew. Wolsey and his rival, Buckingham, walked in outward affability directly behind the ladies.

It was difficult not to be impressed by the vast beauty of Hampton Court. Hosting the royal couple here was an honor for which Wolsey, like all other wise and wealthy courtiers, had openly lobbied for months. It was a state of success in which he now reveled. The group moved past lush clematis and primrose down near a little stone fountain that had been placed by the river. The sky was broad and blue above them, and Bess drew in a deep breath of air, happy that the queen was content once again. When Katherine was newly pregnant, there was optimism, laughter, and music; it was not like usual, when their days were filled only with solemn duty and endless prayer. These times for Bess were like being released from a monotonous prison of order and seriousness. She took in the moment as deeply as the air, which was warm and windless as she walked with Jane Poppincourt, Elizabeth Carew, Joan Champernowne, and Anne Stanhope behind the Countess of Oxford, the Countess of Derby, Lady Hastings, and her sister, Lady Fitzwalter.

Bess watched the queen walk proudly beside her husband now, lightly fingering the heavy silver cross prominent over her chest, as she softly chuckled at something he said. The train of her black cap fluttered lightly on her shoulders.

"Shall we not ask someone then?" Bess heard the king ask his wife. "Surely that shall settle the debate."

The queen was smiling as they paused and turned around. "Lady Carew," the queen said in her cool, deep, thickly accented voice. "Is Wolsey's new Hampton Court more beautiful than any of the king's own fine palaces?"

"Such a thing seems impossible or it would already belong to the king," she replied quickly, forcing a smile.

"Mistress Poppincourt? What say you on the matter?" the king asked.

Jane, who walked behind Wolsey, beside Lady Fitzwalter, was visibly taken aback but calmly replied, "I prefer Richmond, Your Highness, for its grander vistas and more impressive location on the river—one that only a king could possess."

As Jane spoke, her own voice as accented as the queen's, though belying French rather than Spanish roots, Bess watched a muscle in Wolsey's jaw twitch and his small dark eyes narrow imperceptibly. The newly named Cardinal Wolsey was apparently interested in this impromptu test as much as the king.

"And you, Mistress Blount?" the king asked suddenly.

Bess felt her heart stop at the sound of her name on his lips as all eyes suddenly turned upon her. She exhaled, steadying herself. "If you will permit my saying, Your Highness, I find Hampton Court on par with Richmond and exceeding Greenwich," she smoothly replied, surprising herself as she did.

Wolsey tried to stifle a chuckle. Bess could hear Lady Fitzwalter and Lady Hastings whisper haughtily behind her. They had never liked her, and that was becoming clearer now.

"Fool girl," Lady Hastings said softly to her sister. "One can never take enough of the blunt country manners out of the girl to truly make a lady, can one?"

Only Bess had been meant to hear the slight, and she had.

Unexpectedly, however, Henry tipped his head back with a great laugh, pulling her away from the insult.

"You know, Wolsey, I do believe she is right. Your new home *is* lovelier than Greenwich."

The cardinal bowed to the sovereign. "All that I possess belongs to Your Royal Highness, of course, and is to your honor."

"Of course, Wolsey, of course," the king responded, a note of irritation in his voice at the flattery.

Bess caught the nuance but did not have time to mull it over before Jane was upon her.

"You cannot speak so blatantly before them!" she admonished in a hushed tone of indignation while others around her began to whisper.

"I was asked for my opinion, and I gave it," Bess said quietly, feeling for once that she had bested the lovely Jane Poppincourt, at least at something.

"There is not always wisdom in honesty," said the queen, interjecting herself suddenly into the dispute, though neither of them had known she was listening. "Yet controlling one's tongue is *always* a virtue."

"A rather dull virtue," the king grumbled.

"Speaking of virtue, tell us, Mistress Blount, does that French poet de Troyes, whom you endlessly quote, not speak some great pearl of wisdom on the subject in his *Lancelot*?" Lady Hastings asked acidly, clearly trying to highlight Bess's ignorance, or at least her lack of culture.

"I find Master Skelton's work more fitting on that subject," Bess smoothly replied.

"You have read the work of my friend John?" the king asked Bess in surprise.

It was clear he had not expected that of her. Skelton had been an official court poet to Henry's father and also, for a time, Henry's own tutor.

"My favorite are his verses from *The Rewards of Court*, Master Skelton's thoughts on the vices of courtiers. Perhaps more among us should read it," Bess said smartly.

Henry tipped his head and bit back a smile. There was a small silence before he said, "Why, Mistress Blount, I see that you parry with more experienced competitors quite as well as you sing. Perhaps there is a brilliant future ahead for you at my court, after all."

"I am honored Your Highness believes so."

"No one reads Master Skelton's work more often than Master Tailbois," Elizabeth interjected, trying suddenly to champion her dear friend's clearly dying cause of winning Bess.

"And quotes him not only incessantly but incisively," Nicholas seconded. "Nearly as much as he does de Troyes."

"That is only because I introduced him to de Troyes," Bess said proudly.

"To *Lancelot*?" asked the king.

"Lancelot was my very first hero."

"So long as he is not your last hero," returned the king.

"At the moment I am afraid I have no other in mind, Your Highness."

"Perhaps I can offer you a suggestion or two," Henry quipped.

At that moment she saw the king and queen exchange a glance. Katherine's pleasant expression had darkened; everyone seemed to take notice and was silenced by it. Bess had obviously impressed the king more than she had the king's wife—which was most unwise, considering in whose household she served.

On top of that, Bess felt secretly ashamed. She had tried to take credit for Gil's interests, but she had not known that he even liked poetry, or that he had been reading *Lancelot*. She had never thought there might be an element of romance and mystery about Gil at all. He seemed so transparently simple. But she would have to consider his reading interests later. There were more pressing matters at hand.

They began once again to stroll together at the king's lead. But Bess's mind was spinning with fear over the possibility that she might have jeopardized her standing at court. The queen's expression a moment ago had been unmistakable evidence of that.

Katherine waited until the king, Wolsey, Norfolk, and Buckingham took their leave to meet with the rest of the Privy Council. As she sat on a bench with her companion, Maria de Salinas, her mood darkened to match her expression.

"There is to be a banquet this evening hosted by the cardinal to welcome the king and me to his new home."

"There is, Your Highness."

"I find I would not favor *her* among my attendants."

"Mistress Blount?" Maria asked, even though she knew Katherine's desires almost as well as she knew her own.

The queen's dark expression was full of determination, a mirror of her great warrior mother. "I shall not fight every rival my husband puts before me. That would be unseemly, not to mention pointless. But I must do battle with those who pose the greatest danger."

"Your Royal Highness speaks of young Bess Blount as a danger?" Maria was surprised. Jane Poppincourt had seemed much more of a threat than a pretty, country adolescent.

"You know that my mother was a wise queen. She taught me

well," Katherine reminded her most trusted friend. "Half of the challenge in battle, she once told me, is to know your rival. Isabella dealt with that challenge many times with the rulers of France, Scotland, and England, as well as with the emperor. My instincts were instilled in me by her."

"Then Your Highness must trust that."

"I know not why, but there is something about Mistress Blount that causes me to fear her."

"Once you give the king a son, all of your worries shall be gone."

"By God, yes, *a son*." Katherine sighed. "Henry wishes for that more than anything in all the world. Pray that I am the one to give it to him soon or who knows what might become of me."

The next afternoon, Gil was walking back from the tennis courts with Nicholas Carew when Bess found him. He loved seeing her like this, her expression alive with some great revelation she was about to share. The worst of his fears seemed to be behind him now that Brandon was happily married and was no longer a competitor for Bess's affections. In addition, nothing seemed to be coming of his fears about the king and Bess. Gil's heart stirred along with the rest of him at the mere sight of her; carefree, happy, her smooth cheeks slightly rosy with excitement. Elizabeth Carew, who was with her, as well as Nicholas, looked noticeably less happy as the sun lit upon both of their faces, and a soft breeze ruffled the hems of their embroidered satin dresses.

"Look at this, Gil!" Bess exclaimed, thrusting forth a small leather volume tooled intricately in gold. "Can you believe he remembered?"

Gil felt the dread build even as he touched the book. Only

one person at court could have possessed something so exquisitely detailed and costly.

"It is a rare edition of John Skelton's *The Rewards of Court*! I have only ever read a quite-tattered one, and that belonged to my father. I was always reading about court as a girl, hoping to see life here for myself one day!"

Gil tried not to look at her as he thumbed absently through the pages, trying to appear that he cared, though he was devastated that the King of England had entirely undercut him with a gift he could never afford himself. His hand stopped at an inscription: *Since honesty should always be rewarded. H.*

Gil fought back the bile of jealousy rising in his throat. He felt a dark rage building and tried to calm his breathing against it so Bess would not see. He knew Bess was just another of the king's many whims that would not—could not—endure.

No one would ever love Bess as he did—no one.

Nicholas Carew saw Gil's expression and understood it.

"Better Skelton than de Troyes, I suppose," Nicholas said affably, trying awkwardly to make Gil feel better by saying at least they had not purchased the same volume or work of the same writer to give to her.

"My French is atrocious, but I find the prose rather lofty and out of style," Gil said.

"You are misled mightily, Master Tailbois," Bess quickly replied. "Chrétien de Troyes is a legend, one whose prose is as magical and timeless as the tale of *Lancelot* itself. Still, I shall treasure this volume of Master Skelton's work forever, as I will the idea of someone who went out of his way to care about what I read and to give this to me."

Gil must have groaned audibly then, remembering silently all he had done to find her the far shabbier token, only to have angrily surrendered it to the flames at the first opportunity. *You are a fool!* he thought, silently chastising himself for yet another missed opportunity, as well as for unwise fits of jealousy. *You really are your own worst enemy.*

Gil struggled to fashion his expression into something carefree and handed the volume back to her. "Shall we all take a stroll then down by the river, and you can recite the best bits to us?" He forced himself to ask the question. "It might not be the epic adventure from the grand de Troyes, but I am certain a bit of Skelton shall amuse us all."

Her expression darkened almost immediately at the sarcasm, and Gil saw Elizabeth put a hand on Bess's arm. Bess tipped her head for an instant as she studied him.

"Are you mocking me?"

"By my troth, I am not!"

"I would have expected that of anyone else, Master Tailbois, but not of you."

"I honestly did not intend anything of the sort."

Her words and tone were nearly as wounding as her swooning over the king's gift, although he knew he had jealously taunted her into what she had said. Gil literally felt sick as he tried to remind himself she had no idea of his feelings for her, but that really was of no help at all. At the end of the day, he could never be Henry.

Always first, always best, always right . . . always king; such was Henry.

It was like watching something slip down an infinite hill, gaining more momentum as it rolled away, and having no power at all to stop it. Yes, watching her with the king felt exactly like that, Gil thought sadly.

The next afternoon, the king strolled through a long gallery beside Wolsey.

Henry was more anxious than usual about the evening ahead—anxious because Mistress Blount would be there. *Bess*, he thought, rolling her name around in his mind, like something sweet on his tongue. He was watching her grow into the promise of her beauty—and her wit—right before his eyes. What a lethal combination that had always been for him—and delectable.

Tonight he would dance with her, and he would watch her eyes when he asked how she liked the gift. Of course, he knew the answer already, because Henry had learned at a very young age never to ask a question to which he did not already know the answer. Bess looked at him with the same blushing awe as the others, yet there was something more about her. He had still to determine precisely what it was, but Bess stood out from the rest. There was never a day or an evening she was present that he did not notice her or find himself watching her. He delighted in her smile, her laugh, the shy turn of her head, and her body that, in the time she had been at court, had quickly ripened from the flat, long lines of a girl, to the willowy curves of a desirable young woman.

"What of her family, Wolsey?" he asked as they paused at a long window that faced onto the beautifully intricate knot garden below.

"John Blount remains a loyal servant, recovered well from his injuries, and returned fully to service, Your Highness," the recently appointed cardinal replied as he stood behind the king, steepling his fat hands over his new scarlet vestments.

Henry framed the window with his hands and gazed out across the landscape. "Yes, but would they welcome it as a flattering, and potentially lucrative, show of attention to the Blount family from their great sovereign lord, or merely tolerate it as duty?"

"That can only be supposed, of course. And yet perhaps"—he paused for effect—"if Master Blount were to receive an elevation in position, it is likely that his wife's gratitude, as well as his own, would know few bounds."

Henry pivoted toward Wolsey. His deep green eyes glittered in the sunlight. "Have you something in mind?"

"There is one position available as Esquire of the Body in your household, with Sir Thomas Hall gone back to his estates in Cornwall last month. Sir John would suit the position nicely," he dutifully replied.

"Indeed he would." Henry smiled, making his eyes glitter all the more. "Do it then."

"It is done, Your Highness," the cardinal said with a reverent nod, clearly knowing from experience what would come next and what he was meant silently to support.

Later, Wolsey accompanied the king down a wide flight of creaking oak stairs toward another endlessly long corridor leading to the banquet. There they were met by the usual smiling throng of nobles and ambassadors who crowded the doorway. Tiresome, Wolsey thought with great condescension. None of them would ever be able to take his place. He was a cardinal and powerful Lord High Chancellor as well. His face and form had grown fat from more food than prayer, and more women than common sense allowed. The king understood that, and tolerated it, so Wolsey did what he could for the king, particularly where women were concerned, even if at times it felt uncomfortably like procuring them. And besides, if he did not accommodate the sovereign, someone else most definitely would.

As the trumpet fanfare blared and they moved through the carved open doors of Hampton Court, a home he still marveled at possessing, Wolsey silently took stock of the guests. He checked to be sure they were seated in their proper places, making certain that no one important had been slighted. Wolsey quickly discerned who was missing.

The queen, proudly pregnant again, stout, and full faced, sat at the head of the vast, gleaming banquet hall beside the king's larger, still-vacant chair. Wolsey saw with surprise that she was attired stylishly this evening. Instead of one of her usual unadorned black ensembles, Katherine was clothed in an intricately sewn gown of rich ruby velvet, with wide sleeves, a miniver collar, and a band of jewels set in gold mounts. Her usually unadorned fingers flashed with gems as well.

Wolsey felt himself stifle a smile. So, the little queen knew a real rival when she saw one and planned to rise to the challenge. Katherine was not a stupid woman, and she had keen advisers who, of course, would warn her of perceived threats. He was quite certain it explained why, among the ladies gathered around the queen, Bess Blount was nowhere to be seen.

Wolsey finally picked out the king, who was taken up by Don Luis Caroz, the Spanish ambassador, and then by the Duke of Buckingham. Henry did not seem yet to notice Bess's absence. So many brocade- and velvet-clad courtiers and ladies in their jewels, gowns, and pearl-studded headdresses pressed toward him, bowing and curtsying, that it must have been difficult for even so tall a king as Henry to survey all of his subjects. At least Wolsey stood above

the crowd, and above the noxious, mingling fragrances of ambergris, musk, rose-water, and lavender, which masked the true scent of
unwashed flesh. He lifted the silver pomander hanging from a chain
at his round waist and pressed it to his nose. The fresher scent of
dried orange blossom quickly restored him as he proceeded to the
king's side.

Just as Henry was craning his neck finally to glance around the
room, Doña Elvira, the queen's companion, came up on the king's
other side and pressed her fingers gently into his forearm in a way
both familiar and cordial.

"The queen anxiously awaits your company, sire," Wolsey heard
her say in her accented English. Elvira was three years older than
the queen, yet there was a matronly quality about her—pallid skin,
deep-set dark eyes, and a long nose that made her appear much
older. "Her Highness fears she may quickly grow weary and need
to retire."

"Of course," Henry said a bit dismissively as he glanced down
at her. But then Wolsey noted the king's attempt at a compassion-
ate expression. Wolsey knew what that meant. No doubt, he would
retire with her for the evening. At least for now, the queen had won,
as she always would when there was the promise of an heir to inspire
Henry, once again, to hope.

Hope—that was all any of them really had here at court.

And yet it did spring eternal, thought Wolsey, and it fueled
ambitions, desires, and deceits.

He wondered if that was true for Mistress Blount, who was most
likely performing whatever mindless duty she had been given in the
queen's apartments—a strategy no doubt meant to keep her from
the king.

PART III

Step again. . . .

Thrice toss three oaken ashes in the air,
Thrice sit thou mute in this enchanted chair;
Then thrice tie up this truelover's knot,
And murmur soft: "She will, or will she not."

—Thomas Campion

PART III

Chapter Nine

September 1517
Greenwich Palace, Kent

*T*he child born in February of the previous year was a girl, but a strong, living child, who easily survived her first year—an heir at last. Henry and Katherine named her Mary after the king's favorite sister, finally forgiven by Henry and allowed to return home to England with her new husband, Charles Brandon.

For a time, Katherine felt the full weight of her power as mother of the king's child. That was until, once again, Henry began to long for a son. To that end, he doted on his wife exclusively after the birth of the Princess Mary. The queen was now thirty-two years old, and if Henry had hope of a male heir, all the country knew she must become pregnant again quickly.

Bess saw little of the king through that year due to the queen's intervention, preventing her from appearing at most events, which had become commonplace for her. There were the occasional banquets or hunting parties to which she was invited, and where she might catch a random glimpse of him, but beyond that, the flirtation and plays at courtly love he had begun with her fell to obligation and duty.

As the months passed, Bess spent her time, when she was not attending the queen, in the company of Elizabeth, Nicholas, and Gil, as always. They had a comfortable camaraderie after several years of friendship, and Bess missed Kinlet less and less. She wrote to her brother George regularly, and he wrote back with details of life there. Yet even with these descriptions, the images in her mind of the lush and emerald green Shropshire country hills of her girlhood slipped farther and farther away as she ripened more fully into a polished queen's attendant, one who loved life at court and who knew better each day how to navigate it with the dignity and grace of those who came before her.

Gil stood with Nicholas and watched Bess walk down the sloping lawn beside Elizabeth toward a shallow lake across which white swans moved. The sky above them was the color of pewter, and the autumn air was crisply cold, but the long hours of monotonous service were best broken by idle time. The vast gardens at Greenwich were spotted, even on cool autumn days, with more than a few courtiers.

The court was at Greenwich to escape what seemed like a coming epidemic of the deadly sweating sickness. England had not been plagued since the outbreak that had killed the king's elder brother, Arthur. Yet because of that, concern over its return, and whom it might claim next, was never far from Henry's mind.

Wolsey had fallen ill in September, his stout body giving way to both the fever and rash. But within the anticipated twenty-four hours, when one customarily either recovered or died, the cardinal was once again able to say Mass in the king's private chapel. Now, as winter neared, everyone looked at one another with a combination of fear and dread at the first sign of a cough. It was better to be outside, they all believed, amid the restorative air. And so they all walked.

Gil paused for a moment, and raked a hand through his touseled dark hair. He pushed back the pain of his headache and the growing wave of nausea he secretly felt. Surely it was nothing but the copious amount of wine he had drunk last night catching up with him now. Bess wore a gown of rose red brocade with a standing collar that accentuated her graceful neck. The crescent-shaped French hood sat back on her head just enough to show her smooth blond hair above her forehead. Gil tried to concentrate on her to steady himself as Nicholas turned to him in a stylish gray velvet cloak.

"She reads from that volume nearly every day, does she not?" Nicholas asked Gil of the small red leather book of Skelton's work Bess carried with her like a prayer missal.

"Irritatingly so, yes."

He bit back a little smile. "I suspect you would not say it like that if it were your gift and not the king's she carried everywhere. Pity you surrendered yours to the flames before she was ever able to make a choice."

"Between me and the king, there will never be a choice. She is in love with him, just as every other doe-eyed girl at this court. Just as your own wife once was."

Nicholas Carew's affable smile fell. "You need not be caustic. I know how you feel far better than you think."

Gil turned to him, feeling his head throb. "Do you?"

"Once he was finished with her, he forced her to marry me."

"The king? I thought your and Elizabeth's families arranged the matter."

"Your Wolsey organized it, but it was at the king's bidding. I am surprised you did not know."

"There are many things the cardinal and I have never discussed," Gil said, thinking about the details of his own conception, only little bits of which he knew for certain.

He wondered sometimes if anyone else knew about Wolsey's paternity. But Gil doubted it since Thomas Wolsey's image and authority were more important to him than anything else in the world.

"I thought you loved her," Gil finally said. "You certainly always look upon her with great affection."

"I have come to love her, but it is difficult to give your heart to one who can never fully give you hers in return. Elizabeth tolerates me, mainly."

"I had no idea," Gil said honestly.

"It would be a pity if that happened to you one day. Trust me, my friend, it is no way to live."

"I believe it may be too late for that," Gil replied as they looked at the two young women they loved, neither of whom could feel for them what they felt. And for both women this was because of the same man. Gil sighed, and they were silent for a moment.

"Do you believe he has any idea how many hearts he has claimed?"

"I believe he has yet to give his own heart over to anyone, so I imagine His Highness is quite clueless to those sorts of details," Nicholas said.

The wind stirred suddenly, and a carpet of red-gold leaves blew across the darkening landscape before them. Even though it was cold, Gil felt as if he were burning up. He ran a hand behind his neck and forced himself to ignore the growing fever as he continued to watch Bess. Suddenly, she and Elizabeth turned back as if they had heard something. They were both smiling. Both were young, both were so beautiful, and both were so entirely unaware of how their commitment to another man, the king, had affected every one of their lives. As it always did when she looked at him, Gil felt his heart stir, then the familiar ache take its place. Their eyes met as she drew near. Her cheeks were rosy from the cold, and her blue eyes were glittering, even in the flat afternoon light. She reached out and took his hands.

"Let's go exploring inside," Bess said with a note of mischief he knew well, for he had been the one to ignite it four years earlier. "As we did that first time I came here."

"You went into the king's rooms when you first came here. That was not a wise plan," he said, chuckling in response, "and still would not be, if we were to do it again."

"Of course not, silly. That would not be wise at all. But Elizabeth has just told me that the queen leaves on the hour for a pilgrimage to Walsingham with the Countesses of Oxford and Derby to pray for another pregnancy."

"Did she not just return from there last spring?" Gil asked. Everyone at court knew how increasingly devout and evermore serious the queen had become, particularly after the birth of her daughter.

Elizabeth lowered her eyes for a moment. "The poor queen knows time is of the essence at her age, and only God can give her a son now."

"I have heard that the king's sister brought the Boleyn sisters from France with her," Gil said. The four of them began to walk back up the winding brick path toward the stone palace sprawled out like a great sleeping giant before them.

"The Duke of Suffolk has done nothing since they returned but drone on about their unparalleled beauty," Nicholas added, rolling his eyes. "If they were to catch the eye of the king, one or both of them quite likely will be mothering royal bastards before May Day."

"I believe you misunderstand His Highness, as well as insult him, Master Carew," Bess said, sharply, suddenly defensive.

It was still difficult for Gil to remember that, despite Bess's years at court, she continued to be hopelessly romantic, particularly regarding the motivations of men. She was willing to believe the best in everyone, even when faced with the most incriminating of evidence. While it was one of the many things he loved about her, it was also the thing that caused him to fear for her the most. As much as he wanted her to know the truth about the king and his penchant for women, Gil simply could not be the one to tell her. And neither, apparently, could Nicholas nor Elizabeth.

Pray God, someone, somewhere, would tell her, though, before it was too late.

Gil had been behaving oddly all day, Bess thought as she lowered her head against the wind and walked with Elizabeth ahead of Gil and Nicholas. He could be so funny and sweet one minute, then moody and temperamental the next, and all seemingly without reason.

She hated to think what she privately thought—that perhaps his father's increasing dementia was an illness to which he might one day be susceptible. Everyone who had known Sir George Tailbois, a king's Knight of the Body, said that his illness had begun to manifest itself in bouts of depression and sullenness, quite like Gil's present condition. Even so, Bess was always angry with herself when the thought came to her. It felt like a betrayal. But she knew well that she was not alone at court in such unkind conclusions. People had been whispering about it for months.

Her dress swept along the pathway, soft-soled shoes crunching gravel, as she and Elizabeth linked arms. Both of them prattled on and giggled wickedly about which young Boleyn girl overdid her French accent the more, and which possessed the greater air of entitlement from their time spent abroad. Both agreed it was Anne, the fourteen-year-old younger sister with the wickedly brilliant green eyes.

The girls walked together, with the boys trailing behind, down one long corridor, then another, and up a twisted flight of stairs to a floor they rarely visited ornamented with massive tapestries. Bess waited until the two of them were entirely alone before breaking into a sudden full run. Among the things Bess valued most in her dignified life at court were moments like this when she was not required to be so proper. Skirts sailing out behind her, she ran ahead of the others now, with a childlike spirit, bidding them to catch her, or at least keep up as she had done with her siblings back home in Kinlet. Bess passed carved door after door. She was far ahead of the others when she came to an open door, through which she paused to peer.

At first she did not recognize him. He sat on the floor, head in his hands, beside the grand canopy bed—a royal bed. Yes, it was the same one she had seen four years earlier. But he did not look very royal at the moment, hunched over, clinging tightly to something. In this light, as she lingered beneath the doorway, there was the essence of a child about him, a vulnerability she had never seen past all of the puffed velvet, rich brocade, and glittering cascade of gems.

"Today is his birthday. He would have been thirty-one," Henry said gravely. The heavy medallion and chain at his chest glittered like his startling green eyes in the pale light.

At first Bess had no idea whom he meant. Then she realized that the fabric he was clutching was the delicately embroidered cradle blanket she once had taken from this very place.

"My brother would have found you a remarkable beauty," he said, as if seeing her for the first time as he glanced up at her with glazed eyes and a wounded expression.

Bess closed the door, moved across the room then, and sank onto the floor beside him. She could smell the wine on his breath. She felt a twinge of guilt looking at the precious little keepsake she already knew well. A part of another person's heart should never have been open to her like that without an invitation.

"Thank you," she replied with a small catch in her voice.

"I always think of him most when the sweating sickness is upon us."

"Is it again now?"

She tipped her head and studied him. He was not looking at her now. Rather, his gaze had taken him across the vast paneled room, to the fireplace hearth. His coat of arms, flanked by the gods Mars and Venus, was emblazoned above.

"We used to steal away from our nurse and hide in here sometimes when we were boys. Arthur and I would always tell each other secrets here; we knew it was the one place we were not allowed to be and, as children, that felt dangerous and thrilling at the same time."

His tone was suddenly wistful, decorated like the room, with the fabric of long-ago memories. Bess was not certain if Henry realized who was here with him, or to whom he was revealing his most precious secrets. But if he needed a friend, perhaps she could be that for him now. Some part of Henry must have thought so as well, because he continued to look at her intensely. Bess felt an oddly strong connection flare then—one that far exceeded pity.

Suddenly she was in his arms, wrapped in a powerful embrace she had not expected, and about which she had only fantasized. Bess melted against his broad, powerful chest, all reservations gone. Sliding both his hands beneath her chin and not waiting for approval, the king pressed a very gentle kiss onto her lips.

The feeling that he was two very different men—one a powerful, untouchable sovereign, the other a vulnerable son and brother—struck her again, unfastening the hold on her heart. For a moment, his fingers lingered against her trembling jaw.

"God, but you have grown from a child into a stunning beauty, Bess," Henry said in a deep and startlingly seductive tone as the small blanket dropped onto his lap between them.

The way he said her name was seduction itself. It was almost like a growl. She loved how purely male his skin smelled. Ambergris, civet, and musk on him was a heady combination. She drew in a breath, trying to steady herself, but all she could smell was him; all she could feel was her own slim body pressed against his taut magnificent one; all she could taste was his mouth. . . . All she could desire was for him to kiss her again.

"Forgive me," he said then as he pulled away. "It was wrong of me to take advantage of your kindness."

"It is understandable," she said softly, her lips still tingling.

"How can that be?"

"You've an entire country with which to concern yourself. It cannot be a simple task to find time enough to ponder your own heart."

A faint smile turned up the corners of his mouth as his hand fell away from her face. "You surprise me yet again, Mistress Blount."

"I am glad I do." Bess tried to smile encouragingly in return, but suddenly she realized her mouth was still trembling from the way he had kissed her. *Jésu*, but she wanted him to kiss her like that again. His mouth was like nectar, and she did not want ever to be farther away from it than she was now.

"I have many friends: Brandon, Carew, Henry Guildford,

William Compton . . . Wolsey, of course. Affable enough fellows with whom to drink and hunt, lads who are always willing to make mischief with me, always willing to have a good time. But none of them wants to know what troubles me. They cannot hear my heart."

"Do you not have a wife for that?" Bess dared to ask very gently, hoping that she did not insult him by bringing her up yet again.

"I did once, yes," he answered truthfully. "But Katherine is a very different woman now from the one she was when we married. There is no life left in her. Only duty, faith, and fear that she will never give me a son. The fear consumes her."

"And not you?"

"I do long for that, yes. I must have that. . . . But"—he sighed heavily—"I miss the other kind of closeness. I miss—"

He did not seem to want to say what he was thinking beyond that as his words fell away. Instead, he turned from her again, and Bess could feel the distance growing between them. If the moment was over, she thought, this dream would be at an end as well. And that she could not bear.

Surprising herself, Bess leaned over and, with all the tenderness and innocence of youth, touched her lips to his again. She had seen the affection between her parents at home enough to understand what would happen if she did not pull away, but she did not care. Bess understood the man she had come to know these last four years, the man behind the king, and she wanted that part of him—at least that small part the queen could no longer claim.

This time, the king did not let her go. Their kiss ripened quickly into something deep and sensual as he opened his mouth and pressed his tongue against hers. His hands moved from her neck to her hair where he pressed her hood back until its beads and pearls clattered onto the bare plank floor. Silky blond waves tumbled onto her shoulders then, and he tangled a hand deep within the curls.

"I have no wish to hurt you," he whispered huskily as she kissed him back with every ounce of innocent passion she felt.

"I care not at all if you do."

"You might," he warned, even as his skilled hand moved down from her shoulder to the strip of lace across her breasts.

"No, I shall not," she declared, trying to keep the tremor from her voice as his warm fingers trailed a path down to the place between her legs, and she moved with the sudden sensation.

Slowly, Henry lifted her skirts as he very gently pressed her back onto the rich Turkish carpet upon which they sat. Again he kissed her, this time with a demanding hunger she knew he would not let her escape. He had warned her, but it was a warning she did not intend to heed. Henry raised himself up onto her then, bracing his lean torso with thickly muscled arms, arching over her. He touched her, kissed her, and pressed with a steadily growing fury at that untouched place between her thighs that instinctively wanted to draw him in. It was fast and blinding after that, a quick snap of pain, and then the gripping, clawing power of desire took her over completely, drawing her into a powerful surge of pleasure and a universe of new sensations—the full weight of his taut male body; the touch of his smooth, moist skin against hers; and the taste of his mouth as it moved rhythmically with her own.

When it was over and they were still bound by the volumes of fabric from her dress and his doublet, Bess thought how dearly she loved him as she caressed the broad expanse of his back above her. Yes, loved—with her whole heart; with everything. The man, the wounded child within him—even the complex king; whatever he could give her of himself, Bess would love.

She had done it. She had wanted to do it for so long, and now she felt no regret at all.

Bess kissed him again, not just with her lips then, but with her heart. All of it was open to him now, come what may. She would be different from Katherine, she told herself as he held her against his chest, still rising and falling with the exertion. Not pious or sour, or desperate . . . Bess would make him want to come to her . . . and she would pray to God in the meantime that she would not have to sell her soul to do it.

Out in the cobblestoned courtyard that same afternoon, beneath mullioned windows and ivy-draped walls of red brick, the aroma of horseflesh and perfume lingered, and courtiers and servants bustled about. There, the queen, dressed in heavy black unadorned velvet, waited for her favorite riding horse to be brought so that she might begin her planned pilgrimage back to Walsingham to pray for her fertility. She twisted her gloved hands anxiously as she waited.

"You know I would not ask this," she said awkwardly to Mary, the king's sister, who stood beside her, having come out to bid her farewell. "It has always been difficult for me to ask favors of anyone here in England."

"We are family. You know you may ask anything," Brandon's wife said sweetly as she linked hands with the queen.

"Watch after him for me while I am away."

Katherine had meant the request to sound lighter, more nonchalant, but she had always worn her heart on her sleeve when it came to her husband. She did even more so now that she was rapidly changing, well past any resemblance to the young, exotic Spanish princess he once claimed to love. He now increasingly believed he had committed an unforgivable sin, since marrying a brother's wife was strictly forbidden by the Bible. It was laid out clearly in Leviticus, Henry now so often reminded them both.

Katherine knew he believed that, and she tried very hard not to let it break her heart. Of course, he was trying to rationalize the absence of a living son. It was much easier to blame her for such a profound void. That way, the lovers he took did not play so hard on his conscience. Of course, she knew about all of them. Yes, he chose his lovers from her own household. Doña Elvira listened well to all of the gossip. At least her dearest friend was entirely faithful, even if her own husband was not. But beyond that, a wife knew. There were always signs if one was willing to see them, as her mother had often warned her.

"Of course I will look after him for you," Mary replied, and, without needing to say it, Katherine knew that Mary understood the depth of just what she was asking. "But you know my brother as well as I do. He can be a stubborn man."

"That is part of what makes him a magnificent king."

Less so a husband, Katherine was thinking. But she did not say that. She had understood well the risks when she married him. She leaned over then in the cool afternoon air as autumn leaves stirred around them, and she pressed a kiss onto her sister-in-law's smooth, pale cheek.

"Thank you," Katherine said, hearing a telltale catch in her own voice.

"I shall pray that God hears your prayers at last during this pilgrimage, Sister. Now that we have our little Mary, there is much to hope for. You must keep that always in your mind."

"I shall do my best," Katherine replied.

She felt a wellspring of tears at the back of her eyes she had not expected at the thought of her precious little daughter, and all of the years of heartache and loss it had taken to finally bring her into the world. Still, she straightened her back and tipped up her chin, pressing back the tears defiantly. She could not, would not cry in front of anyone, not even Mary, because she had not given up. There was too much at stake, and tears signified weakness. If God would grant her the solitary prayer she prayed by the hour, each and every day, and she could have another child soon—next time a son—all would be well. Katherine would have her husband's heart, as well as his loyalty, returned to her. The way to vanquish any rival, at least from his heart if not from his bed, was to be the mother of the king's son.

After all she had endured, God simply could not intend that honor for anyone else.

Gil had been feeling ill all day, and this was certainly not helping.

Now that the queen was away on her pilgrimage, the king, predictably, was behaving like a carefree adolescent, and he was doing so in front of the entire court. Gil stood in the corner of a banquet hall heavy with candle smoke and the scent of perfume, leaning against a pillar as raucous festivities carried on around him. There, in the center of everything, Bess sat on a fringed velvet stool, her gown overly adorned and suspiciously more elegant than any of the others she had worn before. She was singing with the king, and it was their third tune together that evening. As always, the polite applause had begun to turn to gossip-laden whispers.

Bess's hair was long and golden down her back, her head adorned with a simple cap, and his heart physically ached as he watched her, to think that he would probably never have the opportunity to touch that smooth mane of hair himself, or any other part of Bess, at least not in the way he had longed to for four years. Her embrace on holidays and after a reunion was only that of a sister for a brother. She was entirely unaware that the man she touched was someone who longed to touch her back passionately, and that he would have given anything to possess not just her body, but her heart and soul as well.

Gil thought then, as he stood watching her with the king, of the missed opportunities—the pendant, the de Troyes book. He thought as well of how awkward and certainly too late it was to let her know how he truly felt. Bess Blount was the king's mistress, just as Jane and Elizabeth were before her. Like a coming storm, he could feel it with every fiber of his being. And, as it had been with the two previous impressionable girls, there was not a single thing he could do to stop it. She was especially lost to him now that she had matured. Though Bess understood that she was not the first girl to grace the king's bed, still she would not be dissuaded from the dalliance in the hope that this was the first time the king's heart was involved in the matter. If Gil tried to dissuade her now, it would seem like jealousy, and he would lose even her friendship, which was all he really had of her. That, he could not bear.

The best course left to him had gone unchanged, and his resolve had never wavered. He would be the one to pick up the pieces when it was over, since soon enough, it would be, just as it had been for Jane and Elizabeth. *Jesú, Maria*, what he would not give to have her look at him like that, to laugh with him like that, to touch his arm with such familiarity. Gil's head was still throbbing as if someone were pounding him with a club. And perhaps, in a way, his reason was doing just that, trying to get through to him.

When the song came to an end, the king and Bess rose from the center of the room, their elegant, gold and pearl-studded garments glittering in the fire and candlelight. They went together then, arms linked, to the main table set up on a dais. It was as though Bess, not the unfortunate Spaniard, were queen. Indeed, Bess certainly had the king's interest and his attention.

Yes, like all of the others, she did have that, Gil thought ruefully, at least for the moment.

Across the room, Bess had been stunned by the weight of Gil's cold gaze upon her the entire time she had been singing with the king. Gil's expression hurt, and it disappointed her. If anyone's opinion at this complex, dangerous court mattered at all to her, it was Gil Tailbois's. Still, it surprised her now, in the shadow of his apparent displeasure with her, that she did not feel guilty about what she and the king had done earlier. Her body still throbbed wonderfully from the size and power of him inside her, and she had begun to crave him again almost before they had dressed and left their little sanctuary in the room above the banquet hall.

She watched Henry carefully beside her, feeling the seductive warmth of his hand on her knee beneath the table cover as he laughed and casually conversed with the Duke of Buckingham, who was on his other side. Lord, but the king was magnificent—so purely male, she thought, still overwhelmed as she was by it all. Yet it was not this side of him, but rather the tender vulnerability that had so entirely won her over when they were alone, for which she would do absolutely anything.

Suddenly, as large gleaming silver platters of roast partridge, venison, boiled leg of lamb, figs, sugared almonds, and quince pastries, were laid before the assembled lords, ladies, dukes, earls, and ambassadors, Henry turned to her and leaned nearer.

"Come with me to Beaulieu tomorrow. Since the sweating sickness is growing worse, I am taking only a few of my court to the new palace I have just acquired in Essex from Sir Thomas Boleyn, and I wish very much for you to be with me. It is getting near enough that I, and those I love, must be away from the threat."

She could barely believe he had bought yet another new palace; he already had more than a dozen. The opulence and wealth she would never grow accustomed to. But she wanted desperately to be with him, and she was excited beyond measure to see what mysteries and treasures this new palace, and the days ahead, held for them.

"Are you certain it would be appropriate for me to accompany you?" she managed to ask. "I would not wish to be a complication."

Henry tightened his grip on her knee for a moment, then snaked his hand up near the place between her legs. "I should not wish to go without you," he said deeply, purring the words seductively in her ear and tasting her earlobe for an instant with the tip of his tongue. "Besides, you shall go in my sister's train. The selection of attendants made by the Duchess of Suffolk shall not be questioned."

"Is she not closely allied with the queen?" Bess dared to ask, knowing already how close the two women were, as she fingered the silver stem of her goblet and tried to will herself to concentrate on what he was saying.

"I, not the queen, am ruler of England. It is my wishes, as well as my desires, that must be obeyed," he replied quickly and with a hint of impatience, as his hand that was not on her knee gripped his own silver goblet a little too tightly.

Bess saw a muscle flex in his square jaw as he looked back out across the crowded hall.

"I shall obey all of your commands, my lord," she returned so sweetly then that the small frown that had darkened his expression was replaced quickly by a smile.

"It is what I am hoping for, beginning later this evening after the banquet has ended. I shall send for you then."

"And I shall be anywhere that you ask me to be, tonight, tomorrow, and always," Bess replied, trying in vain to keep the desperate note of pure devotion from her voice.

A small disturbance across the room beneath the archway near the door took her attention then as the king began to dine on sturgeon and Buckingham once again tried to engage him in conversation. Beside the pillar, two men were speaking with Gil. Jane Poppincourt was there as well, and one of the men was holding Gil's arm. But there was concern for him, not censure, in the gesture. A moment later, Gil faltered just as the two men led him from the vaulted banquet hall, one on each side of him in support. Jane quickly followed. Bess thought he did not look well, and her own concern deepened. Still, she could not suddenly leave the king's side to attend to another man's welfare—not when things had only just today deepened between them. It was not long, however, until the choice was made for her. A liveried page bent down behind her. "Lady Carew bids you to come at once, mistress," he said in an urgent tone. "She bids me tell you that it is Master Tailbois for whom she seeks your assistance."

"What is it?" she asked, turning around now to meet his gaze.

The king took note. Henry ceased his conversation and turned to the page as well.

"It may be the sweating sickness," the page nervously revealed. "Pardon me, mistress, but Master Tailbois appears quite gravely ill and Lady Carew felt you would want to know."

"Are you certain it is the sweat?" Henry asked, his deep voice ringing with concern.

Without waiting for a reply, Bess pressed back her chair and stood, her thick skirts moving around her.

"I must go," she declared, surprising herself with the rush of loyalty she felt for Gil, despite what the king might wish.

Without waiting for his approval, Bess left the banquet hall alone then, dashing out into the torch-lit corridor crawling with shadows, and fled up an enormous echoing flight of stairs to Cardinal Wolsey's suite of apartments. There, in a paneled room with two modest oak-framed windows of multicolored glass, she found Elizabeth, Nicholas, Jane, and the cardinal himself. They were gathered at the foot of a canopied bed, while two court physicians attended to Gil, who lay beneath a mound of heavy bedding. He was grimacing as if in enormous pain, but his eyes were closed, so he did not see her.

As Bess advanced, it was the cardinal who looked at her with calm concern and held out a fat jeweled hand to stop her. It was the first time in all these years she had ever seen his fleshy face full of anything but condescension toward her. "Perhaps you should not get too close, my dear. They are quite certain now it is the sweating sickness."

"But he was fine only yesterday!" she cried, feeling tears prick her eyes and the swell of panic move up from her heart. She knew how fatal it could be.

"That is the expected onset, as well as the course of the progression, I am afraid, swift and deadly. The best we can all do for him now is pray," Wolsey said calmly.

His heavy touch on her forearm was full of kindness, but it was clear he intended her to go no farther toward Gil.

"I do beseech you, my lord, allow me to see him," she softly pleaded. The desperation that showed on her face was also in her voice.

"It would not be safe for you," the cardinal calmly argued.

"I do not care about that!"

She exchanged a stricken glance with Elizabeth then, memories of precious times among the three of them flaring, then circling in her mind like birds. "Should we go to the chapel and pray for him?" Elizabeth asked as tears cascaded down her own smooth cheeks and Nicholas tightened his grip around his wife's waist to keep her from faltering.

"He is *not* going to die!" Bess declared, as if her commitment alone could make it so.

"You know what they say," Nicholas gently reminded. "Stricken by supper, dead by dawn."

"Then I am certainly not going anywhere!" Bess stubbornly declared.

The cardinal was looking at her with what she thought was an expression of surprise. But there was also a small spark of respect there, visible in his rich, dark eyes. It was something she had never seen before on the face of anyone at court—at least not directed toward her.

"If you must, then sit with him," Wolsey directed her. "Perhaps you shall bring him some comfort. He is enormously fond of you two young ladies."

Without waiting for a further invitation, Bess advanced toward Gil, pressing past the physicians, both in long black gowns, miniver-edged sleeves, and brimless caps. They stood ominously, cloaked in shadows, talking in a low tone at the side of the bed.

"He is full of fever," one of them declared gravely. "Take care, mistress."

For only an instant, remembering then what had become of the king's brother, did Bess feel any spark of fear for herself. Still, being here for him was far more important. It was everything. He was her friend and her confidant. She simply would not, could not, let him die as Arthur had died. She refused to know that eternal kind of loss.

A candle flickered beside the bed, and he smelled faintly of camphor. There was a large dish of water on the bedside table and a moist cloth near it. Bess ran the cloth through the cool water, then pressed it onto Gil's blazing forehead. He moaned softly but still did not open his eyes, and Bess felt her heart squeeze at the prospect. She could not lose him; she would not.

She and Elizabeth stayed like that all night beside their dearest friend, running moistened cloths over his forehead and taking turns holding his hand. Bess forgot entirely that the king had promised to send for her. It would not have mattered anyway, she thought when she later remembered, since this was where she was meant to be. If, as the ghoulishly cruel saying went, he was to be dead by morning, Bess was determined that Gil not go to that death alone.

When Wolsey placed a hand on her shoulder, it was dawn. The pale pink sunlight spread a blanket of warmth and a glow across the room around her. Elizabeth was asleep in a chair on the other side of the bed, her head back, and her small lips parted. Realizing where she was, Bess instantly bolted forward from her chair to check Gil.

"He has survived the night. He is merely sleeping," the prelate quietly announced. "And his fever broke about an hour ago."

"You were here the entire time?" she asked.

"Of course. He *is* my responsibility, after all."

"He is your servant."

Her charge did not ruffle him. Wolsey stood calmly, towering over her in his smooth silk crimson cassock, his posture, alone, full of more authority than she had ever seen in anyone. "The boy and I have grown close through the years."

Bess thought his tone was odd, belying far more than his words did. Certainly a heart like Cardinal Wolsey's was too hard to have been softened by a young ward with whom he had no family tie. There was clearly something more than a work relationship between them, but precisely what, she did not yet know.

A moment later, Elizabeth woke and, seeing them, lurched forward across the bed.

"Is he . . . ?"

"He has survived," Bess answered her wearily with that same little catch in her voice.

"Oh, praise God! Where has Nicholas gone?"

"To get some sleep," the cardinal announced in a calm baritone. "He said he would return soon."

Elizabeth reached over to touch Gil's limp hand.

"I cannot believe we nearly lost him," she said as a wellspring of tears fell onto her pale cheeks. "I know not what I would have done."

"Nor do I," said the prelate.

Bess glanced up at him and felt compassion. She could see that Cardinal Wolsey truly cared for Gil. Obviously there were many things she still did not know and understand about the world, or even about just the world of the English court. Bess knew she was still considered innocent by many—particularly by those who did not know what was happening between her and the king. But Bess was certain she did know whom she loved and trusted. And after the long night, three of those people were in the room with her.

After Gil woke and they all took turns embracing him and admonishing him never to frighten them like that again, Bess finally stood to stretch her legs, which were cramped and stiff after a full night in a hard chair. She walked to the window to draw open the latch for a breath of morning air. But as she gazed down into the courtyard now that morning had fully broken, she felt her heart lurch, and her breath fall away. The sight below was one she had not expected or, at first, wanted to believe she would ever see. Collected there below the window were dozens of saddled horses, laden carts, and courtiers preparing for travel. Among them was the king himself, who stood very close to Jane Poppincourt, his hand lightly around her waist as they spoke in a low tone together. The king and his entourage were going without Bess to Beaulieu to escape the sweating sickness. It took only a moment more to fully understand. She had been exposed to danger by Gil, and clearly it was too great a risk to include her now in the royal entourage, no matter what the king had proposed yesterday.

Bess stood stone still as she watched a groom hold the polished silver bridle of the king's saddle to steady the horse. Henry leapt easily onto the sleek black stallion without ever once turning around. She watched Jane standing nearby as the king tossed a glance back her way and then nodded to her. Perhaps they were just friends, Bess thought, and with a little jolt of envy she forced herself to press back.

It was understandable—yes, entirely. He feared illness, of course. Who could blame him? His own brother had died of the very same thing, and Henry had been left with a kingdom to rule. At least that was what she told herself as he gave the order, with a gloved hand and a throaty shout, to the blare of peeling trumpets, and galloped off into the dust. He did so without ever having explained himself, or having bid farewell to the girl who had so fully given him her heart, and her trust, only yesterday.

Chapter Ten

May 1518
York Place, London

*E*ight months had passed by the time Bess saw the king again at more than a distance. Over the winter, the threat of illness had passed, so Henry felt safe to join together his traveling entourage with his full court. By April, the queen was yet again pregnant, and again great hope for a son rose up—especially now that at least one of her prayers had been answered. She was finally the mother of a child who, at last, had survived the very fragile first two years.

This was an evening of celebration in honor of both the queen's pregnancy as well as the Treaty of London, which Cardinal Wolsey had painstakingly negotiated between England, France, and the papacy. The peace was to culminate in the formal betrothal of the two-year-old English Princess Mary and François, the three-month-old French *dauphin*. It was whispered that these events had set Wolsey on a course to realize his ultimate dream of one day becoming pope. The celebration following High Mass was to be massive.

From the first moment she saw Henry, Bess felt her anger slip away. He was magnificent as always in jeweled green brocade and a heavy medallion suspended from a thick gold chain around his neck. His eyes twinkled and he tipped back his head, laughing openly at something one of his companions said. Tall, lean, devastatingly handsome, Henry looked even more, she thought, like a young lion ready to devour the world.

Even from a distance, Bess had never seen the king look happier, healthier, or grander. As he saw her draw steadily near, Bess could feel Gil tense beside her. These past months in the king's absence had continued to deepen their friendship. Kindled at first by his illness, the relationship had been enriched by their steady companionship, and a healthy dose of his gratitude.

But tonight everything once again was changing.

Or perhaps, she thought as she looked at the king, it would merely change back, return to what it had been for that brief, magical time that now seemed as if it had not happened. At least that was what Bess prayed from the moment she saw him, his face and smile turned to her in the candlelight. A long line of liveried servants laid out a sumptuous feast for the group gathered in York Place, Wolsey's personal palace in the city. The theme was Roman, with great purple pillows, tasseled in gold, tossed onto the floor before low tables draped in gleaming purple silk. The walls were covered with long sheets of fluttering gold silk so that the entire room resembled the inside of a great columned temple.

"I shall stay when he comes to greet you," Gil said with surprisingly stiff resolve. "The queen will not like him speaking alone to a beautiful girl. The cardinal says she likes that less and less these days, especially when she is with child."

Bess knew by the way he said it that there would be no dissuading him, even though she had dreamed of nothing so much as seeing the king alone. Gil was going to be her protector whether she liked it or not. An instant later, Henry was upon them, his smile still broad and carefree as he took up Bess's lightly trembling hand. The first thing she felt was the cool press of the gold from his many rings on the backs of his fingers. As she dipped into a curtsy, he kissed her knuckles gently. The sensation of his moist lips as they lingered against her skin was seductive, and she tried not to react as she rose and their eyes met. Still, she felt the shiver deeply as they looked at each other.

"It has been too long, Mistress Blount," the king said charmingly as he continued to hold her hand.

"I would agree with Your Highness."

She heard Gil's groan of displeasure beside her.

"You look stunning, as always," he said flatteringly.

She was blushing and she knew it.

"Your Highness is most kind."

"Only observant, mistress, that is all." The king rocked back on his heels for a moment as he glanced over at Gil appraisingly. "So then, Master Tailbois, it has been some time, but you look well recovered, no worse for the wear."

"Thank you, Your Highness. Perfectly well."

The young king's voice went slightly gruff then. "Wolsey tells me you were the only one in his household stricken the last time."

"Apparently that was so, sire."

"How fortunate you were then to have had Mistress Blount and Lady Carew to care for you. I am certain their care only added to the speed of your recovery."

"I should think undoubtedly, Your Highness."

"It would be the only thing *I* would relish about falling ill, to be certain."

It was an odd little exchange, Bess thought, for she heard some small hint of rivalry in it. Odd it was indeed that the King of

England would behave that way with Gil, whose experience with women consisted of his platonic friendships with her and Elizabeth. She glanced over at Gil to see if the king's feelings were mutual, but she saw only the tall, lanky, kind-faced friend from her youth. There was at least some comfort in that, she thought.

Then, suddenly, the king redirected his attention to Bess, drawing her back in. "Mistress Blount, if you could spare but a moment before we dine, I find I could use your counsel on a matter of some urgency."

The way he was looking at her sent a tremor sharply through her body. "Anything I might do for Your Highness." She struggled with the words.

"Come with me," he directed her, nodding coolly to Gil as he turned to leave.

"Take care, Bess," Gil called after her, but she did not turn around. She knew what expression she would find in his eyes if she did, and just now Bess had no desire to see it.

She thought she had lost the king when he moved with long strides around the corner and into the corridor ahead of her. One flash of his jeweled velvet surcoat, and he was gone. But then as she turned the corner, trailing after him, she found him, cloaked in the shadows of a small paneled alcove. Forcefully, he drew her against his hard, lean body and wrapped her up in his powerful embrace. Anticipation arced through her as he pressed her against the cool limestone wall and leaned in against her. She was excited by their recklessness, terrified, and even so, overcome with pure lust. Her thoughts whirled in her mind, mixing with hot desire as Henry's mouth came down hard, parting hers. They did not speak. There were only the directions from his forceful hand and the demand from his hard body pushing against her.

Bess moaned softly as Henry fumbled impatiently with his codpiece first and then her voluminous skirts, the layers of underskirts, and lastly the drawers. She felt his tongue on her neck as he grasped her hips powerfully and lifted her up onto him.

Bess pressed herself against him as he moved, feeling her own feverish arousal in the dark, dangerous alcove where any moment they might be discovered. Pleasure and pain wound themselves up tightly inside her, hard and fast, until his huge body went rigid; then the next instant he groaned and slumped with a great sigh against her.

Less than ten minutes later, they swept back into the banquet hall, a full pace from each other, yet both filled with the reckless passion of the other.

"Mistress Blount?" A sweet-toned female voice came from behind her as soon as they were engulfed by the crowd around them and quickly separated.

Startled, Bess pivoted back and saw Mary, the king's petite, beautiful sister, now the Duchess of Suffolk, standing behind her, dressed in an elegant blue velvet dress with wide hanging sleeves and a plastron of gold brocade down the front.

"I almost did not recognize you," said Charles Brandon's new young wife. "You have changed a great deal since I went to France and returned. You have grown up."

"I thank you, Your Grace. Your beauty is unmatched now as always," Bess answered with the well-schooled aplomb five years at court had given her.

"So my brother chose a wise one this time," Mary observed, and so sweetly that at first Bess did not catch the veiled slight. "You might actually be good for him. If there were not the small matter of the queen."

"I would never do anything to dishonor the queen," Bess declared quickly.

"I bid you, in matters of the heart, be cautious with the word 'never.' I have learned quite well the danger in that."

Bess sought to say that she loved him only as her king. But with her face still flushed from moments ago in the darkened alcove, and her dress still slightly tousled, she simply could not force herself to lie so boldly to her lover's own sister. Bess wondered how Mary knew, as she had only ever been discreet since the brief liaison began, and she had not breathed a word of it to anyone. Yet it was clear that Mary did know. Perhaps it was the king who had confided in his sister. Everyone at court knew they were immeasurably close—that Mary had been the only one ever to boldly deceive Henry VIII and not face his wrath. He could be a gentle and kind man they said, but the King of England did not abide betrayal. She must always keep that in mind, Bess thought. The young woman who had so briefly reigned as Queen of France had risked everything for love with Charles Brandon. Although she was young, Bess was just beginning to understand that particular enduring kind of feeling for a man.

"My brother wishes you to dance with us in the masque he has arranged after supper," Mary said as she looked at Bess appraisingly. "I had planned to dissuade him for the queen's sake—family loyalty and all of that. I should not allow myself fondness for one of you, but perhaps exceptions can be made."

"*One of you?*" Bess dared to repeat, forced to remember that there were other women besides Katherine in Henry's life before her, but as the words lay unanswered on her lips, the trumpets sounded the call to dine.

The moment and the question were both lost then as Mary smiled graciously at her before she turned away.

Bess took the seat to which she was directed near the king, though she was not seated directly beside him. That honor went to Cardinal Wolsey. On his other side sat Charles Brandon, returned to prominence now, having been forgiven. Still, the king and Bess watched each other from a distance. It was a seductive dance of flirtation as music, laughter, plumes of candle smoke, and the rich aroma of spiced and cooked meats permeated the air of the beamed and vaulted hall.

As the evening progressed, she would catch Henry's glance upon her, only to see him run his tongue slyly along his lower lip, smile, then turn to Wolsey with a calm expression. It did not take long for Bess to join the little game. In response, she pressed a bite of lamb between her teeth, letting a bit of the juice drip down her chin. When she knew the king was watching, Bess trailed a finger over her lips, then pressed it into her mouth and let it linger there.

She felt a burst of triumph when she saw him shift in his chair, take a long swallow of wine, then exhale deeply. While Bess was still largely inexperienced, she knew her growing love for Henry made her want to do anything, everything, that would please him. And she would be a swift learner, she had promised herself. Bess Blount longed to be the perfect student.

"My wife was good at the king's little game as well," Nicholas Carew said, observing Bess's behavior. "Pity she does not put that much effort into my desires."

He put a hand on her knee then, and she quickly slapped it away. "I am still a rake, lovely Bess," he slurred with a wink. "It is what I do best—that is, at least for now."

Nicholas, who had never tried anything untoward before, was clearly drunk. Elizabeth was on his other side, chattering away and laughing so loudly with Lady Fitzwalter that she had not heard her husband or seen his advance. Nicholas seemed to see what she was thinking.

"Even if she could hear me, my lovely young wife would not care. I can never be the king, so I can never really matter to her."

Bess's glance cut from one to the other of them as the full implications of his words settled upon her, and she felt the heavy burden of an awful realization. The music and laughter were growing increasingly loud, and the aroma of cooked meat was quickly becoming nauseating. She could not have heard correctly. She had put all of her trust in Henry.

"Are you trying to suggest that Elizabeth and the king had more than a court flirtation or perhaps . . . a dalliance?"

"Oh, I am not suggesting it," he said ruefully. "I am stating it quite boldly, as fact. Jane Poppincourt and then, of course, Lady Hastings before her. Fool girls all thought they could tame the mighty King of England."

"I do not believe you. His Highness is not like that at all. Besides, Elizabeth would have told me if she had been something significant to him. If she had actually been his"—she felt herself choke on the word—"his mistress."

"Would she now?" He arched a pale brow and paused for a moment as Bess's world seemed to stop. The nausea deepened, and the taste in her mouth was sour like bile. She had all along understood that a king took lovers and had indiscretions; she was not that much of a fool after a bit of time at court. But to Bess's mind, a mistress was something more, and Henry had supported her notion. It implied some element of the heart being involved, an emotional attachment, and the moment she had fallen for Henry, Bess had not wanted to believe he had ever given that to anyone but the queen. "She certainly never told me either."

"Then how do you know it to be true?" she shot back, anger suddenly pulsing past the shock and nausea.

His blue eyes narrowed upon her, and his words became glacial. "Because the great Cardinal Wolsey came to me himself and ordered me to marry her by command of the king, who had tired of her."

Carew drained another goblet of wine, then beckoned the steward standing with a large silver flagon behind them. "You see, while the king does play, he knows he must pay. Her father, Sir Thomas Bryan, my friend and now my father-in-law, is too close to our little inner circle not to have made a fuss after the king had her, especially for as long as he did, without her being well married off. Alas, I was available and so duly elected."

She had never heard Nicholas sound so caustic. This was nothing like the carefree Carew she had come to know. Bess's head was spinning with dark, dreadful thoughts. That it all could have been so calculated, so unbelievably cold . . . Elizabeth and Nicholas were both so young and golden that Bess had always assumed if it had not been quite a love match, it was at least a sound one between them.

All of her assumptions were tumbling down like cards around her. Elizabeth was not the girl Bess had believed she knew so well, and Henry had openly lied to her about having taken mistresses. The thought doubled around in her mind: An occasional lover was one thing, but a mistress—a true lover who had one's heart and who was steady and constant—was a very different thing.

Betrayal arced through her, and the urge to run was very strong. It was almost as strong as the need to vomit—to force up the lies, the deceit, as well as the embarrassment of being achingly naive.

Bess shoved back her tall chair, sprang to her feet, and bolted for the tall carved doors on the other end of the room. She did not know if the king saw her go, and at that moment she did not care. The cradle blanket . . . His brother . . . The piece of his heart she had believed in but never really had . . . *Fool*, she thought to herself. *You are such a fool for believing the fairy tale! As if anything could ever truly be like* Lancelot.

It seemed as if everyone was laughing at her as she passed them, although she knew they were not. It was out in the corridor, amid flaming torches that cast golden shadows onto the walls, that Gil found her and drew her forcefully into his arms, letting her sob against his chest. He stood with her like that, completely motionless, a sudden pillar of strength, full of compassion, his long, lean arms wrapped protectively around her until at last he carefully spoke.

"Do you want to tell me?" he asked her in a voice marked with as much compassion as the love he so long and faithfully had felt for her.

"She lied to me. They all did." The word almost would not cross her lips. "Elizabeth was not just a flirtation or even a dalliance. She was actually the king's mistress!"

"Yes," Gil answered simply, but the sound of that single word, the affirmation, held more poison to Bess than any other ever could. She pulled away sharply, her expression full of incredulity directed at this man, her safe harbor, the only person at court she had believed she could fully trust.

"You knew?"

She saw the unmistakable discomfort on his face as his jaw tightened and, for a moment, he closed his eyes, then slowly reopened them. His pained gaze landed unsettlingly once again upon her. "Most everyone did, Bess."

"Everyone, apparently, but I."

"You would not have wanted to know."

"Do you not think I should have made that choice for myself? You, whom I trusted? You, who have been as close to me these years as my own brother?"

"I never wanted to be your brother."

Both shocked at what he was implying within that single declaration, and so many other revelations just now at hand, they gazed at each other, their conversation at a complete standstill as a young liveried page approached.

"The king is calling for you, Mistress Blount. It is time for the masque."

As she looked at the young servant, Bess saw that this moment signaled a profound crossroads for her. Dance with the king now and she would belong to Henry VIII, body and soul—no matter the compromise to her soul. Or walk away, and accept the deceptions of her two dearest friends, saving what she could of her dignity but losing the king.

Bess could hear the change of the music down the corridor at the banquet hall. The page held out a mask for her. She must decide. It was too late now for regrets, she realized, as she looked at the delicate mask, white and gold, studded with pearls. It was too late to go back. Her innocence was already lost.

Henry had lied brashly to her. But his life was enormously complicated. There were so many demands upon his every waking hour. Should allowances not be made for that when he was so much more than an ordinary man?

She knew what Gil would say. She knew now what had happened to Elizabeth. But was it not possible that Bess was different to him? That the king could now be different because of her? After all, history was full of magnificent men, leaders, who had been changed by love. The queen, sadly, was not enough for him. But as she stood there then, the mask glittering in her hands, the memory of a dozen romantic tales still dancing in her head, and Gil looming behind her, so symbolic of her other choices in life, Bess had every intention in the world of trying to be just that to the king . . . come what may.

The king sent for her later that night. Bess was taken by two male esquires she did not recognize up a back set of stairs down a dimly lit corridor that smelled heavily of musk and slightly of mildew. Neither man spoke to her as they trod half a pace ahead of her with heavy-footed strides; nor did they speak to each other. One carried a lit candle lamp that only slightly brightened the way. As she walked, Bess's excitement began slightly to dim in the face of the clandestine nature of their encounter.

Their liaisons had been impetuous, spontaneous, and wholly exciting. Now, as the small rounded door was opened before her, and on the other side the corner of a tapestry pulled back, she realized how fully all of that was about to change. This was a secret door, hidden away, through which she had been brought. Everything about the moment had all the trappings of calculation, planning, and deception. She wondered if Elizabeth had walked through this same door . . . and Jane before her . . . and Lady Hastings before her. For the first time, Bess felt a little shudder of revulsion. Still, it was not enough to change her mind as she was ushered into the king's bedchamber, lit now by a dozen shimmering and long white tapers placed around the massive tester bed. There was a fire blazing in the hearth beneath a gold crown over the grand stone mantel. When she saw him in his bed, smiling now as he waited for her, Bess's heart quickened, and the hesitation vanished as instantly as if a bubble had burst.

"I thought of nothing but this moment all evening," he said seductively as he held out a hand to her.

"Nor I," Bess replied truthfully, drawing near.

"I am sorry about how you were brought, but in this palace the queen's apartments are only just down the hall," Henry explained. Then a smile broke across his square face. "Ah, but then you already know that."

Snuffing out a flicker of shame, Bess sank onto the edge of the bed, feeling strangely shy all of a sudden. But when he touched her cheek and she leaned against his palm, she felt wanton and full of reckless desire again.

"Here, let me help you with your gown. I think it is high time I see all of you properly, do you not agree?"

It was an odd thing to ask, Bess thought, feeling a bit like a mare being trotted out for bidding. But of course he had not meant it like that. He cared for her. She knew it. She still read each day from the book he had given her; she kept it at her bedside so that it was the very last thing she saw each night and the first thing the next morning.

"I love you," she could not help softly saying with childlike devotion as he unlaced her gown. "I want so much to make you happy and for you to forget all of the burdens you have, even if it can only be for a little while."

He ran a fingertip along her bare spine, then kissed the sleek column of her neck. "You do make me forget, Bess," he murmured. "But love is a fleeting thing. Never let that rule you."

Henry pressed her forward then, pleasantries abandoned. He straddled her harshly, tossing her dress into a tangled heap on the plush carpet beside the firelit bed. *Desire,* she thought in response. She was no longer a child or an innocent. *Sensual, wicked, yes, wonderful desire* . . . Perhaps it would be enough. It might have to be—for now, at least.

"And it would be dangerous to love me," he warned as he touched the soft rise of her backside just before he reached down powerfully to anchor himself on her slim hips.

"'Tis a bit too late for that, I am afraid," she breathlessly responded to the king, feeling the glorious, all-consuming force of him.

Katherine knelt beside her own canopied bed, droning out the last of her nightly whispered prayers. Soon it would not be safe for her to kneel. The child inside her would be too big; the risk too great. And she must do absolutely nothing to lose this child, hopefully, a son. *Dios mío, let it be a living son this time.*

Henry was slipping through her fingertips like water. She knew it was the Blount girl this time. Of course, Katherine had seen it coming, for all of the good it had done. Perhaps the knowing was worse, like seeing a death and being entirely unable to stop it. They did say ignorance was bliss, and perhaps they were right. This was a death of sorts—a death of her love, of her marriage, of a sense of peace for the rest of her life. He was different with Bess than he had been with the others; there was something indefinable about their relationship, yet she knew it was there.

Katherine had fought so valiantly for him, waited so long after Arthur, endured so much. How foolish she had been to believe that if only he married her, made her his queen, she could make him truly happy.

Doña Elvira helped her back onto her feet, then straightened the lace hem of her white muslin nightdress. "How are you feeling? May I bring Your Highness anything?" she asked Katherine in Spanish.

"I am feeling surprisingly well. Perhaps I should not get my hopes up, but this one does feel like a boy, *amiga*. It has not felt like this since our first child. There is a way he is sitting, low, not at all like my little Mary. That gives me hope."

"Then pray God it is to be a prince this time."

Doña Elvira's tone held reserve, and Katherine heard it instantly, because they did not easily hide things from each other.

"I haven't many more chances, have I?" Katherine asked in a fragile voice few were allowed to hear.

"That is up to God, Your Royal Highness."

"But he shall soon stop wanting me if this is not a son. He shall stop trying, and there shall be even more women, or more prominence of place with this one."

"Our king knows his duty, and Your Highness knows yours. You cannot give up; nor can he."

"Is she with him now?" Katherine asked, trying hard to keep the tremor from her voice.

"I believe she is."

"Dios me salve," she wept, but even Katherine knew that God could not save her from Mistress Blount—at least not until she had run her course, and the next one turned her husband's eager head . . . or until Katherine gave him a male heir at last and silenced all of her rivals.

"She knows the truth. It seems that great volumes of wine have a way of unlocking Master Carew's lips," Gil announced blandly to Elizabeth.

They were alone in the Carews' small apartment on the second floor with a view past the jewel-shaped, leaded windows down onto a small duck pond by which a flock of birds now flew. Nicholas would not return tonight. They both knew that. When he drank as much as he had that night, Nicholas more than lived up to his reputation as one of the king's most reckless companions. He was a dreadful husband, but Gil had been her confidant long enough to know Elizabeth was no stellar wife. She had largely rejected Nicholas's affection, being only acceptably pleasant, in favor of her memories with the king. He waited for the revelation to descend fully on her.

"He told Bess?"

"It was only a matter of time before she discovered it. Where gossip is concerned, this court is an incredibly small world."

"Has the revelation ended things between them then?" She wanted suddenly to know, and he heard the hopeful tone in her voice.

"Alas, no. If anything, it has seemed to spur her on. Bess has a spark of defiance about her. We should have seen that with our first challenge. I suspect they are together now, since she is not here or in her chamber, as she normally would be."

Elizabeth Carew gazed out the window into the falling blackness of the night, and Gil could only imagine what she was thinking. But she had brought it on herself, just as Bess had.

What was it about Henry that trumped all logic and reason for a woman, he wondered, even now? Certainly, he was a king, handsome, athletic, musically gifted, and humorous. But he was irrevocably married until death separated him from the queen. Thus, it could only ever end badly for anyone else who came to love him.

"Does Bess hate me, do you believe?" she asked in a broken tone.

"I suspect it is not hate she feels, so much as betrayal. But, of course, upon that I can only guess."

"You have never betrayed her," Elizabeth said, finally turning back to look at him standing there in the center of the room, arms limply at his sides while he waited dutifully as he always did for what was meant to come next. He was strong, solid, never wavering.

"No. But then I love her."

"I love her, too," she said tearfully. "I am so worried for her, for where this might lead if she stays in this."

"We both fear for her. But no one can stop her any more than they could have stopped you."

"The king has a power. I do not quite know how to explain it." She sighed, her voice full of knowing. "I made some very foolish choices."

"And yet would you not make them all again?"

She wiped the tears from her eyes and exhaled a steadying breath. "In a heartbeat, if he desired me," she admitted.

"Quite likely that is what our Bess feels. All we can do is be here for her to collect the broken pieces and help her continue on when it ends."

"As you did for me," she said.

"As I did for you," he echoed.

Gil was a trusted friend. Being that for those he loved mattered deeply to him. He thought it was a pity, though, that no one seemed to see him as much of anything more. Perhaps they never would.

Bess and Elizabeth did not speak of the situation after that night, but a palpable tension had developed between them. Where once there had been camaraderie and trust between the two girls, there now was a wall of distrust. In fact, they barely spoke at all as they sat in the queen's privy drawing room, both of them doing needlework at separate tables, each with other maids of honor, when once they would have sat together, bursting with private stories, laughter, and gossip. Occasionally, Bess would look at her friend, but her glance would instantly cut away if Elizabeth looked up in her direction. She still could not quite believe that Elizabeth had lied to her, and about something so important as her having had an affair with the king.

Elizabeth Carew's life had been constructed upon a shaky foundation—a lie. Her seemingly secure position in the queen's household, her marriage, and her liaisons, were all smoke and mirrors. Yet she had sought to share none of that with Bess, once her dearest friend.

As she pressed a needle through the thin cotton fabric, Bess tried hard not to imagine them passionately together. She tried not to imagine her doing with Henry the intimate things Bess herself had now done. But the images crept into her mind anyway; erotic, dark, unnerving images. Bess tried to focus on her needlework, but the tedium of it made her thoughts vulnerable. What she had with Henry was special. It was unique. And he truly did care for her. She believed that. . . . She must steadfastly continue to believe it, because she loved him.

Suddenly, Agnes de Venegas, her uncle Lord Mountjoy's wife, was beside Bess, speaking something softly into her ear. "The queen wishes you to attend her presently."

The directive was startling to Bess, considering her thoughts of the queen's husband at that moment. Bess turned around with a start, dropping the needlework onto her lap.

"Are you certain it was I she asked for, madam?"

"*Sí*, Mistress Blount, you."

As trepidation rose quickly within her, Bess pushed back her chair, stood, then straightened her skirts to steal herself a few moments to collect herself. When she saw that everyone was looking at her, her sense of dread deepened. But there was no escaping the royal command. Somber-faced Agnes, with her sleek black hair pulled away from her face and her perfect, noble carriage, was standing beside her like a jailer, intent on seeing Bess to her incarceration. And surely it would feel that way when she went to see the queen, Bess thought.

For her, the queen's secret rival.

A dozen scenarios played across her mind as they walked silently over heavy carpets, with floorboards creaking beneath. Bess's heart was racing, and it felt as if a stone were lodged in her throat. If she had displeased the queen somehow, she could be easily replaced by one of a dozen willing daughters of other waiting nobles, then sent home to Kinlet, returned to the monotonous and idle country life in which she had all but forgotten how to exist, where she would never be able to see the king again. If that happened, her parents would be furious, since it would seem a slight upon them, on Lord Mountjoy, on all of the Blounts who depended upon the king and queen for every aspect of their livelihood.

Fear that the queen had discovered her deception—fear she had long felt—spiked through Bess as she was led past the posted row of guards in their green tunics, each adorned with silver gilt and a red Tudor rose. The expressions on the faces of some of the senior ladies she passed nearby, including the sisters, Lady Hastings and Lady Fitzwalter, were harsh as each glanced appraisingly at her, then casually turned away. God save her, she knew. They all knew!

"Ah, there you are," the queen said coolly as Bess was issued into her privy chamber.

The door clicked to a close. Katherine was seated on a carved throne with a massive gold and purple tester emblazoned with the king's coat of arms and a Tudor rose hung dramatically behind her. There was a collection of Spanish crucifixes on the wall, and the room was unnaturally chilly. The queen's dress, as it was most days now, was stiff black silk, edged with ivory-colored lace. At her chest was another large silver jewel-studded crucifix suspended from a heavy pearl and silver chain. Bess dipped into a deep curtsy and held it. Finally, she rose and waited. She felt as if she were holding her breath. She certainly could not breathe. The stone of fear was still too deeply lodged in her throat. Even though the queen had a small reserved smile, everything about this moment held danger.

"Your Royal Highness," Bess properly acknowledged, willing her voice not to crack.

"It has been a while since we have spoken, has it not, Mistress Blount?"

"Regrettably, it has, Your Highness."

She saw the queen and Maria de Salinas exchange a little glance. "And you have been well?"

"I have been, Your Highness. Thank you kindly for inquiring."

"I have concern for all of my ladies, Mistress Blount, their health, their lives . . . their activities."

"Your Highness is most considerate."

Katherine arched a dark, thick eyebrow suspiciously and paused before she said, "It is important for a queen to know what goes on around her at all times. Would you not agree?"

"It would seem impertinent of me even to imagine what would be required of a queen, Your Highness."

"An excellent point." She grinned in an oddly forbidding way. "After all, there can only ever be one queen for Henry, and I shall forever be that."

"We are blessed that it is so."

"*Sí bueno*. I am gratified to know that we are in accord," Katherine replied. "You know, Mistress Blount, my mother was an extraordinary queen herself."

"Queen Isabella is already a legend."

"*Sí*, I would agree with you. And do you know, Mistress Blount, one of the most important lessons my legendary mother taught me as a girl—the thing I took to this country, this role, and this life, tucked most indelibly into my mind and heart?" She leaned forward slightly, her elbows both balanced now on the arms of the chair and her hands joined together at just the proper angle so that her wedding ring glinted in the sun through the large window beside her. "My mother taught me never to underestimate a rival."

Words of self-defense threatened to push past her lips, but Bess stubbornly pressed them back down. This was meant as a polite, only slightly veiled, warning. The queen was a wise woman, one Bess had always respected, even liked. If she did not know about Bess and the king, she quite obviously suspected it. This little performance proved that. It was meant to throw Bess entirely off her game, and it had succeeded.

"I am certain it was an honor to know such a wise woman, and to have been schooled by her," Bess said instead.

The queen's thick brows merged slightly, in a discerning way. "Mistress Blount, unfortunately, you shall never have any idea how true that is," she said abruptly. "The best advice I can give to you is to always be mindful, as well as cautious, of those who have been well schooled in many things. Know well your limitations, and your rivals, or believe me, they *will* be your undoing."

Katherine of Aragon's words were final, and Bess knew the

audience she had been given was at an abrupt end. As Doña Elvira took a step forward, Bess dipped into a second low and proper curtsy.

"I shall always remember that, Your Highness," she said.

"*Splendido*. It is pleasant for me to see you are still the wise young woman I thought you were from the start. But, just in case . . . I shall be watching."

Bess felt the chill in her words. What she would do about that beyond the proper curtsies, the proper backward exit, and the smiles, remained to be seen.

The king himself had organized the little hunting party. It was to be a small group of only his most intimate friends this time, those around whom Bess would feel at ease, and those around whom he would feel entirely free. That meant mainly those who would not gossip to the queen, which was a small number in a court where some element of avarice and ambition reigned supreme in nearly everyone. Therefore the hunting party would include Brandon, Sir William Compton, Sir Henry Guildford, and Sir Edward Neville. And to make his intentions only slightly less obvious, and to give him the appearance of propriety, Lord Mountjoy and Elizabeth Carew's father, Sir Thomas Bryan, had been selected as well.

Henry drew on his tooled leather riding gloves in his bedchamber and admired himself in the full-length, gold-framed looking glass. Carew, who was now a Groom of the Chamber, stood formally and stiff behind him, hands linked behind his back. Nicholas was not quite the companion he once had been, before that nasty Elizabeth episode. But how could the king have known that the silly girl would actually fall in love with him, and that it would become necessary to call Nicholas, his friend, into service to marry her? At least Jane Poppincourt had possessed the good sense to have seen their dalliance for what it was. And, after all, everyone had won in it. For as long as it had lasted, and for their discretion, he had showered each of the young ladies in his life with jewels and other rewards. Last winter, he had given Jane a rare beaver cloak and a purse full of gold coins. Henry was a bit ashamed of himself that all that he had given Bess was a little trinket necklace and a book. But there was still time, after all. He winked at his own reflection, and the thought, then smiled.

She was still so deliciously uncorrupted, so eager to please him, he thought a little cruelly, as he forced away the true, unsettling vulnerability he had felt that first time they had kissed beside his bed. That had been a mistake—how unprepared he had felt, at least. His brother's birthday had brought it all to the fore. Henry had been swept up by powerful emotions he knew he could not allow himself to feel. Emotion made him too fragile. It made him feel the hurt and insecurities of his boyhood. And a king, this king, could not afford anything but total control. Ah, how he did want to control her! Bess was quite delectable, really, which was why he so readily suffered her guileless expression, and her overly eager smile every time he approached her. Had that mother of hers never taught her the advantages of the wanton, slightly removed seductress? *Ah, my kingdom for a mistress like that!* Bess was probably a bit too much like Elizabeth for her own good, or his. But for now, Bess Blount was far and away the most interesting diversion his court provided.

They strolled along the long corridor, down the stone stairs, and out into the courtyard where the air was crisp and cool. Perfect for walking, and other things, he thought, with a little self-satisfied grin. He could not wait until they arrived at that wonderful little clearing beside the lake. A hidden jewel, he thought—one his wife knew nothing about. Katherine would not have appreciated that place anyway. Romantic little gestures like that had never interested her. Only two things really did: pregnancy and prayer, and not always in that order.

Bess came out of the little rounded door and moved into the gravel-covered courtyard as Henry stood readying her horse for her, his own personal gift from the Marquis of Mantua, a sleek bay called *Governatore*. Henry had to admit to himself, particularly in this light, that Bess was extraordinarily pretty. He had timed their departure perfectly, the moment Katherine was attending to her devotions. There would not be much time for conversation, at least not here.

"So pleased you could join us," Henry said as Bess approached him in her green velvet riding gown and matching plumed hat. He was standing with his own prized Arabian, holding fast to the silver-studded reins.

"Had I any choice in the matter?" She smiled slyly.

Henry watched her cheeks flush. Then she lowered her eyes in a way that was surprisingly flirtatious. "I would hope not. It would be a frightfully lonely hunt without you." He ran his hand along the haunch of the horse, then gave it a little slap. "I have chosen a spirited mount for you. He is one of my newest, my own prized possession, actually. Do you believe you can handle a Mantuan bay?"

"Spirit is a good thing, is it not?" Bess asked with a surprisingly coquettish little smile that instantly stirred his loins. Yes, it had been a good thing he had waited for her to grow into her beauty and her confidence.

For a moment, a mellow ray of sunlight filtered through the tall stand of courtyard oaks and highlighted her eyes—stunning, brilliant blue eyes with long lashes sweeping over them. Oh, indeed spirit was a good thing. So were beauty and her unquenchable desire to please him.

"Shall we be off then?" Henry asked, helping her into the saddle.

"'Tis Your Highness who leads the way."

He was still holding on to her tiny waist as he said in a very low voice, "Oh, we shall have to do something about your form of address, Mistress Blount. At least in private."

"I am at your disposal in all things, my lord," Bess replied, smiling down and very nearly enchanting him completely. It was a sensation Henry shook off swiftly, one full of a sincerity he could not afford to feel.

The little group rode for an hour after that until streams dotted the lush woodlands shaded by tangles of tall dark trunks and heavy branches full of bristling leaves. As her horse trotted behind his, Henry glanced over and saw with concern Bess's attempts to maneuver an animal obviously more spirited than even he had realized. In spite of his concern, however, it was endearing to watch her silent determination to remain in control. Bess had a beautifully strong pride he had not bothered to see before, and Henry began to realize as they rode that Bess was like a beautiful new rose unfolding before him, with layers like petals peeling back to reveal something new underneath. Perhaps she really was a bit different from all the others, if such a thing were possible. He shook his head and smiled to himself. He was most definitely getting too soft for his own good, especially where a girl was concerned.

The group, led by Brandon, made its way then down a small embankment, thickly carpeted by long grass and well shaded from the sun. Many of the entourage were talking in low tones among themselves, when Bess's horse suddenly stumbled on a rock and reared up in powerful defense, whinnying out a warning. In that single instant following, the animal dashed forward at a gallop, churning mud, leaves, grass, and fear in her wake.

"Go after her, Brandon!" The king called out the command to his friend who was in the lead as he kicked the haunches of his own mount and sped into a gallop.

"Go with it! Lean into him!" Henry called to her.

He was not certain if Bess could even hear him beneath the wind and the sound of the harness jangling, and the thundering of his own heart. As he and Brandon galloped, neck and neck behind her, Bess's green velvet skirts flew out like a sail, and she struggled not to fall from the frightened, charging animal.

"I cannot!" she cried out.

"You can!" Henry urged, surprised at his own building sense of panic.

He was nearly upon her, nearly able to grab hold of the reins, when the horse quite suddenly jerked to a halt, tossed its powerful head, and whinnied again, as though to cast off harm. Caught unawares, Bess lost her grip on the reins and was catapulted suddenly forward, landing in a heap on the ground.

"The king! The king comes!"

Henry Norris, the king's redheaded, freckle-faced principal page, was given the task of being first to the door of a modest two-story thatch and timber cottage that sat in the clearing just past where Bess had fallen. Two of the king's scouts stood at Norris's side as the king's band of friends collected in the small courtyard amid ducks and chickens. The riders were removing their gloves as Henry himself held Bess limply in his arms.

Even from this distance, Henry could hear the pure terror in the voice of the stout, balding man who stood beside his wife and called out a warning to the rest of his family as they stood, modestly dressed, their faces full of shock, at the open front door with an unexpected royal guest before them. There was much scurrying then, along with shrieking, clattering of furniture being moved, and doors slamming, as the man moved forward and his wife disappeared with a little shriek back into the house.

"Your Most Magnificent Highness, my lord, and king," the man sputtered as he bowed awkwardly, his porcine face still white with shock.

"Yes, yes, all of that. I must have a place for her to rest, and it seems that you are to be so honored."

Henry's tone was flippant and he knew it as he stood at the door holding an unconscious Bess. He had not meant to strike such a tone, but he feared for her. He had not thought she had hit her head, yet there was a small gash on her temple that worried him since he had not brought along a physician who could have allayed his fears and properly tended to her.

The house past the low threshold was modest but tidy. There was a large room furnished with only a table, chairs, and a sideboard dotted with pewter pieces. Another room beyond it looked to be a large kitchen, and there was a staircase that likely led to bedchambers upstairs.

Humble, Henry thought, yet it would have to do. He ignored the rest of the family and servants who were all bowing and murmuring as he glanced around the house to survey the scene, then brushed past them all and swept up the stairs with Bess still tight in his arms. She began to moan, but she still had not opened her eyes. Only Brandon followed him, their boot heels clopping on the bare stairs as they quickly walked. The others in the king's hunting party were directed to remain downstairs.

"Send for my physician at once," Henry called out to Brandon as he found the larger of two bedchambers and placed her gently on the feather bed.

"'Tis done, sire," he responded formally.

"And have some wine, a basin of water, and fresh cloths sent up."

"All of it already well on the way."

They covered Bess over with a quilt that had been neatly folded on a traveling trunk beneath the window. The room smelled of must, Henry noticed, but there was also the faint fragrance of rosemary from an herb garden below the window, and thus the house was not without a certain charm he might have appreciated in other circumstances.

"Thank you, Charles, for not admonishing me about Katherine," Henry said as he heaved a huge sigh.

"It is the least I can do, considering."

"Indeed, you are right about that," Henry quickly countered.

They both knew what he meant. The bitterness over how he had married the king's sister without his permission was still too fresh in both their minds.

"Do you . . . love this girl, Hal?" his old friend then dared to ask.

"I cannot afford to love anyone. I have a duty. That is all there is."

"A duty as king, perhaps," Charles cautiously observed. "But as a man, do you not have a duty to your heart? I have seen the way you have looked at her for years."

"I can have no heart, Charles. I have a wife, remember? And England has a queen. Like the end of a story, that is all there is. All there ever shall be."

Henry looked back at Bess, who seemed to be coming slowly

back around finally. Only then did he realize that he was squeezing her hand very tightly.

The woman he had seen at the door came into the room with her two adolescent daughters just then. They were bearing wine, the basin, cloths, and each girl wore an innocent but openly flirtatious smile. Henry surprised himself, realizing that, as the two younger girls left the room, he had barely even looked at them for concern over Bess. That was something new for him. When he glanced back at Bess, he saw that her eyes were open at last—those beautiful blue eyes that always stopped him, even before he'd had a mind to admit it.

"What happened?" she softly croaked.

"You took a rather nasty fall, sweetheart."

Henry gently lifted her head and helped her take a sip of wine as the woman silently ran a cloth through the water, rung it out, then handed it to Charles Brandon to give to the king.

"Does your head hurt?"

"Not so much as my pride," Bess softly admitted. "I thought I could ride him."

"It is my fault for having chosen such a horse, for putting you at risk like that. Forgive me."

"You did me a great honor. You cannot be sorry for that." She tried to smile.

Henry took the cloth from Charles, then placed it very gently on her forehead. "I have sent for my physician and for a more tame horse for you to ride back."

"That is entirely unnecessary, and I cannot hold up the others. They were expecting a hunt. So were you."

"I care nothing about that. Besides," he said with a smile, "there shall be plenty of time for more hunting parties. I am sending them all back to court soon anyway."

"And Your Highness?"

God, he wished she would not look at him, at least not like that. Attraction to her was one thing, but he simply could not afford to actually care.

"Perhaps I shall remain," Henry answered a little more gruffly than he had meant to. "If you would not object, that is. The mistress below is making some delectable stew or other."

"It smells delicious."

"That seems a good thing if you have an appetite," Henry said uncomfortably.

"I do, my lord, for many things."

Henry softened a bit more beneath her gaze and the wanton sound of her declaration. Struggling was futile. He leaned across the bed to gently kiss her. He could hear the others still behind him near the door: the wife, the daughters, and Charles. They left the room then, and the door squeaked as it swung to a close on its hinges.

Safe within their private moment, Henry kissed her again, this time more passionately as he slid up onto the bed and lay down beside her. Filled with desire at her nearness, he ran a hand down the length of her body, feeling very carefully for the willowy shape of her beneath her dress, the petticoats, and the cambric chemise. Then suddenly his hand stilled. He could make himself go no further. A moment later, he pulled away.

"What is it?" Bess asked with a soft tone of surprise.

"You are injured."

"Only my head, sire, I told you. Not the rest of me." She smiled seductively, her long hair soft around her shoulders now that he had removed her hood and her shoes.

"It would not be right," he persisted.

"Neither is anything else we have done together, apparently," she said with a slight note of defeat in her voice.

"It is not that I do not want you, because I do, desperately. But I cannot take advantage of you like this."

Bess coiled her hands in the hair at the nape of his neck and tried to draw him forward. "That is my favorite thing that you do," she wantonly teased.

Henry weakened for a moment, kissing her passionately again and pressing his full weight against her. He felt the force of his own desire, but Henry was the sum total of many things beyond his unquenchable lust. He was a son who had learned the power of restraint from a mother he had adored, and he was a boy who had learned to place duty above all else from a father he respected. Achingly, he moved away from her again and, with a little groan, rolled onto his back and closed his eyes.

"You do have an increasing power over me," he murmured truthfully.

"It seems quite the opposite," she countered, and again he could hear her disappointment.

Henry took a moment to collect himself, his body still burning for want of her. He needed to control himself if he was going to even look at her again. He waited for his racing heart to slow and the heat of his desire to cool by a degree at least.

"That is just the point. In the past, I have cared nothing for a girl's welfare. I was a bit of a reprobate, I suppose, in that regard."

"You told me once that you did not take mistresses, and I believed you, you know."

"I may be a king and a husband, but sadly I am also a man. They were lovers only, momentary dalliances, not mistresses, Bess. There is a distinct difference."

"Is there?"

He thought about how he had slept with Anne, Lady Hastings, Jane, and Elizabeth, but how he had never had deep or lasting feelings for any of them. "Lovers satisfy the body, but with a mistress there is something more. She is acknowledged. Honored. Special. A part of his life, not just his bed."

"Which one shall I be?" she asked, the full power of her bright blue eyes descending on him then and filling him with a mixture of desire and fear that in spite of his reserve he would come to care too much for her.

Bess turned onto her side, moving herself against his body, then running a hand along his smooth, beardless jaw.

"You are far more than a lover to me, Bess."

"Then am I the mistress of Henry the Eighth, King of England?"

Something about her words undid him. Unable to hold himself back any longer for the raw chemistry between them, Henry drew her forcefully onto him, anchored her delicate face in his powerful hands, and opened her mouth with his powerful kiss. When he pulled away, he looked deeply into her eyes.

"It appears so," Henry declared.

PART IV

Step. . . .

*Thus, Lancelot drove him back and forth in whatever
direction he pleased, always stopping before the Queen, his lady,
who had kindled the flame which compelled him.*

—Chrétien de Troyes, *Lancelot*

Chapter Eleven

November 1518
Richmond Palace, Surrey

*W*hile the king was at the little country cottage tending to Bess, the queen was at Richmond Palace giving birth to another daughter. Katherine had dared to call the girl Isabella after her own powerful mother, in hope that the name might portend good things. She knew, even as she did, however, that it was futile. The child died within days.

Full of bitterness at his wife for continuing to withhold the one thing he needed most, Henry became more flagrant in parading his mistress before her as punishment. Some part of him, of course, knew it was cruel and wrong, but he felt incapable of stopping. He still needed a son; he must have an heir. England was dependent upon his securing the succession, or all that his father had battled for a generation earlier would be forever lost without it. But if God meant to go on punishing him for the sin of marrying his brother's widow, Henry decided there was no point in avoiding pleasure—or in denying it.

When Katherine was well enough recovered to leave court for Windsor to mourn the loss of the child privately, Bess's world quickly shifted. Not only did Henry call for her to be brought to his bedchamber every night after the court had retired, but each day she was directed to join him at everything from prayer to tennis to evening banquets as his companion. While he did not parade her before any of his foreign ambassadors or political dignitaries, there were few at the English court who did not fully understand her new place of prominence. The proof most noticeably was on the faces of the queen's own ladies and maids, who had been left behind to attend Bess.

Bess recognized that now as she was dressed and ornamented for supper in the king's privy chamber. She much preferred these evenings to the grander displays at banquets where not only were her every move and every sip of wine marked by courtiers, grooms, and pages alike, but by the local citizens who, stuffed raucously into the gallery above, were given the honor of viewing the event. On those occasions, she always felt like a trapped deer in a pen, observed, judged, even ridiculed. Still, she would have done anything for Henry, and she meant to keep him—to fascinate him and enchant him for as long as she could, even if she had to endure the endless scrutiny.

She regarded herself proudly, dressed now in a chestnut-colored brocade gown with long bell sleeves and an underskirt of gold tissue, as her own mother laid a heavy gold chain woven through with pearls across the square neckline. A stamped, gold medallion filled with jewels was suspended from it. Catherine Blount tried desperately to smile at her daughter standing before her in the shimmering lamplight, but the expression looked more like a grimace. In the reflection, Bess could see her mother willing herself to project an air of approval over a situation that, while financially and socially advantageous for the entire Blount family, could not ever end the way a mother felt it should for a beloved daughter. The king might smile upon his mistress for a moment in time, Catherine had long ago counseled her before sending her to court, and he might shower her with attention and riches; however, in the end, she would never be his wife. She would never be anything but a complication to him—and a concession to the man who came afterward. No matter, Bess thought. Her mother did not understand what was between them; no one did.

"It is a gift from the king," Catherine whispered evenly in her daughter's ear. "His Highness has directed you to wear it this evening."

Bess saw the overwhelming hesitation on her mother's face, now marked by more pronounced lines, and eyes less brilliant than they had once been. Behind her mother's image in the looking glass, she could see Lady Hastings and Lady Fitzwalter standing together watching. Lady Hastings certainly could say nothing about Bess's change in circumstance, since it had recently become widely known throughout the court that she, the married sister of the Duke of Buckingham, had been carrying on a torrid affair herself with the king's Chief Gentleman of the Bedchamber, Sir William Compton.

Bess bit back a smile, remembering well the condescending sneers from the two sisters when she had first come to court, and several times since, as well as from maids of honor such as Anne Stanhope and Joan Champernowne. They certainly were not mocking her now, she thought as she saw their shocked expressions at the priceless jewel that had been placed across her chest. Now Bess was someone with whom to be cautious, if not to respect, for her ongoing intimacy with the king; she loved the advantage this turn of the tables at last had given her.

"Be careful, Daughter," Catherine whispered as she looked again at Bess's reflection in the mirror, and the expressions of the others around them. "But Father and I both know well what determination it takes to survive here at court, and we are proud of that, even if we are worried about your heart in this."

Proud . . . She tipped her chin up in response as her mother adjusted the little French cap on her head and the silk fall behind it. "My heart is full. You needn't worry," Bess sweetly replied.

Henry smiled brightly when she was shown into his presence chamber, already filled with his favorite courtiers. As she advanced, Bess was aware of their slightly more appreciative and welcoming expressions. Wolsey and Brandon were there, as were Sir Henry Guildford, Sir Edward Neville, and Elizabeth Carew's father, Sir Thomas Bryan. The king's most prized band of gallants, she thought with a smile as she nodded to each of them in turn. The great Duke of Buckingham, however, was not present, which seemed to Bess something of an indictment.

Nicholas and Elizabeth were noticeably absent as well. They had gone home to Beddington Park in Surrey. Bess was told by Gertrude Blount, her cousin, that the king had personally seen to their return home. He wanted nothing to upset her or remind her of that earlier indiscretion. Of her original friends, she still spoke with Gil, but the nature of their relationship had been altered, on her side, by his deception, and on his side, by her intimate relationship with the king. Still, she would have given anything to have him there with her. In spite of their smiles, the king's friends were not her friends, and she knew it.

Henry embraced her, kissed her cheek, then wrapped his arm around her waist in a familiar fashion that surprised even Bess. No one there could have missed seeing it. By the gesture, he was making her status known among his circle of friends. Even Mary, the king's sister, who came into the room late, acknowledged Bess with a solicitously polite smile.

A group of musicians began to play something light and appealing as silver dish after dish of aromatic, steaming delicacies was placed before them.

While Henry ate heartily beside her, Bess only picked at the delectable offerings. It was an odd sensation, having everyone staring, judging, paying attention to whether she ate or not. She still was not accustomed to it. She touched the coolly reassuring jewel at her throat and tried to remember the honor this was rather than giving in to her apprehensions.

As the king ate and conversed casually with the others, she glanced at the door when Thomas Boleyn drew forward in a velvet cape and plumed cap, accompanied by two young girls, each dressed with striking elegance in sweeping brocade dotted with pearls. They were pretty girls, dipping into practiced curtsies before the king. One was slightly older, with a fuller face, but possessed of beautiful blue eyes and a small, sweet mouth. The other was remarkably petite, but with a woman's shape already, a flawless face, and haunting dark eyes. Bess had not seen either of them for a while, but she knew only too well who they were.

"Your Highness, as you requested, these are my daughters. May I present my younger, Anne," he said of the smaller girl. "And this is my elder, Mary."

With a quick sideways glance, Bess could see that Henry's smile was broad and full of interest. She felt her throat constrict and her spine stiffen slightly.

"I would not have recognized either of you," the king affably replied as he set down his heavy silver, jeweled goblet. Since their return from France, they had been at home at Hever Castle in Kent, and so he had not had them in his company. "You have grown into lovely young women. Your family has done well by you both."

"Many thanks, Your Royal Highness," they said in unison, each bobbing into little curtsies.

Bess felt her stomach churn. Henry was staring a little too admiringly for her taste at Mary, the elder Boleyn daughter, who was blushing like a child at the attention as Anne held back a strangely confident little smile.

"Were you able to speak to the queen or perhaps with Doña Elvira about an appointment before they left for Windsor?" Henry asked their father with interest.

"There was no time, I'm afraid, sire. Her Highness departed rather quickly after . . ." Boleyn let the words fall away. "Forgive me, sire."

"No, no, we are all saddened by the latest turn of events here," Henry replied magnanimously, with a little wave. "So then, Mary, is it?"

"It is, Your Highness." She was still smiling; still blushing.

"Can you sew?"

"I can, sire. Tolerably well, I am told."

"She does remarkable needlework as well as embroidery, Your Highness," Thomas Boleyn said, interceding proudly.

"That is imperative since the queen takes to that particular pastime by the hour. Is that not so, Mistress Blount?"

Bess was startled and could only sputter out a reply. "'Tis true, sire."

"And prayer, Mistress Boleyn, there is a great deal of that as well," he warned.

"I welcome any chance to commune with our Lord God," Mary replied softly and, Bess thought, flirtatiously.

"When the queen and I reunite at Greenwich for Christmastide, I shall see to it myself that she has a place," Henry decreed, and drew up his heavy silver chalice again.

"Many thanks, sire. It will be an honor to our entire family," Thomas Boleyn said as he dipped into his deepest, most courtly bow yet, and Bess felt a sweeping and intense wave of nausea take her over completely.

From where it had come she had no idea, other than it made her ill to see the king look at anyone else as he looked at her. She was not easily given to nausea or illness. Was this what the queen felt when she saw the king with her? Bess suddenly felt ashamed. She had been so increasingly taken up by her attraction and growing love for Henry that Bess had nearly forgotten how the queen might feel. But just as she was a true rival to the queen, could not the elder Boleyn girl easily become a rival to her as well?

Bess shifted in her seat, forced herself to remain silent, and willed herself to smile as serenely as if she were the queen herself. Like Katherine, Bess would not lose what she had of the king over a pointless show of jealousy now. No, she must trust herself, and him, more than that. And then later tonight, when they were alone in his bed and she was pleasing him as she had been taught well to do, Bess would find the assurance she craved. She would make him remind her that Katherine was his duty and his queen, but *she* was his love. The nausea began to fade and her racing heart began to slow as the three Boleyns backed away and Charles Brandon affably advanced.

"May I tempt Your Highness with a hunt tomorrow morning?" Brandon asked. "I rode this afternoon and found the park here is brimming with deer and wild boar."

"Tempt away, Charles. That is one of my favorite things, after all," he said with a laugh. Bess was uncertain whether he meant the hunt or temptation, but perhaps he intended the ambiguity.

Near dawn, as they lay, sated and happy in each other's arms, whispering and laughing, as lovers do, Henry kissed her breast at the place where the necklace still lay. She was naked except for the jewel, her willowy young body highlighted only by gold, pearls, and the glittering ruby pendant.

"God's blood, woman, but you are seductive in nothing but jewels."

"Only for you," she said sweetly.

"Ah, Bess," Henry said with a sigh. "I need to be carefree like this, always. As I am with you."

"You can be." She kissed his cheek tenderly.

"If only there were not the real world beyond those doors waiting for me. Life. Commitment. Duty . . . Responsibility." He let out another heavy sigh and rolled away from her.

"But you have so much that is good to balance it all out, do you not?"

She was desperately hoping he would say he had her.

"I do have everything but the thing I need most. *A son.* It is all I can think of, all that matters. The Crown is not safe until the queen gives me an heir."

"But you have the Princess Mary."

"A girl cannot rule."

"The queen's mother did," she gently reminded him.

"Alongside a powerful husband."

"Perhaps your Mary shall one day have that."

"I *need* a son, Bess. England shall never be truly secure without it!" He suddenly raged, sitting up and casting off the heavy bedcovers and gazing at the ceiling, as if to the heavens. The moment of tenderness was lost for now to reality. "How it does plague me in my sleep, in my every waking moment, that I displeased You, God, by marrying her! Am I to be eternally punished for making Katherine my bride after Arthur? Arthur! *Arthur!*" His brother's name came forth like a chant as he stalked the length of the bedchamber, lit now by only the faint red glow of embers in the fireplace hearth. "A son is not just an heir. A living son is the only sign from Him that will tell me I did not commit so grievous a sin in marrying her!"

Instinct alone sent her to him then, padding silently across the cold wood floor. Bess put a hand gently on his bare, warm shoulder, and he reached up silently to take it.

"Forgive me," he said in a very low voice. "I have no right to burden you with this."

"I am happy you feel you can speak to me of it."

"Strangely, I do feel as if I can. I used to confide in my sister. But things have changed between us since . . . since Mary went to France and married Brandon."

"I thought you forgave them for that?" Bess cautiously asked as he turned around and drew her back into his arms.

"I did, of course, eventually. But sometimes when something is broken, it can never be fully restored. Do you understand?"

I pray that is never the case with you and me, she thought, but instead of saying it, she kissed his cheek very tenderly, then laid her head on his shoulder as he drew her powerfully against him. Aside from her usual feelings of lust and love, she suddenly also felt a strong sense of loyalty.

"Then I am all the more pleased I can be here for you," she said. "And I always will be."

"Perhaps you are too young to realize that you should not make promises you might not one day wish to keep."

"Oh, I will wish it, always, Hal," she assured him with all the tenderness and love in her voice that she felt in her heart.

Bess awoke alone in Henry's grand bed the next morning, feeling as if she was about to be sick. The reflex was too powerful to avoid when an overpowering wave of nausea struck her. Quickly, she scrambled beneath the bed for the king's chamber pot and wretched until she collapsed beside it.

It was Sir William Compton, Chief Gentleman of the Bedchamber, who came into the room a moment later and gently helped her to her feet.

"Are you all right, mistress?" he asked, helping her to sit on the edge of the bed as he called for the king's Groom of the Stool to dispatch the pot. Compton was a sharp-eyed, quiet man with an air of experience, yet genuine kindness as well, making it plausible, Bess thought, that Lady Hastings would risk her marriage for him.

"I am fine. Perhaps something I ate disagreed with me. Where is His Highness?"

"Gone hunting, mistress, with the Duke of Suffolk."

She remembered last night—the duke; Thomas Boleyn; the flirtation with his daughter; the silent but powerful jockeying for position. Her stomach began to feel enormously sour again.

"Perhaps I should call the king's physician?" he said. "You're pale as linen."

"I am fine, truly. Nothing more than a chill."

"His Highness most assuredly shall not want to hear that. You know how he is about illness of any kind in his presence."

"I do indeed," she replied, remembering what had happened with Gil, and how swiftly the king had left court.

"May I offer a different possibility?" he said carefully as he helped her on with her cambric shift, then her dress with no hint of impropriety, only duty. "Is it possible you are with child, Mistress Blount?"

"No, it is most certainly not possible," she flared without thinking.

"Can you tell me this is the first time you have vomited in the morning?"

"I need tell you nothing, my lord."

"True enough," he conceded, gazing up at her as he knelt beside the bed to slip the soft blue shoes back onto her feet for her. "But are there many others in whom you would be free to confide if you changed your mind?"

"I am not free to confide in you. You serve the king."

"We all do, Mistress Blount, to one degree or another. In spite of that, I do understand. Remember, I have been here in the morning to tidy up for a very long time now."

She knew he meant with other women, and although the notion disgusted her now more than ever, there were more important thoughts plaguing her at the moment. Bess could not deny that she was frightened by even the remote possibility of a pregnancy. There was nowhere else she could think to turn. She did not tell Sir Compton, but her flux had not come this month, and she had long been as regular as nightfall.

"What if I am?" she asked then, almost too softly to hear her words herself.

He helped her to her feet. "There is a woman downstairs in the kitchens. She knows of such things. You shall see her."

"But no one can know about it if I do," she said, giving in to her rising panic. "That would ruin everything."

"I shall take you to her myself. There is a private passageway," he calmly replied. "She shall do as she is bid, and I shall see that she is quiet about it."

"And if I am, my lord," she repeated the question, "what then?"

"That, I cannot say, mistress," Compton answered honestly. "Since you would be the first. The king has yet to sire a child by anyone but the queen. We cannot know quite how he would react under those new and complicated circumstances."

Hawking calmed Henry and brought him a sense of peace that few other sports did. It was an activity of oneness with the bird, his father had always said, and Henry found that to be true. He stood beside Brandon on a bluff overlooking the forest, a sleek, black hawk on his gloved forearm and his attendants a full pace behind them. A brisk late-autumn wind tossed the parts of their hair showing beneath their plumed caps and the hems of both their doublets. Henry felt himself smile. He was happy. At first he had not recognized the feeling because it had been so long.

"Since when do you smile so broadly at hawking?" Brandon asked, his new red-gold beard starting to take shape, making him appear more mature and worldly.

"Apparently I do now."

"The Blount girl, is it?"

"You know well who it is."

"Yet I saw you looking at Boleyn's daughter yesterday, as everyone else did."

"She is a comely thing. No one can contest that," he conceded. "But Bess is different. Certainly she is nothing like Jane, thank God, who has gone to France in order, I assume, to torment de Longueville once again. Nor is she like Carew's wife."

"She is only Carew's wife because you tired of her," Brandon reminded him as they bantered in the familiar way that had come about over many years.

"I am well aware of that, but thanks be to God, Wolsey came up with that plan or she would likely still be chasing me around corridors and gardens with those lovesick tears in her eyes."

Henry's words sounded callous, but they were not his true feelings. If anything, he had felt attraction, guilt, and loss when Elizabeth began to get close enough that he felt the need to be rid of her. He must keep guard against those feelings to prevent his own

undoing. He lifted his arm and sent the ebony hawk into the cloud-
less pewter sky.

"You asked me once if I thought I loved Bess."

"I remember."

"Last night at supper, I saw Tom Bryan watching her. I felt a
kind of rage I have never felt before."

"Jealousy?" Brandon carefully asked.

"Who's to say if it was that? But what I do know is, in that moment,
I had the most unstoppable urge to run him through with my own
dagger. It really was quite a powerful, if unfamiliar, sensation."

"And you think that is love?"

"Well, is it not? Of a sort, at least? I want to be with her all the
time. I crave not only her body, which I am mad for, but her opinions,
and to have her keep my confidences. In that, I have been quite free
with her. I favor talking with her over anyone else these days, even you.
I adore seeing her laugh . . . and when she tumbled from that horse . . ."

"'Tis true then. Saints above."

Henry settled his eyes on his childhood friend. "I do love her,
in a manner."

"So it would seem." Brandon's smile lengthened above his thick-
ening copper beard. "What of the queen?"

"She need not know. At least, not what is in my heart for Bess.
But, yes, she is bound soon enough to understand that I am about
to bring a mistress into our lives, and hopefully she can accept that
with grace. Although I will be discreet, as my father before me
always was. I have no wish to humiliate Katherine. She has tried her
best to be a good wife."

"And to give you a son?"

"She has failed miserably at that," Henry suddenly growled.

"The pursuit of that elusive child destroyed things between us long ago. Every waking moment that woman is not pleading with me to bed her, she is on her knees pleading with God for a son. It does not bode well for passion."

The hawk returned, and Henry surrendered the bird to the keeper who was waiting at the ready behind him.

"Is Bess the kind who shall be happy as your mistress and want no more when the time comes?" Brandon asked as they each began to remove their heavy leather hawking gloves as the wind stirred.

"She shall have to be, as there is really no more I can give her than that."

"Would you if you could?"

Henry shrugged, and for a moment he truly considered the question. "Perhaps it is my prick talking and not my logic, but yes, right now I would do nearly anything for Bess. Although if you told her I said that, I would deny it to the death," Henry quipped, then winked, drawing a mask once again over the emotions he struggled not to feel.

Bess sat at the backgammon table across from her cousin, Gertrude, Marchioness of Exeter, and tried to will herself not to be sick again. Appearance was everything in the tight-knit court where people had little else to do but gossip and scheme. The nausea, however, had not abated since the old woman downstairs had made her pronouncement.

It had been life changing.

"Aye, you are indeed with child, mistress, and two months gone already."

Those could have been joyous words.

If only she were Katherine of Aragon and not Bess Blount of Kinlet.

"'Tis your move again," Lord Mountjoy's putty-faced daughter prompted as they sat in a cavernous room, dotted with other young ladies at game tables or embroidery hoops, and an autumn rain lightly pelted the windows as though with tiny pebbles. It made everything around them feel damp in spite of the grand fire blazing in the hearth across the room.

"Are you going to make a move or not?" Gertrude pressed, her flat, wide forehead wrinkling with prominent frown lines.

Not only was her nausea, as well as her circumstances, a distraction to Bess, but she had been made even more ill a moment ago by Mary Boleyn. The pretty girl had come into the room with her mother, the daughter of Thomas Howard, the influential Earl of Surrey—and a more highly placed lady-in-waiting to the queen than Bess's own mother, Catherine. She even walked with an air of entitlement. It did not help that Bess had seen how Henry had looked at the elder Boleyn daughter the night before.

At Gertrude's prodding, Bess made a cursory move as mother and daughter strode through the room. Her mind was too distracted to do anything else. What would Henry do when he knew about the child? His *bastard* child? Would he be rid of her, and every other Blount and Mountjoy who depended upon his favor? He had sought to be rid of Elizabeth when that affair displeased him. That precious, first sense of pride she had felt was swiftly being replaced by horror and shame. *Jesú,* she missed Elizabeth and the easy confidence of a trusted friend. She, of all people, would understand, and know what Bess should do because, God help her, Bess herself had no idea.

"Ach, your head is in the clouds!" Gertrude grumbled at her in frustration. "No one would have made so foolish a move otherwise!"

Bess glanced down at the backgammon board and realized that Gertrude was right. Fearing another wave of nausea at any moment, or a wellspring of tears, Bess pushed back her chair and stood. She had never felt more alone in her life, or more frightened. There was only one person who could help her now, one person she could trust to tell—the one person left at court who would help her, and she must find him.

Every other person she passed as she swept down the corridor, every person who came to her mind, was someone to be feared or avoided. Focused on her purpose, she went to Wolsey's grand apartments, which took up almost the entire west wing of the second floor, overlooking the hawk mews. There she found Gil, as she had known she would, attending to two of the prelate's long, crimson cassocks. One look at her across the room, and Bess knew he understood there was something very wrong. Calmly, Gil led her by the arm to a chair, his own thin face piqued with concern. He drew up a stool with a padded cushion and tassels on it and sat with her.

"Tell me," he bid her simply.

She exhaled a breath and when she did, the tears spilled forward like a sudden torrent and her bottom lip began to quiver. "I am going to bear the king's child."

Gil was silent for a moment—a moment that stretched into an eternity for her, the declaration echoing before both of them.

"Are you certain?"

"Very."

"Let's speak with the cardinal. He will know how to proceed from here."

"I cannot possibly! Cardinal Wolsey frightens me. I would not know what to say."

He took her hands and held them tightly. "Then do you trust me to speak with him on your behalf? He knows everything about this court and its workings. And I would trust him with my life."

Bess looked at Gil, a friend for so long, her eyes still misted with tears. "It is as I trust you."

She saw that same small muscle tighten in his jaw as it always did when he was holding back emotion. Otherwise he showed very little of his feelings. He was, she thought, as dispassionate and steadfast as a stranger. Perhaps that was what she needed just then, because her own life seemed to be falling apart.

"I am so sorry, Gil," she said brokenly then.

"Sorry for what?"

"For not being a better friend."

He leaned nearer, and she saw that he was trying to smile. As usual, it was probably to make her feel better. "You have been a fine friend. Perhaps you have not always said the things I wished to hear," he said with a shrug, "but they were most often the things I needed to hear."

"Odd. I was going to say the very same thing of you."

"So," he asked, "will you want to have the child? If not, there are women who—"

"I could never do that to Hal's child!"

She saw by his grimace her power to wound him, and suddenly his face was flooded with that elusive show of emotion.

"I'm sorry, but I love him."

"So did Elizabeth."

Bess shot to her feet, angry suddenly at the declaration. A rush of emotions passed across her face. "That was cruel of you."

"What do you expect to gain by loving him? He is married, and King of England."

"He'll not forsake me after he grows accustomed to the idea of this child. He cares for me."

"He told Elizabeth that, as well"

"She was not his mistress!" Bess declared in childish defiance. "A lover is a very different thing."

He arched a brow. "Is it, truly?"

"I need to believe it is." Her voice broke. "Especially now."

Gil was still holding both her hands as he drew them up, pressed them to his chest, then let out a heavy sigh. "Shall I speak to Wolsey then? Shall I ask him what to do?"

"I do not believe he likes me very much," she said, hesitating.

"The cardinal is first a man of God, Bess. He will not steer us wrong in this. You said you trusted me."

"I do trust you. There is no one else."

Bess was so confused that she had not heard him say the word "us." Nor had she seen the look in his eyes. If she had, Bess would have seen the expression of total devotion—one that marked his enduring love for her.

Wolsey had developed the habit of eavesdropping as a child and had honed it into a fine art form later in his life. He stood hidden now behind the heavy crimson velvet drapery, tasseled in gold. It was the very shade of his own cassock, rendering him virtually invisible— or as invisible as a stout prelate in crisp, shimmering crimson ever could be. There was always a payoff for the objectionable practice of listening to others' conversations. That obviously was as true now as when he was a boy in Ipswich and he had discovered family secrets.

So then, the little trollop was about to give the king a bastard. What a terrible irony that would be if the child were a boy. He mulled the thought over. He felt compassion for the poor queen, with so many indignities and disappointments heaped upon her. Nonetheless, though he pitied Katherine, he realized she held no utility for him. And though he remembered Bess's kindness toward Gil when he fell ill, he knew Bess was even less useful to him. But what precisely was he meant to do with this kernel of information, the very thing they were about to entrust him with?

As Gil escorted Mistress Blount to the door and whispered something to her that he could not hear, the prelate's mind began to work very quickly. The ramifications of a royal illegitimate pregnancy, and what he might gain from it, filled his thoughts. The king had come to care deeply for Bess. That much he knew for certain from his one-time rival, Charles Brandon, from whom nearly any information could be bought since he now had a dowager French queen to keep. Henry was also disenchanted with the queen on many levels, and Wolsey could actually envision a scenario where the man behind the title would seek an annulment, follow his sister's lead, and marry someone beneath him for love—if the Bible could provide an avenue for that annulment, and especially if her little bastard were a son.

This could never be allowed to come to pass. Wolsey would have to see to that.

His ultimate power stemmed from his skill at diplomacy. Henry had come to trust that completely. If Katherine of Aragon were one day to be ousted as queen, a French, Italian, or German princess of Wolsey's choosing could be negotiated for the throne, thus his own power base retained. A wise match, well made, could secure him a high enough profile on the world stage, and thus pave the way for his election to the papacy once the old pontiff died. He had negotiated Mary's marriage to the King of France as well as the agreement for Henry's little daughter, Mary, and France's dauphin. He had crafted peace after the war of 1514. He needed one more shining accomplishment now, like a crowning glory, which the world could look upon favorably so that he might shine as the most likely papal candidate. Mother of Henry's child or not, Elizabeth Blount simply did not fit into any of the intricate layers of his future plans for himself. The child might not be a boy anyway, and then concern would be as pointless as intervention. Yet, if it were to be a son—the thing Henry wanted most in the world, the thing he needed—ah yes, that would change everything. Forever.

The wise man avoids evil by anticipating it. Evil, thought Wolsey . . . and defeat.

That night, Bess laid her head on Henry's bare shoulder and fingered the coils of red-gold hair on his broad chest as his breathing gradually slowed. The firelit bedchamber smelled strongly of beeswax candles, wine, and lovemaking, and it was all too strong now for her senses. Everything seemed to make Bess feel ill. She had tried a dozen times tonight to tell him about the child, but the words would never come. There would be no turning back, and both their lives would be changed forever once she did. The responsibility in that was overwhelming, and he had been so passionate tonight, so much more tender than ever before.

Then he had done it; he had whispered, "I love you," the thing she had dreamed for years of hearing, and her courage had slipped farther away. Pray God that Cardinal Wolsey had a plan once Gil confided in him. Her whole world, everything, was tied up in the two of them.

"Are you asleep?" she softly asked him as she glanced at the quarter moon through the window.

"No, just enjoying the dream this is to me." He kissed the top of her head tenderly and drew her closer against his chest. "When we are like this, I want nothing so much as to shut out the entire world."

Bess knew Henry's attention was taken up by the recent death of Maximilian, the Holy Roman Emperor, and his own ambitions to replace him. He could think or speak of little else at dinner, on their long walks, or here in bed. He had begun to campaign with other rulers for the honor. Five years earlier, Maximilian had been so taken with the young, dynamic king that he had spoken of even symbolically adopting Henry. Following Maximilian's death, memory of that intention was what first had put the notion of being emperor himself in Henry's head.

After all, a son was a son; he could become heir if need be, no matter how that came about.

As Holy Roman Emperor, Henry would be monarch of not just England, but all of Christendom. There was no greater power, no higher honor, in all the world. Henry was not only devout but an ambitious man, and if he wanted that, he knew Bess would want it for him.

"Go away with me," he bid her suddenly as she lay pressed tightly against him, both their bodies still awash in perspiration.

"What? Go where?" she said with a giggle, her face lighting at the prospect of the impetuous, slightly dangerous invitation.

"We are invited to Surrey, to Carew's manor there. I am advised that the locals have been preparing for the possibility since last spring. We could give them all a thrill."

"We?"

"Well, all right, I was invited," he conceded. "But you are a part of me now, are you not? And besides, would you not like to see Carew's wife again? The two of you were quite close once, as I recall. You must miss her."

Bess thought then how he spoke with detachment of Elizabeth as Carew's wife; yet she was a girl he had known intimately. She was not certain if it was a slight to Elizabeth or a show of deference to her. There was so much about Henry she had not yet come to understand. Bess shivered as she thought of his brother's cradle blanket, a memento he still kept. She thought of the gentleness behind that. Yet she could not forget that he had treated both Jane and Elizabeth with callous disregard when he no longer fancied them. Try as she might, with that knowledge in her mind now, Bess could not reconcile the two men she knew him to be. She secretly feared them both—even the gentler Henry, because that one could so easily bow to the other.

"I would like to see her, yes." Bess forced herself to say the words with a smile as she pushed away the disturbing thoughts. "If it would please you to take me with you."

Henry rolled on top of her, drew her back into his arms, and gazed down at her deeply. His eyes glittered in the candlelit darkness. "Everything about you pleases me, Bess; that is the problem."

"I love you, my lord, *all of you*. So the problem, I am afraid, is yours alone," she declared in a voice clearly marked by her devotion to him.

"What, I wonder, would my life have been like if I had met you before Katherine?"

"Your Highness would have met a very small child," she said with a wicked little giggle.

"You certainly could not have called me Hal then. But you must do so from now on."

He trusted her with so much. But would he still trust her, she wondered, as he began to kiss the slim column of her neck, when he discovered what she, Wolsey, Gil, and Sir William Compton already knew? Or would he become as cold as he was with Jane and Elizabeth?

When they returned from their trip, he would have to be told. But did she not deserve a few days' peace and a last bit of happiness before doing so? Bess decided swiftly that she did. The future was far too uncertain not to give herself at least that much before reality took over with a vengeance.

"He'll not want her once he knows," Gil declared as he sat across from Wolsey at the cardinal's carved writing table. It was at the same moment Bess lay in bed with the king.

"No, he'll not."

"She will be so hurt."

"Undoubtedly. They all are hurt in the beginning. And I am certain there will be others after Mistress Blount. But time does heal all wounds."

"Platitudes, Father? Even with me?"

"You know very well you are not to address me that way, Gilbert, not ever. And I speak with the sage wisdom and the gift of insight with which I address everyone. If that requires platitudes, then glory be to the Lord Almighty. You should be accustomed to that habit of mine by now, if not fond of it."

"I will want to marry her when the king is done with her, and she with him," he declared.

"Entirely out of the question," Wolsey grumbled, and cast down his pen. "Speak to me no more, ever again, of that foolhardy notion."

Chapter Twelve

December 1518
Beddington Park, Surrey

*B*ess withdrew swiftly from the horse litter and sailed into Elizabeth's open arms, the past, for the moment, swiftly forgotten. Elizabeth had been standing with her husband, Nicholas, in the courtyard of their impressive brick manor house on a broad expanse of green near the village of Croydon when the king's entourage arrived. Both Bess and Elizabeth clung to each other and wept like little girls as Henry and Carew embraced beside them, each man in finely embroidered doublets and heavy neck chains. A collection of household staff and townspeople stood in awe of the royal visitor in their midst after a month of preparation and anticipation. No one even seemed to notice that the king's companion was not the queen, so stunned they were that someone of such great import was here at last.

"It has been too long," Henry declared of his friend as he slapped his back affably.

"Your Highness," Elizabeth said properly as she dipped into a low curtsy in a gown of rose-colored damask dotted with pearls and trimmed with lace. It pooled at her ankles on the gravel beneath her dainty shoes.

Bess saw how formal they were with each other now. It was as if the former lovers were virtual strangers. Yet there was a civility, even a kindness in Henry's eyes as, at last, he took Elizabeth's hand and brought it to his lips for a brief, chaste kiss of truce. It helped to see that, Bess thought, and to know that perhaps bygones truly could be just that for the two of them as well.

They went inside together afterward, and the large contingent of Yeomen and other guards who had accompanied the entourage were posted outside. The manor inside was befitting a companion of the king, with its tall entrance hall paneled in dark wood, and massive staircase with an oak banister. Bess could smell the strong scent of beeswax, oil, and fresh flowers. There were sweet peas, columbines, and roses set out in great pewter dishes everywhere. She found it easy to imagine just how much work had gone into preparation for this visit, since her family had done nearly as much once, years earlier, when the Duke of Buckingham had ridden through Kinlet. And this was a reception for the king.

"Your home is lovely," she said.

"I miss court," Elizabeth countered. "Country life is so achingly dull."

"Then you must return. 'Tis not the same without you," Henry said with a happy smile. "Especially for Bess."

The two girls exchanged a little glance, the rivalry between them fully gone for Bess now in the face of the king's open devotion only to her.

They went together then into the great hall with another soaring, magnificent beamed ceiling. Henry and Nicholas sat in two tall upholstered chairs beside a roaring fire. Bess and Elizabeth took two needlepoint-covered stools opposite them as wine was brought on a grand silver tray by a servant dressed as formally as if he were at court.

"The townspeople have organized a grand banquet in your honor for tonight, sire." Nicholas smiled as he revealed the plan.

"I shall be pleased to accommodate them then," Henry replied, accepting a large silver goblet emblazoned with the Carew family crest. "It is a difficult thing to reject adoration."

"And you, Bess?" Nicholas suddenly asked, turning his attention to her. "Will you be up to such an event, or would a rest better suit you at this stage?"

Henry exchanged a quizzical glance first with Bess, then with Elizabeth. "And why would a rest better suit her? My girl here is the very picture of youth and good health."

"And yet surely it is not every day that a woman comes to Sussex carrying the king's child." Nicholas chuckled. "Or is that to be kept a secret from the others for a while longer?"

In the silence that quickly fell, Nicholas's glance slid from Bess to his wife, then to the king. His smile fell. "I assumed only since Mistress Blount was accompanying Your Highness publically that you—"

Henry shot to his feet.

Elizabeth gasped as Bess went very pale.

She did not have time to think of how Nicholas knew of her pregnancy. She was unprepared for the blow. Bess could not breathe. She felt the familiar nausea swell. The moment stretched on forever as Henry's gaze settled hard upon her. He was no longer smiling.

"Sire, I meant no harm, truly, only to share what my wife's mother wrote from court, which is becoming widely known in court circles. You do know how swiftly gossip there spreads," Nicholas rambled nervously, glancing back and forth.

"Is it true then?" Henry gruffly asked.

Nicholas and Elizabeth stood, then slipped together from the vast room. "Forgive me, Hal. I was afraid to—what I mean is, I did not know how to tell you. The time had simply never seemed right." Bess began to sputter as tears and a flush of panic colored her pale face. "I know it sounds foolish, unimaginable really, but I never once thought this would happen."

He touched her face gently with the back of his hand. The mood suddenly shifted. "Nor did I, honestly. The situation with the queen had made me think the time for children, for heirs, was nearing an end." Henry pressed his other hand lightly against her abdomen. "This *is* to be my heir, is it not?" he asked her with endearingly gentle concern.

"It could be no one else's but yours, my love," Bess replied with a tentative smile, brushing the tears with the back of her hand.

An instant later, Henry drew her against him and embraced her so forcefully that she could not breathe. But she did not care. "I am so sorry for the complication," she whispered, feeling the tears come again. This time there was no way to stop them.

"It certainly is unplanned, but not unwanted, sweetheart," he said. "A child of God, of ours, could never be that . . . if it is to be a son, *my son.* . . ." Henry, overcome with emotion, let the words trail off.

"He shall never be king."

"But he shall be as glorious and powerful as the King of England can make him."

"You desire any son that badly?"

"And his mother as well." He kissed her tenderly then, a light brush of his lips, like a small devotion. "Who at court knows of this? Did you write to the Carews of it on your own?"

"My Lord Compton and Cardinal Wolsey, only."

"Wolsey knows?"

"Well, the cardinal and Master Tailbois."

"Ah, yes." He smiled oddly. "Master Tailbois, who looks at you as if you are his."

"He is my friend, Hal. Only that. I knew not where else to turn."

"You could have turned to me, of course." Henry began to smile more broadly then, his joy outweighing everything else. "But Wolsey is a tolerable second. He is my friend, as Tailbois is yours."

"I shall accept that. Or try to. But the cardinal frightens me."

"Wolsey is not to be feared—at least not by you. You can trust him, too, Bess," he said, full of faith. "More than anyone else in my court, I trust Thomas Wolsey."

As the king and Bess dined with the Carews in Sussex that evening, Wolsey rode with great speed to Windsor Castle in the beating autumn rain to see the queen. He knew now what he must do to protect himself and his ambitions. Katherine was a part of that plan. Although the details were complex, and the plan would be somewhat distasteful to sell to a pious woman who still loved her husband, there was no other way—not if he ever had a chance of one day becoming pope. Power and position were everything for someone who had begun his life in obscurity. At the court of Henry VIII, there was no one more powerful now despite the eager contenders—including the king's mistress and her unborn son. No, he had no equal, and he had every intention of keeping it that way.

Wolsey nodded to the two guards posted at the intricately carved doors to the queen's apartments, then stepped inside, his flowing crimson cassock the only splash of color amid a room dotted with religious-themed tapestries, hanging crucifixes, and quiet women dressed in unadorned black, gray, or deep green dresses. When he found her, Katherine was sitting near a large window reading a prayer book. Thank the Lord there would be no need to finesse his way past the steel-tempered Doña Elvira today, he thought.

"Your Royal Highness," he said, bowing to her more deeply than usual.

After a moment, she looked up calmly, closed the book, and set it on her lap. "My Lord Cardinal. What brings you to Windsor? Has something happened to the king?"

"The king is well, Your Highness, but I do come on a matter of some urgency."

"*Por favor,*" she intoned, indicating the empty chair beside her.

Wolsey gratefully sat and drew up the heavy silver cross at his chest, placing it just beneath his chin. It was something he did at times when he needed to consider very carefully what he would say next. He knew he must be exceedingly gentle now, and that was certainly not his forte with regard to women—or with anyone, for that matter. Most of the time, he only played at the emotions others felt. He had found that a useful device.

Wolsey looked at her closely then, summoning his best expression of heartfelt concern. He pursed his lips with regard for her, lowered his eyes thoughtfully, then exhaled deeply.

"It is Mistress Blount, my queen."

Wolsey watched her expression darken as she steepled her simply adorned hands. Her eyes were discerning as she gazed at him, yet impossible to decipher at the same time. "Tell me."

"She is to bear the king's child."

He did not dare to move, or even breathe, as he waited for her reaction. Only then, once she gave him anything, could he know positively what to say next. "And you have come all the way to Windsor to bring me this news for some reason of value to you, I presume?"

"I have indeed, Your Highness. But the value is to us both. I have always believed in the maxim that one should keep one's friends close and one's enemies closer."

"That was one of my mother's favorite sayings."

"To vanquish an enemy, he, or she, must be dealt with as a friend."

"You have a plan in mind?" she asked, her voice very low, almost husky, and suddenly cunning.

"You cannot rid yourself of her just now when the king craves the fantasy of sons more than all else. But I believe you *can* alter the fantasy, which may gain you your desire in the end."

Silence fell between them then as Wolsey let his words play out in her mind without having to engage in the objectionable practice of spelling it out entirely.

"You propose to unseat one rival with another?"

Indignation flared strongly in her eyes with the question, and Wolsey felt a burst of respect for the queen Katherine of Aragon had always meant to become.

"Perhaps not so much to replace as put a new option more clearly before him," Wolsey clarified.

"Is there a distinction?"

"If Your Highness will forgive my being frank, once one has tasted the forbidden fruit, there is little hope of losing the craving for it. The king may believe he wants a son badly enough to claim a bastard, if it comes to that. But if we act in concert, we can see to it that the child is only ever that—a bastard."

"If I do not act, you believe the king might actually attempt to divorce me, or annul our marriage in favor of her?"

"Forgive me, my lady, but there have been whispers of those options for some time, and that was before there was the hope of a living child." His expression changed to display just the right amount of contrition as he shifted his gaze out the window and to the forest beyond.

He must give her time to believe the idea was her own.

"I knew from the first the Blount girl was a rival to be feared. Now she will truly be so if she bears Henry a son."

Wolsey saw her stiffen at the sound of her own declaration. He waited a moment to respond. "Not if his affections have been weakened while she has gone to childbed."

Doña Elvira appeared predictably before them then, and Wolsey waited in silence while the two women conversed in a low tone. He spoke not a word of Spanish, but he did not believe the queen had told her confidante why he was there, for Doña Elvira never once looked at him before she nodded, then retreated once again across the room in a sweep of severe black silk. A moment later, Katherine looked back at the cardinal.

"And now you shall tell me precisely how *you* are to benefit from this, why you brought yourself all the way to Windsor. And do not bother telling me, Cardinal, that it is your loyalty to me."

"It is not that alone, madam. I would not dishonor you with a lie." He pinched the cross at the point of his broad chest more tightly in order to pace himself. "It can be no secret to you that I am an ambitious man."

"Are your ambitions not alone to grow closer to God?" she asked judgmentally, arching a brow.

"Alas, my queen, they are. I wish—rather, I dearly pray—one day to be fortunate enough to be elected pope in order to glorify our gracious God. To do that, I must walk a thin line in diplomacy, not angering the French, the Italians, or the Spanish—that, for Your Highness's sake, of course." *Nor can I allow the king to waste a future match, which I would otherwise negotiate, on a country maiden like Mistress Blount*, he thought. "The world sees me as counsel to the king. If he were to divorce you and marry someone such as her, only because of a child, my own credibility on the world stage would be dangerously diminished."

"But a rival for Mistress Blount? Have you one in mind strong enough to unseat her, yet one who would not be my undoing?"

"I do indeed. I believe I know of the perfect girl for the temporary diversion we both require," Cardinal Wolsey affirmed with only the faintest glimmer of a smile.

Henry had told Bess that he was glad about the child. And after all, it was not a complete lie. Although the prospect of a baby changed everything, he was glad. While Bess and Elizabeth strolled in the gardens beyond the grand windows, he and Nicholas sat by the fire, drinking Rhenish wine from large tooled silver cups. They were trying to laugh and converse as if Elizabeth, and a royal command to marry her, had not long ago come between their friendship.

"I truly did assume you knew about the child," Carew finally said apologetically. "Elizabeth's mother can, upon occasion, be a bit more free with details than she should be. I remember that well enough."

"Bess said she was frightened to tell me, so you only did me a favor."

"Do you know yet what you are going to do, sire?"

Henry paused for a moment to watch Bess outside the window—lovely, smiling Bess, her face shining in a mellow ray of autumn light as the ermine collar at her throat fluttered gently beneath her chin. He never should have come to care for her. He should have taken her to his bed, but not to his heart. He was old enough to have known better. But it was too late for that now.

"She shall need to go away until after the child is born. It would be cruel to the queen otherwise. I would imagine Wolsey already has a place in mind."

"The cardinal knows as well?"

"Bess confided in him," Henry confirmed. "And even if she had not, he makes the workings of the court, and the country, his business, and I am glad of it. There is still no one I trust more. Except, perhaps, Bess."

"And after the child is born? What will happen then?"

Henry settled his gaze upon Carew, and only then did he realize why the courtier had asked. He believed it would end for Bess the way it had ended for Lady Fitzwalter, Elizabeth, and Jane Poppincourt before her. Carew assumed he would soon be casting her aside, and thus a suitable husband such as he would need to be cajoled and bribed into marrying another of the king's former liaisons. The difference was that Henry had actually fallen in love with Bess. And although he was not supposed to feel such things, the king was clearly ecstatic about their child.

"I have no idea what the future holds for either one of us, honestly, Carew," Henry said, feeling that his friend had an odd right to press him on this, so he did not object.

Nicholas Carew was a good man, an honorable man. Henry's sense of guilt over what he had asked of him, with regard to Elizabeth Bryan, was one of the factors in his visit to Sussex, a visit distinguished by bringing the most important guest his friend would ever be able to boast of to his neighbors in the coming years.

As Henry saw it, each had now done the other a favor.

The women returned shortly after that, and Henry pulled Bess affectionately onto his knee, which was covered in dun-colored nether hose of Burgundian silk. "Did you enjoy your walk, sweetheart?"

"The grounds are lovely," Bess said, her innocent face still lightly flushed and brightened by a happy smile.

Henry loved to see her like this, yet in some ways it made the guilt worse, since he knew, no matter how he spoke of divorce and annulment, or even dreamed of it, he could never make Bess a proper wife—not his own wife anyway.

Still, Henry thought as he drew her closer, trying to hold on to the last vestiges of their brief and bittersweet love, there must be a way to make this right. Yes, he must do that—for Bess's sake.

He was not a bad man, he told himself; he was just one who had learned well to understand reality, his place, and the heavy price of both.

PART V

Step. . . .

Time, which strengthens friendship, weakens love.
—JEAN DE LA BRUYÈRE

Chapter Thirteen

*H*enry Norris, a favorite Page of the Chamber, dark-haired and reed thin, scrambled down the staircase, taking the carpeted steps two at a time. Nearly tripping over his own slippered feet at the landing, he then broke into a full run down the paneled corridor beyond. He darted then into the warm summer sun and headed quickly toward the garden in search of the king. A moment later, out of breath from running, he swept into a low bow before the king, the sovereign's pretty, new companion, Mary Boleyn, and a group of his friends, who were all laughing and joking.

"I come with news from Jericho, Your Highness!" Norris announced in a breathy, excited voice that caused the king to glance up.

The conversation and the laughter around him fell away as everyone else looked at Norris as well. Henry released Mary's hand and slowly stood. Everyone surrounding the king, his most intimate circle, knew Jericho as the euphemism for the moated brick estate in Essex that the king kept in secret at a place called Blackmore. It was a romantic house on the river Can where Wolsey had recommended that Bess be taken six months earlier in order to wait out her pregnancy.

"Well?" he asked, eager yet almost afraid to know the answer.

"Would you not prefer to hear it in private, sire?"

"Anything you have to say these people can hear," Henry answered.

"The child is a boy, Your Highness. Word is, he is a strong child, too, with a healthy shock of copper hair."

Henry had not expected the news. Not once that he could remember in the past ten years with Katherine—the false hopes, the stillbirths, the deaths, and then the birth of their single living daughter—had Henry had the urge to weep. Yet he did so now, and the very last place he wished to show weakness was beside his latest dalliance. Mary Boleyn, with her round face and large, expressive eyes, was sweet, sensual, and certainly eager enough to please. Still, at the heart of it, she was not Bess. Henry had missed Bess these past months. He missed talking with her, laughing with her; he missed the needed escape that being with her had become for him when he faced so many ongoing challenges. But he had been able to make himself visit her only a month ago. Seeing her so heavy with his child had been a dose of reality he had not anticipated, and it had not gone down well.

As he moved away from his friends now, he could not stop himself from weeping. His tears were for dreams lost, for innocence gone . . . and for other things that could never be—things he might once have wished for but could no longer allow himself to covet. Hence, there was Mary Boleyn now—a buffer between his heart and the reality of his duty.

Mary tried to follow him, with her sweet, slightly vapid expression of concern, her silk skirts billowing behind her, but he waved her away with a swipe of his hand and his long, fur-lined bell sleeve. He had not so much betrayed Bess with Mary, he thought, as he had saved his heart, as well as his marriage. Bess would never understand that once she knew. The betrayal she would feel would be brutal. And he despised knowing he would be responsible for that. But she would recover. He would find her someone suitable, as he always did. Better yet, he would have Wolsey do it.

Wolsey always knew the right thing to do.

In the meantime, he really should see the boy—his flesh and blood; a son, at last. Or perhaps he should wait to see that the child remained a living son. There was always, after all, danger to be feared.

Bess's smile flashed in his mind. Then came the sound of her laughter. Guarding against the image and the memory, he pulled Mary toward him and began to laugh blithely at something Sir William Compton had said. Although he had no idea what that was, he must pretend. So much of his life was about pretending, after all.

He was the king's son, the vaunted male child, at last.

Five days after his birth, Bess still held tightly in disbelief to the fragile, glorious little creature who was hers, not quite prepared yet to surrender him to his cradle. And she could not quite stop staring. His little face was round, smooth, his features perfect, and the fuzz on the top of his head was the same copper shade as his father's. In some ways, it was like looking at Henry.

Bess's mother, Catherine, sat on the edge of the bed, watching them together. Her expression bore a mix of fear and pride as George, Bess's brother, grown almost to manhood now, lingered at the heavily carved footboard.

"Is he going to visit? It has been days."

It was clear to them all that George had meant the king. Bess narrowed her eyes on her brother in defense of the king.

"He is a busy man. He does have an entire country to care for, after all. I am certain he will come in time."

"Are you?" George moved a step nearer. His blond hair was now thick and full of waves, as hers was. His expression became very gentle then. "Forgive me, Sister, but they are saying he has taken a new mistress already."

"George!" said their mother, intervening with a growl of disapproval.

"'Tis the truth, Mother, and you know it as I do. Has she not a right to know what the rest of us know? Having her locked away out here is unfair to her!"

Bess shot her mother an anxious glance, praying she would find denial in the warm, maternal eyes she trusted.

"He would not do that to me, to our child. He loves me."

"I am quite certain the queen thought the same thing more than once," George put in. Their mother sprang from the bed and shot him a silencing glare in response.

"George, that will do."

His arms went out in pleading. "You would rather she be a laughingstock than face the truth, Mother? Has your love of the luxury and power that has gone along with her position so colored your perception that you cannot think clearly about the future?"

"She'll not have a future if any of us angers the king!" Catherine Blount cried.

So it was out between them, glaring, cold, but every bit the bitter truth.

When the infant in Bess's arms began to cry, Catherine called to the door for the wet nurse who waited outside.

"No, Mother," Bess objected in a tone of absolute determination she rarely used.

"And when His Highness comes, you will want him to see you like that? Nightdress open, milking the child like a Welsh sow?"

"This is the king's son," she answered indignantly, straightening her back like a board in response. "His Highness shall praise me when he arrives for not handing over my precious duty over his son to a stranger, and he shall do so with me looking spectacularly well, radiating from the experience, and ready to bear him another, if it should please him."

George and Catherine exchanged a glance.

"Well, what at least are you going to call the boy?"

"I shall let Hal decide that when he sees his son." There was an awkward little silence before she said, "I know he will come in time. I know it."

"Do you not even want to know who your rival is?" George pressed. "How on earth can you do battle with her if you do not know who it is?"

There was an uncomfortable little silence before she replied. "She might possess his body while I am away, but she is not my rival for Hal's heart. That much I trust, with everything I am."

"Seriously, Sister! Think!" George bid her pleadingly. "Do not be a love-struck fool! Did the king ever tell you that he loved you?"

"He did, once, yes."

"If it was in the throes of passion, that hardly counts," he said condescendingly.

"I know what the king said. I know what I heard," Bess persisted defensively. "He shall come. You both shall see. I am not wrong in this. . . . His Highness shall not forsake his son."

"But will he show *you* the same favor as the child?" Catherine Blount asked her daughter, giving in to her fear in the strained silence, where no answer rose to meet her question.

Wolsey rode beside Gil, horses paired exactly, harnesses jangling, yet he was careful not to speak. He could almost see the thoughts churning in the boy's head for the deep frown on his slim face. While he had never understood either Gil's or the king's attraction to Mistress Blount, Wolsey had to manufacture some sympathy for it.

The Lincolnshire forest through which they rode was deep, wooded, and filled with shadows and shafts of sunlight. Unseen birds trilled from the lacy branches above them, and the horses broke twigs and crunched fallen coppery leaves beneath them with their heavy, regular hoofbeats.

Once, long ago, he was the Dean of Lincoln, but Wolsey had not been back for a good many years. It had been even longer since he had seen *her*. The uncertain youth he had been was now well hidden beneath self-imposed layers of duty, ambition, and the heavy, powerful cloak of the clergy. Two months earlier, Wolsey, having been named papal legate, had come one step closer to his dream of one day becoming pope. His ecclesiastical power now, like his political influence, was unparalleled, surpassing even the influential Archbishop of Canterbury. The prominent jewels on his fingers sparkled in a shaft of midday sun weaving its way through the branches. He was really not so different from the king when he considered it all. Perhaps that was why they understood each other's weaknesses. At the end of the day, duty took the place of all else.

But as a youth, he had cared for her. Elizabeth Gascoigne . . . Her name moving through his mind was as lyrical now as it had been back then. Wolsey's attraction to the lovely blond, green-eyed Elizabeth had become love, but it had never been love enough to alter the path that lay before him back then. Certainly, though, it had been enough that he was honor bound to do well by their son— the first of his bastard children.

And so he had gone to the king five days ago and convinced Henry that he alone understood the dilemma, as well as the decision Henry was making in regard to Bess Blount. After all, Elizabeth Gascoigne had been *his* Bess Blount.

Duty and affection had led Wolsey to find a suitable husband for her.

And now he would do so, in kind, for the king's whore.

The brick Lincolnshire manor house up to which they rode appeared smaller now than he remembered it. But perhaps that was to be expected, considering the gargantuan size of his own prized Hampton Court. As he stood there surveying the property, and remembering, Wolsey let one of his own servants take the reins of his horse, then those of Gil's as well, and lead the animals together toward the smaller stables, which were to the left side of the L-shaped property, amid trees and thick shrubs.

He was oddly nervous as he drew off his tooled black riding gloves and broad-brimmed clerical hat and stood unmoving for a moment. At forty-five, Wolsey had changed a great deal, and he knew it. He had grown more stout with the years than he should have. His dark eyes had always been intense, but they were more so now, pressed into the fleshy folds of a fattened face that had deepened. Unlike the king, Wolsey despised physical exercise and grew tired just watching the sovereign strut about his royal tennis courts.

When she came to the door and ran with open arms toward Gil, Wolsey very quickly saw that she had not allowed the same fate to befall herself. After all these years, Elizabeth was still lovely. While her blond hair was not so bright as it once was, shot through now with a few early streaks of gray, she still possessed the same gentle beauty that had drawn him to her all those years ago. Her eyes were the color of jade, and her figure was as slim as a girl's.

It took her another moment, still smiling and embracing her son, before she saw him standing in the courtyard, arms falling limply at his sides.

"Your Grace," she said, falling to her knees before him, trying to kiss his ring, the crimson cassock a venerable barrier between people who once had shared love and a child.

"Now, none of that," he said, extending his jeweled hand and helping her rise.

"It is good to see you, Thomas," she said very softly and humbly with only the slightest hint of a smile.

"How is he?" Wolsey asked of her husband, a man he knew now to be fully ravaged by his decade-long struggle with dementia.

"George has his bad days, as well as his good."

"It is a blessing from our Lord then that he has you."

Wolsey realized only then that Gil was listening, watching, scrutinizing.

"I am glad you've come," Elizabeth Tailbois said in a gentle tone that drew Wolsey back across the years.

"It has been too long," he replied in a low voice.

They went inside then, and Gil left them at the table, already laid with their best pewter pieces and decanters full of Malmsey wine, to see the man he called his father.

Elizabeth and Thomas sat facing each other as her maid, dressed in plain gray cloth with an ivory apron, poured him wine, and then excused herself with a proper nod.

"Forgive me, I know 'tis nothing at all like the wine you drink at court."

"Yet it is pleasingly familiar to me just the same," he said.

"So there must be a reason you have come out here after all these years."

"There is. And yet seeing you should be reason enough. You have not changed at all."

Neither blushing nor smiling, she simply leveled her jade eyes on him. "It is not difficult to see how you have risen to such heights and so swiftly with flattery of that kind."

"You know me too well to argue that," Thomas conceded with a nod and a slightly impish smile as he drank more of the local wine. Seeing her again, he was grateful at the moment for its immediate and palliative effect. "The boy is going to tell you that he wishes to marry. 'Tis why we have come."

He could see that she was surprised. "Gilbert has not written to me of having a girl."

"That is because he does not have her. Not yet. At the moment, she belongs to the king."

He watched her sweet face go very pale, then judgment disturb her features. "My son wishes to marry a whore?"

"She is more than that. She is mother of the king's new son."

Elizabeth Tailbois stiffened. "God's blood, Thomas! You must tell him that he cannot! His life, and his reputation, shall lie in utter ruins!"

"The girl needs a husband, and the king needs an escape. Therefore it would be an honor. He wants to do this, Elizabeth." Wolsey reached across the table to take her hand, but she drew it sharply away.

She stood very stiffly, glowering down at him. "So, this is really why you have come then? To convince me to betray my son with a lie?"

"You know very well he is my son as well as yours, and I wish the best for him. Why else would I have brought him to court and kept him there as my own ward where he mingles with dukes, earls, lords, and countesses?"

"And whores? You cannot do this to him, Thomas!" she hotly declared.

"It is already done, I am afraid. Gilbert believes he is in love with the girl, and if she will have him, sooner or later, he *will* marry her."

"And the great Cardinal Wolsey benefits how from this abomination? Perhaps by being the one who rescues the king from his unfortunate indiscretion?"

"In part, yes. But it is to the queen's advantage as well, so I win all around," he replied, allowing just a hint of calculation back into his voice.

Gil came downstairs then, leading George Tailbois along by the arm. Gil was obviously grateful that his adoptive father had been returned home, not consigned forever to the hospital where Gil had seen him last. That was his mother's doing, and for the respect she showed a man she did not love, Gil had told Wolsey he would forever be awestruck.

George was a frail gaunt-faced man now, the shadow of his former soldier self, one who had once so proudly served on the battlefield in his dashing uniform beside the king. Instead, he wore a dun-colored tunic, white shirt, loose trousers to the knee, and plain black slippers as he padded toward the table. His dark hair was wild now from the hours spent in his bed, whispering to the ghosts of his mind, and the memories of his past that he tearfully swore to his wife were real.

His eyes were vacant, looking at nothing, as he came to his own dish loaded with food while Elizabeth angrily faced Wolsey. George did not seem to recognize the cardinal, his rival for the heart of the woman who sat between them.

A moment later, Gil sat down on his other side, then glanced up expectantly at his mother and Wolsey.

"Have you told her?" Gil asked, taking a cautious sip of wine.

"I have, my boy."

"Mother, please, be happy for me. I do not require your blessing, but I would very much wish it."

"Has this"—she paused intentionally—"this *girl* a name?"

"Elizabeth, Mother, like your own. But she is called Bess."

"And if she accepts you, what will you do with the king's bastard?"

Wolsey calmly intervened. "There have been no decisions yet made about that. It is early days. It is not even certain that His Highness will acknowledge the child as his own. And if he does not, her husband shall be called upon to step in."

"History does repeat itself," she shot back flippantly.

Gil placed a wide spoon in George Tailbois's spindly hand. "Does he remember me at all?" Gil asked his mother as she finally sank back into her chair, letting go of the worst of her anger and lifting her cup of wine. As she replied, she looked at Wolsey discerningly.

"Fortunately for your father, he lives mainly in a world of his own conjuring now, recalling very little of his former life, or ours."

Gil gently pressed the hair back from his father's face as he ate, then smoothed the rest of it down with tender little movements of his fingers, uninterested in his own meal, which sat untouched before him.

"He is missed at court," Gil said. "It is not the same without him."

"At least you have the good cardinal in his stead," Elizabeth retorted, the bitterness rising again in her voice. "I am certain someone as powerful as he is a comfort."

"This is my decision, Mother, not his," Gil said, defending himself.

"I am certain that it is," she countered. "At least in your mind, and that is really all that matters anyway."

Henry's mind was much too full. Along with Wolsey, he had negotiated the marriage of his little daughter, Mary, to the French king's infant heir, thus hopefully cementing, for England's sake, a lasting alliance between the two warring countries. But weighing most heavily upon him was the precious little boy in Jericho who was now ten days old—a boy whom he had yet to see or claim as his son.

Henry sat beside the queen, squirming in his chair like a boy, as his musicians played his own composition, his body and mind physically aching to be there and not here in the vast, cold music room at Windsor. Even the sound of his own tune, usually a comfort, grated in his mind as something he wanted to escape.

Jésu Cristo! Where was Wolsey when he needed the cardinal's good counsel so desperately? Gone to see to personal affairs, his servants had explained apologetically. Henry played with the fringe at his long bell sleeve, wanting desperately to rip the delicate thing apart as Katherine, drawn by his fidgeting, finally glanced over at him. She was smiling and nodding, enjoying the tune, until she saw her husband's expression.

After the performance was over and the polite applause of their guests had faded, Katherine rose in a dignified sweep of black damask adorned conservatively with pearls, and Henry rose with her. She was no longer smiling. They walked together out into the great gallery beyond the music room, and once the others were well behind them, Katherine spoke.

"You are not going to see her."

It had sounded something like a question, but it was very clearly a command, and Henry knew it.

"The child is my son."

"And I am your queen."

"One has nothing to do with the other, Katherine."

"On the contrary, they are intricately bound. If you go to that girl and her little bastard now, I shall write personally to the pope informing him that the King of England is unfit to be considered as next Holy Roman Emperor, and he shall never sanction it."

"On what grounds?" Henry scoffed, though seeing as he did that her days of silent acquiescence were over.

"On the grounds that you are a weak ruler driven far more by your carnal desires than by more clearheaded ambition. Have you learned nothing in all these years from Cardinal Wolsey? Your friend is a master at it."

His copper brows arched, and his lower lip dropped in an expression of disbelief. "You would betray me?"

"Only as you have betrayed me, *mi amor.*"

"What is it you wish?" he asked coldly, scowling now.

"Send her away. Marry her off. I care not what you do with her. Only do not bring this rival back into my household ever again."

"What difference does it make whether it is Bess who attends you, Lady Hastings, Mistress Carew, Mistress Poppincourt, or even

Mistress Boleyn, for that matter? Aside from Bess, I have never flaunted any of them in front of you. My liaisons have all been largely private matters."

"Because Mistress Blount is the only one who has claimed your heart, Hal. Now she is mother to the king's son. You cannot possibly expect I would welcome her back as one of my own ladies."

"My son shall not be denied by me, Katherine. I have waited too long for him."

"Your *bastard* son," she clarified in an accent that grew heavier with her anger, and the speed with which she attempted to banter.

"Just because Bess gave me the one thing you could not, do not seek to punish her now for that."

"I shall do whatever I must to vanquish a rival and to save my marriage."

Henry stopped near a tapestry of a hunting scene, hung on a heavy iron rod, his tall, taut body rigid with fury. "You cannot save something, madam, that is already lost to you."

Elizabeth Carew had heard the entire exchange as she stood a few feet away with Lady Elizabeth Howard, wife of Thomas Boleyn, waiting in the shadows of the paneled corridor to attend the queen. Both of them had pretended not to hear. It was the first time Elizabeth could remember being glad she was no longer the king's lover. She was glad especially that she was filled with her own husband's child, and not Henry's. She lived a life of calm predictability now, and she was almost happy. She did not adore her husband, or the life she had made with Nicholas, but at last Elizabeth had made her peace with it. She certainly no longer envied Bess for the uncertain future that lay before her, and she had stopped punishing her husband for not being the king.

It had taken Elizabeth a long time to stop believing she loved him. Henry was a powerful force for her heart to let go of. Distance and time away from court had helped. And somewhere along the way, she had actually come to care for, and at least respect, the man against whom she had fought so hard and had been forced to wed.

"She will not be back," Mary Boleyn's mother, Lady Howard, put in crudely, overhearing the same thing Elizabeth had. "Poor Bessie Blount," she mocked. "She appears destined for the annals of obscurity now, when once she showed such promise as a true courtesan."

Elizabeth shot her a censuring look as the king and queen walked farther away from them down the hall. But she did not say anything in response since, at the heart of it, she really could not argue the point. It appeared that while Mary Boleyn's star had begun to burn very brightly, Bess Blount's was destined now to fade gradually, and quite unremarkably away.

Chapter Fourteen

*B*ess and her brother George walked, arms linked, up the sloping lawn from the mossy bank of the small lake while their mother remained with the baby. After sixteen days' time, Bess craved a bit of fresh air, as well as a break from the duties of motherhood she found all-consuming. Henry might not have come, and she might have been cast over for Mary Boleyn for now, but Bess was too in love with her son to concern herself with any of that at the moment. From the very first instant the midwife had laid him on her breast, Bess's world had shifted. Her son was the love of her life, and having him with her healed a great many other wounds that nothing else ever could have.

She saw the horses in the distance as they came into the courtyard, banishing all thoughts of that. She knew by the livery and the large group of riders that the sizable cortege had come from court. Her heart quickened with the realization, and she gripped her brother's arm more tightly.

"Stay calm now, Bess," he bid her. "It'll not do to have you full of expectation. He is married, after all."

"I knew he would come," Bess said softly, her heart filling once again with every bit of the love she had so long felt for Henry.

No one understood what they meant to each other; how it was when they were alone together, in spite of everything that was against them. And their son, the image of his father, was a reminder of that. She began to walk more quickly up the little flagstone path, the warm summer breeze ruffling the hem of her dress. George strained to keep up with her as Bess broke into a run then—until she saw him. *Them.* Her guest was not the king after all; instead, there were two guests, Cardinal Wolsey and Gil Tailbois.

When Gil saw her approaching, he called out to her with a wave. Bess forced herself to wave back, because it was not his fault that with every part of herself she wanted him to be someone else.

"You look wonderful," he said happily as they embraced, his lanky body pressing fully against her.

Bess smiled at him in response, then turned and dipped into a low curtsy before the cardinal, who stood stoically, silently, and, she thought, formidably—a stout, towering sight in his bright crimson cassock and biretta.

"You did not write to me that you intended to come," she said to Gil.

"I thought it better to surprise you. But Cardinal Wolsey did write to your mother of our intention to travel here."

Of course her mother would do that—try to make Gil's trip into some romantic and heroic rescue of a maiden in distress now that there was a child involved. Was that not why he had brought the cardinal to accompany him here? No matter how much she cared for Gil, and his friendship, Bess had grown. She had matured these last years. She had come into her own, and she did not plan to be pawned off by anyone against her will as Elizabeth Carew had been—not even by the king's command.

"May I see him?" Gil asked of the baby who still, sixteen days after his birth, had yet to be named.

They began to walk together up to the large carved-oak entrance of the king's secret house. A royal servant silently opened the door for them, and they all passed by without acknowledging him.

"I would like you to see him," Bess answered, meaning it. It felt important to her that at least someone who cared for her had taken the time to come here when the king had not. "He is absolutely gorgeous, Gil; you'll not believe it."

"He is your son. That surprises me not at all."

He gently pressed a hand against her back to guide her up the stairs. After everything, she thought, he still cared for her. After six years of trust and dear friendship, she was not certain why that surprised her, yet it did.

"He sleeps well already and eats just like his father," Bess happily reported.

"Then he had better become fond of a sporting life, if he does."

Even Wolsey chuckled at that.

They found the baby asleep in a cradle in Bess's bedchamber and Catherine Blount reading from a prayer book as she sat in a chair beside the cradle. Seeing Wolsey, Bess's mother immediately stood, then dipped into a reverent curtsy.

"It was good of Your Grace to make the journey here."

The prelate advanced, then hovered over the sleeping infant for a moment. "He is indeed the very image of the king."

"It is a disappointment that His Highness has not come here to see that for himself," George put in.

His mother swatted at him, and yet the words could not be unspoken.

"His Highness is very busy presently, especially with planning the upcoming summit with France to solidify the peace."

"Yet it is said that he finds time for Mistress Boleyn," George persisted.

The cardinal frowned at him, and there was a sudden awkward silence. "What is your name, young master?"

"I am George Blount, Your Grace. Bess is my sister."

"Then you have defended her honorably. See only that you do not overstep your bounds with your ambition to sound clever."

George had no choice but to acquiesce with a silent and deferential bow. Wolsey went downstairs, with Catherine and George following behind him, and Gil remained behind. He was happily transfixed, it seemed, by the infant whose deep, beautiful Tudor eyes had opened and seemed strangely trained upon Gil.

"May I hold him?" Gil asked.

"I am surprised you would want to do that. He is another man's son, after all."

"But you are his mother, and that shall always be what makes him special to me."

She felt a twinge of guilt, just as she always did, knowing that he felt emotions for her that she could never return. Still, he was her dear friend, and he had come out here when Henry had not, she reminded herself again. She owed him some gratitude for that.

Gently, she drew the docile child from his cradle and handed him to Gil.

"Pray God, I do not break him!" Gil smiled in awe as he carefully cradled the infant in his gangly velvet-sleeved arms.

"You'll not. You are far too gentle a soul to ever hurt anyone," Bess said sincerely.

She watched him more closely than she had intended to as he pressed his thumb across the baby's cheek.

"Marry me, Bess."

He had blurted it out so suddenly that she was certain at first that he had not meant to say it, and she felt a burst of pity for him. But then he turned his earnest gaze upon her.

"I would be a good father to the boy, and I would try with all my heart to make you happy. Although I know it is doubtful that you could ever actually love me, in time, you might find, as Nicholas and Elizabeth do, that—"

"Oh, dear." Her lower lip turned out a little, and she struggled not to frown or do anything that would make him feel rejected. He was making her such a wonderful offer, but her heart still wanted Henry so badly that she could not allow herself even to consider accepting it.

"Gilly, my friend, my dearest friend, please understand that I cannot."

It would never be an ideal situation. She knew that. Bess was not a fool or an innocent any longer. But she did not quite believe that Mary Boleyn had fully replaced her. There was still enough of the romantic child left in her to believe in him and his past declaration of love. Until the day came that she learned otherwise, if it ever did, it would not be fair to Gil to use him that way.

"Very well," Gil said with a sad smile, as if he had expected it. "But if you change your mind, you know where to find me."

"I thank you, more than you know."

He handed the child back to her then, and after she had returned him to his cradle, Gil drew a small velvet pouch from his doublet.

"If you would not mind, I would like to give you something anyway."

Bess glanced up at him, uncertain of what to say. His kindness made the guilt of rejecting him that much worse. "Please. I want you to have it," he urged, handing her the pouch. "It belonged to my mother, given to her many years ago by a suitor she did not marry either."

Hesitantly, Bess drew out a delicate ruby and pearl pendant. It was so exquisite, so delicate, that she actually gasped. It was far too detailed and valuable to have been given by any country squire to a lady. There had to be an extraordinary story behind it.

"I cannot accept this, Gilly. It is too precious."

"I have waited years for the right time to give it to you. I tried once, long ago, but I lost my courage about it, so Wolsey has kept it for me since," he said with a chuckle, and she could tell that he was trying to put her at ease. Still, she could see his devotion to her behind the easygoing smile, and there was something incredibly heroic in it. "It was to be your betrothal gift, if you accepted me. But I think now it shall make an even better remembrance for the birth of your son."

Bess wiped away the tears in her eyes, despising herself a little for not being able to love him the way someone so honorable very richly deserved to be loved.

"Try it on?" he urged, moving the drape of her cap and clasping it at the nape of her neck. "Ah, there. Exquisite, you see? Just as I knew it would be."

"You really are too good to me."

"True," Gil returned with a sly little crooked smile that made her chuckle.

It was much later that day when Cardinal Wolsey called for Bess to come and speak with him in the apartments he had set up in the Priory of St. Lawrence with the monks. Going to him was, of course, designed to give him the advantage. She had learned that much from her years around the powerful prelate, but now she was in no position to contest his demands.

She was shown alone into a room, stark by contrast to what she knew him to inhabit at the various other royal palaces. Wolsey was sitting in an imposing, straight-back black oak chair beneath a forbidding tapestry depicting David slaying Goliath, hung on a heavy black iron rod. Wolsey was reading from a prayer book, bound in crimson leather, a color that matched his cassock exactly. At first he did not look up despite the swishing sound of her heavy silk dress.

"Your Grace," she finally said, dipping low into a curtsy.

It was another moment before he granted her the favor of glancing up.

"Ah, yes. Mistress Blount." He said her name in a perfunctory tone as he casually set down his book. "How are you faring these days?"

"I am quite well, Your Grace."

"It seems childbirth agrees with you."

"As motherhood does."

"That is certainly a far bigger role, one best overseen by a child's father."

Bess narrowed her eyes at him, feeling a new yet strong maternal flicker of suspicion.

"I intend to be a devoted mother to my son, Your Grace, in spite of who his father is."

"I am told you have refused a wet nurse."

"It is my duty, as well as my pleasure, to feed my son myself."

She could tell she had surprised him, because he paused for longer than he ever had in speaking to her. Thomas Wolsey was certainly not known for ever being at a loss for words.

"Very well then. We shall take it all a day at a time, for now. As I am certain you know, the boy needs a name."

"I am waiting for the king to decide that," she countered in a brittle tone.

"And indeed he has, Mistress Blount. I have been sent to see to the child's christening. Your mother has called to court for Lady Exeter, your cousin, to come and stand as godmother. I have been appointed by His Highness as godfather."

"When will the king be arriving?"

Wolsey's lips tightened as if he were forcing back a smile. It was, she thought, an oddly cruel reaction as he balanced his chin on a jeweled finger. "I'm sorry, Mistress Blount, but His Highness will be unable to attend the christening, as he is quite occupied right now in dealings with complications over the betrothal of his daughter, the Princess Mary."

Bess felt her own lip quiver, fending off tears. The king was giving in to the very world from which he had always sought to escape with Bess. As Wolsey stared unblinkingly at her in the echo of his announcement, she thought he was almost daring her to cry. But she was too proud.

"And the name the king has chosen for our son?" she asked, steadying her voice by squeezing her hands into fists hidden by the folds of her skirts.

"He is to be christened Lord Henry Fitzroy."

She knew that Fitzroy meant "son of the king," and Bess felt herself confused by the contradiction. Henry was going to bestow that dignity on their child, yet he could not be bothered to attend the christening to see his son, or her?

Anger, hurt, disappointment—all of the emotions wound themselves tightly around her heart then, squeezing tightly. Did Henry actually mean never to see this son he had so longed for? Was this grand honor given only in order to allay his sense of guilt?

"I see." She struggled to respond, feeling that if she said more, the cardinal would actually see her heart breaking.

It was her own fault. She had been a fool. Bess knew that. She had meant to try to become a rival to a queen. This now, apparently, was her punishment—or at least a part of it. She could not bear just then to imagine what more might be in store for her.

Her family stood around her in the nave of the Chapel of St. Lawrence, a show of great support for a young woman who was weakened and wounded. But, for her son's sake, she must not let it show. For him, she must learn swiftly how to survive this and thrive.

The vaulted nave was drafty even for July, and Bess felt herself shiver. She watched silently then, feeling helpless as Wolsey took the baby and held him gently over the baptismal font so that the prior could pour the warm oil on his head.

"In nomine Patri et Filii et Spiritus Sancti . . ."

The chanted words echoed through the vaulted nave as she felt tears behind her eyes once again aching to fall. *You should be here,* she urged silently, angrily, to her son's father. *You may not owe me anything, but you do owe him that.*

Bess glanced over at Gil who stood beside Wolsey. Her friend was the second godfather to the king's son. She studied him more intensely in that bittersweet moment than she had in a very long time. It surprised her to see pride so well-worn into his once-youthful expression, maturing his face, as he looked down at the child, silent, precious, and full of innocence in Wolsey's arms. Bess had not understood it before this moment. She had never taken the time to see it. But Gil's love for another man's child was unconditional. The moment she realized it, she felt light-headed, as though she had been struck. It set her off balance, and for a moment she could think of nothing else.

After the service they went outside, and Bess was quickly warmed by the summer sun, and by the reassuring feel of her child back in her arms. This little boy was her lifeline no matter what else happened. He would keep her strong and make her heart safe again. She had every intention of doing the same for him. Bess gently brushed a finger across his cheek. In response, he opened his eyes, yawned, then looked up at her. He had impossibly wide, trusting eyes. From pain and disappointment, she thought, came enormous joy, and that would be enough.

There is no fear in love; but perfect love casteth out fear.

The passage from John ran through her mind then, because she knew the baby, whom she intended to call Harry, was an example of absolute perfect love. She would protect that, and him, no matter the risk.

As Wolsey introduced George and their parents to the prior, Bess went to Gil who was standing alone near a splashing white stone fountain. It struck her symbolically as it had in the chapel that he was here once again for her, while Henry was not. This time the realization was even more profound than the last, and she felt everything shift. It was the right thing to do. She knew that now.

"Hold him?" she asked with a tentative little smile.

Without hesitating, Gil drew the baby back into his long arms and cradled him expertly within the reassuring folds of his puffed slashed silk and velvet sleeves. When he looked down at Bess, she said very softly and simply, "If there is still an offer, I would be honored to accept and to marry you."

She would grow to love him in time, she told herself even as he gazed down at her with an easy, confident smile, as if he had known this was meant to happen all along. A real, secure, and loving family as she'd had was what was best for Harry—what was best for her as well. It was even what was best for the queen, who did not deserve an unfair advantage from the mother of the king's son. It was best for Henry, too, that she bow out of his life.

At least, that was what she told herself as Gil pressed a tender kiss onto her cheek and smiled. "I thought you would never ask," he said.

Chapter Fifteen

*H*enry ultimately lost his bid to become Holy Roman Emperor. Like the legitimate heir he had so craved, this was the loss of yet another thing he desired but could not have. Instead of England's king, in June of 1519 it was the queen's own Spanish nephew, Charles, who was elected. The ruling powers that threatened England were now this new emperor, Charles V, and the new French king, François I. François had previously turned away from attempts at an exclusive English-French alliance, even the betrothal of their children, in favor of an alliance with this new young Spanish emperor.

Wolsey had convinced Henry that making peace with France or Spain now in order to keep England safe was more important than ever. Because he could not bear the thought of the rival who had beaten him, Henry chose to try once again to align himself with François. The cardinal's intense negotiations at last led to a planned meeting between the two young rulers to be held near Calais. Henry's bravado got in the way nearly as much as François's did. For months, like two peacocks in a yard, the two sides leaked details about the grandeur they each planned to display to impress the other. In addition to vast pavilions and tents to house the events that would take place, the English court even brought a temporary palace constructed of timber and canvas. No amount of opulence was to be spared. But no matter how much Henry planned to spend on great lengths of costly gold cloth, jewels, jousts, and lavish banquets, the one thing he did not have was an heir to match the two that François and his queen had already produced. Adding insult to the injury of being rejected as Holy Roman Emperor the year before, Henry had been given the honor of being godfather to the French king's second son.

It seemed to him a taunt that François had even named the boy Henry.

"But Your Highness does have a son," Wolsey reminded him.

"For all the good the boy does for me, out there in the Lincolnshire countryside with Bess and that lad of yours she married."

"Surely Your Highness recalls that the Tailbois family is a venerable one. A sound match was made for your son's mother."

"And what advantage does that bear me, given that I have never even seen the boy? How old is he now?"

"Lord Fitzroy is a year old next month, sire," Wolsey answered calmly as the king's agitation grew.

Henry cast down the pen with which he had been signing documents all morning, as a warming gold sun streamed in through the diamond-shaped panes of window glass, one ornamented prominently with a red Tudor rose. "I should see the boy," he declared suddenly.

"Your Highness chose not to do so in the past, in order to give Lady Tailbois time and distance to settle into her new circumstances."

Hearing the reminder, Henry laid his head back against the chair and sighed as he looked at the cardinal. "How is she, Thomas? How is she truly?"

"Gilbert writes to me that she is well, and expecting a second child."

He tried not to feel the little wave of jealousy again, but, for a moment, it was impossible to press back. He had let her go, fully and completely, more than a year ago now, but that had not stopped him from missing her or thinking about her nearly every day since. Bess had always deserved better than what he could give her, and so he had forced himself to let her go and he would keep to that. Their son was another matter. The approaching summit made that more pressing at the moment.

Among the hundreds already slated to accompany the French king, no doubt François meant to parade his heir, and the son who bore his name, to Calais in order to taunt him. All along, Henry had planned for Katherine and Mary, his own sister, as well as Brandon and Wolsey, to join him, so why not *his* son? He had acknowledged the boy, named him, and dared to begin hoping a son of his might actually grow to manhood.

Little Henry might not be the queen's progeny, he silently reasoned as he sat slump shouldered at his writing table, but he was a natural child, a boy, to hold up to François in less than a month's time.

"I want to take him with me to Calais," Henry firmly announced.

Wolsey paused, and for a moment it did not seem he was going to answer. "She and the boy are close, sire. I visit often, and I can see that she has been an extraordinarily devoted mother to him."

"Then it is my turn to be a father to him."

"But Your Highness, the queen and her retinue are to attend you in Calais."

"My wife knows I have a son, Wolsey," he said with an irritated snap.

"If you will forgive me, sire, oftentimes 'tis one thing to know something and quite another to be faced with it head-on."

"Well, unlike the others, this son of mine is meant to survive, and the queen seems to be unable to produce any sort of competition, so I intend to bring my son into my life, and honor him as the rightful and acknowledged son of the king."

"You would tear such a small boy away from his mother, sire?"

Henry rolled his eyes peevishly. "For a cleric, you have such an overly dramatic way of stating your case, Wolsey. . . . No, I do not intend that. At least not initially. The boy may return to Lincolnshire after Calais. Besides, from what you say, his mother is soon to be taken up with the birth of her next child. I would be granting Lord and Lady Tailbois a favor by giving them time with *their* child once it arrives."

"If you truly intend to do this, sire, then I shall ride to Lincolnshire with you. It may make the transition a bit easier for the boy's mother," Wolsey carefully offered.

"Oh, I do not intend to go myself, not with Bess half gone already with her husband's child. That would seem inconsiderate of me, as well as exceedingly awkward." Henry pushed back his chair, stood, then walked slowly to the window, below which he could see the queen walking hand in hand through the knot garden with their four-year-old daughter, Mary. *If only you had been a son at last*, he thought of the little girl with her mother's dark hair and strong features. It was that absence that plagued him, the void in his life that was coming ever strongly to define him. But, praise God, there was Henry Fitzroy now, tangible proof that he was not a failure. He *must* have that at any cost.

"I am not certain I should go in your stead, sire. The boy is yet small and accustomed to the care of a woman."

"Then send Mistress Carew. Bess will trust her."

Wolsey's eyes widened incredulously. "But, Your Highness, they are friends. Can you ask one dear friend to take a beloved child away from the other?"

"As you wish. Then send someone less fond of my son's mother. Lady Hastings or Lady Fitzwalter, perhaps," he countered belligerently.

Wolsey cringed at the suggestion. Then with no other choice, he nodded his acquiescence. "As Your Highness commands, I shall go to Mistress Carew at once," he said.

After nearly a year's time as mistress here, Goltho Hall in Lincolnshire, with its warm brick facade and climbing pink roses, felt truly her home, from the manicured gardens, the special Belgian carpets Gil had insisted she buy, to the staff she personally had selected. On their wedding day, he had told her he meant her to be comfortable here; he was, as in all things, a man of his word.

Bess watched Harry sitting on a blanket in the corner of her bedchamber with Mistress Fowler, the nurse she had selected on her own for her son from a dozen candidates.

Antonia Fowler was an attractive, childless butcher's wife from the nearby village of Kyme. She had won the position over the stern objections of Wolsey, who had argued valiantly that someone from court needed to attend the child.

"The king should concern himself with his daughter. Harry is my worry," Bess always replied. Eventually with Gil's support, the cardinal gave up the argument.

Bess stood watching the child from a place near her bed as Antonia pushed a ball toward him and he giggled in response. It was such a blessing to see that Harry was happy, she thought, already feeling the weight and responsibility of the child she was carrying. And she planned to make the full experience of her next lying-in very different than the last.

Here, Bess refused to bow to the custom of darkening the bedchamber and lighting it with candles only before the child's arrival. She felt better even now, moving around with the windows thrown open, so that was what she did. Her parents had gone back to court last year, so there was no one here to tell her to do otherwise. And though her household servants often raised a critical eyebrow behind her back, no one dared contradict Lady Tailbois, to whom each owed his position. Nonetheless she found it could still be lonely at times, pacing the floors of these rooms with only her own thoughts and the sound of her shoe heels on the inlaid wood to keep her company. She then went to her son, who looked more every day like his father, and bent over to draw him into her arms.

"Oh, my lady should not!" Mistress Fowler declared. "The strain could be dangerous to the babe."

"It would be more dangerous if I do not hug my son at just this very moment." Bess smiled happily, pulling him close enough to smell his sweet baby skin and the faint scent of rose oil that had been combed through his coils of red-gold hair.

"Ma." He giggled and poked a finger between her lips.

Bess pretended to bite him in a playful way but then kissed him instead. It was their little game.

A firm knock at the door brought the tender moment to an end. "You have a guest downstairs, my lady," said the servant dressed in gray trunk hose and a doublet.

Bess handed Harry back to his nurse. But she always did so with a strange hesitation, as if it might be the last time. "Did you not say, as you were instructed, that your mistress had begun her lying-in and so does not receive guests at present?"

"I did of course, my Lady Tailbois, but your guest has come from court."

The announcement that once had made her heart race now brought dread. She did not wish to hear news of court from anyone. She could not bear to hear how happy the king was with Mary Boleyn, in spite of his marriage—and Mary's.

The last time she'd had a visit from court by her mother, Bess had been unintentionally tormented with lurid details of how, even though Sir William Carey had been called upon to marry Mary Boleyn, the king's affair with the Boleyn girl continued long afterward, and still did now. There were even whispers that Mary was with child not by her husband, but by the king. The thought of Mary sickened Bess as much now as it had then.

Henry had meant none of what he had told her. In the end, she was just another pawn; just another expendable beauty. Her childish dreams of Lancelot were an embarrassment.

Before she could object further, she heard Elizabeth Carew's sweet soprano voice float like music into the bedchamber before Bess even saw her. "Look at you!" she exclaimed, her embroidered blue gown sweeping across the floor. "Should you not be reclining at the least?"

"I feel better when I stand, so I stand. It is a blessing to be able to decide things for myself." Bess smiled back, embracing her friend whom she had dearly missed.

"Well, at least sit with me while I am here, will you? So that I do not end up feeling responsible in case something were to happen."

Gil lingered at the door, proudly watching his wife. It was the same expression he had worn on his slim, beardless face every day since they had married, she thought. And it was becoming more difficult every day not to love him just a little bit for it.

"You did not write that you were coming," Gil said as he moved nearer and joined them in the small sitting area lined with books and a collection of polished cushioned chairs.

"There was not time. I only spoke with the king yesterday."

"The king?" Gil asked, and Bess watched the happy, proud expression on her husband's face disappear swiftly. "What has he to do with your visiting my wife?"

Elizabeth looked dignified and very adult to Bess now as she sat between them. Her gaze slid from one of them to the other as her own smile fell. It was a moment more before she made the announcement.

"I am to bring his son to London. His Highness wishes Lord Fitzroy to accompany him to Calais in three days' time for his summit with the French king."

Bess felt dark bile rise up from the pit of her stomach, and she tried hard to press it back down. "No."

"Please understand, Bess," Elizabeth said gently as she reached out a hand to Bess's arm, which had tightened as she clutched the chair. "I was not to present it as a request."

"He means to rip my son away from me now after a year's time when he has never so much as come to meet him?" She sprang to her feet, then faltered, so that Gil went to her side.

"Nicholas and I are to be a part of the entourage, and Harry knows me," she offered hopefully.

"Not well enough. No. I shall not allow it!"

"He has authorized me to show you this. It is a proclamation stating that the town of Rugby shall become yours, along with all of the titles and proceeds therein," she said as she tentatively handed her a scrolled paper, stamped with the king's large red seal. "It is a great honor."

"I desire nothing from him now," she raged, full of indignation.

"With or without it, I am commanded to take him, Bess."

"Over my own dead body."

"Bess, I beseech you, there is a contingent of the king's guard downstairs. We are not to leave Lincolnshire without the king's son."

"*My* son," she declared, her high voice breaking with emotion.

"He will be returned here by month's end, Bess. The boy has a right to know his father."

"Harry *has* a father!" she cried out on a choking sob, clinging to Gil and feeling the weighty press of her second child as she did.

The world was turning. Her head was spinning too fast. She could not catch her breath. All Bess could think of, all she could feel, was the prospect of the unendurable nights without her child— her precious son, safe here beneath this roof with her.

Part of her, buried deeply inside, had always known a day like this might come, but as the months had passed, Bess had dared to believe that the king had moved on, not just from her, but from the greatest tie between them.

"You . . . must take his favorite little ball." Bess wept brokenly now, the full force of what was ahead of her descending, the words across her own lips making it horrifyingly real that her child, her heart, was about to be taken from her, and brought into the world of the king—the very center of privilege and power—and she was powerless to stop it. And this was only the beginning of the sacrifices that lay ahead of her to make. She knew the time had now come to pay God fully for what she had done to the queen.

Katherine knelt alone in the dark shadows of early evening inside the king's privy chapel of cold stone. Beneath her unadorned black gown she had taken to wearing the hair shirt of the Order of St. Francis to increase her discipline and self-punishment. She knew she would be left safely alone here since Henry would be with *her*— Anne Boleyn: temptress, beauty, thief. One Boleyn sister had not been enough, so now these past weeks he had begun to show favor to the other. Yet Katherine had realized she could work with Wolsey to put a dozen ambitious girls like her in that place, and, at the heart of it, none of them was the mother of the king's only son. Damn her! Bess Blount remained a rival miles away in Lincolnshire, even now, a year later, because of that boy he had found the gall to call Henry. *Be careful what you wish for*, her father used to say. How fateful were those words, Katherine thought now. She had prayed and prayed that Henry would be given the joy of a son, and so he had. Now her husband meant to bring the little love child into her very midst, into her own household, and parade him proudly about like the great long-sought-after prize. Katherine knew it because she knew Henry. She alone knew the depth of his longing for the son she had been unable to give him.

He had loved her once. He had been faithful once . . . but none of that mattered any longer. Nor would it ever again. Her humiliation was nearly complete.

Katherine lowered her forehead against her icy steepled hands again and closed her eyes. There were not enough prayers in the world to ever take away the damage Bess Blount had done to her marriage, by her fertility alone. The vindictive side of her against which she now prayed, and for which she suffered the discomfort of the hair shirt, was glad that the Blount woman must live with the knowledge that, as Katherine had been replaced, now she as well had been replaced by the beautiful Boleyn daughter, who had more ambition and hubris than either of them.

Tonight the child was to arrive here, and Katherine had been warned that Henry meant to show him off to the entire court. A banquet was to be held in the boy's honor. And because the French ambassador was present, Katherine was being commanded to be present for the abomination as well.

She had always understood that natural children were the likelihood of a sovereign king who dallied with other women. But poor little Mary, four already, was the child of her heart. She was a true Tudor heir. Still, Henry spent only as much time with his daughter as he must—whatever decorum dictated, and little more. There was a part of Katherine now after all these years that, God save her, made her glad she had not given him a legitimate son. She was glad she had denied him that greatest satisfaction even though it had been her ultimate duty to do so.

Doña Eliva Manuel brought a hand to Katherine's shoulder then, breaking the moment and terminating her repetitious prayers.

"The boy has just arrived, Your Highness," Elvira whispered in Spanish in the nave of the hollow stone chapel. "The king sent word that he wishes you to come and join in welcoming him. Shall I present your refusal then?"

Katherine breathed a heavy, steadying breath and tipped up her full chin proudly. She made the sign of the cross over her chest, which had become more broad and flat with the years. Then she gripped the top of the prayer kneeler. This was certainly not the first bit of adversity she had faced in her life; and, doubtless, it would not be the last. She was a Spanish princess, she reminded herself with steely determination, accustomed to facing challenges head-on and enduring them with grace. She would not insult her beloved mother's memory by displaying anything less than that now. If Henry wished to flaunt his love child before everyone at court, and he wished her to be a part of it, she would give him his desire; the final victory still would be hers. Katherine alone was his wife until death, and therefore Henry would never have a legitimate son, no matter how he pretended otherwise with his whore's boy. One day her daughter, Mary, would rule England as queen, just as Mary's grandmother had so proudly ruled Spain. The hope for a Tudor king was dead with Katherine's own dying fertility, and just now Katherine felt like celebrating with a bit of strong wine. If it appeared she was toasting the little Fitzroy bastard in their midst, she thought, so much the better.

"She is exquisite," Gil exclaimed with tear-filled eyes focused on his daughter, who was only minutes old.

"She has your eyes," Bess wearily observed, her face still glistening with the perspiration from childbirth as she proudly watched.

"So long as she does not have my nose, she will be blessed since you are her mother."

"Harry will adore her, do you not think?" she asked, aching for her other child in a way she had never believed possible. It was as if a part of her was actually missing in his absence. "How long has he been gone? It feels a month's time already."

"Only three days, my love," Gil replied tenderly. "But he shall be back with us before you know it."

"I *do* know his loss already, Gil, and I ache for him so desperately. I am not whole with him gone. Every night since he was taken,

I wake and think I hear him calling for me. Even this precious little girl cannot change that," she said, cradling her newborn daughter as her eyes filled with tears at the overwhelming emotions she felt.

"The king will be good to Harry, you shall see." Gil tried to reassure her, nestling in gently beside her and pressing the wet blond hair back from her forehead.

"Why did he wait so long to see him then if he truly cared for my child?"

"Wolsey says it is because he lost so many others in his life. It is said the loss of his brother was the most difficult to bear and changed him most. He is hesitant about whom he loves now because of it."

She did not want to believe anything tender about Henry any longer. She wanted to have the hardened heart she felt for him, since it was what had helped to lessen the pain of his betrayal. Yet Bess could still not stop herself from remembering the little child's blanket unearthed so long ago, and the way the man beneath the crown once had trusted her enough to confide in her about it. Had even that been a ruse to seduce her into their affair?

Bess despised herself now for how much she had so naively loved him.

She took Gil's hand then and squeezed it to chase away her thoughts. She was happy now to be his wife; happy to have found this life when once it was the last thing she thought she desired. Theirs had never been a romance, but rather, a slow and steady kindling of affection and trust, and now, after all these months, Bess believed she loved her husband—not passionately, perhaps, but steadfastly and enduringly.

"My love, we must make a decision soon about Rugby. The town and the manor there will be in need of direction soon."

"It is payment for my son, Gil. I cannot take that."

Gently, he rubbed her temple and prepared to reason with her. "This house has been in my family's possession for more than a hundred years, and it will always be our home. Doubtless, Harry will receive advantages from his father as he grows to manhood. Accepting Rugby is something we could do for our daughter. It could be her dowry since, if we are blessed in time with a son, Goltho Hall will be his. Should we not give this precious child as close to the same advantage Harry will have, if we can?"

Bess was silent for a moment; then she turned her lower lip out in a little mock pout. "I really do despise it when you make sense."

"Elizabeth deserves this, Bess," he lightly insisted. "The king wants you to have it, and I want our daughter to have the best I can give her."

"She has a name already?" Bess smiled.

"It could be no other, my love, than your own."

"How do you know the king will provide for Harry? He has not shown much of an interest until now, after all."

Gil glanced down at his daughter, her eyes wide and inquisitive upon him. "Because now I know what it is to be a father. There is nothing I would not do for my child. I am certain once the king sees his son for the first time, his life will be changed forever, just as my own now has been."

Henry's green eyes shimmered with tears as he knelt in the courtyard before the now-toddling boy, dressed in his best little black velvet trunk hose, doublet, and white collar to meet the king, an ensemble so small a child would never have worn otherwise. *God's blood!* It was not just himself the boy resembled, but Arthur.

He had planned so many things, dreamed of them, before this moment. He had meant to declare to the boy that he was his father. He had intended to embrace him. Now all Henry could do was stare with awe at the little wide-eyed child, his own heart cut open and raw now by the startling resemblance to his beloved brother.

"Do you see it, Mary?" he asked his sister, who stood behind him with her husband, Charles, as the little boy held fast to a nurse's hand. Mary herself was pregnant with her fourth child and full of the emotion that family connections brought. Henry knew she understood how much he had longed for this moment. It felt safe having her here as the tears came.

"I am Henry," he finally said gently, afraid to move a muscle nearer the boy who looked positively dazed by all of the eyes upon him, and the unfamiliar adults crowded around. "You're called Henry, as well, are you not?"

He watched the wide green eyes, fringed with long lashes, suddenly glisten with tears as well, and the little rosebud of a mouth begin to quiver in response.

"Ma," he said very weakly, barely managing to utter the word.

He stood as bravely as could a child his age, yet still the tears fell in two long ribbons down his full ivory cheeks at the mention of his family left behind.

"Ah, well. My family has always called me Hal, but I think I like Harry much better."

When he noticed his son transfixed by the heavy gold medallion hanging across his ornate doublet, he drew it off without a thought and carefully placed it over the little boy's head.

"There now, that looks splendid." He smiled. "Bring a looking glass!" he bellowed, and there was a great deal of scurrying behind him to comply. "Would you like to see?"

Harry nodded and wiped his own tears clumsily with the back of his small hand.

"I received that from my father after my first military battle," Henry explained, sharing a deeply held memory he knew the child could not possibly understand nor would he ever remember. "Having to meet all of us at once like this certainly qualifies as your first great challenge. This shall mean absolutely nothing to you, but I have wanted to meet you since the very day you were born."

The mirror was brought then and held before the child, with his downy soft mop of copper curls. He began to smile just slightly at the grand, glittering jewel weighty across his chest.

"You cannot have meant to give that to him, can you?" Mary asked her brother as little Henry Fitzroy, every bit his father's son, began to admire his own reflection.

"Why not? It shall be his one day, after all."

"And if the queen bears you a son?"

"Have we all not given up *that* ghost by now?" he shot back coolly.

"I do not suppose Katherine has."

"Then that is a bad bit of fortune for her."

"Mama?"

The small voice before them was clear in its request and interrupted their bickering as the king and his sister looked back down at him in surprise.

"We are going to Calais first, my boy, to show you off to the King of France."

Harry's lower lip began to quiver again. "Mama," he repeated in a more desperate tone

"*I* am your—"

Mary's fingers pressing into his shoulder stopped him from

letting the final word fall from his tongue—at least for now. Mary had warned her brother when he came seeking her counsel on the matter that delicacy with a small child was of the essence.

He stood slowly and turned to his sister. "It is just not right. He should know who he is. He should understand his role," he whispered desperately to her.

"He is only a small child, Hal. He shall understand in time, if you do not quite frighten him to death first," she whispered back.

"What can I do?"

"Why not show him the aviary? It is an amazing place your daughter has always loved. Then after that, perhaps your marmoset and the dogs?"

"Of course." He smiled and kissed her cheek. "Thank you."

"No thanks required. He *is* my nephew, after all." Mary smiled back at him. "I want Harry to be happy for as long as he is with us."

"Oh, he is not returning to Lincolnshire," Henry firmly declared. "A son of the king must be brought up at court, being properly educated and trained for the role ahead of him."

"Role?" Mary asked with a note of surprise. "Hal, he'll not succeed you as your heir."

"And yet he is the son of the King of England, acknowledged and so named. There shall be titles, grants, gifts, and, when the time comes, an important match to be made, possibly even a strategic one. I waited too long for a son, Mary. I'll not let this one go."

In the silence broken only by the sound of the swish of her skirts, she led him a few steps away from the boy, who stood looking at them quizzically as the strangers they were to him.

"Wolsey promised Lady Tailbois the child would be returned to her by month's end," Mary said.

"He should have made no such promise," Henry snapped.

"The cardinal had no reason to believe otherwise, Hal, since the child is a year old already and this is the first interest you have ever shown in even seeing him."

Henry walked to the window, braced himself on the sill, then looked back at his son, who was being spoken to quietly by Charles Brandon. A giant of a man like the king, Brandon had knelt before the boy and was showing him the jeweled scabbard he had drawn from the hilt on his jeweled belt while brother and sister spoke in low tones.

"Every single waking hour since I knew he had drawn his first breath at Jericho, I have longed to see him, to hold him in my arms, and to make him my son," Henry declared passionately.

"Then why did you not?" Mary asked him.

He closed his eyes for a moment before answering. "For Bess's sake, of course. She was in love with me, and I knew it. I used her badly, Mary. I was selfish and cunning, knowing just exactly how to win her. And then, somewhere along the way, I know not even where, I truly began to care for her. And that caring became love. It was not the same with Lady Hastings, Jane, or Elizabeth. It is not the same now with Boleyn's daughters, willing as they are."

He glanced at his small son again, already the haunting image of Arthur. "Perhaps I was idealistic. I know not. I was definitely foolish with Katherine and her expectant tear-filled gazes as well as the constant praying, damning me to hell. But I came to feel a fool for Bess. . . . For a moment, Bess, I suppose, was like starting over. God help me, but she loved me, and I allowed her to love me." He drew in a breath and exhaled it deeply, looking back at their son once again. "Letting Bess heal from that injustice . . . Giving Tailbois a chance with her heart . . . Those were the only honorable steps to take."

"And not tempting your own heart in the bargain?" she gently asked with a knowing tone.

"Selfish again, I suppose."

"Very. But I do understand."

"You are probably the only one who does. Bess quite likely despises me now, and she will despise me even more when she learns about the boy's future. But she has just had another child already, and she and Tailbois will have their own sons in time. It seems with Katherine, however, that I shall not have any more chances. Unless perhaps she were to die and I could marry again, Harry shall be my only son. He is my hope, my legacy. . . . He is Arthur to me."

"Should you not go to Lincolnshire and reason with her yourself then? Perhaps that way she will come to understand the things that a life at court can provide for him that she and Lord Tailbois never can. She will want that for her child if she knows how much we all will love him," Mary proposed with hope as she, too, looked back at the little boy, the essence of innocence, mingling brightly there with his Tudor heritage.

"I have never been so instantly in love with anything in my life as I am with that child," Henry said. "Bess is the one who brought that precious gift into my life, and I shall be forever grateful. But I cannot risk the pleading I know I will hear to dissuade me from my course. Wolsey is better at all of that. Besides, he is quite unnaturally close to the Tailbois lad. It shall be easier on them both coming from him, of that I am certain."

When she saw the cortege of riders this time, and a banner from court, Bess gasped, then cried out. She knew the king would not be among them, but she no longer cared whether Henry was in her life or not, so long as their son was finally returned to her. It had been nearly a month of silence and waiting. The hours had become days, and those had stretched into eternity as she worried after Harry's eating, his sleeping, and whether he missed her even half so much as she missed him.

Gertrude, her cousin, had sent her a letter from court a few days earlier about the meeting of the two kings in France at what had been called the Field of Cloth of Gold. She knew Mary, the king's sister, had been a guest, as had Thomas Boleyn and his two daughters, Mary and her younger sister, Anne. There was a time, nearly two years earlier, when she would have envied anyone who had been asked to attend that sort of important and sumptuous event—and she would have felt contempt for her successor.

Now all Bess wanted, all she craved, was her son, and to see the little boy's first meeting with his new baby sister.

As all of that played across her mind, Bess could not help herself. Seeing the riders in her courtyard from her window upstairs, she drew up the sides of her dress and bolted like a child herself down the grand carved oak staircase. Mistress Fowler and her own lady's maid were already there with Gil and Cardinal Wolsey as Bess burst into the sun-splashed courtyard. The shocked expressions on all of their faces stopped her.

"What is it? What is wrong? Where is my son?"

She looked at each of them in turn and felt a swiftly escalating panic.

"Where is Harry?" Bess asked her husband, because he was the one who, she knew for certain, would tell her the truth as always. He was the only one in the world whom she trusted now.

In response, Gil put his arm around her and drew her against himself very tightly. When no one spoke, Bess tried to pull free so that she could find the little child among the tangle of adults getting off horses, out of carts, and milling about. But Gil only held on to her more tightly, bracing her.

"Harry is to remain at court," he said very gently. "The king feels it would be best for his education and—"

Bess's legs began to go weak. She could not breathe until she heard her own horrified gasp. "The king *feels*? To the devil himself with what the king feels! What the king wants! Harry is *my* son!"

"And his," Wolsey added stoically, speaking out for the first time. "Keep in mind, it is indeed an honor, my Lady Tailbois, to have a natural child who has been acknowledged by the king himself."

Bess began to sob as indignation crawled up through her like a black, evil thing. "He would not *dare* to deny Harry, especially when he is his own mirror image!"

"And that, perhaps, is the point. Harry is every bit the king's son. He wants the boy with him," the cardinal calmly countered. His tone was controlled, and as condescending as ever, she thought through a blaze of her own fury.

"Well, he cannot have him!" she sobbed with open defiance. "The great king can play with my heart as he pleases, but not with our child's. Harry needs his mother. No one will know how to be with him as I do. He needs things—favorite things only I know!" she cried out as the desperation took her completely over and she crumpled against Gil like a rag doll.

Wolsey took a step nearer, the movement stately, grand, and forbidding in the sweep of crimson silk. "Forgive me, my lady," he said, "but it is already done. In time the king shall know those things as well. It is his will."

"No! God in heaven, no! He cannot have Harry and my heart as well."

Bess could not breathe; she could not reason. Each heartbeat in her chest felt like the blow of a death knell, and it was so because, with her child's loss, her own death could not be very far away.

A moment later, her legs gave way, and Bess collapsed into the biting gravel and a swirl of dust, everything around her going as black as the death she feared.

PART VI

Step. . . .

There is no fear in love; but perfect love casteth out fear.

—1 JOHN 4:18

Chapter Sixteen

*T*here were five winters more, and as many summers, before the worst of the pain of Bess's great loss eased even a little. There were two children to follow after Elizabeth. First, a boy called George was born after Harry was taken to court. A second son, called Robert, arrived shortly after that.

When Harry was first taken, Bess could only exist by the hour. Gil rarely left her side in those early, dark days for fear she might do something desperate. It helped when, through his emissaries, the king recommended Bess's two brothers, George and Robert, go to London to live as companions to their royal nephew and, thus, to offer Bess reports more unbiased than Wolsey's might have been concerning her son's progress. In her mind, Bess silently thanked Henry for the gesture, but her wounded heart, still full of the child's loss, was not fully ready to forgive.

From George, Robert, and Cardinal Wolsey, Bess learned that Harry was accorded every possible dignity and, in fact, far more than most Englishmen considered reasonable for any natural son of the king. Henry doted on his now six-year-old son by establishing for him his own household, staffed to the brim with servants, tutors, a nurse, and his two Blount uncles; surrounding him with luxurious carpets and furnishings; and stuffing his wardrobe with opulent costumes.

George sent letter after letter detailing the fine Spanish silks and Burgundian velvets Harry was afforded and how well he could already speak Latin and French. Gradually, Bess began to see, through the filter of her own grief, the advantages her sacrifice had provided.

One sunny spring afternoon, she stood back a few feet, watching with a mix of pride and wary curiosity as Gil and Wolsey embraced in the grand open doorway to their home. The cardinal always came with news from court, and this time would likely be no different. They had learned during his last journey that the king's affair with Mary Boleyn had ended entirely at last. Most at court believed Mary's two children to have resulted from this relationship. Curiously, however, Henry did not publicly acknowledge them.

It was so different from how Bess and her son had been treated. Perhaps, Wolsey had supposed, it was because the king had now entirely set his sights on Mary's younger sister, Anne, and did not want to endanger his courtship with one sister by formally acknowledging the affair with the other. It was a sordid business from which Bess felt very far away now—just as she did from the competition, danger, and the grandeur of court life.

After Gil and Thomas had embraced, the portly cardinal turned to her. Smiling warmly this time, he kissed her cheek, then held her arm in a fatherly gesture before they went inside.

"Tell me first any news you have of Harry," she excitedly bid him, the animosity between them all but dissolved now. "Is he eating well? How is his health? You never write to me with nearly enough details of his life. I want to know everything!"

"He does tolerably well. He is a tall, healthy-looking young boy. In fact, I have brought you something by order of the king, to prove it."

The king. The sound of it still had the power to wound her. She leaned a little nearer to Gil in response once they sat together in the cozy nook near the fireplace hearth that was brimming with fragrant summer flowers rather than fire on this warm summer afternoon.

Wolsey drew open a leather satchel he carried and brought out a miniature framed in gold leaf, studded with small pearls and emeralds. "It was painted last month at Richmond when they were all together there."

"All?" Gil asked protectively on behalf of his wife as she took the miniature from the cardinal and gazed down at the image she knew without needing to ask was her son. He had been painted in a boy's white cap and an exquisitely detailed lace shirt. She could see Henry in him instantly, but he had her brother George's eyes more obviously now.

"His Highness, the boy, Mistress Anne, and her father, Sir Thomas Boleyn, primarily," he finally answered, and with great hesitation.

"I see," Bess replied coolly, feeling the edges of her calm beginning to fray slowly.

"Remarkable that the king thought at all to send a picture to his son's mother when he is so occupied elsewhere," Gil said defensively.

"On the contrary, he thinks of you often, my lady. I know because he speaks of you regularly, and still quite fondly."

Her eyes searched his face for truth as he sat stiffly in an uphol-stered wood chair, hands curled over the arms. Wolsey had changed, Bess thought. He was older now and even more stout, and his face had wizened. Lines and fleshy folds made him more endearing to her. He was someone she had come almost to trust for his connec-tion to Gil, in spite of how he once had not seemed to care for her.

"He makes certain that the child writes to you often. I am to report to His Highness personally of it weekly."

"How generous of him," Bess responded, unable to keep the sour note of sarcasm from her voice.

"You are, of course, invited at any time that might suit you to visit him."

It was an offer the king always extended, and one she always declined. With three small children, Bess saw that her greater duty now lay here. She was certain Henry knew that, and this likely was why he extended the offer in the first place, she thought with a little more animosity than before.

It was a game of bluff for a child they both wanted.

And there was something more. Bess was not certain she was strong enough yet to see Harry again, even if she did go. Her heart, her joy, her love, she thought, glancing down again at the painted image, wide-eyed and half smiling, in that comfortable regal way.

"In the meantime, however, I have come with other news." As if sensing her hesitation, Wolsey added, "This news is quite extraordi-nary. I know you and Gilbert shall be most pleased."

He drew something else from the satchel. It was a document sealed with red wax stamped with the king's personal seal. He handed it to Bess, but, when her hands began to tremble, Gil took it from her and broke the seal with his thumb. She watched his eyes widen and his lower lip drop open in shock.

"The king has made Harry a duke!" Gil declared with incredulity as the paper fell from his hands and drifted down onto his lap.

"And an earl as well," Wolsey calmly added. "Your son is heretofore Earl of Nottingham as well as Duke of Richmond and Somerset."

"He is a six-year-old child!" Bess gasped, looking back and forth at each of them.

"He has also been granted appointment as Lord High Admiral," Gil read on incredulously.

"The king wishes there to be no question in the court, or in the country, as to the high regard in which he holds his son. Those titles elevate him to the second most powerful position in all of England."

Bess was on the edge of her seat, glancing back and forth to the miniature in her hands and then to the cardinal and her husband.

"He cannot make Harry his legitimate heir," Gil said, intervening, "so he is doing the next best thing."

"Precisely," Wolsey replied with a nod. "The king has not always behaved wisely in his personal dealings; he is well aware of that. But our sovereign, while a fallible man, is a pious one as well—one who places honor very highly, just as his father and brother did before him."

"Is Harry still happy, though? Is he allowed opportunities just to be a little boy with all of that heaped upon his shoulders?" She heard her voice break, as she ached to know.

"Your brothers take him daily either to play his favorite game of shuttlecock or primero, and when he is with the king, they spend hours making games with all of the maps they both so fancy."

"I did not know he could play a card game like primero," Bess said sadly.

"He is a growing boy with a sharp mind, swiftly changing," Wolsey carefully told her.

"We do appreciate your always coming here, Thomas, asking Bess for her opinions on decisions about the boy," said Gil, intervening again when Bess was no longer capable of speech. "It is very good of you for both their sakes."

"You are like my own family, both of you," the cardinal replied, keeping the full truth just out of Bess's reach, for decorum's sake. Yet he had clearly grown fond of her through the years and let go of whatever judgments had fueled his condescending behavior toward her early on.

"The queen cannot be happy about this," Gil said. "A natural child with so many honors and privileges bestowed upon him right in her midst."

"I would suppose it is torture for her. But the queen is a woman whose faith has long sustained her, since the king himself no longer can."

Bess felt a spark of guilt hearing that, knowing what part she had played. She could tell herself she had been young and innocent, but at the end of the day she had done it more than willingly. She had wanted him. She had wanted what had happened, and more.

Katherine ached for the days of Bess Blount.

It was the same sensation she'd had many times these past few years when she was faced with this new rival for her husband. The following winter became a spring five times over, and she watched her husband walk hand in hand down in the garden below for what she knew would be the last time she ever would have to witness it. And for that alone she was grateful.

Anne Boleyn had managed a great deal in the years she had come to possess Henry's heart. Knowing the evil temptress for what she was, Katherine very nearly hoped that somehow the Blount girl and her little bastard boy would triumph over Anne, even now. At least Bess was an enemy she knew. Of course, Henry meant to divorce his queen, no matter how fiercely Katherine battled against it. He had given up trying, and waiting. He had made that abundantly clear. It was why today she was being sent away.

Poor Hal. He was such a fool for love. He always had been. But there was something. A last glimmer of hope, Katherine thought, even as she watched them now, arms around each other, warmed by their heavy layers of rich velvet and priceless fur as they paused beneath her window. Why had Hal lavished upon his son all of those unbelievable honors five years earlier if the rumors were not true? Were the dukedom, the earldom, the palaces, and the important posting as Lord High Admiral all the first steps in seeing the now ten-year-old Henry Fitzroy made heir for lack of a legitimate son? That Rome would ever grant Henry an annulment seemed increasingly unlikely, since Charles V, the Holy Roman Emperor, was Katherine's nephew, and the emperor ruled Pope Clement. But even if Henry did receive an annulment, there was no guarantee that the little Boleyn she-devil would be fertile.

Katherine bit back an uncharitable smile. One thing was guaranteed: If Anne Boleyn wanted her husband, she was going to have a royal fight on her hands, particularly that hand with the evil little extra finger. Katherine had certainly suffered rivals before, and she knew precisely what to do, if not to win, then at least how to make her rival's life a living hell of waiting and indecision. And in the end, without a divorce or an annulment, Anne Boleyn would be unable to marry Henry and become queen.

But there was another pressing matter. After Katherine was banished, she would need a well-placed ally who would remain here and see, by whatever means necessary, that Henry Fitzroy did not become heir in place of her own daughter, Mary. She needed Cardinal Wolsey. Yes, Wolsey was duplicitous, self-seeking, and ambitious to a fault. That went without saying. But, outwardly at least, he was also a pious man of God. Plus, there was something else that might well motivate him to help her cause.

Katherine had long heard the whispers, as everyone else had, that there was more between the great cardinal and the young Baron Tailbois than just a relationship of master and ward. Thus, there might be some secret loyalty to Bess Blount's bastard son she could use as motivation as well.

She watched with an oddly voyeuristic interest then as the king's favorite horses were brought and one of his dearest friends, Nicholas Carew, joined him. Anne and Henry were laughing now, so carefree. There would be a price to be paid for that, Katherine knew, but what it would be, only time would tell. It was the first time in all of their married years that Hal had left one palace for another without bidding her farewell, if for nothing else than polite courtesy. Apparently, for her resolute refusal to divorce him, he would no longer extend even that.

His silence now spoke volumes. Anne Boleyn believed she had won. Henry believed it, too. What would happen next, only time, and God, would tell.

"I wish to stop on the way to Woodstock and visit with my son," Henry informed his party of elegantly dressed riders, guards, and servants, as they set off on horseback, trotting away from the great palace of Windsor.

Anne Boleyn, cloaked in elegant velvet and ermine, and a

matching hat that framed her striking face, began immediately to pout.

"But we have just seen the boy," she declared with a petulant whine. "I do not fancy that diversion at all, my lord."

Henry cast a glance across at her as they rode beneath heavy branches blanketed with snow. Only a shaft of winter sun that broke through the gray canopy of clouds warmed them all.

"That was an entire month ago," he reminded her.

"Truly, it feels like only yesterday," she sniped.

"'Tis your duty to join me silently and proudly, Nan."

"Other women's children are tedious creatures. And Richmond is not your proper son anyway," Anne taunted him dangerously.

She had Henry twisted in knots and well she knew it. So did he, but he felt powerless against it, and against her. Finally it seemed he was meant to pay fully for toying with women's hearts by having his own heart toyed with this way, like a cat with a mouse. Passion and frustration mixed daily with pure delight inside him so that he could think of almost nothing else but having her for the challenge she presented. He had certainly met his charming, arrogant match in Anne Boleyn. Henry still was not certain that he actually loved her—not as he had once loved Bess, or even Katherine. But his powerful, unrequited passion for the proud, clever girl he called Nan certainly eclipsed everything else in his life at the moment.

If only Anne would surrender herself, finally he would be able to see if this power she had over him was simply lust or if it was truly love. He had certainly never let anyone speak to him as he had Nan, or withhold so much, reducing him one day to a raging bull and a teary-eyed boy the next. He had grown a beard because Anne fancied the French style over the English, cut his hair short, and begun dousing himself in ambergris exclusively because she said the fragrance excited her more than any other. Henry knew he was pathetic, but he could not stop himself from wanting the challenge. He lusted for her, carnally, powerfully, and completely. Until he had her at last, she was the absolute master of his soul, and she well knew it.

"He is my son, Nan, and if you ever truly expect to be queen, you shall learn well to honor that," he said, trying his best to sound commanding with her.

"Perhaps she wisely tolerates him, but a queen does not *honor* a bastard. Katherine certainly exemplifies that."

"You would be wise to leave Katherine out of this."

"She had better be well out of it. You told her to be gone by the time we returned to Windsor, did you not? You know I shall never warm to the notion of anything intimate between us with her always there, watching us," Anne warned, her high voice going suddenly low.

Henry rolled his eyes, trying in vain to steel himself against the lure of her body that she kept always just beyond his reach. "I'll not hold my breath," he said, bristling, as they wound over hills and through pastureland covered in dirt and melting patches of snow. "You have made me wait five years already with little more to show for it than a stolen kiss."

They rode out ahead of the others, and Henry was glad they could not be overheard for the jangle of silver harnesses. It was unseemly for a sovereign to be so manipulated, and he knew it.

Sensing that, Anne leaned over and ran her hand down his forearm with a deliberately slow sweep. "Well, once Katherine is gone for good, there are certainly things that I can do, that we can do, to . . . satisfy you. At least until the divorce is secured."

"You still plan to make me wait to have you?" he growled, tensing in his saddle.

"I'll certainly not end up like Mistress Blount or my sister," she haughtily declared, drawing back her hand sharply as the sun went back behind the clouds.

"Best to leave Lady Tailbois out of this," he warned, growing angry at how easily Anne could play him.

"And why would I when you bring her son into it every single day of our lives? I shall bear you sons when I am your queen, Hal, but I'll not stand for their being anywhere behind the Duke of Richmond in the line of succession."

Henry ran a gloved hand behind his neck, feeling tense and irritated suddenly. He did not like thinking about Bess—certainly not when he was with Anne. It had been the same with Mary Boleyn. And he certainly did not like threatening references to his son's mother. It may have been nearly eleven years since that final weekend with the Carews, when he had allowed himself the excitement of a man in love about her pregnancy, but in some ways that felt like only yesterday.

There was little he did not recall about Bess—the sweet, gentle sound of her laughter; the light fragrance of rose water in her hair; the sensation of her adoring wide-eyed gaze fixed upon him; or how it felt to have her touch him so wantonly as she had learned to. He closed his eyes for a moment to vanquish the images. The memory was more difficult to let go, and he breathed a small sigh that he knew Anne did not hear because she did not care enough to perceive subtleties. They continued over a vast hill, and a broader patchwork of snow and dirt, and she began to chat with one of her attendants.

If it was possible for a man to love two women, then Henry did, although in very different ways. And there were moments even now with Anne beside him, when part of him regretted he had not considered divorce for Bess's sake as he now did for Anne. After all, Bess had already given him her body, her heart . . . and his son.

He had loved Bess Blount, yes. But a child had been a complication. His queen had seemed irreplaceable. Back then much had seemed impossible. . . . Now he glanced at Anne. Beautiful, brash, demanding . . . unattainable, and he felt a moment's fear for what lay ahead if he were actually to be granted the annulment by Rome. Henry could hardly see past his craving for her, and he knew it. Yet now, in this instant, with her disregard for his son so fresh in his mind, it was all so clear. Henry shook his head. It was pointless. Bess was another man's wife. He had done all he could to honor and care for her, for her husband as well, by making Tailbois a baron, and for their child—his own precious son. Yet how different might their lives all have been—the fleeting thought came to him when he heard Anne's hollow laugh—if he had met Bess, not when he did, but rather when he had met Anne Boleyn. . . .

Chapter Seventeen

April 1530
Goltho Hall, Lincolnshire

*H*e had been ill for three days. Now, as she sat at his bedside, Bess had begun to fear the worst. The weakness, the fever, then death. If anything should ever happen to Gil, she was quite certain her own life would come to an end. After two decades, first as her dearest friend, then her husband, Gilbert Tailbois was her soul mate. It had taken three perfect children and a contented life away from the temptation of court to realize that. She had been a fool. She had wasted too much time; time she could never regain.

She held his veined, limp hand now and watched him sleep, content to see the reassuring rise and fall of his chest as heavy snow flurries and a harsh wind pelted the bedchamber windows, shaking them and turning the sky gray and bleak outside. A fire nearby in the grand stone hearth warmed the room and steamed the diamond-shaped panes of leaded glass. Their children came in and out of the chamber, offering her support and inquiring about their father's condition. His physician did the same, but Bess would not leave his side.

"You really should get some sleep," Gil said weakly, startling her because Bess had not known he was awake. She leaned nearer and caressed his cheek. There was still the raging fever that would not break. But at least he was awake and speaking enough so she could hold out hope that he would recover from what the physician gravely told her was most probably consumption.

"Do you think perhaps we should send word to Wolsey?" he asked his wife then.

Bess stiffened in response, refusing reality. "Why would we trouble the cardinal with something so minor as a temporary malady? You, of course, are going to recover any day now, and he has his own critical circumstances with which to deal at the moment," she gently reminded him.

And that was an understatement. From such a mighty height, Thomas Wolsey had fallen far this past year when Anne Boleyn successfully convinced the king that it was due to Wolsey's poor negotiating skills that the pope had refused to grant an annulment so that Henry could marry her instead. Impatient with not getting his way, and eager for a scapegoat, Henry had stripped his old and dear friend of his palaces in London and Hampton Court as well, and there were whispers now that Anne was urging that the cardinal be tried for treason.

"You do know that he is my father," Gil mouthed very softly.

Bess had always suspected it but never knew for certain. He and Gil were so alike in certain ways, and the cardinal had always been fair with her, if a little brusque in the beginning. Now she understood fully why Wolsey had made the effort. He had done it because his son loved her. Through the years, he had written directly to her of Harry's progress, keeping her involved, giving her detailed accounts of his health, his education, and asking for her counsel in decisions that concerned the young duke. She often wondered if the king knew of her involvement in their son's life, but she never asked because, at the heart of it, she could not bear to lose what little she had of her Harry. Yet never a day, an hour, barely a moment that went by, did her heart not grieve for the child she had lost—the one she had given up to a father who had seemed to need him more.

"I will personally send word to the cardinal myself the moment you are well recovered so that we can bring him happy news for a change. He would delight in that."

"I believe you are right. . . ." Gil sighed. For a moment his eyes closed and he was still. Bess lurched forward, feeling a flood of relief when he looked at her again. "What day is this?" Gil asked her.

"It is Sunday."

"No, the date . . . What is the date?"

"March twenty-fourth."

"Ah, so I thought. Your birthday," he replied, his eyes crinkling at the corners and a faint smile dawning on a face that now was gaunt, creased with lines, and marked by his bouts of ill health. "In the drawer," he said, indicating the carved bedside table.

Bess opened the drawer and drew from it a small red leather-bound volume. *Lancelot* was printed on the cover in heavy gold lettering. As he saw her looking at it, in a hollow voice he said, "Many years ago at court, I bought you a far less perfect edition of the same work, but I tossed it into the fire one night in a fit of jealous rage."

She assumed he meant his jealousy about the king, and she felt a flush of regret for such youthful foolishness.

"I know he gave his personal copy of John Skelton's poetry to you, but you often said this was your favorite book," he revealed, giving a weak little chuckle, nothing at all like the robust sound she was accustomed to hearing. "You were right to want the fantasy of a life like the one de Troyes wrote about in these pages."

"Yes, and *you* gave it to me. Thank you for that. And for this beautiful book," she said, squeezing his hand. "It shall always be dear to me."

"As dear as I am?" he asked in a whisper, a hint of his old, youthful sweetness shining through.

"Never even close to that much," Bess replied as her weary eyes filled with tears at the bittersweet truth of it. "I love you," she declared in the same soft whisper as his eyes closed again, and she said a silent prayer that it was not for the final time—not yet. She was not ready. She would never be ready for that.

It was just after dawn, and it had at last stopped snowing.

The first thing Bess saw through the grand window of their bedchamber when she woke was the canvas of bright white stretched across the undulating horizon, lit by soft, glittering sunlight. She had fallen asleep in the chair beside their bed, still holding Gil's hand, but it had gone cold, and slackened against her fingers. Bess felt her heart begin to race, knowing before she looked what had happened.

Gil's face was relaxed now, smooth and free of pain. Bess leaned over to touch his waxy cheek and saw that the burning fever had cooled as well. With the connection of her warm hand against his face, she felt something break inside her. It was sharp, like splintered glass, as the horrendous realization descended on her. The physician, old and stern, was standing at the foot of the bed. She did not know how long he had been there; nor did she care. Gil was her husband and her love. He had given her respectability and three beautiful children. All of the years, the joys, the struggles, and the memories, and in an instant he was gone, and their last moment, just like all the rest, could never be shared with anyone.

Instinctively, Bess reached over and drew the bedcovers up over his shoulders as if to warm him. She smoothed back a bit of hair near his temple; then for a moment, her hand stilled there. *My love*, she thought. *Thank you for saving me.*

Gil's death was the most difficult on Elizabeth, their eldest child, who would not eat or sleep and refused to come downstairs to greet guests and mourners who came in the days following the funeral. Townspeople as well as friends from court made the long, cold journey to Lincolnshire over a winter landscape, spotted with slush and patches of snow. Twigs, branches, and bare tree trunks peeked out from the white as if trying to recover from winter. Nicholas and Elizabeth Carew were the first to come in their heavy fur-lined cloaks, mufflers, and hats. Lord Mountjoy and his wife, Agnes de Venegas, followed, embracing Bess with tear-filled eyes and somber, murmured condolences. Yet none of them really understood what Gil meant to her.

Dressed in a mourning costume of unadorned dark gray velvet, with a high stiff collar, Bess stood looking out the tall, second-floor library window as an impressive train of riders and horses trapped in silver drew up and came to a stop in the gravel-covered courtyard below. Ahead were four riders in yellow and blue livery and another four at the back. On the door of the grand horse litter, which she saw before it was opened by a gloved guard, she caught a glimpse of the emblem, a lion bursting forth from a Tudor rose. It could not be, she thought with a numb, strangely calm realization, not after all these years. Yet it was; of course it was. It had taken the sudden death, two days before Gil's passing, of the once great Cardinal Wolsey, on the cleric's journey to London where he would have faced a charge of treason, to engender enough nostalgia apparently to bring him here to her at last, Bess thought with a flaring spark of bitterness she had not expected to feel.

She felt herself stiffen as the king was helped from the litter. But it was a very different monarch who stood in her courtyard now than the one she had seen for the very last time all those years ago. Henry had grown noticeably stockier during their separation. His hair was short now, the red-gold hairline receding at his forehead, and he wore a neat red beard beneath a heavier, square jaw. But the eyes were the same. They were deep, clear, intensely focused sea green eyes that had so often tormented her. If rosemary was for remembrance, then to Bess it would always be the deep scent of ambergris and the way he wore it that brought the past flooding back, as it came now, with a vengeance, especially when she looked into those eyes of his. . . . *Windows to the soul* they were. . . . Even looking at Henry in a rich, large-patterned brocade doublet, trunk hose, and a feathered hat that seemed more garish than elegant, brought her back.

Suddenly, she saw the slim, copper-haired boy of eleven, dressed in the finest blue velvet, emerge after the king, and the surprise heightened to panic. *Harry.* God, Harry had come home with him, at last.

Bess faltered, bracing herself on the frame of the window as the rosary she held tumbled onto the heavy carpet beneath her feet. She tried to suck in gulps of air, but little would come. After ten years, Hal himself had actually brought their son home. The prospect alone was almost more than she could bear, for how hard she had battled against that dream. She felt tears rise in her eyes.

The moments after that became disjointed. Each instant was full of fragmented sensations. The call of the yeoman suddenly at the door behind her, announcing the Duke of Richmond and the king, was solemn. Bess's heart was pounding in her chest so forcefully that she almost could not hear. Each beat brought such pain. Sensation after sensation pelted her. The feel of wet on her own cheeks as she hurriedly ran back across the room swiftly cooled the heat of shock on her face. The taste of the bitingly cold air as she struggled again to draw in a full breath was bracing. The thought, the last one, before she turned around, was that she was not at all prepared for this meeting; yet there was the knowledge as well calling from deep within her, like an old friend, that she could never be ready for something like this.

Slowly, Bess forced herself to move forward into the courtyard. She linked her hands together and squeezed them to try to quell the overwhelming trembling that swiftly overtook her as her gaze passed over Henry and settled heavily on the boy she knew was her Harry. At last . . . Ah, yes, Harry.

He was his father's son, indeed, so much a Tudor—from the close-cropped copper hair, to the vivid green eyes, and the tall, lean frame. He was so like the king the day they first met that it made her shiver again remembering. Harry stood before her soberly, though. In that, he was nothing like the brash young king from years ago. For a moment Bess was not certain Harry knew who she was. To collect herself, she dipped into a deep, sustained curtsy, praying that her legs would not give way.

"Your Grace," she said, not quite to the king, but as properly as a lifetime of skills had taught her to do in the presence of someone above her in rank.

But as she rose back up, it was the boy, not the king, who acknowledged the movement and advanced. Stiff-spined, formal, and smooth, almost regal, she thought.

"Mother," he said, extending a small hand as the other hand went behind his back in a nuance she knew he had been taught. "I have wished to meet you for such a very long time," he said with the crisp, schooled diction of a royal.

"And I you." Bess felt herself murmur the response despite her impossibly dry throat as she greedily scanned every element of her precious lost child, trying at the same time not to stare. That, however, was nearly impossible.

It was no more than an instant that felt like a lifetime before the king took the same three steps forward, crossing the chasm of years and bitterness to bring her into his commanding embrace.

"Bess," he whispered, the scent of ambergris she had expected punctuating the absolute maleness of him and, for a moment, overpowering her with memories. "I am so deeply sorry."

He seemed to be referring to Gil, but the way he spoke, the words seemed to hint at something more. Was it an apology finally for having taken her heart, her youth, her innocence, her son?

Bess entirely lost her ability to think in this odd, jarring moment.

"He is a grand boy, do you not think?" Henry asked her, not quite letting go of his hold on Bess, yet turning back to Harry, his expression full of marked pride.

There was an odd desperation in their interaction, she thought, though linked inextricably with the old familiarity. No matter how much his hair changed or he grew in stature, he was still the same Hal she once had loved so desperately. And somewhere inside herself, beyond the maturity and wisdom of years, she was still the young and hopeful Bess Blount from Kinlet come to the court of the great King Henry VIII with images of romances like *Lancelot* dancing in her head.

"My greatest condolences about your husband. Lord Tailbois was a man of true honor, as Cardinal Wolsey was. No matter what happened to the cardinal in his later years, I shall always remember Wolsey's greater qualities." Finally he let go of Bess and turned back to glance fully at their son. "Still, it was an odd coincidence that they should die so closely to each other after the deep connection they shared in life."

"My husband was extremely fond of Cardinal Wolsey," Bess answered honestly, trying very hard to keep her voice from trembling against the onslaught of memories that surfaced now, taunting her from every direction. "The cardinal treated him like a son for most of his life," she added, though unwilling to reveal too much of the truth out of respect for both men who were now gone. She felt in charge, strangely now, of a secret that had died with them, and she meant to keep it that way.

"Indeed he did," Henry replied in agreement.

"I, too, am sorry about your husband, Mother," Harry said suddenly and more sincerely than she would have expected. "My uncle George, your brother, tells me that, as a small boy, I knew Lord Tailbois well and that he was good to me."

Her eyes filled again with tears at the recollection—that one brief, precious year; a jewel lost, never to be reclaimed.

"Indeed, he was that," she answered softly. "He was very good to you. He treated you as a son, just the way Cardinal Wolsey treated him. 'Tis a pity you do not remember him at all."

"I am certain that is true," Harry said maturely. Only then did she notice it around his neck, hidden in the layers of silk and lace. It was the ruby and pearl pendant Gil had given her, and which she had sent to Harry for his birthday, three years after he left Lincolnshire. Contrary to everything she had believed, Henry had allowed her a place in Harry's life, and the gift symbolized that. Also, he had not called her Lady Tailbois as he might, but Mother, and as directly and matter-of-factly as if he had done it thousands of times before.

"I brought a small coterie of men with me," her son said, changing the subject and reminding her that they had traveled under the banner of the Duke of Richmond, not the King of England. "I hope I have your leave to feed them and allow them to rest?"

She looked back at the child she had ached for and about whom she had wondered and worried for so many years. She was quite unable to take her eyes from him.

"Of course, my lord, if it is at His Highness's pleasure."

Henry grinned. "Now, have we truly gone and gotten so formal with each other just because of a few years between us?"

Bess thought to herself what determination it must have taken to tell Anne Boleyn that he intended to reunite with his former mistress and with the child they shared while Rome still endlessly debated the finer points of his current threat to leave the Church altogether and begin his own church in England. It made Bess sad to think of the queen. The betrayal Bess had knowingly committed had been bad enough, but never once had she sought to replace Katherine of Aragon as Henry's lawful wife in precisely the way Anne Boleyn was now doing.

Bess had heard the lurid details from both her mother, who still served at court, and from Elizabeth Carew, who did as well. She had decided it was a good thing Gil had never known of Wolsey's death. Bess had intended to tell Gil once he recovered, but that moment never came. The queen had lost her Catholic champion in Cardinal Wolsey, Bess had lost a friend, and Anne Boleyn was on the verge of full victory now that all of her competition was out of the way.

It was too cold for them to walk outside, and the pathways were slick with frost, so Bess invited them to take a cup of ale beside the fire. To her surprise, the king declined, saying he preferred to attend to a few of his more pressing dispatches, but that he would join them soon. It had not been so long, Bess thought, that she did not understand that Henry was trying to give her time alone with their son. What should have produced a feeling of gratitude instead brought a swell of distress, as she sat with her son, each of them in one of her two imposing, velvet-covered high-back chairs. She was looking into the eyes of a boy who was in most ways a stranger to her now. Yet he was a boy nonetheless who had sought his mother out in her darkest hour, and there was some comfort to her in that.

"So then, Your Grace. You are such an important person now, elevated to the peerage as a duke. I am told by all of these honors and positions, His Highness has actually made you the second most powerful man in England."

Harry smiled. "I am not very popular with Mistress Boleyn, but I am told that as well, yes. The king has shown me great honor. But with you, I am simply called Harry."

Bess felt another painful tug at her heart. "I gave you that name myself."

"Father told me. He told me all about you, actually. How kind you are, how clever, and how lovely."

"Yet you stopped writing to me and never sought to meet me before now."

It was the first time she had noticed any discomfort on his smooth young face. He waited a moment before he responded. "He has always told me what a noble thing you did, allowing me to be raised at court so that I could be better prepared for my role as the king's son. My uncles, both George and Robert, said my leaving had upset you, but that your life was full with your other children now. I assumed that was why you never came to London to see me."

Her fingers splayed out across her lips in a gesture of surprise as she saw a hint of true emotion in his expression. "Not one of my three other children could replace you, Harry, nor shall they ever," she murmured, the tears of so much emotion splashing onto her cheeks. Bess tried to steady herself enough to continue. "When you were a little boy of barely a year, you did not want to leave here, and I did not want to let you go." She began to wring her hands, squeezing them so tightly that her wedding band cut into the flesh of her finger. "There was nothing more difficult than watching you leave that day. And George is quite right. I am not certain I could ever have survived that a second time. So while I did not come, I heard everything about you."

She tried very hard to smile through her tears, but when she saw his sweet young face now, fully defined by emotion, that became impossible. She sniffed and wiped the back of her hand across her eyes, determined to continue. She had waited a lifetime for this moment with her child.

"I know which foods you like, which you do not—particularly salmon pastry, if I am not mistaken? Which subjects you are best at with Master Palsgrave, and which you favor the least. While your French accent is perfect, you do not often apply yourself in French conversation. You prefer discussions on Plato, much like the king, and in fact, you regularly debate with him, always acquitting yourself quite well. You are not good at bowls, and you cannot yet be bothered with the focus archery requires, but you love to ride and are a master at dice as well as primero. And in your bedchamber beneath your bed, there is a small red ball that you were given here as a child in order to remind you of something you believed you had lost, just as the king once similarly kept something dear to him beneath his own bed." She wept openly, surrendering her face to her hands as he came and sank onto his knees before her.

"Cardinal Wolsey told me of that ball here in this house, the sound it made on the wood floors, how I loved it. . . . I do not remember it myself, I'm afraid, but some part of me does remember *you*," he confessed.

"Forgive me for not being strong enough to come to see you," Bess said, still weeping.

"You are stronger and more noble than any other woman I know."

"More so than Mistress Boleyn?" she asked suddenly with a crooked, slightly guilty little smile as she sniffled, needing to defuse the intensity of the moment for both their sakes.

"She is positively horrid," Harry said very low, but with a crooked smile of his own. "I truly hope the king is not granted his divorce if it means having to answer to her, even though he is threatening to leave the Church to get it. But please do not tell him I said that."

"Of course not." Bess took his hand then; so soft and smooth it was, not yet the hand of a man. "Are you happy there—at court, and in your own world as a duke with a vast household, staff, and so much duty and responsibility, I mean?"

He tipped his head, considering the question thoughtfully. He was still at her knees, still holding her hand. "It has all come in stages, I suppose. The king acted wisely in that, so it has not seemed a bother."

"You have heard the whispers, I trust, that if he does not soon produce a legitimate son, he may seek to change the laws so that you actually may be named his heir."

Wolsey himself had told her that, the very last time he had come to Lincolnshire.

"He has Mary. She shall succeed him if he has no sons."

"But you *are* his son."

"Yes," he said with the sudden calm maturity of a much older boy. "And I shall serve the king in any way that I am called to do. If it ever comes to that, I shall be prepared, thanks to your great sacrifice, Mother."

If he truly believed her actions had been a benefit to him, then she was glad of it. But Bess was not certain she would ever believe it could be worth the loss of those years with her child, and all that had cost her.

Later that night, when the grand old house was quiet and everyone had gone to bed, there was a light rap on Bess's bedchamber door. She settled back onto her lap the volume of *Lancelot* from Gil that she liked to read each night, for the calm, happy memories it brought.

"Come in," she said in a tentative voice, knowing well who it would be.

The king opened the door, lingering hesitantly beneath the jamb, dressed still in the long white cambric undershirt he had worn beneath his doublet, shoes, and heavy wool tights. But she could see that he was relaxed and that he had been drinking.

"May I come in?" he asked her.

"Would I dare to deny you?"

"Perhaps it would have been better if you had."

When she smiled, he advanced and sank onto the bed, moving to the empty place beside her, as though it had been a fortnight, not nearly twelve years, since he last had lain with her.

Henry picked up the book from her lap and examined it. "From Tailbois?" he asked.

"A birthday gift. Our last."

"I truly am sorry, Bess. Gilbert was a good man."

"There was no one better." The slight to Henry was intentional in the moment, but he disregarded it. Instead, he touched the side of her face with a single finger and leaned nearer.

"I am sorry as well about the boy. I should have given you more of a voice in what happened after I took him to France."

"'Tis true, you should have."

"That is an incredible boy we made, Bess," Henry said with great affection. He turned onto his side familiarly then on her bed and propped his head on his hand.

"You have honored him greatly, Hal. But all of England, I think, has been abuzz as to why, when you certainly did not honor your children with Mary Boleyn in the same manner."

"Those are William Carey's children," he said, bristling. "Harry was always mine."

"You never did deny him for even an instant; that is true. And for that, I am grateful."

"Nor shall I ever deny my son. I loved his mother dearly, after all. We were good together, Bess."

"Not so good that you now find yourself with Mary Boleyn's sister."

Henry fell back onto the pillows and moaned as though he had been struck. He sighed then but with a slight smile. "Ah, yes, that. 'Tis complicated."

"Do you love her, Hal?"

"I wish I knew. . . . She confounds me, certainly. She knows how to make me do things . . . say things, I never believed I would."

He looked over at her honestly, and there was the depth of years, and their experiences, mirrored back to her in his expression. "Some say Anne Boleyn is a witch. But I only think you are bewitched by her," she said.

"That much is true. She wishes to be queen before—"

"Before she does what I so willingly did without it, or any other promise?"

Henry averted his eyes, and she thought he looked like a guilty schoolboy, even behind the beard and the lines of a grown man that now so defined his features. "I truly was in love with you."

"It is enough now that *you* believe that," she said.

He turned again then and kissed her. But it was a chaste, gentle kiss, full of more nostalgia than passion.

"Will you divorce the queen and even break with Rome to do it?"

"If I want sons, I must." He caught himself then. "Heirs to carry on the Tudor legacy."

She could see by his expression that he knew what she was thinking. "Come back to court," he suddenly bid her. "There is a place for you there alongside your mother again. You can spend more time with Harry . . . and with me."

"And with Mistress Anne?"

She caught just a glimmer then of a charming, slightly arrogant smile. It was the same smile that had won her so long ago when life had seemed full of excitement and that dangerous innocence had ruled her. "I suppose we could see if she is up to the challenge of having you around her apartments. It might be good fun."

Bess arched a brow and bit back a half smile of her own. "You would use me as in a bearbaiting?"

"Forgive me." He sighed more heavily then. "I should not have assumed such a thing would be your desire as well after all these years."

This time it was Bess who turned toward him, willingly, and with the greatest affection. She placed a hand on his shoulder. "I did not give my heart, or my body, casually to you."

"You would not have been the Bess I loved if you had. Come to court," he pleaded again.

"I have the children, and a life here now, Hal. There are so many responsibilities and obligations."

"You are far too young and vital, the mother of the king's son, to settle out here in the country forever. Write to your family, bid them to come and manage Goltho Hall, or ask it of Mistress Carew for a while."

"Have we not, the two of us, used Elizabeth quite enough?" she asked pointedly.

"I am asking only that we pass a bit of time together again, Bess. It seems I can tell you what I can tell no one else. I am at a crossroads in my life, and it is a fateful juncture. That much I do know."

"I believe I would fear for my safety if I did return," she said, trying to pass off his plea as nothing more than a whim or a moment of nostalgia.

"I will keep you safe and well cared for. Have I not always done that?"

She thought of the life she had now as the widow of a baron; a woman of stature and of some note; a woman still young, still beautiful, with possibilities ahead. It was true; much of that really was to do with Henry VIII and the loyalty he had shown her.

"If I came to court, would I not complicate your decision about Mistress Anne?"

"Please do complicate it," he bid her without hesitation. "Does the mother of the king's much-loved son not have that right?"

Before she could respond, Henry kissed her, but this time it was not a chaste or harmless union of their lips. Rather it was the expression of things long held and now remembered, and it flared powerfully between them.

Suddenly, though, Bess pressed him back, her expression not one of passion but of conviction. "I cannot, Hal. Not here in his bed. Not ever."

Henry exhaled a steadying breath, then ran a tender hand along the line of her jaw. "And it is one of the things I loved most about you, your sense of honor."

"Thank you," she whispered, letting him tenderly kiss her cheek.

"But I would still like to stay and lie here for a little while and just talk with you, if that would be all right."

Bess felt the same desire to protect this strangely precious moment in time, one that would be gone soon enough once he and Harry left Lincolnshire. She had no idea whether to go to court, as he had bid her, or what dreadful thing might occur if she did. The only thing Bess knew for certain at this oddly bittersweet moment was that, in spite of everything, it felt so good to be with Henry again after all this time.

The next morning, she came downstairs to see that Henry and Harry were already sitting at the large cloth-covered trestle table in the grand dining hall, waiting for her to join them. Going well against custom, the three Tailbois children—young Elizabeth, little

George, and their brother, Robert—had been brought to partake of the morning meal with the king and Harry rather than being left to dine in the nursery as usual with their nurse. None of the king's servants, or the duke's attendants, was there to attend them at the moment as Bess lingered at the open door. She knew that was intentional.

She felt her heart squeeze as Harry sat talking and laughing with George, who was not quite eight, and she could hear the king patiently testing Elizabeth on her Latin verbs. Happy, odd little family, she thought. If only it were real. As soon as Harry glanced up and saw his mother, he stood politely and nodded to her.

"Good morning, my lady mother," he said, showing a deference not due her, which she thought made it all the more sweet. "Have you slept well?"

"I scarcely slept at all," she replied, not daring to glance at the king who, true to his word, had remained with her through the night, talking, laughing, and reminiscing but taking no other liberties.

"Your home is lovely," Harry happily countered as he began to eat. "My sleep here was deep and peaceful, not unlike how I imagine death well might be."

He did not realize how his response sounded, three days after a funeral, until he saw the faces of Elizabeth and George, as the two elder children of Gil Tailbois exchanged pained little glances.

"Bollocks," Harry cursed at himself in response, his smile having quite fully and swiftly fallen. "Forgive me, Mother, please. I have been brought up better than that."

"Indeed you have," the king calmly chided his son.

"It is just so peaceful, so utterly bucolic here, nothing at all like the busy roughness of London, from which we have just come."

"There is no need to explain," Bess assured Harry as one of her own liveried servants, stiff-spined and silent, came formally into the room. She then drew back her chair so she could sit. "It is a world away from London in so many respects," she said with a smile, trying as well as she could to help rid him of the horrified expression on his smooth boy's face. How lacking she, too, had been in self-confidence at that age, she thought, remembering how awkward and unsure she had felt that first time Henry spoke to her.

Bess sat silently after that, watching all of her children interact with one another, as if it had always been that way. And Henry, King of England, sat happily at the head of her table, dining, laughing, and talking with them. She wanted to capture the moment and preserve it like a rose sealed between the pages of a book, protected forever.

Since they had come in the duke's entourage, rather than in that of the sovereign, Henry and their son were able to join Bess for Mass that morning in the local stone church down in the village. Covered in an unadorned yet fashionable gray wool cape and a low, wide French cap, England's king passed unnoticed beside the young duke. As prayers were offered up for the soul of Baron Tailbois, Henry somberly lowered his head and made the sign of the cross.

"I wish I had known him," Harry said to Bess afterward as they walked, arms linked, out into a wet and cold gray morning where the low-lying fog rolled at their ankles.

The king, Elizabeth, and George were behind them, and Bess relished this precious moment alone with her eldest son.

"He was an extraordinary man," Bess confirmed.

"His Highness tells me he has asked you to return to court."

"It seems a foolish thing even to consider with Mistress Boleyn there," she countered, unable to keep a hint of rivalry from her voice at the thought.

"They are saying he will start his own church and annul his own marriage to the queen, and then marry her," Harry said in a tone much lower than before. "Unless, of course, there is someone to prevent all of that."

Bess glanced over at him, surprised at how worldly wise this young boy sounded to her just then. For an instant, she allowed herself to actually imagine him one day King of England because of it.

"I shall try to come to court," she replied with a sideways glance and a crooked smile. "But only to see you."

Harry matched her smile. That much of him was thoroughly Blount. "We shall begin there," he said. And that was every bit his father. "I like my brother George," he added. "We are similar in many ways."

She felt it deeply in her heart that he would think of the two of them as brothers.

"I would like him to come with you as my companion," he suddenly declared. "If, of course, you would agree."

A mix of emotions flared within her again at the sudden prospect of losing another child, another son to Henry's influential court.

"It is certainly something to consider," Bess hedged, keenly aware of the gentle, understanding image of his mother with which she wanted him to leave; something special he could take away and keep, and hopefully upon which they could build.

"Do you two not look intense," Henry affably remarked as he came up behind them. Pressing himself in between them, he linked each of their arms through his own and continued to walk over the ordered gravel pathway. "Is it a private conversation or may anyone join in?" he asked with a smile and a sly little wink.

"Not just anyone," Bess replied. "But certainly you may."

"I was just telling Mother how much we both would like her to come to court. And when it is time for me to return to my own estates, I would like her to see them as well. And I would very much like it if she would bring my brother George with her. There are not many others my own age, and it would be so lovely to have a companion. A bit of family."

"Ah, yes. Just as I had Brandon when I was a boy."

"Precisely." Harry smiled, and Bess could see the lovely ease between them. She did not like admitting that his father had been good for him. She had been full of anger for such a long time.

"Well, I think it is a splendid idea. If your mother agrees, that is," said the king.

"I shall certainly consider it."

"And you will come to court?" Harry badgered hopefully.

Bess gave a wan little smile as she was pressed by what felt like two errant boys. "I shall try," she replied finally. "Perhaps later in the spring."

Chapter Eighteen

he powerful forces of the clergy in Rome threatened excommunication in response to Henry's claim that he would break with the Church over the issue of divorce from Katherine of Aragon. On one side of him, Anne Boleyn pleaded and cried, threatening to withhold her favor forever, which drove mad a man accustomed to having everything he desired. On the other side were Henry's son and Bess—a ready-made family, taunting his heart and his conscience with a choice of lust or love.

"It is true, sire, if you were to marry the Lady Tailbois, it would give legitimacy to the Duke of Richmond and ease him, with no difficulty should you choose, into the line of succession," Thomas Cromwell cautiously advised. "And Mistress Anne is still most unpopular with the people."

Since the disgrace and death of Cardinal Wolsey, and the death of another confidant, the Earl of Essex before that, and with Brandon and Mary living away from court much of the time, Henry now relied almost exclusively upon Cromwell to help him navigate the turbulent waters of divorce, annulment, and excommunication—not only with Rome, but with his conscience.

Katherine was left alone now at Richmond with only a few of her servants. It was her punishment for continually refusing to say she had slept with Henry's brother, Arthur, an admission that would have rendered her marriage to Henry invalid and provided grounds for annulment, and also for refusing to accept that Henry would eventually divorce her. Meanwhile, Henry, Anne Boleyn, and his court were luxuriously installed at Wolsey's elegant former London palace, York Place, where they meant to pass the spring without the queen. He was no monster, he assured himself daily. But he had a choice to make, and that choice no longer included Katherine of Aragon. He would have to decide which way to go once the divorce was granted.

Yes, he could marry Bess. That would make things simple. It would calm so much of what tortured him as well. A part of him still did love her after all these years. He had satisfied himself about that question last April when he had gone to Lincolnshire with Harry. *But Nan* . . . Fiery, unpredictable, sensual Nan, how his blood did burn for her! Yet had his passion become real, enduring love? Or was it simply still his pride and that love of the hunt that had always ruled him?

Henry had written to Bess, asking her once again to come to court. He needed to see her again now that her yearlong mourning period was at an end. He needed to be with her as they once had been to see if the love between them could extinguish the passion he felt for Anne. Bess had written back that she would come for the May Day celebration. And yet, he thought now even as he waited, perhaps memories were just that—something better left to the corners of the heart and not paraded up to the vulnerable center.

His plans for a law passed by Parliament to bring his son into the line of succession would certainly destroy his chances with a woman like Anne—if he planned to marry her and have sons with her. But if he did not do it, Harry would not be assured his rightful place—a place for which Bess had sacrificed so much.

So there was a risk either way.

Henry glanced beyond the window glass and down into the vast gardens below, full of neat brick pathways and conically shaped juniper trees. Anne was there with several of Katherine's former ladies, now her attendants, along with Henry's own Groom of the Stool, young Henry Norris. When he saw the handsome, dark-haired Norris, Henry's smile fell. The look was intense between Nan and the boy. They were laughing, and she had touched her hand playfully to his chest. Henry leaned back in his chair as Cromwell droned on, delving into details he did not care to hear. So the king was not the only man at court with a passion for Anne Boleyn, he thought, jealously focusing on Norris. *Come to court soon, Bess*, he thought again as he had so many times already that day.

"My Lady Tailbois, there is a gentleman downstairs. He says he is your neighbor, although I do believe I would remember him if he were."

Stout and silver-haired beneath her gabled hood, Mistress Fowler stood in the doorway to the music room, and Bess looked up from the virginal where she had been listening with the music teacher as her daughter played a piece. Elizabeth stopped playing and looked toward the door as well.

"Has this gentleman a name?" Bess asked with a hint of irritation at how flustered the married woman was apparently by the prospect of the waiting guest.

"He called himself Lord Clinton, my lady. But I did always believe Lord Tailbois, God rest his soul, to be the only nobility around this area."

Bess stood and straightened her skirts.

"Shall I show him upstairs?"

"I shall come down. Where is he now?"

"In the foyer, my lady Tailbois. I tried to show him to the drawing room, but he insisted this was not a social call."

Bess rolled her eyes, irritated to be called upon by a stranger who clearly was not any more pleased to be in her house than she was to have him here, whatever his reason. There was enough to do maintaining a family and a household this size without being bothered by mundane interruptions. Bess did not descend the stairs gracefully, rather taking each step with purpose, and also a hint of irritation as the hem of her skirts swirled at her ankles. But as she reached the landing, she saw him. The sight of him stopped her fully. He was familiar, though a total stranger. And all the activity in her house, servants moving about, children laughing—all of it ceased in that moment.

He was tall, young—magnificent. He was stunningly prepossessed for someone his age, as he held his gloves in one hand, glancing at the Tailbois coat of arms on the wall beside the door and thus giving her an instant more to take in the details of his extraordinary face. He was twenty, perhaps younger, but he exuded such command that age was irrelevant. His square face, dominated by sleepy, seductive ice blue eyes, was framed by strong brows and tamed waves of wheat-colored hair, which she watched him casually rake back from a broad, smooth forehead as he waited. He had a slight whisper of a beard at his chin, and, below his nose, only enough of a mustache to show he could grow one. When he glanced up and saw her, Bess had reached the bottom step and paused, gripping tightly the polished banister with the hand that still wore her wedding band. She felt not entirely connected to her own body. It was as if she were viewing herself and this man from an outside perspective. And then, seeing her, he smiled. The gesture was refined, small, with just a slight turn upward of his lips. Bess saw a spark of impishness in it, and the way his eyes crinkled at the corners.

He bowed crisply to her then, linking his hands behind his back as he did. "My Lady Tailbois, I am Edward Fiennes, Lord Clinton, your neighbor to the south."

"I had no idea I possessed a noble neighbor to the south," she said, not certain at all the moment she spoke them what words she had actually said. He made her feel more foolish and girl-like than she had ever felt before, even with the King of England.

"Our lands adjoin each other's, although it is at a rather great distance. I often dealt with your husband on border issues."

The mention of Gil reminded her of too many things she did not wish to think about at this moment, and she saw by the sudden slight frown on his face that he sensed that.

"I am most sorry for your loss last year, my lady. Please accept my condolences. Lord Tailbois was a fine and great man."

"He was indeed. Thank you." She moved down the final step and faced him. He was tall, but not in Henry's imposing way. This man—this Edward—seemed to her perfectly proportioned, as if a sculptor had fashioned him, knowing to what a widowed woman, with no prospects of passion, would be drawn.

"Would you like to come in, take a cup of wine perhaps, and rest after your ride?" she asked him, struggling with the words and feeling instantly awkward. She had not been a young, uncertain girl for a very long time. And yet there was a sense of destiny in her question, like nothing she had ever felt in her life—as if she had known him, or been meant to know him, all along.

"Thank you," he replied, moving forward with her. "Several of the sheep that graze out on your pastureland have in recent days wandered onto my adjoining property, which is much closer to that thick stretch of deep woodland than yours is." He shifted his weight casually from one leg to another, but he did not take his eyes, his sleepy, piercing, exquisite eyes, from her. "I am afraid several of your sheep have been killed on my land. But just this morning, my man and I caught the fox red-handed and took him down."

"Thank you," Bess said softly, still trying to process his claim.

"I cannot say, of course, if there is more danger to your animals, so perhaps we might consider some sort of barrier along that far pastureland."

"Perhaps I should ride out and take a look at it myself," Bess said.

His eyes met hers. There was still that tiny upturn of the lips she saw even then. It was not so much a smile, she realized now, but rather a spark of satisfied self-possession. "Under the circumstances, it would be much wiser for my servants and me to accompany you, if you mean to do so."

"Lord Clinton, I have my own servants, and we have only just this moment met," Bess demurely said, knowing that she sounded like a child, rather than the confident mother of four children she had become.

Edward Fiennes's smile widened at that, and the crinkles beside his sleepy crystal blue eyes deepened, making her feel, for a moment, utterly foolish for the way she knew she was staring at him. "That much is true," he concurred. "However, if you and your children were to agree to accompany your good neighbor to the May

Day celebration in the village next week, we would be strangers no longer."

It had been more of a statement of logic than a proposal, and Bess felt powerless to contest. It was so logical, in fact, that she laughed.

"May I take that as your acceptance, Lady Tailbois?" he asked, arching a brow as his crooked smile deepened.

It was not brash arrogance that he showed, she thought, but simply utter self-confidence. She had not felt anything like this, the pull of a smile, and her heart beating swiftly, for a very long time— not since she met the king for the first time, all those years ago.

Anne Boleyn was playing a game with his heart better than a game had ever been played, and Henry did not like it at all. He craved her, he dreamed of her, he fought for her, and he was willing to surrender everything for her, if she would only surrender just a small bit of herself in return. But even that she continued to withhold as the great lure.

Henry stood now at the edge of his grand tennis courts at Richmond Palace, dressed in an elegant russet-colored doublet accented with heavy slashed sleeves, a grand sable collar, and a gold medallion. He was every bit the elegant ruler, yet always a man underneath. He was watching his son compete against the boy's older and stronger uncle, the thirty-three-year-old George Blount, who, in spite of the difference in age, had remained Richmond's most faithful companion. Harry was growing into such a magnificently strong and handsome boy that it startled Henry sometimes to see him like this, tall, athletic, and healthy, because it kindled hope.

And it kept his memories, and questions, of Bess alive.

The pope in Rome had continued flatly to refuse Henry's call for the annulment no matter what threat he dangled, and as he waited to be with Anne fully, Henry could not help continuing to consider Bess—and the possibility of making her his bride instead. She had not come to court for the May Day celebration after all, but she had sent him a gift of local Lincolnshire wine like the kind they had shared on his April visit following Gilbert Tailbois's death, along with a letter, which had pleased and enticed him. Bess was still such an alluring and beautiful woman. And unlike Katherine, Bess had produced three healthy sons and a daughter as well. His mind played at the scenarios daily. Could he, after all this time, marry his son's mother and make her queen?

Thomas Cromwell stood calmly beside him. Every bit as ambitious as Wolsey had been to maintain his power base, and slightly more ruthless, he was a fat-faced man with dark, snake eyes, a long nose, and small pursed lips.

"Richmond is playing well today," Henry quietly observed.

"He plays like his father," Cromwell noted, touching his blunt-cut sable-colored hair to see that it had stayed in place with the breeze.

"Has there been any further word from Parliament on the question of Lady Tailbois?" the king asked without taking his eyes from the game.

Cromwell rubbed his smooth, hairless jaw between two fat fingers. "Once the annulment question is settled in Rome, or within a new church here in England, based on the premise that your marriage to Katherine was never valid in the first place, then His Grace, the Duke of Richmond, would automatically be legitimized and, thus, become your heir. If you were to marry his mother, that is."

"England would have an heir, and the succession would be made secure with the presence of a healthy son to follow me."

"But you would need to sacrifice Mistress Boleyn to do it."

Such a thing as Cromwell suggested was unthinkable . . . *or was it?*

The challenge of Anne excited him still. It also exhausted him, and most days he was a man driven by unfulfilled passion, not intellect or reason at all. He raked both hands through his now-short copper hair as he continued to watch his son and to consider the grand, life-changing choice before him, one that had presented itself more prominently since Tailbois's death. A king must be wise, calm, and thoughtful to rule a country, and most days now, Henry felt more like a wild dog going after a bitch in heat. It was not good for his country, and it was even worse for his soul.

"Has there been any word back from Lady Tailbois as to whether she favored my return gift to her?"

He had sent her a jewel-encrusted gold chalice. While Anne withheld her body from him as part of her game, Henry played his own match. He could recall only too well the passionate nights, and afternoons, with Bess—her small, perfect body open to him, along with her heart. He felt himself harden at the memory.

"I am afraid there has yet been no word from Lincolnshire, sire."

Henry let out a heavy sigh. He felt as if he were holding the weight of the world with the decision before him, and he did not want to make a second matrimonial mistake. "How would *you* counsel me, Cromwell? Could I actually marry Bess? Could I be happy? It would solve so many things if I could be."

"Your heart alone knows the answer, sire," he calmly replied. "There is, of course, that other path still to be considered."

No matter how patiently Cromwell laid it out each time, or how many times he tried to consider it as a way to protect the succession and his country, the prospect always made him slightly ill.

"The boy *will* need a powerful alliance at some point, you know." Cromwell pressed the issue, seeing how the king's expression had so swiftly hardened against it.

"True, but a marriage with his own sister? Thomas, that is far worse, by any biblical standard, than what I did with Katherine."

"Still, canon law does approve of such a unique match, sire. The position from Rome is such that if you drop the issue of your own divorce and annulment, and stop threatening to leave the Church, Pope Clement could well honor such a request on behalf of your son. And after all, the Princess Mary is only Richmond's half sister."

Henry shifted his weight from one leg to the other, feeling weakened even by the thought. The other option currently on the table was also from the pope who had proposed his own young niece, Caterina de Medici, as a bride for Harry.

"If you arranged a marriage between your daughter, Mary, and Richmond, it would ensure a Tudor heir, from either vantage point. You would certainly need never worry again about any foreign claim to the throne, and your need for another male heir would be voided, and thus your need for a divorce," Cromwell said, carefully pressing the issue until Henry sharply cut him off.

"But I am not prepared to agree that my marriage to Katherine was ever legal, much less valid in the eyes of God! You know well the same passage I do."

"*If a man shall take his brother's wife, it is an unclean thing . . . and they shall be childless,*" Cromwell dourly repeated, knowing the passage as well as anyone else who dealt with the king and took a side on the great debate.

Harry came off the court then, flushed, smiling, and triumphant, bringing the debate for now to an end. Henry embraced his son. "You played splendidly, just as you were taught to, my boy."

"I was slow in the third round, and he nearly had me," Harry panted, bright-eyed and perspiring.

"But he did not. That is what matters," Henry reminded him.

"Your Highness." George Blount, dressed in a white lawn shirt with leather laces, dun-colored hose, and a brown belt, just as Harry was, swept into a deep and proper bow.

"You gave the Duke of Richmond a good turn, Master Blount," Henry praised.

"Not so good as he gave me, sire," George returned, wiping the perspiration from his temple with the back of his hand.

They were alike, especially around the eyes, and with that same strong essence, Henry thought as he looked at Bess's brother. *Sweet Bess . . .* These constant thoughts and memories of her only made his decision more difficult. In the beginning, it had seemed unfathomable that he might actually marry his son's mother. But now a way seemed more clearly paved, and thus two distinct paths were still tauntingly before him.

They began to walk with one another then, George and the others following behind, and Henry draped an arm across Harry's still-slim shoulder. Just as he himself had; just as Arthur might have, if God had given his brother that chance, Harry would grow into his bones, Henry thought with pride of his increasingly tall and lanky son.

"I have had a letter from my mother today," the boy revealed with a tentative smile.

Henry glanced at him. "Splendid. Any great news from Lincolnshire to share with me?" he asked nonchalantly, yet finding as he did that he did truly wish to know.

"As it happens, there is. Surprising news, actually. My mother, it seems, is going to ask for your approval of her marriage."

For an odd, impossible moment, Henry thought that Harry had meant a marriage to him. He had not expected to feel the strong wave of bitterness he did when he realized that was not at all what Harry had meant, but the bitter wave swiftly followed anyway.

"Who in heaven's name would she marry?" he growled.

As he glanced over again, he saw his son's reaction. His tone had been needlessly harsh.

"He is Lord Clinton, sir. I know little else of him."

"Of course. Her neighbor." Henry nodded gruffly, patting the boy's shoulder as they walked.

"Will Your Highness give it then?"

"What?"

"Your approval of her marriage. My mother has been widowed for a year now."

When one door closed another might well open, Henry thought, but it was the door that remained closed that would ever tantalize him. Yet Bess was not to blame. He had not gone after her. He had never made a stand. It was only hindsight and perspective that had finally brought the thought to meet and match the desire. He should be ashamed of himself. He deserved this. She had let Harry go for his sake. Now if Bess truly wanted this, he must make a sacrifice in the same way and do this in return for her.

"Yes, of course I shall approve it," Henry said with a tone of resignation he did not feel. "There are few people in all the world who more deserve happiness than she."

PART VII

Step. . . .

Wait for that wisest of all counselors, Time.

—PERICLES

Chapter Nineteen

*B*ess read the letter again, taking in every word, each detail of the event she had missed. Harry's wedding to Mary Howard, the young daughter of the Duke of Norfolk, held at Hampton Court, had been a small affair attended by only a few guests. It had not really been a proper wedding anyway since Harry had not yet reached the age of fifteen. But the king and his wife, Anne Boleyn, had attended to sanction the match. The new queen was said to be a ragingly jealous woman, which had precluded inviting former mistresses to court, even if they were the mother of the bridegroom.

Harry did not like Anne any more now than he had in the beginning, and it caused him to keep his distance, touring his own estates much of the year, and visiting Lincolnshire, rather than remaining at court to be badgered by the queen and the new royal heir—a daughter they had chosen to call Elizabeth.

Bess folded the letter again, and Edward studied her. He was lying beside her in their bed, a grand canopied structure draped with heavily fringed crimson velvet and gold ties. In the early-morning autumnal light, her husband resembled a god, Bess thought; scandalously young and dangerously handsome he was. It still amazed her, after two years, that her long-fallow body had come so alive again beneath his passionate touch, and she loved Edward Fiennes with a focus and intensity that rivaled anything she believed she had felt for Henry or Gil.

"I'm sorry we could not be there, my love," Edward said, stroking her cheek with the back of his hand. "I know it would have meant something to the boy."

"Moreover, it would have been a reason for the new queen to make a scene, and that was Harry's day."

"And also, we have to protect our own little investment," he returned, smiling that devilish smile that could still melt her even now as he pressed his hand down against the hard little knot at her belly, the beginnings of their growing child.

Neither of them spoke about it being a youthful power alliance between the king's son and the Duke of Norfolk's daughter, not a true marriage. Harry and the girl, one of Anne Boleyn's favorite maids of honor, had barely met when she was selected to become his bride. And based on his youth, it would be some time before he was allowed to reap the full carnal benefits of marriage either.

Edward tenderly kissed his wife, then drew her nearer. "What is it that is really bothering you?" he asked, his voice full of tender concern.

"Harry has changed. He is no longer my gentle little boy who I would carry through the meadow with me, smelling all of the flowers. Nor even the one who came here after Gil died. Now, the tone in his letters is more clipped, more formal than when last we met. He speaks with an air of entitlement now about how bored he is with this or that. After all, my son is a duke."

"Second most powerful personage in all of England, no matter his age," Edward unnecessarily reminded her. There was no one in England allowed to forget who Harry was.

Bess sighed. "I suppose he is simply growing into his role as the son of a king. I should have known life at court would change him. I know not why I expected anything different."

"Because you are his mother, and even from afar you will always love him for the child he was," Edward tenderly answered. "And a part of you will forever be tied to his father."

"After the annulment question was finally made moot by the king's marriage to Anne Boleyn, and the commencement of his own church, so it was no longer necessary for Harry to be married off to the Princess Mary. I suppose I just expected the king to make a better match for his only son."

"You said it yourself—Anne Boleyn's influence over him is strong. Since she will soon be with child again, I suspect his hope for a legitimate heir is all he can think about. All of England knows what he has sacrificed for that opportunity."

"His faith . . . His conscience . . . His queen . . . Even his dignity," Bess murmured sadly.

What the king had become was so different from the man, Hal, she had known as a young girl. It was still difficult to believe he had changed so much. Now their son was changing as well, growing into his role in ways she had not expected. But she had permitted that destiny when she let him go to a future that seemed bigger and brighter than any she might have given him here—the son of a woman whose only mark on history was her affair with a married king.

Very gently, Edward took the letter from her and placed it on the carved side table for her. Finally, Bess sat up and flung her legs over the side of the bed. Her long, still-shimmering blond hair fell onto her shoulders as she gazed out the window, wondering exactly where her eldest son, her sweet Harry, was at that very moment and whether he was thinking of his mother, or of the new bride she had yet to meet. There would doubtless be a new, volatile rivalry at court now among the girl's father, Norfolk, Cromwell, and the queen. Seeing that might almost make the danger of a visit worthwhile, after her own child came, she thought with a smile. Yes, perhaps a visit should be made.

Bess and Edward went together then into the nursery where Robert and George were playing. It was such a sweet scene, she thought, content with the peace she had so unexpectedly found here in the countryside with Edward. Elizabeth, who was thirteen now, came quickly away from the virginal she had been playing in a swish of heavy yellow silk and a happy, adolescent smile to greet them. Gil's daughter was becoming a beauty, with her mother's shimmering blond hair, wide blue eyes, and a dusting of freckles over her flawless features.

"It sounded lovely," Bess said with a smile, one that matched her daughter's own. "You have entirely worked out that troublesome spot in the center of the piece."

"Thank you, Mother," Elizabeth said sweetly. "But may I ask you if you have decided yet?"

Bess knew of course what she meant since it was not the first time her daughter had asked. The invitation for George, her son, to join Harry for the Christmastide holiday at court had gone unanswered for days. Elizabeth, who adored her younger brother, had made it her goal to champion the cause of his going. Edward gave a tepid smile, and Bess shot him a censuring look in response.

"I have made no decision."

"But court, Mother." Her eyes glittered dreamily at the prospect.

"All of the fine dresses, the jewels, the music, the banquets . . . the gentlemen. Think of it!"

"I need not think of it, child. I remember it well enough."

"I wish he had invited me instead of Georgie. It would be a dream to walk with the duke, my brother, through the corridors of a great royal palace at Christmas."

"Court is also a place of great vice, greed, and temptation, so, alas, it shall remain a dream for you since I shall never allow it to tempt you."

Elizabeth frowned at her mother's sharp response, and she stiffened her spine stubbornly. "You were tempted there, and now have a life that is better for it. Even Grandmother says so."

Bess was suddenly angry at the child for bringing up those dark years. "You know nothing of what I endured, or what I am better for."

"But you are a lady now, though you went to court only as Mistress Blount. Grandmother has told me the entire story, and about your glorious romance with the king as well."

"After all of her own years there, your grandmother should have learned to hold her tongue."

"Are we not to know of you, Mother, what the rest of England already does?" Elizabeth pressed, leaning slightly forward in a combative stance, and her eyes mirroring for Bess some of the youthful ambition she, too, once felt.

"Yes, Mother, answer her that," George seconded as he came up behind them.

And in the echo of her children's bidding, Bess felt herself cringe. Truthfully, she was not ashamed of her youthful indiscretion, or of the life she had lived at court. But now, at thirty-one, she felt very far away from that world—that love—and from the naive adolescent she once had been.

"You well know the story, both of you. No one here has kept it from either of you," Edward calmly defended his wife. "Your mother simply chooses not to dwell in the past."

"Yet did not *her* past make up *our* legacy?" Elizabeth asked.

"The king is not your father. Nor George's either. You have no tie to court," Bess quickly interceded to defend herself.

"And yet the Duke of Richmond is still our brother, and he has invited me to come to court, and I do so wish to go, Mother; I truly do," George said with respectful boldness.

For the first time in her life, Bess felt silenced by her children—because they were right. Thoughts, memories, and images of losing Harry moved through her mind with the darkness of a death dance, as they always did at even the mention of his name. But she must do it. She could not ask George to pay for her mistakes or to try to heal her wounds for her. She left the nursery without answering his request, but she knew what she would do.

It was too cold to take the horses out, but Bess still wanted to walk. She needed to be outside to clear her mind with the cold snap of winter air that she knew would instantly surround her. Cloaked in heavy velvet, lined with luxurious sable, she walked alone down the winding brick path blanketed by slick frost, a path through the dormant gardens, as a low-lying fog swirled at her ankles and colored her breath white each time she exhaled. Bracing herself against the clear, bitingly cold winter morning, Bess drew the fur collar up around her neck and shoved her other gloved hand into the pocket of her cloak. She had not worn this for a very long time. Gil had given it to her to celebrate their first year of marriage, and for a long period after his death it had made her sad. But today it had seemed all right. He had been such a grand part of her life, more important to her in many ways than the king. She smiled now, feeling his presence returning strongly with it.

He would have trusted their son.

Bess knew she must do that also. Letting go of things was part of life's progression—especially letting go of children. They were not a mother's, but rather they all belonged to God.

Bess glanced up then at a broad, clear winter sky, thinking of Gil somewhere there looking down at her. *You would like Edward,* she thought. *He is young, but a good man. And I do love him . . . though I will never forget all we had together during our years at court, and our long and happy marriage afterward.*

She and the king were still, after all of these years, on good terms. He always remembered her at Christmas with a suitably grand gift, and except for recently, since he had married Anne Boleyn, the invitations to court had continued, regularly and sincerely. But Bess preferred the country now. In her youth, court had brought her excitement, but the predictability of her life here brought her peace. And that was enough. She would write to her brother, and also to her uncle Mountjoy, bidding them both to keep watch over George. He would have the same opportunities she once had been given, and the same protections as well. What he made of his chance would be up to him. And secretly Bess envied him that—she envied him a beginning.

Chapter Twenty

*K*atherine of Aragon had been dead for five months. Anne Boleyn had been executed four months after her death, and eleven days after that there was yet another new Queen of England as Henry continued to look for that elusive thing he had only glimpsed once long ago with Bess Blount.

Jane Seymour was shy, pretty, and very much like Bess. Also like her, Jane had been there, quietly waiting in the wings for her moment. While it was a moment that had never come fully for Bess, Henry knew that their son wrote to his mother, telling her that he liked Jane's gentle sweetness, and he was happy that the boy felt as he did. Harry and his own young bride, Mary, spent a great deal of time now with the royal couple, along with Mary's increasingly dominant father, the Duke of Norfolk. The balance of power in the English court was shifting again, and the king's son had grown to become an even more integral part. At seventeen, Harry was called Richmond mainly now; handsome, healthy, well married, and increasingly powerful. The king had done well by the boy, and Harry had not disappointed his investment in him. Landed baron, peer of the realm, Lord High Admiral, privy counselor; the king's son was all these things, but to his father, he was still Harry—Bess's little boy who stood so bravely before him that day, resigned to meeting his destiny in France with the king.

Your mother had that same gentle sweetness as Jane, Henry thought as he made his way with an increasingly gruff demeanor toward the long polished Privy Council table. Among the other counselors he saw his son already seated there, clothed in rich velvet, fur, and a jeweled collar. He was leaning back in his chair, confident and completely at ease. Seeing him always brought sweet thoughts of Bess, even though he was content with Jane.

They all stood and bowed as Henry moved on, passing each of them, on the way to his tall leather-covered throne positioned at the head of the massive table. The room was warm, and the press of bodies beneath so much velvet, silk, and heavy jewels, along with the rank odor of flesh, irritated him today more than usual. His council members blathered on about things until Robert, Earl of Sussex, once again took up the familiar debate regarding the line of succession. It was always a topic at the forefront of Henry's mind, and as much so now that his two daughters had been declared illegitimate when he invalidated his two previous marriages. In fact, he managed to think of little else most days but who would next be king.

Henry suddenly heard Sussex making a declaration. "All that I am saying regarding the matter is that if the queen does bear a male child, then glory be to God, that royal issue would be resolved. However, until that time, it would be wise for our sovereign king to have a safeguard in the line of succession."

"I quite agree," said the Duke of Norfolk.

Sharply ambitious and full of cunning, Norfolk was a man who was cleverly and steadily gaining power by solidifying key alliances. Since his daughter's marriage to Richmond, Norfolk had pushed Cromwell aside easily as overseer of the Duke of Richmond after Wolsey, guiding and encouraging the boy himself in a steady, familial manner.

"Since all three of His Highness's children are now considered to have been born out of wedlock, the three of them are on an even field, legally speaking," Sussex continued. "I suggest only that a son would be preferable to daughters when considering succession, if one is able to choose."

"Here, here," Norfolk chimed of his friend and supporter who was brave enough to declare what everyone else was thinking. "A wise and prudent observation."

Only Charles Brandon, whose children, born of the king's sister, had legitimate Tudor blood, frowned now, shaking his amber-bearded chin. "England need not look to bastards, either female or male, when the king has three undisputed blood relations—two in my own daughters; the third in the niece Your Highness and I share through Margaret, your sister," he declared in a deep-voiced grumble.

"Still, they are females of the line, and we all sit here at this moment in the very presence of the king's honored and acknowledged son, the Duke of Richmond. A male of the line. It would seem we need look no further than our own midst," Norfolk said, lightly pressing the point and letting Sussex take the previously agreed-upon lead in the matter.

Henry listened keenly to the debate. Even knowing beforehand that it was to be brought up, he was still uncertain what to do. The two had spoken for him perfectly, yet a question remained. Harry had certainly been properly groomed, impeccably educated, then strategically if not magnificently married. But if Jane should have a child, and of course in time she would, could he then withdraw from his precious Harry the honor that had been dangled before him since the day he had first come to court as a little boy? Could he take that away from Bess as well, after she had sacrificed him as she had been forced to do?

All of those thoughts worked their way around in his mind, latching on and then falling away as he sat, trying to pretend he had heard every word of the ongoing debate by men whose agendas he knew of course were personal. His neatly bearded chin balanced on his hand, he began to watch Thomas Seymour, Jane's younger brother, most closely as the others went on debating.

Obviously, the Seymour family would not be in support of naming Harry, as it would be a risk to their own growing power base. But how precisely would Thomas eventually object? Boldly and directly? Or more underhandedly? Seymour most certainly possessed that quality to be underhanded in his dealings. There was something about Jane's brother he knew instinctively was not trustworthy. Henry scratched his chin and silently waited.

"It seems a rather grand waste of parliamentary time, since my nephew shall next be king," Thomas Seymour finally said, yet so blandly that it might not have mattered if Henry had not been focusing on him. In the ensuing silence, Thomas exchanged a quick glance with Edward, his older brother.

"Your unborn nephew," Norfolk icily amended.

"Not born and not yet even conceived," Sussex chimed in at great risk.

Henry shot them both a glare for the words that had seemed a swipe at Henry's manhood, but he did nothing more because he knew they were right.

Norfolk lowered his head, but clearly he had no intention of showing more contrition than that. Fortunately for Norfolk, the side he had chosen to champion so boldly was Harry's.

Henry IX ... Henry imagined the title, rolling it around in his mind as he regarded his son, a boy who grew more powerfully and surely into manhood each day. Was that why God had not blessed him with another son? Was there meant to be this Henry IX after him?

Before he decided, Henry must see Bess. He had had enough of this stalling. She simply must come to court. She could bring her husband, and she should. That would make it far easier on Jane, but he needed her counsel on the matter. If she approved of putting their son into the line of succession, knowing that he might one day be reduced if Jane bore a child, then he must do it. It had been seventeen years, and if Bess agreed, it was well past time to honor their son in that way.

Elizabeth Carew smiled to herself and walked with a spring in her step up the east-wing steps of Greenwich Palace. She was grateful to be back for a time amid the vibrance of court, thanks to her husband, who, praise God, was still tightly allied with the king. She had missed the activity, the gowns, the energy, and the gossip. The only thing lacking here was Bess, and the echo of her presence upon this place was sorely missed. As she walked gracefully through the halls that she knew well, there was still the outline of the beauty Elizabeth once had been—stunning enough for a little while to capture a king. Her face was flawed by only a few light lines at the corners of her eyes and mouth, and the strands of gray that wove their way through her thick blond hair were well captured beneath the stylish

French hood to match her gown. The years and childbirth had been kind to Elizabeth, and she returned to court each time she was called, her head held high.

And so now Bess was to return for a visit as well. That could be no small thing to have been invited, or for Bess to have finally accepted. She knew through Nicholas that they had always kept up a correspondence and that they had never ceased through the years to exchange gifts at Christmastide. Theirs was a unique and enduring bond, certainly. But this . . . This was something else entirely. Elizabeth Carew could feel it like a coming north wind down to her very core. The king was rarely in London in summer, due to the heat, dust, and the threat of fatal disease. But now he intended to be. Was he actually making that grand concession in order to see Bess?

It clearly had to do with Richmond. The situation, and the king's lack of a firm stance on the matter of succession since the execution of Anne Boleyn, had been the fodder for debate for months.

The court would move from Greenwich to London in four days' time, and they would all know soon enough.

While they wrote often, it had been several years since she had seen Bess, and she had never met Lord Clinton, so the excitement for Elizabeth was a charged thing. All of those thoughts whirled like a top in her mind as a collection of elegantly dressed men, speaking in low tones, came toward her, crossing the other way down the corridor. She stopped and stepped back behind the drapery. A childhood of games in these halls made the move instinctual.

"What if Jane cannot bear a son and the king tires of her just as he did of Katherine and Anne?" Thomas Seymour, the queen's brother, was asking. "Where will our family be then?"

"He does seem to intend finally naming Richmond as his heir," Edward drily confirmed.

Their footfalls were heavy and stalking as they neared her. Elizabeth held her breath.

"You know how the king adores him. Bringing any harm to the boy would be a treasonous crime," Edward continued.

"True, *if* a crime were committed," Thomas Seymour coolly returned. "Yet it is summer, we shall be in London soon, and you know there is always a chance that even a perfectly healthy young man could fall ill very suddenly there."

"It does happen," Edward said, voicing his agreement in an oddly callous tone.

Elizabeth saw the men pause to glance at each other. Then their looks cut guiltily away. Her blood ran cold at what was unsaid between them, and the inference there. She shrank back against the heavy velvet drapery, feeling her legs go very weak beneath her. They would not dare. The Seymour brothers could not be that desperate, she thought, her mind a great boiling pot of confusion. What to do? What could she do now in the wake of a circumstance where they had said everything and yet nothing at all?

Their heavy presence lingered along with the deep scent of ambergris and perspiration, and the sense of conspiracy, even after they had gone on down the corridor. They left Elizabeth Carew suddenly with far more concern now than excitement about going on to London. God keep safe the child of her friend's heart, she thought frantically then, for such would Richmond ever be for Bess.

PART VIII

The Final Step . . .

The path of a good woman is indeed strewn with
Flowers; but they rise behind her steps, not before them.
—JOHN RUSKIN

Chapter Twenty-one

July 1536
Kyme Castle, Lincolnshire

*G*rief was an odd thing, Bess thought as she sat alone before the high altar, beside one of the columns near the nave of the little Norman church in Sleaford, not far from the castle where she lived with Edward. Nevertheless, she was still praying to a God who had taken her son away twice, this time for good. Grief was a force that pulled and sucked the life out of those left behind, reducing them to wish they were the ones who had died instead. Yet life continued.

For five days, she had gone through the motions, receiving condolence after condolence, bearing embraces, and seemingly sincere concern for her health from people who had never cared for her. Even Edward had offered little real comfort to her as he sat beside her in silent support for hours, until she had insisted he rest. The only one she had not yet seen since Harry's sudden and slightly mysterious death was her son's father. Nicholas Carew gently told her the king was too grief-stricken to see anyone. Even Queen Jane had been barred from the king's privy apartments. Few outside of court yet even knew that the young Henry Fitzroy, Duke of Richmond, so full of promise, was suddenly, mysteriously, dead. Henry seemed in limbo about what to do. Days had gone by. Three had become four. That now became five, as they all waited silently for the king to react, for a funeral to be planned, a burial to be designed.

Praise God, she had been given at least those two precious days with Harry and his young wife. While not an incredible beauty, the Duke of Norfolk's daughter was kind and gentle, and Bess had been pleased with the match. Her heart ached now to wonder what sort of mother Mary might one day have been to her son's children if she had been given that chance. But, as with so many other things, that as well was not to be.

Bess closed her eyes, then opened them again, settling them on the great gold crucifix on the altar before her. Harry's had been a life full of promise left unfinished. That would forever haunt her, and she knew it.

But decisions must be made. If Wolsey were still alive, she could send him to counsel with the king. But there was no one else. She and the king were his parents. What they had begun together they must finish now in the same way.

She must see him. It would be the final step in a journey both of them had made.

Slowly, Bess rose from the pew, colored light thrown upon her face from the colored glass of the mullioned windows, one containing the image of a kneeling knight asking prayers for his soul. She was thinking suddenly of how many times Katherine of Aragon, her former great rival, had sat in places just like this, praying endless prayers for things that were impossible, as she herself had just done. In so many ways, they had been kindred spirits, not rivals at all.

Bess left the chapel then and was met by Edward, who had waited for her outside. Even for her husband she did not lift the veil.

"I must go to Greenwich," she announced brokenly.

"The king is there."

"I must see him, alone. There is much to be decided."

"Let me take you. I shall feel much better if you are not alone. You have not eaten for days, and you have barely slept."

Through the black gauzy fabric she looked at him. Young, handsome, sent by God, he was a touch of human perfection, she had always believed. Yet she would have given him up, and a dozen other wonderful men like him, to have had Harry back in this world. Harsh as that was, it was the truth.

"Ride with me if you wish," she responded quietly, accepting his offer, because she knew how much he would worry if she declined, but Bess and Henry alone had to take this step. Alone they had to close this chapter.

Bess was silent inside the drawn litter on the hot, jostling ride across rutted roads from London to Greenwich, knowing the king probably would not agree to receive her. Elizabeth had argued against her going, pleading that his strange outbursts of grief-stricken temper might flare before her. But there was a way. A fitting one, she thought, as she glanced at Edward. He had been clutching her hand in silent support. She could feel his strength through his fingers, firm, sleek, and so masculine, just like the rest of him.

"Are you certain you are prepared for this?" he asked deeply, his voice rich with true concern, as they paused at the guard tower beside the palace gates, then with a courtly nod of approval, were issued inside the vast grounds. She remembered this place so well.

"I only pray that I am, because I must do it. There is no other choice."

The secret stairwell leading to the king's bedchamber to which Cromwell showed her, then left her on her own, was narrower than her memories and the years made it. Each step felt steeper. *One . . . two . . . three . . . four . . . five . . . six . . .* Each footfall was full of such bittersweet memories, as if each contained a part of her life.

Bess found him then, as she might have known she would, slouching low in a huge oak chair that was covered in blue velvet and studded with gilt nails. He was turned from her, facing the window, a man like any other man; a father full of grief, like any other who had lost a son. He did not move or acknowledge her presence even as the floorboards creaked beneath each gentle step that drew her near to him.

He was so different now than the young king with whom she had fallen so boundlessly in love; a king who now had sanctioned execution, murders, changed laws, and broken rules. As she came up beside him and placed her hand on his shoulder, Henry did not move, even as he realized it was Bess. The moment was a quiet eternity. And then silently, as he reached up to take her hand, the tears came. She wanted to shout out her fear that Harry had been poisoned. The court was full of such envy and malice. It came now from every direction for a boy who threatened the goals of so many. She wanted to accuse someone—anyone. There were several she suspected, but there was no proof.

"It should not have happened this way," he murmured in a broken whisper full of anguish. He did not glance up, yet he knew now it was she. "He was meant to be king. I was going to see him made king."

The grand declaration made it all real in a way that the gossip never could have, and Bess felt the bitter fall of her own tears. She knew Henry meant it. From the beginning, he had honored their child, and through that their love. She knew Henry well enough to know what he would say next.

"He must be well honored. It shall be a state funeral." He sobbed out the words. "A funeral fit for the king Harry might well have been."

"No."

Bess stopped him then in a voice as gentle as it was firm.

"I have never asked you for anything, Hal. I have given and given . . . and given to you. My heart, my soul . . . and then my precious son. Harry was raised a Tudor. Let him rest in peace a Blount," she asked quietly as he finally looked up at her brokenly, defeated, his face wet with tears.

It seemed an eternity that they gazed at each other, sharing the past, sharing this torturous moment of the present—all of it; everything that had led them here.

"His wife's family has requested he be buried in Norfolk at the Thetford Priory there. But I knew that much must be up to you. I knew I had to see you. I simply did not know how to ask you for another single thing, even coming here."

"In death, he is mine again, and I want no ceremony to mark his return to me. Take him on a cart in a plain coffin, and covered over with straw so no one knows. He will be better protected at the priory, so let him be taken there," she replied in tearful agreement.

The decision, heartbreaking, final, had been made. He was not a king. He was not the heir.

He was Duke of Richmond, all he would ever be.

There was another long silence marking his agreement, before she knelt at his feet and Henry took her hands into his own. She searched his tear-moistened face, and he searched her glistening eyes. But there were no answers there for either of them. She hoped he had a son with Queen Jane—many sons. Henry had waited so long for that gift. And she hoped this marriage would endure. She hoped it all but could not bring herself to say any of it in this silent, shadow-filled moment, full as she was of too much grief and remembrance.

Finally, she stood and stepped back from his chair as Henry surrendered his face to his hands and wept anew by the light of a dozen flickering tapers that lit the drapery-darkened room. That so mighty and powerful a king could be reduced like this for love of a child gave Bess an odd peace as she lingered for another moment. The sound of footsteps and the creak of floorboards beneath the weighted steps beyond the closed door finally brought the encounter to a close. As she turned to go back behind the curtain and through the secret door, she heard him.

"No," Henry commanded, yet with a voice that trembled in a way only she could hear. "Leave properly . . . through the gallery door this time."

"But the queen—"

"You were the mother of the king's son long before there was Jane," Henry declared. "Leave by the proper door and be as proud as I am of what we once had, and the magnificent person we created together."

When she hesitated, he nodded, urging her. She reached out one last time then to touch the top of his head amid the burning candle flames and the light that danced between them like a thousand little sparks of what might have been. She stroked him tenderly for a moment more, remembering everything, and wishing once again for all that might have been but could never be because they had reached the final step of their long journey together. She was so thankful even then for the life to which she would now return, a life that lay waiting just beyond the gallery door below . . . and she was so thankful for the happiness she had found after Henry. The journey had been a long one.

"Leave me now. But you shall never know how glad I am that, across this long road we have often together trod, you found your way back to me. For a little while, at least," he said without meeting her gaze.

There was a small silence between them then, one full of things she thought to say, thought to do, but could not, before Bess finally and firmly turned away.

Author's Note

$\mathscr{B}$ess Blount died in 1540, at the approximate age of thirty-eight, of apparent consumption. It was likely the same ailment that took the life of the Duke of Richmond rather than something more nefarious—the subject of theory and conjecture for centuries. The truth is lost to time and no one can say for certain; however, the very real possibility of Fitzroy succeeding Henry VIII, after passage of the Act of Succession in 1536, created envy and concern enough in the various court factions to have made such speculation a viable scenario.

Bess did give birth to Lord Clinton's three daughters, Bridget, Catherine, and Margaret, and she lived as his wife for four years more following her son's death. As per her request, and in agreement with the king, the body of Henry Fitzroy, Duke of Richmond, was transported in a plain cart with no ceremony to Thetford Priory. Bess was buried, as she had lived, away from her first child, at the Blount family estate at Kinlet.

While there is no direct proof that Thomas Wolsey fathered Gilbert Tailbois, the powerful cardinal was known to have maintained several mistresses and to have fathered several children throughout his life. In addition, young Tailbois was curiously close to the powerful prelate throughout his youth as well as his adolescence, and he did hold a prominent place at court as his ward, in spite of his having had his own father, who was well placed enough to make the sustained connection curious. In addition, the month of his death was here altered. Thomas Wolsey died in November of 1530.

After his wife's death, Edward Fiennes, Lord Clinton, survived another forty-five years and went on to an illustrious career himself at court as Lord High Admiral of England.

Diane Haeger is the author of several novels of historical and women's fiction. She has a degree in English literature and an advanced degree in clinical psychology, which she credits with helping her bring to life complicated characters and their relationships. She lives in Newport Beach, California, with her husband and children.

The
Queen's Rival

IN THE COURT OF HENRY VIII

DIANE HAEGER

QUESTIONS
FOR DISCUSSION

1. Prior to reading *The Queen's Rival*, what, if anything, did you know about Bess Blount or her son Henry Fitzroy? Many people know about Henry VIII's legitimate children, Mary, Elizabeth, and Edward, but did it surprise you that a son shown such favor by so famous a king has been rendered so much more obscure throughout history?

2. Discuss how Bess's relationship with Gilbert Tailbois evolved and was enriched throughout the novel. Why do you think Bess could not initially see Gil's true feelings for her, or even earlier on, when others around them so easily did? Do you think her blindness to it was intentional?

3. When faced with a choice, Bess, knowing how illness frightened the king, chose to risk not only her life and her standing at court, but her place in Henry's heart, in order to nurse Gil back to health. Why do you think Bess made that choice for one man when she believed herself in love with the other?

4. Bess allowed herself to believe that the king's lovers were not mistresses, and therefore not serious rivals to her place in his heart. Why do you think she allowed this of herself, in spite of

having been raised by seasoned courtiers? Does this seem characteristic of the Renaissance with a girl from the country? Or was there something more at play for Bess?

5. Bess felt great compassion very early on for Queen Katherine. How and why do you think Bess allowed herself to compromise her conscience to become the mistress of a married man who brought her hope of marriage only at the expense of the woman she admired?

6. Elizabeth Carew went to great lengths to keep her relationship with Henry VIII a secret from her best friend, Bess. What do you believe motivated Elizabeth? Do you believe she was naive in a different way than Bess was regarding the king?

7. How were Bess Blount and Elizabeth Carew different as two of Henry's early mistresses? How were they similar?

8. Henry continued to have strong feelings for Bess Blount long after their affair ended, yet not so with Elizabeth Carew, Jane Poppincourt, or Lady Hastings. Do you believe the source of those feelings was that she bore his child? There has long been conjecture that Mary Boleyn bore him children as well. What do you believe made the two circumstances different?

9. Henry VIII's desire for an annulment from Katherine of Aragon is a running theme throughout the novel. Prior to reading

The Queen's Rival, what did you know about how the Church of England was formed? Did you realize this one royal marriage was pivotal in the formation of the American Episcopal Church as well?

10. Do you believe that, had Henry married Bess instead of Anne Boleyn, he might have remained content with her throughout the remainder of his life? If so, how would his life have been changed by a woman who loved him and whom he loved in return?